One

"You want me to marry Kanza the Monster?"

Aram Nazaryan winced at the loudness of his own voice.

Not that anyone could blame him for going off like that. Shaheen Aal Shalaan had made some unacceptable requests in his time, but *this* one warranted a description not yet coined by any language he knew. And he knew four.

But the transformation of his best and only friend into a meddling mother hen had been steadily progressing from ignorable to untenable for the past three years. It seemed that the happier Shaheen became with Aram's kid sister Johara after they had miraculously reunited and gotten married, the more sorry for Aram he became and the more he intensified his efforts to get his brother-in-law to change what he called his "unlife."

And to think he'd still been gullible enough to believe that Shaheen had dropped by his office for a simple visit. Ten minutes into the chitchat, he'd carpet bombed him with emotional blackmail.

He'd started by abandoning all subtlety about enticing him to go back to Zohayd, asking him point-blank to come *home*.

Annoyed into equal bluntness, he'd finally retorted that Zohayd was Shaheen's home, not his, and he wouldn't go back there to be the family's seventh wheel, when Shaheen and Johara's second baby arrived.

Shaheen had only upped the ante of his persistence. To prove that he'd have a vital role and a full life in Zohayd, he'd offered him his job. He'd actually asked him to become Zohayd's freaking minister of economy!

Thinking that Shaheen was pulling his leg, he'd at first laughed. What else could it be but a joke when only a royal Zohaydan could assume that role, and the last time Aram checked, he was a French-Armenian American?

Shaheen, regretfully, hadn't sprouted a sense of humor. What he had was a harebrained plan of how Aram could *become* a royal Zohaydan. By marrying a Zohaydan princess.

Before he could bite Shaheen's head off for that suggestion, his brother-in-law had hit him with the identity of the candidate he thought *perfect* for him. And *that* had been the last straw.

Aram shot his friend an incredulous look when Shaheen rose to face him. "Has conjugal bliss finally fried your brain, Shaheen? There's no way I'm marrying that monster."

In response, Shaheen reeled back his flabbergasted expression, adjusting it to a neutral one. "I don't know where you got that name. The Kanza I know is certainly no monster."

"Then there are two different Kanzas. The one I know, Kanza Aal Ajmaan, the princess from a maternal branch of your royal family, has earned that name and then some."

Shaheen's gaze became cautious, as if he were dealing with a madman. "There's only one Kanza…and she is delightful."

"Delightful?" A spectacular snort accompanied that exclamation. "But let's say I go along with your delusion and agree that she is Miss Congeniality herself. Are you out of your mind even suggesting her to me? She's a kid!"

It was Shaheen's turn to snort. "She's almost thirty."

"Wha…? No way. The last time I saw her she was somewhere around eighteen."

"Yes. And that was over ten years ago."

Had it really been that long? A quick calculation said it had been, since he'd last seen her at that fateful ball, days before he'd left Zohayd.

He waved the realization away. "Whatever. The eleven or twelve years between us sure hasn't shrunk by time."

"I'm eight years older than Johara. Three or four years' more age difference might have been a big deal back then, but it's no longer a concern at your respective ages now."

"That may be your opinion, but I…" He stopped, huffed a laugh, shaking his finger at Shaheen. "Oh, no, you don't. You're not dragging me into discussing her as if she's actually a possibility. She's a monster, I'm telling you."

"And I'm telling you she's no such thing."

"Okay, let's go into details, shall we? The Kanza I knew was a dour, sullen creature who sent people scurrying in the opposite direction just by glaring at them. In fact, every time she looked my way, I thought I'd find two holes drilled into me wherever her gaze landed, fuming black, billowing smoke."

Shaheen whistled. "Quite the image. I see she made quite an impression on you, if after over ten years you still recall her with such vividness and her very memory still incites such intense reactions."

"Intense *unfavorable* reactions." He grunted in disgust. "It's appalling enough that you're suggesting this marriage of convenience at all but to recommend the one…creature who ever creeped the hell out of me?"

"Creeped?" Shaheen tutted. "Don't you think you're going overboard here?"

He scowled, his pesky sense of fairness rearing its head. "Okay, so perhaps *creeped* is not the right word. She just… disturbed me. *She* is disturbed. Do you know that horror once went around with purple hair, green full-body paint and pink contact lenses? Another time she went total albino rabbit with white hair and red eyes. The last time I saw her she had blue hair and zombie makeup. *That* was downright creepy."

Shaheen's smile became that of an adult coddling an unreasonable child. "What, apart from weird hair and eye color and makeup experimentation, do you have against her?"

"The way she used to mutter my name, as if she was casting a curse. I always had the impression she had some... goblin living inside her wisp of a body."

Shaheen shoved his hands inside his pockets, the image of complacency. "Sounds like she's exactly what you need. You could certainly use someone that potent to thaw you out of the deep freeze you've been stuck in for around two decades now."

"Why don't I just go stick myself in an incinerator? It would handle that deep freeze much more effectively and far less painfully."

Shaheen only gave him the forbearing, compassionate look of a man who knew such deep contentment and fulfillment and was willing to take anything from his poor, unfortunate friend with the barren life.

"Quit it with the pitying look, Shaheen. My temperature is fine. It's how I am now.... It's called growing up."

"If only. Johara feels your coldness. I feel it. Your parents are frantic, believing they'd done that to you when you were forced to remain with your father in Zohayd at the expense of your own life."

"Nobody forced me to do anything. I chose to stay with Father because he wouldn't have survived alone after his breakup with Mother."

"And when they eventually found their way back to each other, you'd already sacrificed your own desires and ambitions and swerved from your own planned path to support your family, and you've never been able to correct your course. Now you're still trapped on the outside, watching the rest of us live our lives from that solitude of yours."

Aram glowered at Shaheen. He was happy, incredibly so, for his mother and father. For his sister and best friend. But when they kept shoving his so-called solitude in his face, he felt nothing endearing toward any of them. Their solicitude only chafed when he knew he couldn't do anything about it.

"I made my own choices, so there's nothing for anyone to feel guilty about. The solitude you lament suits me just fine. So put your minds the hell at ease and leave me be."

"I'll be happy to, right after you give my proposition serious consideration and not dismiss it out of hand."

"Said proposition deserves nothing else."

"Give me one good reason it does. Citing things about Kanza that are ten years outdated doesn't count."

"How about an updated one? If she's twenty-eight—"

"She'll be twenty-nine in a few months."

"And she hasn't married yet—I assume no poor man has taken her off the shelf only to drop her back there like a burning coal and run into the horizon screaming?"

Shaheen's pursed lips were the essence of disapproval. "No, she hasn't been married or even engaged."

He smirked in self-satisfaction at the accuracy of his projections. "At her age, by Zohaydan standards, she's already long fossilized."

"How gallant of you, Aram. I thought you were a progressive man who's against all backward ideas, including ageism. I never dreamed you'd hold a woman's age against her in anything, let alone in her suitability for marriage."

"You know I don't subscribe to any of that crap. What I'm saying is if she is a Zohaydan woman, and a princess, who didn't get approached by a man for that long, it is proof that she is generally viewed as incompatible with human life."

"The exact same thing could be said about you."

Throwing his hands up in exasperation, he landed them on his friend's shoulders. "Listen carefully, Shaheen, because I'll say this once, and we will not speak of this again. I will not get married. Not to become Zohaydan and become your minister of economy, not for any other reason. If you really need my help, I'll gladly offer you and Zohayd my services."

Shaheen, who had clearly anticipated this as one of Aram's answers, was ready with his rebuttal. "The level of involvement needed has to be full-time, with you taking the top job and living in Zohayd."

"I have my own business…"

"Which you've set up so ingeniously and have trained your deputies so thoroughly you only need to supervise operations from afar for it to continue on its current trajectory of phenomenal success. This level of efficiency, this uncanny ability to employ the right people and to get the best out of them is exactly what I need you to do for Zohayd."

"*You* haven't been working the job full-time," he pointed out.

"Only because my father has been helping me since he abdicated. But now he's retreating from public life completely. Even with his help, I've been torn between my family, my business and the ministry. Now we have another baby on the way and family time will only increase. And Johara is becoming more involved in humanitarian projects that require my attention, as well. I simply can't find a way to juggle it all if I remain minister."

He narrowed his eyes at Shaheen. "So I should sacrifice my own life to smooth out yours?"

"You'd be sacrificing nothing. Your business will continue as always, you'd be the best minister of economy humanly possible, a position you'd revel in, and you'll get a family…something I know you have always longed for."

Yeah. He was the only male he knew who'd planned at

sixteen that he'd get married by eighteen, have half a dozen kids, pick one place and one job and grow deep, deep roots.

And here he was, forty, alone and rootless.

How had that happened?

Which was the rhetorical question to end all rhetorical questions. He knew just how.

"What I longed for and what I am equipped for are poles apart, Shaheen. I've long come to terms with the fact that I'm never getting married, never having a family. This might be unimaginable to you in your state of familial nirvana, but not everyone is made for wedded bliss. Given the number of broken homes worldwide, I'd say those who are equipped for it are a minority. I happen to be one of the majority, but I happen to be at peace with it."

It was Shaheen who took him by the shoulders now. "I believed the exact same thing about myself before Johara found me again. Now look at me…ecstatically united with the one right person."

Aram bit back a comment that would take this argument into an unending loop. That it was Shaheen and Johara's marriage that had shattered any delusions he'd entertained that he could ever get married himself.

What they had together—this total commitment, trust, friendship and passion—was what he'd always dreamed of. Their example had made him certain that if he couldn't have that—and he didn't entertain the least hope he'd ever have it—then he couldn't settle for anything less.

Evidently worried that Aram had stopped arguing, Shaheen rushed to add, "I'm not asking you to get married tomorrow, Aram. I'm just asking you to consider the possibility."

"I don't need to. I have been and will always remain perfectly fine on my own."

Eager to put an abrupt end to this latest bout of emotional wrestling—the worst he'd had so far with Shaheen—he started to turn around, but his friend held him back.

He leveled fed-up eyes on Shaheen. *"Now what?"*

"You look like hell."

He felt like it, too. As for how he looked, during necessary self-maintenance he'd indeed been seeing a frayed edition of the self he remembered.

Seemed hitting forty did hit a man hard.

A huff of deprecation escaped him. "Why, thanks, Shaheen. You were always such a sweet talker."

"I'm telling it as it is, Aram. You're working yourself into the ground...and if you think I'm blunt, it's nothing compared to what Amjad said when he last saw you."

Amjad, the king of Zohayd, Shaheen's oldest brother. The Mad Prince turned the Crazy King. And one of the biggest jerks in human history.

Aram exhaled in disgust. "I was right there when he relished the fact that I looked 'like something the cat dragged in, chewed up and barfed.' But thanks for bringing up that royal pain. I didn't even factor him in my refusal. But even if I considered the job offer/marriage package the opportunity of a lifetime, I'd still turn it down flat because it would bring me in contact with *him*. I can't believe you're actually asking me to become a minister in that inhuman affliction's cabinet."

Shaheen grinned at his diatribe. "You'll work with me, not him."

"No, I won't. Give it up, already."

Shaheen looked unsatisfied and tried again. "About Kanza..."

A memory burst in his head. He couldn't believe it hadn't come to him before. "Yes, about her and about abominations for older siblings. You didn't only pick Kanza the Monster for my best match but the half sister of the Fury herself, Maysoon."

"I hoped you'd forgotten about her. But I guess that was asking too much." Wryness twisted Shaheen's lips. "Maysoon was a tad...temperamental."

"A tad?" he scoffed. "She was a raging basket case. I barely escaped her in one piece."

And she'd been the reason that he'd had to leave Zohayd and his father behind. The reason he'd had to abandon his dream of ever making a home there.

"Kanza is her extreme opposite, anyway."

"You got that right. While Maysoon was a stunning if unstable harpy, Kanza was an off-putting miscreant."

"I diametrically differ with your evaluation of Kanza. While I know she may not be…sophisticated like her womenfolk, Kanza's very unpretentiousness makes me like her far more. Even if you don't consider those virtues exciting, they would actually make her a more suitable wife for you."

Aram lifted a sarcastic brow. "You figure?"

"I do. It would make her safe and steady, not like the fickle, demanding women you're used to."

"You're only making your argument even more inadmissible, Shaheen. Even if I wanted this, and I consider almost anything admissible in achieving my objectives, I would draw the line at exploiting the mousy, unworldly spinster you're painting her to be."

"Who says there'd be any exploitation? You might be a pain in the neck that rivals even Amjad sometimes but you're one of the most coveted eligible bachelors in the world. Kanza would probably jump at the opportunity to be your wife."

Maybe. Probably. Still…

"No, Shaheen. And that's final."

The forcefulness he'd injected into his voice seemed to finally get to Shaheen, who looked at him with that drop-it-now-to-attack-another-day expression that he knew all too well.

Aram clamped his friend's arm, dragging him to the door. "Now go home, Shaheen. Kiss Johara and Gharam for me."

Shaheen still resisted being shoved out. "Just assess the

situation like you do any other business proposition before you make a decision either way."

Aram groaned. Shaheen was one dogged son of a king. "I've already made a decision, Shaheen, so give it a rest."

Before he finally walked away, Shaheen gave him that unfazed smile of his that eloquently said he wouldn't.

Resigned that he hadn't heard the last of this, Aram closed the door after him with a decisive click.

The moment he did, his shoulders slumped as his feet dragged to the couch. Throwing himself down on it, he decided to spend yet another night there. No need for him to go "home." Since he didn't have one anyway.

But as he stretched out and closed his eyes, his meeting with Shaheen revolved in his mind in a nonstop loop.

He might have sent Shaheen on his way with an adamant refusal, but it wasn't that easy to suppress his own temptation.

Shaheen's previous persuasions hadn't even given him pause. After all, there had been nothing for him to do in Zohayd except be with his family, who had their priorities—of which he wasn't one. But now that Shaheen was dangling that job offer in front of him, he could actually visualize a real future there.

He'd given Zohayd's economy constant thought when he'd lived there, had studied it and planned to make it his life's work. Now, as if Shaheen had been privy to all that, he was offering him the very position where he could utilize all his talents and expertise and put his plans into action.

Then came that one snag in what could have been a once-in-a-lifetime opportunity.

The get-married-to-become-Zohaydan one.

But…should it be a snag? Maybe convenience was the one way he *could* get married. And since he didn't want to get married for real, perhaps Shaheen's candidate *was* exactly what he needed.

Her family was royal but not too high up on the tree of

royalty as to be too lofty, and their fortune was nowhere near his billionaire status. Maybe as Shaheen had suggested, she'd give him the status he needed, luxuriate in the boost in wealth he'd provide and stay out of his hair.

He found himself standing before the wall-to-wall mirror in the bathroom. He didn't know how he'd gotten there. Meeting his own eyes jogged him out of the preposterous trajectory of his thoughts.

He winced at himself. Shaheen had played him but good. He'd actually made him consider the impossible.

And it was impossible. Being in Zohayd, the only place that had been home to him, being with his family, being Zohayd's minister of economy were nice fantasies.

And they would remain just that.

Miraculously, Shaheen hadn't pursued the subject further.

Wonders would never cease, it seemed.

The only thing he'd brought up in the past two weeks had been an invitation to a party he and Johara were holding in their New York penthouse tonight. An invitation he'd declined.

He was driving to the hotel where he "lived," musing over Shaheen dropping the subject, wrestling with this ridiculously perverse sense of disappointment, when his phone rang. Johara.

He pressed the Bluetooth button and her voice poured its warmth over the crystal-clear connection.

"Aram, please tell me you're not working or sleeping."

He barely caught back a groan. This must be about the party, and he'd hate refusing her to her ears. It was an actual physical pain being unable to give Johara whatever she wanted. Since the moment she'd been born, he'd been a *khaatem f'esba'ha,* or "a ring on her finger," as they said in Zohayd. He was lucky that she was part angel or she would have used him as her rattle toy through life.

He prayed she wouldn't exercise her power over him, make it impossible for him to turn down the invitation again. He was at an all-time low, wasn't in any condition to be exposed to her and Shaheen's happiness.

He imbued his voice with the smile that only Johara could generate inside him no matter what. "I'm driving back to the hotel, sweetheart. Are you almost ready for your party?"

"Oh, I am, but…are you already there? If you are, don't bother. I'll think of something else."

He frowned. "What is this all about, Johara?"

Sounding apologetic, she sighed. "There's a very important file that one of my guests gave me to read, and we'd planned to discuss it at the party. Unfortunately, I forgot it back in my office at Shaheen's building, and I can't leave now. So I was wondering if you could go get the file and bring it here to me?" She hesitated. "I'm sorry to take you out of your way and I promise not to try to persuade you to stay at the party, but I can't trust anyone else with the pass codes to my filing cabinets."

"You know you can ask me anything at all, anytime."

"Anything but come to the party, huh?" He started to recite the rehearsed excuse he'd given Shaheen, and she interjected, "But Shaheen told me you did look like you needed an early night, so I totally understand. And it's not as if I could have enjoyed your company anyway, since we've invited a few dozen people and I'll be flitting all over playing hostess."

He let out a sigh of relief for her letting him off the hook, looking forward to seeing them yet having the excuse to keep the visit to the brevity he could withstand tonight.

"Tell me what to look for."

Twenty minutes later, Aram was striding across the top floor of Shaheen's skyscraper.

As he entered Johara's company headquarters, he

frowned. The door to her assistants' office, which led to hers, was open. Weird.

Deciding that it must have been a rare oversight in their haste to attend Johara and Shaheen's soiree, he walked in and found the door to his sister's private office also ajar. Before he could process this new information, a slam reverberated through him.

He froze, his senses on high alert. Not that it took any effort to pinpoint the source of the noise. The racket that followed was unmistakable in direction and nature. Someone was inside Johara's office and was turning it upside down.

Thief was the first thing that jumped into his mind.

But no. There was no way anyone could have bypassed security. Except someone the guards knew. Maybe one of Johara's assistants was in there looking for the file she'd asked him for? But she had been clear she hadn't trusted anyone else with her personal pass codes. So could one of her employees be trying to break into her files?

No, again. He trusted his gut feelings, and he knew Johara had chosen her people well.

Then perhaps someone who worked for Shaheen was trying to steal classified info only she as his wife would be privy to?

Maybe. Calling the guards was the logical next step, anyway. But if he'd jumped to conclusions it could cause unnecessary fright and embarrassment to whomever was inside. He should take a look before he made up his mind how to proceed.

He neared the door in soundless steps, not that the person inside would have heard a marching band. A bulldozer wouldn't have caused more commotion than that intruder. That alone was just cause to give whomever it was a bit of a scare.

Peeping inside, he primed himself for a confrontation if need be. The next moment, everything in his mind emptied.

It was a woman. Young, slight, wiry. With the thickest

mane of hair he'd ever seen flying after her like dark flames as she crashed about Johara's office. And she didn't look in the least worried she'd be caught in the act.

Without making a conscious decision, he found himself striding right in.

Then he heard himself saying, "Why don't you fill me in on what you're looking for?"

The woman jumped in the air. She was so light, her movement so vertical, so high, it triggered an exaggerated image in his mind of a cartoon character jumping out of her skin in fright. It almost forced a laugh from his lips at its absurdity yet its appropriateness for this brownie.

The laugh dissolved into a smile that hadn't touched his lips in far too long as she turned to him.

He watched her, feeling as if time was decelerating, like one of those slow-motion movie sequences that signified a momentous event.

He heard himself again, amusement soaking his drawl. "I hear that while searching for something that evidently elusive, two sets of hands and eyes, not to mention two brains, are better than one."

With his last word, she was facing him. And though her face was a canvas of shock, and he could tell from her shapeless black shirt and pants that the tiny sprite was unarmed, it felt as if he'd gotten a kick in his gut.

And that was before her startled expression faded, before those fierce, dark eyes flayed a layer off his skin and her husky voice burned down his nerve endings.

"I should have known the unfortunate event of tripping into your presence was a territorial hazard around this place. So what brings you to your poor sister's office while she's not around? Is no one safe from the raids of The Pirate?"

Two

Aram stared at the slight creature who faced him across the elegant office, radiating the impact of a miniature force of nature, and one thing reverberating through his mind.

She'd recognized him on the spot.

No. More than that. She *knew* him. At least knew *of* him.

She'd called him "The Pirate." The persona, or rather the caricature of him that distasteful tabloids, scorned women and disgruntled business rivals had popularized.

She seemed to be waiting for him to make a comeback to her opening salvo.

A charge of electricity forked up his spine, then all the way up to his lips, spreading them wider. "So I'm The Pirate. And what do you answer to? The Tornado? The Hurricane? You did tear through Johara's office with the comparative havoc of one. Or do you simply go with The Burglar? A very messy, noisy, reckless one at that?"

She tilted her head, sending her masses of glossy curls tumbling over one slim shoulder. He could swear he heard them tutting in sarcastic vexation that echoed the expression on her elfin face.

It also poured into her voice, its timbre causing something inside his rib cage to rev. "So are you going to stand there like the behemoth that you are blocking my escape route and sucking all oxygen from the room into that ridiculously massive chest of yours, or are you going to give a fellow thief a hand?"

His lips twitched, every word out of hers another zap lashing through his nerves. "Now, how is it fair that I assist you in your heist without even having the privilege of knowing who I'm going to be indicted with when we're caught? Or are formal introductions not even necessary? Perhaps your spritely self plans on disappearing into the night, leaving me behind to take the fall?"

Her stare froze on him for several long seconds before she suddenly tossed her hair back with a careless hand. "Oh, right…I remember now. Sorry for that. I guess having you materialize behind me like some genie surprised me so much it took me a while to reboot and access my memory banks."

He blinked, then frowned. Was she the one who'd stopped making sense, or had his mind finally stopped functioning? It *had* been increasingly glitch riddled of late. He had been teetering on the brink of some breakdown for a long time now, and he'd thought it was only a matter of time before the chasm running through his being became complete.

So had his psyche picked now of all times to hit rock bottom? But why *now,* when he'd finally found someone to jog him out of his apathy, even if temporarily; someone he actually couldn't predict?

Maybe he'd blacked out or something, missed something she'd said that would make her last words make sense.

He cleared his throat. "Uh…come again?"

Her fed-up expression deepened. "I momentarily forgot how you got your nickname, and that you continue to live down to it, and then some."

Though the jump in continuity still baffled him, he went along. "Oh? I'm very much interested in hearing your dissection of my character. Knowing how another criminal mastermind perceives me would no doubt help me perfect my M.O."

One of those dense, slanting eyebrows rose. "Invoking the code of dishonor among thieves? Sure, why not? I'm charitable like that with fellow crooks." That obsidian gaze poured mockery over him. "Let's see. You earned your moniker after building a reputation of treating other sentient beings like commodities to be pillaged then tossed aside once their benefit is depleted. But you reserve an added insult and injury to those who suffer the terrible misfortune of being exposed to you on a personal level, as you reward those hapless people by deleting them from you mind. So, if you're seeking my counsel about enhancing your performance, my opinion is that you can't improve on your M.O. of perfectly efficient cruelty."

Her scathing portrayal *was* the image that had been painted of him in the business world and by the women he'd kept away by whatever measures necessary.

When his actions had been exaggerated or misinterpreted and that ruthless reputation had begun to be established, he'd never tried to adjust it. On the contrary, he'd let it become entrenched, since that perceived cold-bloodedness did endow him with a power nothing else could. Not to mention that it supplied him with peace of mind he couldn't have bought if he'd projected a more approachable persona. This one did keep the world at bay.

But the only actual accuracy in her summation was the personal interactions bit. He didn't crowd his recollections with the mundane details of anyone who hadn't proved worth his while. Only major incidents remained in his memory—if stripped from any emotional impact they might have had.

But...wait a minute. Inquiring about her identity had triggered this caustic commentary in the first place. Was she obliquely saying that he didn't remember *her*, when he should?

That was just not possible. How would he have ever forgotten those eyes that could reduce a man to ashes at thirty paces, or that tongue that could shred him to ribbons, or that wit that could weave those ribbons into the hand basket to send him to hell in?

No way. If he'd ever as much as exchanged a few words with her, not only would he have remembered, he would probably have borne the marks of every one. After mere minutes of being exposed to her, he felt her eyes and tongue had left no part of him unscathed.

And he was loving it.

God, to be reveling in this, he must be sicker than he'd thought of all the fawning he got from everyone else—especially women. Though he knew *that* had never been for *him*. During his stint in Zohayd, it had been his exotic looks but mainly his closeness to the royal family that had incited the relentless pursuit of women there. After he'd become a millionaire, then a billionaire… Well, status and wealth were irresistible magnets to almost everyone.

That made being slammed with such downright derision unprecedented. He doubted if he would have accepted it from anyone else, though. But from this enigma, he was outright relishing it.

Wanting to incite even more of her verbal insults, he gave her a bow of mock gratitude. "Your testimony of dishonor honors me, and your maligning warms my stone-cold heart."

Both her eyebrows shot up this time. "You have one? I thought your species didn't come equipped with those superfluous organs."

His grin widened. "I do have a rudimentary thing somewhere."

"Like an appendix?" A short, derogatory sound purred in the back of her throat. "Something that could be excised and you'd probably function better without? Wonder why you didn't have it electively removed. It must be festering in there."

As if compelled, he moved away from the door, needing a closer look at this being he'd never seen the likes of before. He kept drawing nearer as she stood her ground, her glare one that could have stopped an attacking horde.

It only made getting even closer imperative. He stopped only when he was three feet away, peering down at this diminutive woman who was a good foot or more shorter than he was yet feeling as if he was standing nose to nose with an equal.

"Don't worry," he finally said, answering her last dig. "There is no reason for surgical intervention. It has long since shriveled and calcified. But thank you from the bottom of my vestigial heart for the concern. And for the counsel. It's indeed reassuring to have such a merciless authority confirm that I'm doing the wrong thing so right."

He waited for her ricocheting blitz, anticipation rising. Instead, she seared him with an incinerating glance before seeming to delete *him* from her mind as she resumed her search.

By now he knew for certain that she wasn't here to do anything behind Johara's back. Even when she'd readily engaged him in the "thieves in the night" scenario he'd initiated, and rifling through the very cabinets he himself was here to search…

It suddenly hit him, right in the solar plexus, who this tempest in human form was.

It was *her*.

Kanza. Kanza Aal Ajmaan.

Unable to blink, to breathe, he stood staring at her as she kept transferring files from the cabinets, plopping them down on Johara's desk before attacking them with a speed and focus that once again flooded his mind's eye with images of hilarious cartoon characters. He had no clue how he'd even recognized her. Just as she'd accused him, his memories of the Kanza he'd known over ten years ago had been stripped of any specifics.

All he could recall of the fierce and fearsome teenager she'd been, apart from the caricature he'd painted for Shaheen of her atrocious fashion style and the weird, bordering-on-repulsive things she'd done with her hair and eyes, was that it had felt as if something ancient had been inhabiting that younger-than-her-age body.

A decade later, she still seemed more youthful than her chronological age, yet packed the wallop of this same primal force. But that was where the resemblance ended.

The Mad Hatter and Wicked Witch clothes and makeup and extraterrestrial hair, contact lenses and body paint were gone now. From the nondescript black clothes and the white sneakers that clashed with them, to the face scrubbed clean of any enhancements, to the thick, untamed mahogany tresses that didn't seem to have met a stylist since he'd last seen her, she had gone all the way in the other direction.

Though in an opposite way to her former self, she was still the antithesis of all the svelte, stylish women who'd ever entered his orbit, starting with her half sisters. Where they'd been overtly feminine and flaunting their assets, she made no effort whatsoever to maximize any attributes she might have. Not that she had much to work with. She was small, almost boyish. The only big thing about her was her hair. And eyes. Those were enormous. Everything else was tiny.

But that was when he analyzed her looks clinically. But when he experienced them with the influence of the being they housed, the spirit that animated them…that was when his entire perception changed. The pattern of her features, the shape of her lips, the sweep of her lashes, the energy of her movements… Everything about her evolved into something totally different, making her something far more interesting than pretty.

Singular. Compelling.

And the most singular and compelling thing about her was those night eyes that had burned to ashes any preformed ideas of what made a woman worthy of a second glance, let alone constant staring.

Though he was still staring after she'd deprived him of their contact, he *was* glad to be relieved of their all-seeing scrutiny. He needed respite to process finding her here.

How could Shaheen bring her up a couple of weeks ago only for him to stumble on her here of all places when he hadn't crossed paths with her in ten years? This was too much of a coincidence. Which meant…

It wasn't one. Johara had set him up.

Another realization hit simultaneously.

Kanza seemed to be here running his same errand. Evidently Johara had set her up, too.

God. He was growing duller by the day. How could he have even thought Shaheen wouldn't share this with Johara, the woman where half his soul resided? How hadn't he picked up on Johara's knowledge or intentions?

Not that those two coconspirators were important now. The only relevant thing here was Kanza.

Had she realized the setup once he'd walked through that door? Was that why she'd reacted so cuttingly to his appearance? Did she take exception to Johara's matchmaking, and that was her way of telling her, and him, "Hell, no!"?

If this was the truth, then that made her even more interesting than he'd originally thought. It wasn't conceit, but as Shaheen had said, in the marriage market, he was about as big a catch as an eligible bachelor got. He couldn't imagine any woman would be averse to the idea of being his wife— if only for his status and wealth. Even his reputation was an irresistible lure in that arena. If women thought they had access, it only made him more of a challenge, a dangerous bad boy each dreamed she'd be the one to tame.

But if Kanza was so immune to his assets, so opposed

to exploring his possibility as a groom, that alone made her worthy of in-depth investigation.

Not that *he* was even considering Shaheen and Johara's neat little plan. But he *was* more intrigued by the moment by this…entity they'd gotten it into their minds was perfect for him.

Suddenly, said entity looked up from the files, transfixed him in the crosshairs of her fiercest glare yet. "Don't just stand there and pose. Come do something more useful than look pretty." When she saw his eyebrows shoot up, her lips twisted. "What? You take exception to being called pretty?"

He opened his mouth to answer, and her impatient gesture closed it for him, had him hurrying next to her where she foisted a pile of files on him and instructed him to look for the very file Johara had sent him here to retrieve.

Without looking at him, she resumed her search. "I guess pretty is too mild. You have a right to expect more powerful descriptions."

He gave her engrossed profile a sideways glance. "If I expect anything, it certainly isn't that."

She slammed another file shut. "Why not? You have the market of *halawah* cornered after all."

Halawah, literally sweetness, was used in Zohayd to describe beauty. That had him turning fully toward her. "Where *do* you come up with these things that you say?"

She flicked him a fleeting glance, closed another file on a sigh of frustration. "That's what women in Zohayd used to say about you. Wonder what they'd say now that your *halawah* is so exacerbated by age it could induce diabetes."

That had a laugh barking from his depths. "Why, thanks. Being called a diabetes risk is certainly a new spin on my supposed good looks."

She tsked. "You know damn well how beautiful you are."

He shook his bemused head at what kept spilling from those dainty lips, compliments with the razor-sharp edges of insults. "No one has accused me of being beautiful before."

"Probably because everyone is programmed to call men handsome or hunks or at most gorgeous. Well, sorry, buddy. You leave all those adjectives in the dust. You're all-out beautiful. It's really quite disgusting."

"Disgusting!"

"Sickeningly so. The resources you must devote to maximizing your assets and maintaining them at this…level…" She tossed him a gesture that eloquently encompassed him from head to toe. "When your looks aren't your livelihood, this is an excess that should be punishable by law."

An incredulous huff escaped him. "It's surreal to hear you say that when my closest people keep telling me the very opposite—that I'm totally neglecting myself."

She slanted him a caustic look. "You have people who can bear being close to you? My deepest condolences to them."

He smiled as if she'd just lavished the most extravagant praise on him. "I'll make sure to relay your sympathies."

Another withering glance came his way before she resumed her work. "I'll give mine directly to Johara. No wonder she's seemed burdened of late. It must be quite a hardship having you for an only brother in general, not to mention having to see you frequently when she's here."

His gaze lengthened on her averted face. Then suddenly everything jolted into place.

Who Kanza *really* was.

She was the new partner that Johara had been waxing poetic about. Now he replayed the times his sister had raved about the woman who'd taken Johara's design house from moderate success to household-name status, this financial marketing guru who had never actually been mentioned by name. But he had no doubt now it was Kanza.

Had Johara never brought up her name because she didn't want to alert him to her intentions, making him resistant to meeting Kanza and predisposed to finding fault with her if he did? If so, then Johara understood him better than Shaheen did, who'd hit him over the head with his intentions and Kanza's name. That *had* backfired. Evidently Johara had reeled Shaheen in, telling her husband not to bring up the subject again and that she'd handle everything from that point on, discreetly. And she had.

Another certainty slotted into place. Johara had kept her business partner in the dark about all this for the same reason.

Which meant that Kanza had no clue this meeting wasn't a coincidence.

The urge to divulge everything about their situation surged from zero to one hundred. He couldn't wait to see the look on her face as the truth of Johara and Shaheen's machinations sank in and to just stand back and enjoy the fireworks.

He turned to her, the words almost on his lips, when another thought hit him.

What if, once he told her, she became stilted, self-conscious? Or worse, *nice?* He couldn't bear the idea that after their invigorating duel of wits, her revitalizing lambasting, she'd suddenly start to sugarcoat her true nature in an attempt to endear herself to him as a potential bride. But worst of all, what if she shut him out completely?

From what he'd found out about her character so far, he'd go with scenario number three as the far more plausible one.

Whichever way this played out, he couldn't risk spoiling her spontaneity or ending this stimulating interlude.

Deciding to keep this juicy tidbit to himself, he said, "Apart from burdening Johara with my existence, I was actually serious for a change. Everyone I meet tells me I've never looked worse. The mirror confirms their opinion."

"I've smacked people upside the head for less, buddy." She narrowed her eyes at him, as if charting the trajectory of the smack he'd earn if he weren't careful. "Nothing annoys me more than false modesty, so if you don't want me to muss that perfectly styled mane of yours, watch it."

Suddenly it was important for him to settle this with her. "There is no trace of anything false in what I'm saying—modesty or otherwise. I really have been in bad shape and have been getting progressively worse for over a year now."

This gave her pause for a moment, something like contrition or sympathy coming into her eyes.

Before he could be sure, it was gone, her fathomless eyes glittering with annoyance again. "You mean you've looked better than this? Any better and you should be…arrested or something."

Something warm seeped through his bones, brought that unfamiliar smile to his lips again. "Though I barely give the way I look any thought, you managed what I thought impossible. You flattered me in a way I never was before."

She grimaced as if at some terrible taste. "Hello? Wasn't I speaking English just now? Flattering you isn't among the things I would ever do, even at gunpoint."

"Sorry if this causes you an allergic reaction, but that is exactly what you did, when I've been looking at myself lately and finding only a depleted wretch looking back at me."

She opened her mouth to deliver another disparaging blow, before she closed it, her eyes narrowing contemplatively over his face.

"Now I'm looking for it. I guess, yeah, I see it. But it sort of…roughens your slickness and gives you a simulation of humanity that makes you look better than your former overly polished perfection. Figures, huh? Instead of looking like crap, you manage to make wretched and depleted work for you."

He abandoned any pretense of looking through the files and turned to her, arms folded over his chest. "Okay. I get it. You despise the hell out of me. Are you going to tell me what I ever did to deserve your wrath, Kanza?"

When she heard her name on his lips, something blipped in her eyes. It was gone again before he could latch on to it, and she reverted back to full-blast disdain mode. "Give the poor, depleted Pirate an energy bar. He's exerted himself digging through his hard drive's trash and recognized me. And even after he did, he still asks. What? You think your transgressions should have been dropped from the record by time?"

"Which transgressions are we talking about here?"

"Yeah, with multitudes to pick from, you can't even figure out which ones I'm referring to."

"Though I'm finding your bashing delightful, even therapeutic, my curiosity levels are edging into the danger zone. How about you put me out of my misery and enlighten me as to what exactly I'm paying the price for now?"

Her lips twisted disbelievingly. "You've really forgotten, haven't you?" At his unrepentant yet impatient nod, she rolled her eyes and turned back to the files, muttering under her breath. "You can go rack your brains with a rake for the answer for all I care. I'm not helping you scratch that itch."

"Since there's no way I've forgotten anything I did to you that could cause such an everlasting grudge..." He paused, frowned then exclaimed, "Don't tell me this is about Maysoon!"

"*And* he remembers. In a way that adds more insult to injury. You're a species of one, aren't you, Aram Nazaryan?"

Before he could say anything, she strode away, clearly not intending to let him pursue the subject. He could push his luck but doubted she'd oblige him.

But at least he now knew where this animosity was coming from. While he hadn't factored in that this would be her stance regarding the fiasco between him and Maysoon, it seemed she had accumulated an unhealthy dose of prejudice against him from the time he'd been briefly engaged to her half sister. And she'd added an impressive amount of further bias ever since.

She slammed another filing cabinet shut. "This damn

file isn't here." She suddenly turned on him. "But you are. What the hell are you doing here, anyway?"

So it had finally sunk in, the improbability of his stumbling in on her here in his sister's office.

Having already decided to throw her off, he said, "I was hoping Johara would be working late."

She frowned. "So you don't know that she and Shaheen are throwing a party tonight?"

"They are?" This had to be his best acting moment ever.

She bought it, as evidenced by her return to mockery. "You forgot that, too? Is anything of any importance to you?"

He approached her again with the same caution he would approach a hostile feline. "Why do you assume it's me who forgot and not them who neglected to invite me?"

"Because I'd never believe either Johara or Shaheen would neglect anyone, even you."

When he was a few feet away, he looked down at her, amusement again rising unbidden. "But it's fully believable that I got their invitation and tossed it in the bin unread?"

She shrugged. "Sure. Why not? I'd believe you got a dozen phone calls, too, or even face-to-face invitations and just disregarded them."

"Then I come here to visit my sister because I'm disregarding her?"

"Maybe you need something from her and came to ask for it, even though you won't consider going to her party."

He let out a short, delighted laugh. "You'll go the extra light-year to think the worst of me, won't you?"

"Don't give me any credit. It's you who makes it exceptionally easy to malign you."

Hardly believing how much he was enjoying her onslaught, he shook his head. "One would think Maysoon is your favorite sister and bosom buddy from the way you're hacking at me."

The intensity of her contempt grew hotter. "I would have

hacked at you if you'd done the same to a stranger or even an enemy."

"So your moral code is unaffected by personal considerations. Commendable. But what *have* I done exactly, in your opinion?"

Her snort was so cute, so incongruous, that it had his unfettered laugh ringing out again.

"Oh, you're good. With three words you've turned this from a matter of fact to a matter of opinion. Play another one."

"I'm trying hard to."

"Then *el'ab be'eed*."

This meant *play far away*. From her, of course.

Something he had no intention of doing. "Won't you at least recite my charges and read me my rights?"

She produced her cell phone. "Nope. I bypassed all that and long pronounced your sentence."

"Shouldn't I be getting parole after ten years?"

"Not when I gave you life in the first place, no."

His whole face was aching. He hadn't smiled this much in…ever. "You're a mean little thing, aren't you?"

"And you're a sleazy huge thing, aren't you?"

He guffawed this time.

Wondering how the hell this pixie was doing this, triggering his humor with every acerbic remark, he headed back to Johara's desk. "So are we done with your search mission? Or going by the aftermath of your efforts, search-and-destroy operation?"

"Just for that," she said as she placed a call, "you put everything back where it belongs."

"I don't think even Johara herself can accomplish that impossibility after the chaos you've wrought."

She flicked him one last annihilating look, then dismissed him as she started speaking into the phone without preamble. "Okay, Jo, I can't find anything that might be the file you described, and I've gone through every shred of paper you got here."

"You mean *we* did." Aram raised his voice to make sure Johara heard him.

An obsidian bolt hit him right between the eyes, had his heart skipping a beat.

He grinned even more widely at her. He had no doubt Johara *had* heard him, but it was clear she'd pretended she hadn't, since Kanza's wrath would have only increased if Johara had made any comment or asked who was with her.

And he'd thought he'd known everything there was to know about his kid sister. Turned out she wasn't only capable of the subterfuge of setting him and her partner up, but of acting seamlessly on the fly, too.

Kanza was frowning now. "What do you mean it's okay? It's not okay. You need the file, and if it's here, I'll find it. Just give me a better description. I might have looked at it a dozen times and didn't recognize it for what it was."

Kanza fell silent for a few moments as Johara answered. He had a feeling she was telling Kanza a load of ultra-convincing bull. By now, he was 100 percent certain that file didn't even exist.

Kanza ended the conversation and confirmed his deductions. "I can't believe it! Johara is now not even sure the file is here at all. Blames it on pregnancy hormones."

Hoping his placating act was half as good as Johara's misleading one, he said, "We only lost an hour of turning her office upside down. Apart from the mess, no harm done."

"First, there's no *we* in the matter. Second, I was here an hour before you breezed in. Third, you *did* breeze in. Can't think of more harm than that. But the good news is I now get to breeze out of here and put an end to this unwelcome and torturous exchange with you."

"Aren't you even going to try to ameliorate the destruction you've left in your wake?"

"Johara insisted I leave everything and just rush over to the party."

So she was invited. Of course. Though from the way she was dressed, no one would think she had anything more glamorous planned than going to the grocery store.

But it was evident she intended to go. That must have been Johara and Shaheen's plan A. They'd invited him to set him and Kanza up at the soirée. And when he'd refused, Johara had improvised find-the-nonexistent-file plan B.

Kanza grabbed a red jacket from one of the couches, which he hadn't noticed before, and shrugged it on before hooking what looked like a small laptop bag across her body.

Then, without even a backward glance at him, she was striding toward the door.

He didn't know how he'd managed to move that fast, but he found himself blocking her path.

This surprised her so much that she bumped into him. He caught an unguarded expression in those bottomless black eyes as she stumbled back. A look of pure vulnerability. As though the steely persona she'd been projecting wasn't the real her, or not the only side to her. As though his nearness unsettled her so much it left her floundering.

A moment later he wondered if he'd imagined what he'd seen, since the look was now gone and annoyance was the only thing left in its place.

He tried what he hoped was the smooth charm he'd seen others practice but had never attempted himself. "How about we breeze out of here together and I drive you to the party?"

"You assume I came here…how? On foot?"

"A pixie like you might have just blinked in here."

"Then I can blink out the same way."

"I'm still offering to conserve your mystic energies."

"Acting the gentleman doesn't become you, and any attempt at simulating one is wasted on me since I'm hardly a damsel in distress. And if you're offering in order to score points with Johara, forget it."

"There you go again—assigning such convoluted motives to my actions when I'm far simpler than you think. I've decided to go to the party, and since you're going, too, you can save your pixie magic, as I have a perfectly mundane car parked in the garage."

"What a coincidence. So do I. Though mine is mundane for real. While yours verges on the supernatural. I hear it talks, thinks, takes your orders, parks itself and knows when to brake and where to go. All it has left to do is make you a sandwich and a cappuccino to become truly sentient."

"I'll see about developing those sandwich- and cappuccino-making capabilities. Thanks for the suggestion. But wouldn't you like to take a spin in my near-sentient car?"

"No. Just like I wouldn't want to be in your near-sentient presence. Now *ann eznak*...or better still, *men ghair eznak*." Then she turned and strode away.

He waited until she exited the room before moving. In moments, his far-longer strides overtook her at the elevators.

Kanza didn't give any indication that she noticed him, going through messages on her phone. She still made no reaction when he boarded the elevator with her and then when he followed her to the garage.

It was only when he tailed her to her car that she finally turned on him. *"What?"*

He gave her his best pseudoinnocent smile and lobbed back her parting shot. "By your leave, or better still without it, I'm escorting you to your car."

She looked him up and down in silence, then turned and took the last strides to a Ford Escape that was the exact color of her jacket. Seemed she was fond of red.

In moments, she drove away with a screech right out of a car chase, which had him jumping out of the way.

He stood watching her taillights flashing as she hit the

brakes at the garage's exit. Grinning to himself, he felt a rush of pure adrenaline flood his system.

She'd really done it. Something no other woman—no other person—had ever done.

She'd turned him down.

No…it was more that that. She'd *rebuffed* him.

Well. There was only one thing he could do now.

Give chase.

Three

Kanza resisted the urge to floor the gas pedal.

That…rat was following her.

That colossal, cruelly magnificent rat.

Though the way he made her feel was that *she* was the rat, running for her life, growing more frantic by the breath, chased by a majestic, terminally bored cat who'd gotten it in his mind to chase her…just for the hell of it.

She snatched another look in the rearview mirror.

Yep. There he still was. Driving safely, damn him, keeping the length of three cars between them, almost to the inch. He'd probably told his pet car how far away it should stick to her car's butt. The constant distance was more nerve-racking than if he'd kept approaching and receding, if he'd made any indication that he was expending any effort in keeping up with her.

She knew he didn't really want to catch her. He was just exercising the prerogative of his havoc-inducing powers. He was doing this to rattle her. To show her that no one refused him, that he'd do whatever he pleased, even if it infringed on others. Preferably if it did.

It made her want to slam the brakes in the middle of the

road, force him to stop right behind her. Then she'd get down, walk over there and haul him out of his car and... and... What?

Bite mouthfuls out of his gorgeous bod? Swipe his keys and cell phone and leave him stranded on the side of the road?

Evidently, from the maddening time she'd just spent in his company, he'd probably enjoy the hell out of whatever she did. She *had* tried her level worst back in Johara's office, and that insensitive lout had seemed to be having a ball, thinking every insult out of her mouth was a hoot. Seemed his jaded blood levels had long been toxic and now any form of abuse was a stimulant.

Gritting her teeth all the way to Johara and Shaheen's place, she kept taking compulsive glances back at this incorrigible predator who tailed her in such unhurried pursuit.

Twenty minutes later, she parked the car in the garage, filled her lungs with air. Then, holding it as if she was bracing for a blow, she got out.

Out of the corner of her eye she could estimate he'd parked, too. Three empty car places away. He was really going the distance to maintain the joke, wasn't he?

Fine. Let him have his fun. Which would only be exacerbated if she made any response. She wouldn't.

When she was at the elevator, she stopped, a groan escaping her. Aram had frazzled her so much that she'd left Johara and Shaheen's housewarming present, along with the Arabian horse miniature set she'd promised Gharam, in the trunk.

Cursing him to grow a billion blue blistering barnacles, she turned on her heel and stalked back to the car. She passed him on her way back, as he'd been following in her wake, maintaining the equivalent of three paces behind her.

Feeling his gaze on her like the heaviest embarrassment she'd ever suffered, she retrieved the boxes. Just as the tailgate clicked closed, she almost knocked her head against it in chagrin. She'd forgotten to change her sneakers.

Great. This guy was frying her synapses even at fifty paces, where he was standing serenely by the elevator, awaiting her return. Maybe she should just forget about changing the sneakers. Or better still, hurl them at him.

But it was one thing to skip around in those sneakers, another to attend Johara and Shaheen's chic party in them. It was bad enough she'd be the most underdressed one around, as usual.

Forcing herself to breathe calmly, she reopened the tailgate and hopped on the edge of the trunk. He'd just have to bear the excitement of watching her change into slightly less nondescript two-inch heels. At least those were black and didn't clash like a chalk aberration on a black background.

In two minutes she was back at the elevators, hoisting the boxes—each under an arm. Contrary to her expectations, he didn't offer to help her carry them. Then he didn't even board the elevator with her. Instead, he just stood there in that disconcerting calm while the doors closed. Though she was again pretending to be busy with her phone, she knew he didn't pry his gaze from her face. And that he had that infuriating smile on his all the time.

Sensing she'd gotten only a short-lived respite since he was certain to follow her up at his own pace, she knew her smile was on the verge of shattering as Johara received her at the door. It must have been her own tension that made her imagine that Johara looked disappointed. For why would she be, when she'd already known she hadn't found her file and had been the one to insist Kanza stop searching for it?

Speculation evaporated as Johara exclaimed over Kanza's gifts and ushered her toward Shaheen and Gharam. But barely three minutes later, Johara excused herself and hurried to the door again.

Though Kanza was certain it was *him,* her breath still

caught in her throat, and her heart sputtered like a mal-functioning throttle.

Ya Ullah... Why was she letting this virtuoso manipulator pull her strings like this?

The surge of fury manifested in exaggerated gaiety with Shaheen and Gharam. But a minute later Shaheen excused himself, too, and rushed away with Gharam to join his wife in welcoming his so-called best friend. She almost blurted out that Aram was here only to annoy her, not to see him or his sister, and that Shaheen should do himself a favor and find himself a new best friend, since *that* one cared about no one but himself.

Biting her tongue and striding deeper into the penthouse, she forced herself to mingle, which usually rated right with anesthesia-free tooth extractions on her list of favorite pastimes. However, right now, it felt like the most desirable thing ever, compared to being exposed to Aram Nazaryan again.

But to her surprise, she wasn't.

After an hour passed, throughout which she'd felt his eyes constantly on her, he'd made no attempt to approach her, and her tension started to dissipate.

It seemed her novelty to him had worn off. He must be wondering why the hell he'd taken his challenge this far—at the price of suffering the company of actual human beings. Ones who clearly loved him, though why, she'd never understand.

She still welcomed the distraction when Johara asked her to put the horse set in their family living room away from Gharam's determined-to-take-them-apart hands. The two-and-a-half-year-old tyke was one unstoppable girl who everyone said took after her maternal uncle. Clearly, in nature as well as looks.

She'd finished her chore and was debating what was more moronic—that she was this affected by Aram's presence or that her relief at the end of this perplexing interlude was mixed with what infuriatingly resembled letdown—when it felt as if a thousand volts of electricity zapped her. His dark, velvety baritone that drenched her every receptor in paralysis.

It was long, heart-thudding moments before what he'd said made sense.

"I'm petitioning for a reopening of my case."

She didn't turn to him. She couldn't.

For the second time tonight, he'd snuck up on her, startling the reins of volition out of her reach.

But this time, courtesy of the building tension that had been defused in false security, the surprise incapacitated her.

When she didn't turn, it was Aram who circled her in a wide arc, coming to face her at that distance he'd been maintaining, as if he was a hunter who knew he had his quarry cornered yet still wasn't taking any chances he'd get a set of claws across the face.

And as usual with him around, she felt the spacious, ingeniously decorated room shrink and fade away, her senses converging like a spotlight on him.

It was always a shock to the system beholding him. He was without any doubt the most beautiful creature she'd ever seen. Damn him.

She'd bet it was beyond anyone alive not to be awed by his sheer grandeur and presence, to not gape as they drank in the details of what made him what he was. She remembered with acute vividness the first time she'd seen him. She *had* gaped then and every time she'd seen him afterward, trying to wrap her mind around how anyone could be endowed with so much magnificence.

He lived up to his pseudonym—a pirate from a fairy tale, imposing, imperious, mysterious with a dark, ruthless edge to his beauty, making him…utterly compelling.

It still seemed unbelievable that he was Johara's brother. Apart from both of them possessing a level of beauty that was spellbinding, verging on painful to behold, they looked nothing alike. While Johara had the most amazing golden hair, molten chocolate eyes and thick cream complexion, Aram was her total opposite. But after she'd seen both their parents, she'd realized he'd manifested the absolute best in both, too.

His eyes were a more dazzling shade of azure than that of his French mother's—the most vivid, hypnotic color she'd ever seen. From his mother, too, and her family, he'd also inherited his prodigious height and amplified it. He'd added a generous brush of burnished copper to his Armenian-American father's swarthy complexion, a deepened gloss and luxury to his raven mane and an enhanced bulk and breadth to his physique.

Then came the details. And the devil was very much in those. A dancing, laughing, knowing one, aware of the exact measure of their unstoppable influence. Of every slash and hollow and plane of a face stamped with splendor and uniqueness, every bulge and sweep and slope of a body emanating maleness and strength, every move and glance and intonation demonstrating grace and manliness, power and perfection. All in all, he was glory personified.

Now, exuding enough charisma and confidence to power a small city, he towered across from her, calmly sweeping his silk black jacket out of the way, shoving his hands into his pockets. The movement had the cream shirt stretching over the expanse of virility it clung to. Her lips tingled as his chiseled mouth quirked up into that lethal smile.

"I submit a motion that I have been unjustly tried."

Aram's obvious enjoyment, not to mention his biding his time before springing his presence on her again, made retaliation a necessity.

Her voice, when she managed to operate her vocal cords, thankfully sounded cool and dismissive. "And I submit you've not only gotten away with your crimes but you've been phenomenally rewarded for them."

"If you're referring to my current business success, how are you managing to correlate it to my alleged crimes?"

She fought not to lick the dryness from her lips, to bite into the numbness that was spreading through them. "I'm managing because you've built said success using the same principles with which you perpetrated those crimes."

His eyes literally glittered with mischief, becoming bluer before her dazzled ones. "Then I am submitting that those principles you ascribe to me and your proof of them were built around pure circumstantial evidence."

Her eyebrows shot up. "So you're not after a retrial. What you really want is your whole criminal record expunged."

He raised those large, perfectly formed hands like someone blocking blows. "I wouldn't dream of universally dismissing my convictions." His painstakingly sculpted lips curled into a delicious grin. "That would be pushing my luck. But I do demand an actual primary hearing of my testimony, since I distinctly remember one was never taken."

Although she felt her heart sputtering out of control, she tried to match his composure outwardly. "Who says you get a hearing at all? You certainly didn't grant others such mercy or consideration."

The scorching amusement in those gemlike eyes remained unperturbed. "By others you mean Maysoon, I assume?"

"Hers was the case I observed firsthand. As I am a stickler for justice, I will not pass judgment on those I know of only through secondhand testimonies and hearsay."

His eyes widened on what looked like genuine surprise.

Yeah, right. As if he could feel anything for real.

"That's very…progressive of you. Elevated, even." At her baleful glance, something that simulated seriousness took over his expression. "No, I mean it. In my experience, when people don't like someone, they demonize them wholesale, stop granting them even the possibility of fairness."

She pursed her lips, refusing to consider the possibility of his sincerity. "Lauding my merits won't work, you know."

"In granting me a hearing?"

"In granting you leniency you haven't earned and certainly don't deserve." He opened his mouth, and she raised her hand. "Don't you think you've taken your joke far enough?"

For a moment he looked actually confused before a careful expression replaced uncertainty. "What joke, exactly?"

She rolled her eyes. "Spare me."

"Or you'll spear me?" At her exasperated rumble, he raised his hands again, the coaxing in his eyes rising another notch. "That *was* lame. But I really don't know what you're talking about. I am barely keeping up with you."

"Yeah, right. Since you materialized behind me like some capricious spirit, you've been ready with something right off the smart-ass chart before I've even finished speaking."

He shook his head, causing his collar-length mane to undulate. "If you think that was easy, think again. You're making me struggle for every inch before you snatch it away with your next lob. For the first time in my life I have no idea what will spill out of someone's lips next, so give me a break."

"I would ask where you want it, but I have to be realistic. Considering our respective physiques, I probably can't give you one without the help of heavy, blunt objects."

The next moment, all her nerves fired up as he proceeded to subject her to the sight and sound of his all-out amusement, a demonstration so...virile, so debilitating, each peal was a new bolt forking through her nervous system.

When he at last brought his mirth under control, his lips remained stretched the widest she'd seen them, showing off that set of extraordinary white teeth in the most devastating smile she'd had the misfortune of witnessing. He even wiped away a couple of tears of hilarity. "You can give me compound fractures with your tongue alone. As for your glares, we're talking incineration."

Hating that even when he was out of breath and wheezing, he sounded more hard-hitting for it, she gritted out, "If I could do that, it would be the least I owe you."

"What have I done *now?*" Even his pseudolament was scrumptious. This guy needed some kind of quarantine. He shouldn't be left free to roam the realm of flimsy mortals. "Is this about the joke you've accused me of perpetrating?"

"There's no accusation here—just statement of fact. You've been enjoying one big fat joke at my expense since you stumbled on me in Johara's office."

His eyes sobered at once, filling with something even more distressing than mischief and humor. Indulgence? "I've been relishing the experience immensely, but not as a joke and certainly not at your expense."

Her heart gave her ribs another vicious kick. She had to stop this before her heart literally bruised.

She raised her hands. "Okay, this is going nowhere. Let's say I believe you. Give me another reason you're doing this. And don't tell me that you care one way or the other what I think in general or what I think of you specifically. You don't care about what anyone thinks."

The earnestness in his eyes deepened. "You're right. I care nothing for what others think of me."

"And you're absolutely right not to."

That seemed to stun him yet again. "I am?" At her nod, he prodded, "That includes *everyone?*"

She nodded again. "Of course. What other people think of you, no matter who they are, is irrelevant. Unsolicited opinions are usually a hindrance and a source of discontentment, if not outright unhappiness. So carry on not caring, go take your leave from Johara and Shaheen and return to your universe where no one's opinion matters…as it shouldn't."

"At least grant me the right to care or not care." Those unbelievable eyes seemed to penetrate right through her as his gaze narrowed in on her. "And whether it comes under caring or not, I do happen to be extremely interested in your opinion of me. Now, let me escort you back to the party. Let me get us a drink over which we'll reopen my case and explore the possibility of adjusting your opinion of me—at least to a degree."

She arched a brow. "You mean you'd settle for adjusting my opinion of you from horrific to just plain horrid?"

"Who knows, maybe while retrying my case, your unwavering sense of justice will lead you to adjusting it to plain misjudged."

"Or maybe just downright wretched."

He hit her with another of his pouts. Then he raised the level of chaos and laughed again, his merriment as potent as everything else about him. "I'd take that."

Trying to convince her heart to slot back into its usual place after its latest somersault, she again tried her best glower. It had no effect on him, as usual. Worse. It had the opposite effect to what she'd perfected it for. He looked at her as if her glare was the cutest thing he'd seen.

She voiced her frustration. "You talk about my incinerating glares, but I could be throwing cotton balls or rose petals at you for all the effect they have on you."

"It's not your glares that are ineffective. It's me who's discovering a penchant for incineration."

Instead of appeasing her, it annoyed her more. "I'll have you know I've reduced other men to dust with those scowls. No one has withstood a minute in my presence once I engaged annihilate mode." She lifted her chin. "But you seem to need specifically designed weapons. If I go along with you in this game you got it in your mind to play, it'll be so I can find out if you have an Achilles' heel."

"I have no idea if I have that." His gaze grew thoughtful. "Would you use it to…annihilate me if you discovered it?"

She gave him one of her patented sizing-up glances and regretted it midway. She must quit trying her usual strategies with him. Not only because they always backfired, but it wasn't advisable to expose herself to another distressing dose of his wonders.

She returned to his eyes, those turquoise depths that exuded the ferocity of his intellect and the power of his wit, and found gazing into them just as taxing to her circulatory system.

She sighed, more vexed with her own inability to moderate her reactions than with him. "Nah. I'll just be satisfied knowing your Achilles' heel exists and you're not invulnerable. And maybe, if you get too obnoxious, I'll use my knowledge as leverage to make you back off."

That current of mischief and challenge in his eyes spiked. "It goes against my nature to back off."

"Not even under threat of…annihilation?"

"Especially then. I'd probably beg you to use whatever fatal weakness you discover just to find out how it feels."

"Wow. You're jaded to the point of numbness, aren't you?"

"You've got me figured out, don't you? Or do you? Shall we find out?"

It was clear this monolith would stand there and spar with her until she agreed to this "retrial" of his. If she was in her own domain or on neutral ground, or at least somewhere without a hundred witnesses blocking her only escape route, she would have slammed him with something cutting and walked out as she'd done in Johara's office.

But she couldn't inflict on her friends the scene this gorgeous jerk would instigate if he didn't have his way. She bet he knew she suffered from those scruples, was using the knowledge to corner her into participating in his game.

"You're counting on my inability to risk spoiling Johara and Shaheen's party, aren't you?"

His blink was all innocence, and downright evil for it. "I thought you didn't care what other people thought."

"I don't, not when it comes to how I choose to live my

life. But I do care about what others think of my actions that directly impact them. And if I walk out now, you'll tail me in the most obvious, disruptive way you can, generating curiosity and speculation, which would end up putting a damper on Johara and Shaheen's party." Her eyes narrowed as another thought hit her. "Now I am wondering if maybe they *didn't* extend an invitation to you after all because they've been burned by your sabotage before."

He pounced on that, took it where she couldn't have anticipated. "So you're considering changing your mind about whether I was invited? See? Maybe you'll change your mind about everything else if you give me a chance."

She blew out a breath in exasperation. "I only change my mind for the worse...or worst."

"You're one tiny bundle of nastiness, aren't you?" His smile said he thought that the best thing to aspire to be.

She tossed her head, infusing her disadvantaged stature with all the belittling she could muster. "Again with the size references."

"It was you who started using mine in derogatory terms. Then you moved on to my looks, then my character, then my history, and if there were more components to me, I bet you'd have pummeled through them, too."

Refusing to rise to the bait, she turned around and stomped away.

He followed her. Keeping those famous three steps behind. With his footfalls being soundless, she could pinpoint his location only by the chuckles rumbling in the depths of his massive chest. When those ended, his overpowering presence took over, cocooning her all the way to the expansive reception area.

Absorbed in warding off his influence, she could barely register the ultraelegant surroundings or the dozens of chic people milling around. No one noticed her, as usual, but everyone's gaze was drawn to the nonchalant predator behind her. Abhorring the thought of having everyone's eyes on her by association once they realized he was following her, she continued walking where she hoped the least amount of spectators were around.

She stepped out onto the wraparound terrace that over-looked the now-shrouded-in-darkness Central Park, with Manhattan glittering like fiery jewels beyond its extensive domain. Stopping at the three-foot-high brushed stainless steel and Plexiglas railings, gazing out into the moonlit night, she shivered as September's high-altitude wind hit her overheating body. But she preferred hypothermia to the burning speculation that being in Aram Nazaryan's company would have provoked. Not that she'd managed to escape that totally. The few people who'd had the same idea of seeking privacy out here did their part in singeing her with their curiosity.

She hugged herself to ward off the discomfort of their interest more than the sting of the wind. He made it worse, drenching her in the dark spell of his voice.

"Can I offer you my jacket, or would I have my head bitten off again?"

Barely controlling a shudder, she pretended she was flipping her hair away. "Your head is still on your shoulders. Don't push your luck if you want to keep it there."

His lips pursed in contemplation as he watched her suppress another shudder. "You're one of those independent pains who'd freeze to death before letting people pay them courtesies, aren't you?"

"You're one of those imposing pains who force people into the cold, then inflict their jackets on them and call their imposition courtesy, aren't you?"

"I would have settled for remaining inside where it's toasty. You're the one who led me out here to freeze."

"If you're freezing, don't go playing Superman and volunteering your jacket."

That ever-hovering smile caught fire again. "How about we both mosey on round the corner? Since you're the one who decided to hold my retrial thirty floors up and in the open, I at least motion to do it away from the draft."

"You're also one of those gigantic pains who love to marvel at the sound of their own cleverness, aren't you?" She tossed the words back as she walked ahead to do as he'd suggested.

His answer felt like a wave of heat carrying on the whistling wind. "Just observing a meteorological fact."

As he'd projected, the moment they turned the corner, the wind died down, leaving only comfortable coolness to contend with.

She turned to him at the railings. "Stop right there." He halted at once, perplexity entering his gaze. "You're in the perfect position to shield me from any draft. A good use at last for this superfluous breadth and bulk of yours."

Amusement flooded back into his eyes, radiated hypnotic azure in the moonlight. "So you're only averse to voluntary courtesy on my part, but using me as an unintentional barrier is okay with you."

"Perfectly so. I don't intend to suffer from hypothermia because of the situation you imposed on me."

"I made you come out here?"

"Yes, you did."

"And how did I do that?"

"You made escaping the curiosity, not to mention the jealousy, of all present a necessity."

"Jealousy!" His eyebrows disappeared into the layers of satin hair the wind had flopped over his forehead.

"Every person in there, man or woman, would give anything to be in my place, having your private audience." She gave an exaggerated sigh. "If only they knew I'd donate the *privilege* if I could with a sizable check on top as bonus."

His chuckle revved inside his chest again and in her bones. "That *privilege* is nontransferable. You're stuck with it. So before we convene, what shall I get you?"

"Why shouldn't I be the one to get you something?"

His nod was all concession. "Why shouldn't you, indeed?"

She nodded, too, slowly, totally unable to predict him and feeling more out of her depth by the second for it. "Be specific about what you prefer. I hate guessing."

"I'm flabbergasted you're actually considering my preferences. But I'll go with anything nonalcoholic. I'm driving." Considering he'd placed his order, she started to turn around and he stopped her. "And, Kanza...can you possibly also make it something nonpoisoned and curse free?"

Muttering "smart-ass" and zapping him with her harshest parting glance, which only dissipated against his force field and was received by another chuckle, she strode away.

On reentering the reception, she groaned out loud as she immediately felt the weight of Johara's gaze zooming in on her. She'd no doubt noticed Aram marching behind her across the penthouse and must be bursting with curiosity about how they'd met and why that older brother of hers had gotten it into his mind to follow her around.

Johara just had to bear not knowing. She couldn't worry about her now. One Nazaryan at a time.

She grabbed a glass of cranberry-apple juice from a passing waiter and strode back to the terrace, this time exiting from where she'd left Aram. As soon as she did, she nearly tripped, as her heartbeat did.

Aram was at the railing, two dozen paces away with his back to her. He was silhouetted against the rising moon, hands gripping the bar, looking like a modern statue of a Titan. The only animate things about him were the satin stirring around his majestic head in the tranquil breeze and the silk rustling around his steel-fleshed frame.

But apart from his physical glory, there was something about his pose as he stared out into the night—in the slight slump of his Herculean shoulders, dimming that indomitable vibe—that disturbed her. Whatever it was, it forced her to reconsider her disbelief of his assertion that he'd never felt worse. Made her feel guilty about how she'd been bashing him, believing him invincible.

Then he turned around, as if he'd felt her presence, and his eyes lit up again with that potent merriment and mischief, and all empathy evaporated in a wave of instinctive challenge and chagrined response.

How was it even possible? That after all these years he remained the one man who managed to wring an explosive mixture of fascination and detestation from her?

From the first time she'd laid eyes on him when she'd been seventeen, she'd thought him the most magnificent male in existence, one who compounded his overwhelming physical assets with an array of even more impressive superiorities. He'd been the only one who could breach her composure and tongue-tie her just by walking into a room. That had only earned him a harder crash from the pedestal she'd placed him on, when he'd proved to be just another predictable male, one who considered only a woman's looks and status no matter her character. Why else would he have gotten involved with her spoiled and vapid half sister? Her opinion of him would have been salvaged when he'd walked away from Maysoon, if—and it was an insurmountable if— he hadn't been needlessly, shockingly cruel in doing so.

Remembered outrage rose as she stopped before him and foisted the drink into his hand. It rose higher when she couldn't help watching how his fingers closed around the glass, the grace, power and economy of the movement. It made her want to whack herself and him upside the head.

She had to get this ridiculous interlude over with.

"Without further ado, let's get on with your preposterous retrial."

That gargantuan swine gave a superb pretense of wiping levity from his face, replacing it with earnestness.

"It's going to be the fastest one in history. Your indictment was unequivocal and the evidence against you overwhelming. Whatever her faults, Maysoon loved you, and you kicked her out of your life. Then when she was down, you kicked her again—almost literally and very publicly. You left her in a heap on the ground and walked away unscathed, and then went on to prosper beyond any expectations. While she went on to waste her life, almost self-destruct in one failed relationship after another. If I'd judged your case then, I would have passed the harshest sentence. In any retrial, I'd still pronounce you guilty and judge that you be subjected to character execution."

Four

Aram stared at the diminutive firebrand who was the first woman who'd ever fetched him a drink, then followed up by sentencing his character to death.

Both action and indictment should have elated the hell out of him, as everything from her tonight had. But the expected exhilaration didn't come; something unsettling spread inside him instead. For what if her opinion of him was too entrenched and he couldn't adjust it?

He transferred his gaze to the burgundy depths in the glass she'd just handed him, collecting his thoughts.

Although he'd been keeping it light and teasing, he knew this had suddenly become serious. He had to be careful what to say from now on. If he messed this up, she'd never let him close enough again to have another round. That would be it.

And he couldn't let that be it. He wasn't even going to entertain that possibility. He might have lost many things in his life, but he wasn't going to lose this.

He raised his eyes to meet hers. It was as if they held pieces of the velvet night in their darkest depths. She was waiting, playing by the rules he'd improvised, giving him a chance to defend himself. He had no doubt it would be his one and only chance. He had to make it work.

He inhaled. "I submit that your so-called overwhelming evidence was all circumstantial and unreliable. I did none of the things you've just accused me of. Cite every shred of evidence you think you have, and I'll debunk each one for you."

Her face tilted up at him, sending that amazing wealth of hair cascading with an audible sigh to one side. "You didn't kick Maysoon out of your life?"

"Not in the way you're painting."

"How would you paint it? In black-and-white? In full color? Or because the memory must have faded—in sepia?"

"Who's being a smart-ass now?" At her nonchalant shrug, he pressed on. "What do you know about what happened between Maysoon and me? Apart from her demonizing accounts and your own no less prejudiced observations?"

"Since my observations were so off base, why don't you tell me your own version?"

Having gotten so used to her contention, he was worried by her acquiescence.

He exhaled to release the rising tension. "I assume you knew what your half sister was like? Maybe the impossible has happened and she's evolved by age, but back then, she was…intolerable."

"But of course you found that out after you became engaged to her."

"No. Before."

As he waited for her censure to surpass its previous levels, her gaze only grew thoughtful.

There was no predicting her, was there?

"And you still went through with it. Why?"

"Because I was stupid." Her eyes widened at his harsh admission. She must have thought he'd come up with some excuse to make his actions seem less pathetic and more defensible. He would have done that with anyone else. But with her, he just wanted to have the whole truth out. "I wanted to get married and have a family, but I had no idea how to go about doing that. I thought I'd never leave Zohayd at the time and I'd have to choose a woman from those available. But there was no one I looked at twice, let alone considered for anything lasting. So when Maysoon started pursuing me…"

"Watch it." Her interjection was almost soft. It stopped him in his tracks harder than if she'd bitten it off. "You'll veer off into the land of fabrication if you use this rationale for choosing Maysoon. Using the pursuit criterion, you should have ended up with a harem, since women of all ages in Zohayd chased after you."

"Now who's taking a stroll in the land of exaggeration? Not all women were after me. Aliyah and Laylah, for instance, considered me only one of the family. And you didn't consider me human at all, I believe, let alone male."

Her eyes glittered with the moon's reflected silver as she ignored his statement concerning her. "And that's what? Two females out of two million?"

"Whatever the number of women who pursued me, they were after me as an adventure, and each soon gave up when I made it clear I wasn't into the kind of…entertainment they were after. I wanted a committed relationship at the time."

"And you're saying that none wanted that? Or that none seemed a better choice than Maysoon for said relationship?"

"Compared to Maysoon's pursuit, they were all slouches. And your sister did look like the best deal. Suitable age, easy on the eyes and very, very determined. Sure, she was volatile and superficial, but when her pursuit didn't wane for a whole year, I thought it meant she *really* liked what she saw."

"Her along with everyone with eyes or a brain wave."

Again she managed to make the compliment the most

abrasive form of condemnation, arousing that stinging plea-sure he was getting too used to.

"I'm not talking about my alleged 'beauty' here. I thought she liked *me,* and that meant a lot then. I knew how I was viewed in the royal circles in Zohayd, what my attraction was to the women you cite as my hordes of pursuers. I was this exotic foreigner of mixed descent from a much lower social class that they could have a safe and forbidden fling with. Many thought they could keep me as their boy toy."

Something came into her eyes. Sympathy? Empathy?

It was probably ridicule, and he was imagining things.

"You were hardly a boy," she murmured.

"Their gigolo, then. In any event, I thought Maysoon viewed me differently. Her pursuit in spite of our class dif-ferences and the fact that I was hardly an ideal groom for a princess made me think she was one of those rare women who appreciated a man for himself. I thought this alone made up for all her personal shortcomings. And who was I to consider those when I was riddled with my own?" He emptied his lungs on a harsh exhalation. "Turned out she was just attracted to me as a spoiled brat would be to a toy she fancied and couldn't have. Most likely because some of the women in her inner circle must have made me a topic of giggling lust, maybe even challenge, and being patho-logically competitive herself, she wanted to be the one to triumph over them."

Kanza's eyes filled with skepticism, but she let it go un-voiced and allowed him to continue.

"And the moment she did she started trying to strip me bare to dress me up into the kind of toy she had in mind all along. She started telling me how I must behave, in private and public, how I must distance myself from my father, whom she made clear she considered the hired help." He drew in a sharp inhalation laden with his still-reverberating chagrin on his father's account. "And it didn't end there. She dictated who I should get close to, how I must kiss up to Shaheen's brothers now that he was gone, play on my former relationship with him to gain a 'respectable' position within the kingdom and wheedle financial help in setting up a business like theirs so I would become as rich as possible."

The cynicism in Kanza's eyes had frozen. There was nothing in them now. A very careful nothing. As if she didn't know how to react to the influx of new information.

He went on. "And she was in a rabid hurry for me to do all that. She couldn't wait to have me pick up the tab of her extravagant existence—which she'd thought so disadvantaged—and informed me that as her husband it would be my duty to raise her up to a whole new level of excess." He scrubbed a hand across his jaw. "In the four months' duration of the engagement, I was so stunned by the depths of her shallowness, so taken aback by the audacity of her demands and the intensity of her tantrums, that I didn't react. Then came the night of that ball."

She'd been there that night. In one of those horrific get-ups and alien makeup. He now remembered vividly that she'd been the last thing he'd seen as he'd walked out, standing there over Maysoon, glaring at him with loathing in her eyes.

There was nothing but absorption in her eyes now. She was evidently waiting to see if his version of that ill-fated night's events would change the opinion she'd long held of him, built on her interpretation of its events.

He felt that his next words would decide if she'd ever let him near again. He had to make them count. The only way he could do that was to be as brutally honest as possible.

"Maysoon dragged me to talk to King Atef and Amjad. But when I didn't take her heavy-handed hints to broach the subject of the high-ranking job she'd heard was open, or the loan she'd been pushing me to ask for, she decided to take control. She extolled my economic theories for Zohayd and made a mess of outlining them. Then she proceeded to massacre my personal business plans, which I'd once made the mistake of trying to explain to her. She became terminally obvious as she bragged how anyone getting on with me on the ground level with a sizable investment would reap *millions*." He huffed a bitter laugh. "For a mercenary soul, she knew nothing about the real value of money, since she'd never made a cent and had never even glanced at her own bills."

There was only corroboration in Kanza's eyes now. Knowing her half sister, she must have known the accuracy of this assessment.

He continued. "Needless to say, King Atef and Amjad were not impressed, and they must have believed I'd put her up to it. I was tempted to tell them the truth right then and there, that I'd finally faced it that I was just a means to an end to subsidize her wasteful life. Instead, I attempted to curtail the damage she'd done as best I could before excusing myself and making my escape. Not that she'd let me walk away."

Wariness invaded her gaze. She must have realized he'd come to the point where he'd finally explain the fireworks that had ended his life in Zohayd and formed her lasting-till-now opinion of him.

He shoved his hands into his pockets. "She stormed after me, shrieking that I was a moron, a failure, that I didn't know a thing about grabbing opportunities and maximizing my connections. She said my potential for 'infiltrating' the higher echelons of the royal family was why she'd considered me in the first place and that if I wanted to be her husband I'd do anything to ingratiate myself to them and provide her with the lifestyle she deserved."

Her wince was unmistakable. As if, even if she knew full well Maysoon was capable of saying those things and harboring those motivations, she was still embarrassed for her, ashamed on her account.

Suddenly he wanted to go no further, didn't want to

cause her any discomfort. But she was waiting for him to go on. Her eyes were now prodding him to go on.

He did. "It was almost comical, but I wasn't laughing. I wasn't even angry or disappointed or anything else. I was just…done. So I told her that I would have done anything for the woman I married if she had married me for me and not as a potential meal ticket. Then I walked away. Maysoon wasn't the first major error in judgment I made in Zohayd, but she was the one I rectified."

He paused for a moment, then made his concluding statement, the one refuting her major accusation. "If your half sister has been wasting her life and self-destructing, it's because that's what she does with her capriciousness and excesses and superfluous approach to life—not because of anything *I* did to her. And she's certainly not spinning out of control on my account, because I never counted to her."

Kanza stared up at Aram for what felt like a solid hour after he'd finished his *testimony.*

She could still feel his every word all over her like the stings of a thousand wasps.

She'd never even imagined or could have guessed about his situation back in Zohayd, how he'd been targeted and propositioned, how he'd felt unvalued and objectified.

And she'd been just as guilty of wronging him. In her own mind, in her own way, she had discriminated against him, too, if in the totally opposite direction to those women he'd described. While they'd reduced him to a sexual plaything in their minds, or a stepping-stone to a material goal, she'd exalted him to the point where she'd been unable to see beyond his limitless potential. She hadn't suspected that his untouchable self-possession could have been a facade, a defense; had believed him confident to the point of arrogance; equated his powerful influence with ruthlessness; and had assumed that he could have no insecurities, needs or vulnerabilities.

But…wait. *Wait.* This story was incomplete. He'd left out a huge part. A vital one.

She heard her voice, low, strained, wavering on a gust of wind that circumvented the shield of his body. "But you ended up doing what she advised you to do. She just didn't reap the benefit of her efforts, since you kicked her out of your life on her ear and soared so high on your own."

"Now what the hell are you talking about?"

She pulled herself to her full five-foot-two-plus-heels height, attempting to shove herself up into his face. "Did you or didn't you seek the Aal Shalaan Brotherhood in providing you with their far-reaching connections and fat financial support on your launch into billionairedom?"

"Is this what she said I did?" His scoff sounded furious for the first time. So this was his inapproachable line, what would rouse the indolent predator—any insinuations maligning the integrity and autonomy of his success. "And why not? I did know that there was no limit to her vindictiveness, that she'd do and say anything to punish me for escaping her talons. What else did she accuse me of? Maybe that I abused her, too?"

Her own outrage receded at the advance of his, which was so palpable she had no doubt it was real. Her answer stuck in her throat.

She no longer wanted to continue this. She hadn't wanted to start it in the first place. But his eyes were blazing into hers, demanding that she let him know the full details of Maysoon's accusations. And she had to tell him.

"She said you…exploited her, then threw her aside when you had enough of her."

His eyes narrowed to azure lasers. "By exploited, she meant…sexually?" She nodded, and he gave a spectacular snort, a drench of cold sarcasm underscoring his affront. "Would you believe that I never slept with her?"

"Last I heard, 'sleeping' with someone wasn't a prerequisite of being intimate."

"All right, I did try to be a gentleman and spare you the R-rated language. But since being euphemistic doesn't work in criminal cases, let me be explicit. I never had sex with her. In *any* form. *She* did instigate a few instances of heavy petting—which I didn't reciprocate and put an end to when she tried to offer me…sexual favors. Bottom line…beyond a few unenthusiastic-on-my-part kisses, I never breached her 'purity.' And I wasn't even holding back. I just never felt the least temptation. And when I started seeing her true colors and realized what she really wanted from me, I even became repulsed."

Every word had spiked her temperature higher. To her ears, her every instinct, each had possessed the unmistakable texture of truth. But sanctioning them as the new basis for her belief, her view of the past and his character was still difficult. Mainly because it went against everything she'd believed for so long, about him, about men in general.

Feeling her head would burst on fire, she mumbled, "You're telling me you could be so totally immune to a woman as beautiful as Maysoon when she was so very willing, too? I never heard that mental aversion ever interfered with a man's…drive. Maybe you are not human after all."

"Then get this news flash. There are men who don't find a beautiful, willing woman irresistible."

"Yes. Those men are called gay. Are you? Did you maybe discover that you were when you failed to respond to Maysoon?"

She knew she was being childish and that there was no way he was gay. But she was floundering.

"I 'failed to respond' to Maysoon because I'm one of those men who recognizes black widows and instinctively recoils from said intimacies out of self-preservation. Feeling you're being set up for long-term use and abuse is far more effective than an ice-cold shower. Of course, in hindsight, the fact that I was not attracted to her from the start should have been the danger bell that sent me running. But as I said, I was stupid, thinking that marriage didn't have to include sexual compatibility as a necessary ingredient, that beggars shouldn't be choosers."

He shook his head on a huff of deep disgust. "Lord, now I know why everyone treated me as if I was a sexual predator. Even knowing what she's capable of, I never dreamed she'd go as far as slandering herself in a conservative kingdom where a woman's 'honor' is her sexual purity, in order to paint me a darker shade of black."

That was the main reason Kanza had been forced to believe her half sister. She hadn't been able to imagine even Maysoon would harm herself this way if it hadn't been true. And once she'd believed her in this regard, everything else had been swallowed and digested without any thought of scrutiny. But now she couldn't even consider *not* believing him. This was the truth.

This meant that everything she'd assumed about him was a lie. Which left her…where?

Nowhere. Nowhere but in the wrong and not too happy about being forced to readjust her view of him.

Which didn't actually amount to anything. Her opinion had never mattered to anyone—especially not to Aram. All this new information would do now was torment her with guilt over the way she'd treated him. She'd always prided herself on her sense of justice, yet she'd somehow allowed prejudice to override her common sense where he'd been concerned.

The other damage would be to have her rekindled fascination with him unopposed by that buffering detestation. Although it wouldn't make any difference to him how she changed her opinion of him, she couldn't even chart the ramifications to herself. There was no way this wouldn't be a bad thing to her. Very bad.

Snapping out of her reverie, she realized he wasn't even done "testifying" yet. "Now I come to my deposition about your other accusation—of enlisting the Aal Shalaan Brotherhood's help in 'soaring so high.'"

She waved him off, not up to hearing more. "Don't bother."

"Oh, I bother. Am bothered. Very much so."

"Well, that's your problem. I've heard enough."

"But I haven't said enough." He frowned as a shudder shook her. "For a hurricane, it seems you're not impervious to fellow weather conditions. Let's get inside, and I'll field all the curiosity and jealousy you dragged us out here to avoid."

She shuddered again—and not with cold. She was on the verge of combusting with mortification. "It's not the cold that's bothering me."

He gave her one of those patient looks that said he'd withstand any amount of resistance and debate...until he got his way. Then he suddenly advanced on her.

Trapped with the terrace railings at her back, she couldn't have moved if she'd wanted to. She was unable to do anything but stand there helplessly watching him as he neared her in that tranquil prowl, shrugging off his jacket. Then, without touching her, he draped her in it. In what it held of his heat, his scent, his...essence.

For paralyzed moments, feeling as if she was completely enveloped in him, she gazed way up into those preternatural eyes, that slight, spellbinding smile, a quake that originated from a fault line at her very core threatening to break out and engulf her whole.

Before it did, he stepped away, resumed the position she'd told him to maintain as her windshield.

"Now that you're warm, I don't have to feel guilty about rambling on. To explain what happened, I have to outline what happened after that showdown at the ball. I basically found myself a pariah in Zohayd, and I very soon was forced to take the decision to leave. I was preparing to when the Aal Shalaan Brotherhood came to me—all but Amjad, of course. They attempted to dissuade me from leaving, assured me they knew me too well to believe Maysoon's accusations, that they'd resolve everything with their family and Zohaydan society at large if I stayed. They did offer to help me set up my business, to be my partners or to finance me until it took off. But I declined their offer."

She again tried to interject with her insistence that she didn't need him to explain. She believed that had been another of Maysoon's lies. "Aram, I—"

He held up a hand. "Don't take my word for it. Go ask them. I wanted no handouts, but even more, I wanted nothing to maintain any ties to Zohayd after I decided to sever them all forever. I'd remained in Zohayd in the first place for my father, but I felt I hadn't done him any good staying, and after Maysoon's stunt, I knew my presence would cause him nothing but grief." He paused before letting out his breath on a deep sigh. "I had also given up on Shaheen coming back. It was clear that the reconciliation I'd thought being in Zohayd would facilitate wouldn't come to pass."

She heard her voice croaking a question that had long burned in the back of her mind. "Are you going to tell me that Shaheen was to blame for this breakup and alienation, too?"

She hadn't been able to believe the honorable Shaheen could have been responsible for such a rift. Learning of that estrangement after Maysoon's public humiliation *had* entrenched her prejudice against Aram, solidifying her view of him as a callous monster who cast the people who cared for him aside.

Though said view had undergone a marked recalibration, she hoped he'd blame Shaheen as he'd blamed Maysoon. This would put him back in the comfortable dark gray zone.

His next words doused that hope.

"No, that was all my doing. But don't expect me to tell you what I did that was so bad that he fled his own kingdom to get away from me."

"Why not?" she muttered. "Aren't you having a disclosure spree this fine night?"

"You expect me to spill all my secrets all at once?" His feigned horror would have been funny if she was capable of humor now. "Then have nothing more to reveal in future encounters?"

"Did I ask you to tell me *any* secrets? You're the one who's imposing them on me."

His grin was unrepentant. "Let me impose some more on you, then. Just a summation, so grit your teeth and bear it. So…rather than following Maysoon's advice and latching onto Shaheen's brothers for financing, connections and clout, I turned down their generous offers. I had the solid plan, the theoretical knowledge and some practical experience, and I was ready to take the world by storm."

Her sense of fairness reared its head again. "And you certainly did. I am well aware of the global scope of your business management and consultation firm. Many of the major conglomerates I worked with, even whole countries, rely on you to set up, manage and monitor their financial and executive departments. And if you did it all on your own, then you're not as good as they say—you're way better."

Again her testimony seemed to take him by surprise.

His eyes had taken that thoughtful cast again as he said, "Though I'm even more intrigued than ever that you know all that, and I would have liked to take all the credit for the success I've achieved, it didn't happen quite that way. The beginning of my career suffered from some…catastrophic setbacks, to say the least."

"How so?"

Those brilliant eyes darkened with something…vast and too painful. But when he went on, he gave no specifics. "Well, what I thought I knew—my academic degrees, the experience I had in Zohayd—hadn't prepared me for jumping off the deep end with the sharks. But I managed to climb out of the abyss with only a few parts chomped off and launched into my plans with all I had. But I wouldn't have attained my level of success if I hadn't had the phenomenal luck of finding the exact right people to employ. It was together that we 'soared so high.'"

Not taking all the credit for his achievements cast him in an even better light. But there was still one major crime nothing he'd said could exonerate.

"So Maysoon might have been wrong—*was* wrong—about how you made your fortune. But can you blame her for thinking the worst of you? My opening statement in this retrial stands. You didn't have to be so unbelievably cruel in your public humiliation of her."

His stare fixed her for interminable moments, something intense roiling in its depths, something like reluctance, even aversion, as if he hated the response he had to make.

Seeming to reach a difficult decision, he beckoned her nearer.

He thought she'd come closer than that to him? Of her own volition? And why did he even want her to?

When she remained frozen to the spot, he sighed, inched nearer himself. She felt his approach like that of an oncoming train, her every nerve jangling at his increasing proximity.

He stopped a foot away, tilted his head back, exposing his neck to her. She stared at its thick, corded power, her mind stalling. It was as if he was asking her to…to…

"See this?" His purr jolted her out of the waywardness of her thoughts. She blinked at what he was pointing at. Three parallel scars, running from below his right ear halfway down his neck. They'd been hidden beneath his thick, luxurious hair. A current rattled through her at the sight of them. They were clearly very old, and although they weren't hideous, she could tell the injury *had* been. It was because his skin was that perfect, resilient type that healed with minimum scarring that they'd faded to that extent.

He exhaled heavily. "I ended my deposition at the moment I walked away, thought it enough, that any more was overkill. But seems nothing less than full disclosure will do here." He exhaled again, his eyes leveled on hers, totally serious for the first time. "Maysoon gave me this souvenir. She wouldn't let me go just like that. I barely dodged before she slashed across my face and took one eye out."

Kanza shuddered as the scene played in her mind. She did know how hysterical Maysoon could become. She could see her doing that. And she was left-handed…

"I pushed her off me, rushed to the men's room to stem the bleeding and had to lock the door so she wouldn't barge in and continue her frenzy. I got things under control and cleaned myself up, but she pounced on me as soon as I left the sanctuary of the men's room. I couldn't get the hell out of the palace without crossing the ballroom, and I kept pushing her off me all the way there, but once we got back inside, she started screeching.

"As people gathered, she was crying rivers and saying I cheated on her. I just wanted out—at any cost. So I said, 'Yes, I'm the bad guy, and isn't she lucky she's found out before it was too late?' When I tried to extricate myself, she flung herself on the ground, sobbing hysterically that I'd hit her. I couldn't stand around for the rest of her show, so I turned away and left."

He stopped, drew in a huge breath, let it out on a sigh. "But my deposition wouldn't be complete without saying that I've long realized that I owe her a debt of gratitude for everything she did."

Now, *that* stunned her. "You do?"

He nodded. "If her campaign against me hadn't forced me to leave Zohayd, I would have never pursued my own destiny. My experience with her was the perfect example of *assa an takraho sha'an wa howa khairon lakkom.*"

You may hate something and it is for your best.

He'd said that in perfect Arabic. Hearing his majestic voice rumbling the ancient verse was a shock. Maysoon had spoken only English to him, making her think he hadn't learned the language. But it was clear he had—and perfectly. There wasn't the least trace of accent in his pronunciation. He'd said it like a connoisseur of old poetry would.

He cocked that awesome head at her. "So now that you've heard my full testimony, any adjustment in your opinion of me?"

Floundering, wanting for the floor to split and snatch her below, she choked out, "It—it *is* your word against hers."

"Then I am at a disadvantage, since she is your half sister. Though that should be to her disadvantage, since you're probably intimate with all her faults and are used to taking her testimony about anything with a pound of salt. But if for some reason you're still inclined to believe her, then there is only one way for me to have a fair retrial. I demand that you get to know me as thoroughly as you know her."

"What do you mean, get to know you?" She heard the panic that leaped into her voice.

He was patient indulgence itself. "How do people get to know each other?"

"I don't know. How?"

The same forbearance met her retort. "How did you get to know anyone in your orbit?"

"I was thrown with them by accidents of birth or geography or necessity."

That had his heart-stopping smile dawning again. "I'm tempted to think you've been a confirmed misanthrope since you exited the womb."

"According to my mother, they barely extracted me surgically before I clawed my way out of her. She informed me I spoiled the having-babies gig for her forever."

His eyes told her what he thought of her mother. Yeah, him and everyone in the civilized world.

Then his eyes smiled again. "It's a calamity we don't have video documentation of your entry into the world. That would have been footage for the ages. So—" he rubbed his hands together "—when will our next reconnaissance session be?"

Her heart lodged in her throat again. "There will be no next anything."

"Why? Have you passed your judgment again, and it's still execution?"

"No, I've given you a not-guilty verdict, so you can go gallop in the fields free. Now, *ann eznak...*"

"Or better still, *men ghair ezni,* right?"

"See? You can predict me now. I was only diverting when you couldn't guess what I'd say next, but now that you've progressed to completing my sentences, my entertainment value is clearly depleted. Better to quit while we're ahead."

"I beg to differ. Not that I am or was after 'entertain-ment.' Will you suggest a time and venue, or will you leave it up to me?"

She could swear flames erupted inside her skull.

"You've had your retrial, and I want to salvage what I can of this party," she growled. "Now get out of my way."

As if she hadn't said anything, his eyes laughed at her as he all but crooned, "So you want me to surprise you?"

"Argh!"

Foisting his jacket at him, she pushed past him, barely resisting the urge to break out into a sprint to escape his nerve-fraying chuckles.

She felt those following her even after she'd rejoined the party, when there was no way she could still hear him.

And he thought she'd expose herself to him again?

Hah.

One cataclysmic brush with Aram Nazaryan might have been survivable. But enduring another exposure?

No way.

After all, she didn't have a death wish.

Five

"I see you've found Kanza."

Aram stopped midstride across the penthouse, groaning out loud.

Shaheen. Not the person he wanted to see right now.

But then, he wanted to see no one but that keg of unpredictability who'd skittered away from him again. Though he was betting she wouldn't let him find her again tonight.

While Shaheen wasn't going anywhere before he rubbed his nose in some choice I-told-you-sos.

Deciding on the best defense, he engaged offensive maneuvers. "*Found* her? Don't you mean you and your coconspirator wife threw us together?"

"*I* did nothing but put my foot in it. It's *your* kid sister who pushed things along. But she only 'threw' you two together. You could have extracted yourself in five minutes if she'd miscalculated. But obviously she didn't. From our estimations, you've spent over five hours in Kanza's company. To say you found her…compatible is putting it mildly."

"*Hold* it right there, buddy." He shook his finger at Shaheen. "You're not even going down that road, you hear? I just *talked* to the…to the… God, I can't even find a name

for her. I can't call her girl or woman or anything that…
run-of-the-mill. I don't know what the hell she is."

"As long as it's not monster or goblin anymore, that's a
huge development."

"No, she's certainly neither of those things." And Kanza
the Monster hadn't even been his name for her. It had been
Maysoon's and her friends'. That alone should have made
him disregard it. He'd adopted it only because he couldn't
find an alternative. And Kanza *had* unsettled the hell out
of him back then. She still did—if in a totally different
way. One he still couldn't figure out. "All night I've been
thinking sprite, brownie, pixie…but none of that really de-
scribes her either."

"The word you're looking for is…treasure."

Aram stared at his friend. *"Treasure?"*

Then he blinked. *Kanz* meant treasure. Kanza was the
feminine form. How had he never focused on her name's
meaning?

Though… "Treasure isn't how I'd describe her, either."

"No?" Shaheen quirked an eyebrow. "Maybe not…yet.
She can't be categorized, anyway."

"You got *that* right. But that's as right as you get. I'm not
about to ask for her hand in marriage, so put a lid on it."

"Your…caution is understandable. You met her—the
grown-up her, anyway—only hours ago. You wouldn't be
thinking of anything beyond the moment yet."

"Not yet, not ever. Can't a man enjoy the company of an
unidentifiable being without any further agenda?"

Knowing amusement rose in Shaheen's eyes. "You tell
me. Can he?"

"*Yes,* he can. And he fully intends to. And he wants you
and your much better half to butt out and stay out of this.
Let *him* have *fun* for a change, and don't try to make this
into anything more than it is. Got it?"

Shaheen nodded. "Got it."

He threw his hands in the air. "Why didn't you argue? Now I know I'm in for some nasty surprise down the road."

Abandoning his pretense of seriousness, Shaheen grinned teasingly. "From where I'm standing, you consider the surprise you got a rather delightful one."

"Too many surprises and one is bound to wipe out all good ones before it. It's basic Surprise Law." Folding his arms across his chest, he shot his friend a warning look. "Keep your royal noses out of this, Shaheen. I'm your senior, and even if you don't think so, I do know what's best for me, so permit me the luxury of running my own personal life."

Shaheen's grin only widened. "I already said I...*we* will. Now chill."

"Chill?" Aram grimaced. "You just managed to give me an anxiety attack. God, but you two are hazards."

Shaheen took him around the shoulder. "We've done our parts as catalysts. Now we'll let the experiment progress without further intervention."

He narrowed his eyes at him. "Even if you think I'm messing it up? You won't be tempted to intervene then?"

Shaheen wiggled one eyebrow. "That worry would motivate you not to mess it up, wouldn't it?"

He tore himself away. "Shaheen!"

Shaheen laughed. "I'm just messing with you. You're on your own. Just don't come crying one day that you are."

"I won't." He tsked. "And quit making this what it isn't. I only want to put my finger on what makes her so... unquantifiable."

Sighing dramatically, Shaheen played along. "I guess it's because she's nothing anyone expects a princess, let alone a professional woman, to be. Before she became Johara's partner, I only heard her being described as mousy, awkward, even gauche."

"*What?* Who the hell were those people talking about?"

"*You* had that Kanza the Monster conviction going, too."

"At least 'monster' recognized the sheer force of her character."

Shaheen shrugged. "I think she's simply nice."

An impressive snort escaped him. "Who're you calling nice? That's the last adjective in the English language to describe her. She's no such vague, lukewarm, *benign* thing."

Shaheen's lips twitched. "After an evening in her company, you seem to have become *the* authority on her. So how would *you* describe her?"

"Didn't you hear me when I said that I don't *know* what she is? All I know is that she's an inapproachable bundle of thorns. An unstoppable force of nature, like a…a… hurricane."

"That's more of a natural disaster."

He almost muttered "smart-ass" in the exact way Kanza had to him. He *was* exasperated with having his enthusiasm interpreted into what Shaheen and Johara wanted it to be. When it was like nothing he'd ever felt. It was as unpredictable as that hurricane in question.

One thing he knew for certain, though. He wasn't trying to define it or to direct it. Or expect anything from it. And he sure as hell wasn't attempting to temper it. Not to curb Shaheen's expectations, not for anything.

"Whatever. It's the one description that suits her."

"That would make her Hurricane Kanza."

With that, Shaheen took him back to Johara, where he endured her teasing, too. And he again made her and her incorrigibly romantic spouse promise that they wouldn't interfere.

Then as he left the party, he thought of the name Shaheen had suggested.

Hurricane Kanza. It described her to a tee.

After he'd compared her effect on Johara's office to one a lifetime ago, she had proceeded to tear through him with the uprooting force of one. All he wanted to do now was hurtle into her path again and let her toss him wherever she would.

But she wouldn't do it of her own accord. She must still be processing the revelations that, given her sense of justice, *must* have changed her opinion of him. But it no doubt remained an awkward situation for her, since her prejudice had been long held, and Maysoon was still her half sister.

Not that he would allow any of that to stand in his way. He fully intended to get exposed to her delightful destruction again and again, no matter what it took.

Now he just had to plan his next exposure to her devastation.

Aram eyed Johara's office door, impatience rising.

Kanza was in a morning meeting with his sister. Once that was over, he planned to…intercept her.

He'd done so every day for the past two weeks. But the sprite had given him the slip each time. He never got in more than a few words with her before she blinked out on him like her fellow pixies did. But what words those had been. Like tastings from gourmet masterpieces that only left him starving for a full meal again.

He'd let her wriggle away as part of his investigation into her components and patterns of behavior. It had pleased the hell out of him that he still found the first inscrutable and the second unforeseeable. But today he wasn't letting that steel butterfly flutter away. She was having a whole day in his company. She just didn't know it yet.

Johara's assistants eyed him curiously, no doubt wondering why he was here, *again*. And why he didn't just walk right into his sister's office. That had been his first inclination, to corner that elusive elf in there.

He'd reconsidered. Raiding Kanza's leisure time was one thing. Marauding her at work was another. He'd let her get business out of the way before swooping in and sweeping her away on that day off Johara said she hadn't taken in over a year. He'd arranged a day off himself. The first whole one he'd had in…ever.

The office door was suddenly flung open, and Johara's head popped out, golden hair spilling forward. "Aram—come in, please."

He was on his feet at once, buoyed by the unexpected thrill of seeing Kanza now, not an hour or more later. "I thought you were having a meeting."

"When did that ever stop you?" Johara's grin widened as he ruffled her hair. "But as luck would have it, the day you chose to go against your M.O., I found myself in need of that incomparable business mind of yours, big brother."

He hugged her to his side, kissing the top of her head lovingly. "At your service always, sweetheart."

His gaze zeroed in on Kanza like a heat-seeking missile the moment he entered the office. Déjà vu spread its warmth inside his chest when he found her standing by the filing cabinets, like that first night. The only difference was the office was in pristine order. It had looked much better to him after she'd exercised her hurricane-like powers.

He noticed the other two people in the room only when they rose to salute him. All his faculties converged on that power source at the end of the office, even when he wasn't looking at her.

Then he did, and almost laughed out loud at the impact of her disapproving gaze and terse acknowledgment.

"Aram."

While it no longer sounded like a curse, it was…eloquent. No, more than that. Potent. Her unique, patented method of cutting him down to size.

Johara dragged back his attention, explaining their problem. Forcing himself to shift from Kanza to business mode, Aram turned to his sister's concerns.

After he'd gotten a handle on the situation, he offered solutions, only for Kanza to point out the lacking in some and the error in others. But she did so without the least contention or malice, as most would have when they considered someone to be infringing on their domain. In fact, there was nothing in her analysis except an earnest endeavor to reach the best possible solution.

Aram ascribed his lapse to close exposure to her, but he was lucid enough to know he was in the presence of a mind that rivaled his in his field. Having met only a handful of those in his lifetime, who'd been much older and wielding far more experience, he was beyond impressed.

As the session progressed, what impressed him even more was that she didn't compete with him, challenge him or harp on his early misjudgment. She deferred to his superior knowledge where he possessed it and put all her faculties at his disposal during what became five intensive hours of discussion, troubleshooting and restructuring.

Once they reached the most comprehensive plan of action, Johara leaped to her feet in excitement. "Fantastic! I couldn't have dreamed of such a genius solution! I should have teamed you and Kanza up a long time ago, Aram."

He couldn't believe it.

How had he not seen this as another of Johara's blatant efforts to show him how *compatible* they were? Would he *never* learn?

He twisted his lips at Johara for breaching their *noninterference* pact again as he rose to his feet. "And now that you did, how about we celebrate this breakthrough? It's on me."

Johara's eyes were innocence incarnate. "Oh, I wish. I have tons of boring, artistic stuff to take care of with Dana and Steve. You and Kanza go celebrate for us."

If anyone had told him before that business with Kanza that his kid sister was an ingenious actress, he wouldn't have believed it. But though he didn't approve of her underhanded methods, he was thankful for the opportunity she provided to get Kanza alone.

He turned to the little spitfire in question, gearing up for another battle, but Kanza simply said, "Let's go, then. I'm starving. And, Aram, it's on me. I owe you for those shortcuts you taught me today."

His head went light as the tension he'd gathered for the anticipated struggle drained out of him. Then it began to spin, at her admission that she'd learned from him, at her willingness to reward the favor.

Exchanging a last glance that no doubt betrayed his bewilderment with Johara, who was doing less than her usual seamless job of hiding her smug glee, he followed Kanza the Inscrutable out of the office.

Kanza walked out of Johara's office with the most disruptive force she'd ever encountered following her and a sense of déjà vu overwhelming her.

In the past two weeks he'd been taking this "get to know him" to the limit, had turned up everywhere to trail her as he was doing now. Instead of getting used to being inundated in his vibe and pervaded by his presence, each time the experience got more intense, had her reeling even harder.

And she still couldn't find one plausible reason why he was doing this.

The possibility that he was attracted to her had been the first one she'd dismissed. The idea of Aram Nazaryan, the epitome of male perfection, being romantically interested in her was so ludicrous it hadn't lasted more than two seconds of perplexed speculation before it had evaporated. Other reasons hadn't held water any better or longer.

So, by exclusion, one theory remained.

That he was nuts.

The hypothesis was loosely based on Johara's testimony.

With his repeated appearances of late, which Johara hadn't tied to Kanza, Johara had started talking about him. Among the tales from the past, mostly of their time in Zohayd, she'd let slip she believed he'd been sliding into depression. Kanza had barely held back from correcting Johara's tentative diagnosis to *manic*-depression, according to that inexplicable eagerness and elation that exuded from him and gleamed in his eyes.

Johara believed it was because he'd long been abusing his health and neglecting his personal life by working so much. Again, Kanza had barely caught back a scoff. In the past two weeks he hadn't seemed to work at all. How else could he turn up everywhere she went, no matter the time of day? Her only explanation was that he'd set up his business with such efficiency that its success was self-perpetuating and he could take time off whenever the fancy struck him.

But according to Johara, he had been working himself to death for years, resulting in being cut off from humanity and lately even becoming physically sick. It had been why she and Shaheen came so often to New York of late, staying for extended periods of time, to try to alleviate his isolation and stop his deterioration.

Not that Johara thought they were succeeding. She felt that their intimacy as husband and wife left Aram unable to connect with either of them as he used to, left him feeling like an outsider, even a trespasser. But she truly believed he needed the level of attachment he'd once shared with them to maintain his psychological health. Bottom line, she was worried that his inability to find anyone who fulfilled that need, along with his atrocious lifestyle, was dragging him to the verge of some breakdown.

But this man, stalking her like a panther who'd just discovered play and couldn't contain his eagerness to start a game of all-out tackle and chase, seemed nothing like the morose, self-destructive loner Johara had described. Which made *her* theory the only credible explanation. That his inexplicable pursuit of her was the first overt symptom of said breakdown.

Not that she was happy with this diagnosis.

While it had provided an explanation for his behavior, it had also influenced hers.

She'd dodged him so far, because she'd thought he'd

latched on to her in order to combat his ennui, and she hadn't fancied being used as an antidote to his boredom. But the idea that his behavior wasn't premeditated—or even worse, was a cry for help—had made it progressively harder to be unresponsive.

"So where do you want to take me?"

Doing her best not to swoon at the caress of his fathomless baritone, she turned to him as they entered the garage. "I'm open. What do you want to eat?"

"You pick." He grinned as he strode ahead, leading the way to his car. Seemed it was time for that spin in his near-sentient behemoth, a black-and-silver Rolls-Royce Phantom that reportedly came with a ghastly half-million-dollar price tag.

She stopped. "Okay, this goes no further."

That dazzling smile suddenly dimmed. "You're taking back your invitation?"

"I *mean* we're not going in circles, each insisting the other chooses. I already said I'm open to whatever you want, and it wasn't a ploy for you to throw the ball back in my court, proving you're more of a gentleman. I always say exactly what I mean."

His smile flashed back to its debilitating wattage. "You have no idea what a relief that is. But I'm definitely more of a gentleman. It's an incontestable anatomical fact."

She made no response as he seated her in his car's passenger seat. She wasn't going to take this exchange that lumped him and anatomy together any further. It would only lead to trouble.

Focusing instead on being in his car, she sank into the supple seashell leather while her feet luxuriated in the rich, thick lamb's wool, feeling cosseted in the literal lap of luxury.

After veering that impressive monster into downtown traffic, he turned to her. "So why did you suddenly stop evading me?"

Yeah. Good question. Why did she?

She told him the reason she'd admitted to herself so far. "I took pity on you."

"Yes." He pumped his fist. At her raised eyebrow, he chuckled. "Just celebrating the success of my pitiful puppy-dog-eyed efforts."

"If that's what you were shooting for, you missed the mark by a mile. You came across as a hyper, blazing-eyed panther."

Those eyes flared with enjoyment. "Back to the drawing board, then. Or rather the mirror, to practice. But if that didn't work…what did?"

And she found herself admitting more, to herself as well as to him. "It got grueling calculating the lengths you must have gone to, popping up wherever I went. It had me wondering if you're one of those anal-retentive people who must finish whatever they start, and I was needlessly prolonging both of our discomfort. I also had to see what would happen if I let go of the tug-of-war."

"You'll enjoy my company." At her sardonic sideways glance, he laughed. "Admit it. You find me entertaining."

She found him…just about everything.

"Not the adjective I'd use for you," Kanza said with a sigh.

"Don't leave me hanging. Lay it on me."

Her gaze lengthened over his dominant profile. She'd been candid in her description of his outward assets. Was it advisable to be her painfully outspoken self in expounding on what she thought of his more essential endowments?

Oh, what the hell. He must be used to fawning. Her truthfulness, though only her objective opinion, wouldn't be more than what he'd heard a thousand times before.

She opened her mouth to say she'd use adjectives like *enervating,* like a bolt of lightning, and *engulfing,* like a rising flood—and as if to say the words for her, thunder rolled and celestial floodgates burst.

He didn't press her to elucidate, because even with the efficiency of the automatic wipers, he could barely see through the solid sheets of rain. Thankfully, they seemed to have arrived at the destination he'd chosen. The Plaza Hotel, where Johara had mentioned Aram stayed.

As he stopped the car, she thought they should stay inside until the rain let up. They'd get soaked in the few dozen feet to the hotel entrance. Then he opened her door, and lo and behold…an umbrella was ingeniously embedded there. In moments, he was shielding her from the downpour and leading her through the splendor of the iconic hotel. But it wasn't until they stepped into the timeless Palm Court restaurant that she felt as if she'd walked into a scene out of *The Great Gatsby*.

She took in the details as she walked a step ahead among tables filled with immaculate people. Overhanging gilded chandeliers, paneled walls, a soaring twenty-foot green-painted and floral-patterned ceiling and 24-karat gold-leafed Louis XVI furniture, all beneath a stunning stained-glass skylight. Everything exuded the glamour that had made the hotel world famous while retaining the feel of a French country house.

After they were seated and she opted for ordering the legendary Plaza tea, she leveled her gaze back on him and sighed. "Is that your usual spending pattern? This hotel, that car?"

"I am moderate, aren't I?" At her grimace, he upped his teasing. "I was eyeing a Bugatti Veyron, but since there are no roads around to put it through its two-hundred-and-fifty-miles-per-hour paces, I thought paying three times as much as my current car would be unjustified." He chuckled at her growl of distaste. "Down, girl. I can afford it."

"And that makes it okay? Don't you have something better to do with your money?"

"I do a *lot* of better things with my money. And then, it's my only material indulgence. It's in lieu of a home."

"Meaning?"

"Meaning I've never bought a place, so I consider my cars my only home."

This was news. Somewhat...disturbing news. She'd thought he'd been staying in this hotel for convenience, not that he'd never had a place to call home.

"But...if you're saying you don't splurge on your accommodations, it would be *far* more economical—and an investment—to buy a place. A day here is an obscene amount of money down the drain, and you've been here almost a *year*."

His nod was serene. "My suite goes for about twenty grand a night." At her gasp, his lips spread wide. "Of which I'm not paying a cent. I am a major shareholder in this hotel, so I get to stay free."

Okay. She should have known a financial mastermind like him wouldn't throw money around, that he'd invest every cent to make a hundred. It was a good thing their orders had arrived so she'd have it instead of crow after she'd gone all self-righteous on him.

She felt him watching her and pretended to have eyes only on the proceedings as waiters heaped varieties of tea, finely cut sandwiches, scones, jam, clotted cream and a range of pastries on the table.

They had devoured two irresistible scones each, and mellow live piano music had risen above the buzz of conversation, when he broke the silence.

"This place reminds me of the royal palace in Zohayd. Not the architecture, but something in the level of splendor. The distant resemblance is...comforting."

The longing, the melancholy in his reminiscing about the place where he'd lived a good portion of his youth, tugged at her heart...a little too hard.

Suddenly his smile dawned again. "So ask me anything."

Struggling with the painful tautness in her throat, she eyed him skeptically. "Anything at all?"

His nod was instantaneous. "You bet."

It seemed Johara had been correct. He did need someone to share things with that he felt he could no longer share with his sister or brother-in-law. And as improbable as it was, he seemed to have elected her as the one he could unburden himself to. His selection had probably been based on her ability to say no to him, to be blunt with him. That must be a total novelty for him.

But she also suspected there was another major reason she was a perfect candidate for what he had in mind. Because he didn't seem to consider her a woman. Just a sexless buddy he could have fun with and confide in without worrying about the usual hassles a woman would cause him.

She had no illusions about what she was, how a man like him would view her. But that still had mortification warring with compassion in her already tight chest. Compassion won.

Feeling the ridiculous urge to reach across the table for his hand, to reassure him she was there for him, even if he thought her a sprite, she cleared her throat. "Tell me about the rift between you and Shaheen."

He nodded. "Did Johara tell you how we came to Zohayd?"

"Oh, no! You're planning to tell me your whole life story to get to one incident in its middle?"

"Yep. So you'll understand the factors leading up to the incident and the nature of the players in it."

"Can I retract my request?" She pretended glibness.

"Nope. *Dokhool el hammam mesh zay toloo'oh.*"

Entering a bathroom isn't like exiting it. What was said in Zohayd to signify that what was done couldn't be undone.

And she was beginning to realize what that really meant.

Living life knowing a man like him existed had been fine with her as long as he'd been just a general concept—not a reality that could cross hers, let alone invade it.

But now that she was experiencing him up close, she feared it would irrevocably change things inside her.

And the peace she'd once known would be no more.

Six

Pretending to eat what seemed to have turned to ashes, Kanza watched Aram as he poured her tea and began sharing his life story with her.

"Before I came to Zohayd at sixteen, my father used to whisk me, Johara and Mother away every year or so to yet another exotic locale as he built his reputation as an internationally rising jeweler. When I told my peers that I'd trade what they thought an enchanted existence in the glittering milieus of the rich and famous for a steady, boring life in a small town, dweeb and weirdo were only two of the names they called me. I learned to keep my mouth shut, but I couldn't learn to stop hating that feeling of homelessness. My defense was to go to any new place as if I was leaving the next day, and I remained in self-imposed isolation until we left."

She gulped scalding tea to swallow the lump in her throat. So his isolation had deeper roots than Johara even realized. And she'd bet she was the first one he'd told this to.

He went on. "I had a plan, though. That the moment I hit eighteen, I'd stay put in one place, work in one job forever, marry the first girl who wanted me and have a brood of kids. That blueprint for my future was what kept me going as the flitting around the world continued."

She gulped another mouthful, the heaviness in her chest increasing. His plans for stability had never come to pass. He was forty and as far as she knew, apart from the fiasco with Maysoon, he'd never had any kind of relationship.

So how had the one guy who'd planned a family life so early on, who'd craved roots when all others his age dreamed of freedom, ended up so adrift and alone?

He served them sandwiches and continued. "Then my father's mentor, the royal jeweler of Zohayd, retired and his job became open. He recommended Father to King Atef…."

Feeling as if a commercial had burst in during a critical moment, she raised a hand. "Hey, I'm from Zohayd and I know all the stories. How your father became the one entrusted with the Pride of Zohayd treasure is a folktale by now. Fast forward. Tell me something I don't know. I hate recaps."

His eyes crinkled at her impatience—he was clearly delighted she was so riveted by his story. "So there I was, jetting off to what Father said was one of the most magnificent desert kingdoms on earth, feeling resigned we'd stay for the prerequisite year before Father uprooted us again. Then we landed there. I can still remember, in brutal vividness, how I felt as soon as my feet touched the ground in Zohayd. That feeling of…belonging."

God. The emotions that suddenly blazed from him… Any moment now she was going to reach for that box of tissues.

"That feeling became one of elation, of certainty, that I'd found a home—that I *was* home—when I met Shaheen." His massive chest heaved as he released an unsteady breath. "Did Johara tell you how he saved her from certain death that day?"

She shook her head, her eyes beginning to burn.

"She was a hyperactive six-year-old who made me age

running after her. Then I take my eyes off her for a minute and she's dangling from the palace's balcony. I was too far away, and Father failed to reach her, and she was slipping. But then at the last second, Shaheen swooped in to snatch her out of the air like the hawk he's named after.

"I was there the next second, beside myself with fright and gratitude, and that kindred feeling struck me. And from that day forward, he became my first and only friend. As he became Johara's first and only love."

She let out a ragged breath. "Wow."

"Yeah." He leaned back in his chair. "It was indescribable, having the friendship of someone of Shaheen's caliber—a caliber that had nothing to do with his status. But though he felt just as closely bonded to me, considered me an equal, I knew the huge gap between us would always be unbridgeable. I grew more uncomfortable by the day when Johara started to blossom, and I became certain that her emotions for Shaheen weren't those of a friend but those of a budding woman in love.

"By the time she was fourteen, worry poisoned every minute I spent with Shaheen, which by then almost always included Johara. Though the three of us were magnificent together, I thought Shaheen's all-out indulgence of Johara would lead to catastrophe, for Johara, for my whole family. Then my anxiety reached critical mass…"

"Go on," she rasped when he paused, unable to wait to hear the rest.

He raked a hand through his dark, satin hair. "We were having a squash match, and I started to trounce a bewildered Shaheen. The more Johara cheered him to fight back, the more vicious I became. Afterward in the changing room, I tore into Shaheen with all my pent-up resentment. I called him a spoiled prince who made a game of manipulating people's emotions. I accused him of encouraging her crush on him—which he knew was beyond hopeless—just for fun. I demanded he stop leading her on or I'd tell his father King Atef...so he'd *order* him never to come near Johara again.

"Shaheen was flabbergasted. He said Johara was the little sister he'd never had. I only sneered that his affections went far beyond an older brother's, as I should know as her *real* one. He countered that while he didn't know what having a sister was like, Johara was his 'girl'—the one who 'got' him like no one else, even me, and he did love her... in every way but *that* way.

"But I was way beyond reason, said that his proclamations meant nothing to me—I cared only about Johara—and that he was emotionally exploiting her, and I wouldn't stand idly by waiting for him to damage her irrevocably."

She couldn't imagine how he'd felt at the time. Sensing the powerful bond between his best friend and sister, having every reason to believe it would end in devastation and being forced to risk his one friendship to protect his one sister. It must have been terrible, knowing that either way he'd lose something irreplaceable.

Grimacing with remembered pain, Aram placed his forearms on the table, his gaze fixed on the past. "Outrage finally overpowered Shaheen's mortification that I could think such dishonorable things of him. His bitterness escalated as my conviction faltered, then vanished in the face of his intense affront and hurt. But there was no taking back what I'd said or threatened. Then it was too late, anyway.

"Shaheen told me he'd save me the trouble of running to his father with my demands for him to cease and desist. He'd never come near Johara again. Or me. He carried out his pledge, cutting Johara and me off, effective immediately."

It was clear the injury of those lost years had never fully healed. And though Shaheen and Johara were now happily married and Aram's friendship with Shaheen had been restored, it seemed the gaping wound where his friend had been torn out had been only partially patched. Because there was no going back to the same closeness now that Shaheen's life was so full of Johara and their daughter while Aram had found nothing to fill the void in his own life. Except work. And according to Johara, it was nowhere near enough.

"Just when I thought Shaheen's alienation was the worst thing that could happen to me, Mother suddenly took Johara and left Zohayd. I watched our family being torn apart and was unable to stop it. Then I found myself left alone with a devastated father who kept withdrawing into himself in spite of all my efforts. I tried to grope for my best friend's support, hoping he'd let me close again, but he only left Zohayd, too, dashing any hope for a reconciliation."

So she had been totally wrong about him in this instance, too. It hadn't been not caring that had caused that breach; it had been caring too much. And it had cost him way more than she'd ever imagined.

He went on. "With all my dreams of making a home for myself in Zohayd over, I wanted to leave and tried to persuade Father to leave with me, too, but I backed off when I realized his service to the king and kingdom was what kept him going. Knowing I couldn't leave him, I resigned myself that I'd stay in Zohayd as long as he lived."

It must have been agonizingly ironic to get what he wanted, that permanent stay in Zohayd, but for it to be more of an exile than a home.

As if he'd heard her thoughts, he released a slow, deep breath. "It was the ultimate irony. I was getting what I'd hoped for all my life—stability in one place, just without the roots or the family, to live there in an isolation that promised to become permanent." *Isolation.* There was that word again. "Then, six years after everyone left Zohayd, I took a shot at forging that family I'd once dreamed of…and you now know what happened next."

She nodded, her throat tight. "And you ended up being forced to leave."

He sighed deeply again. "Yeah. So much happened after

that. Too much. And I've never stayed in one place longer than a few months since. I hadn't wanted to. Couldn't bear to, even. Then three years ago, Shaheen and Johara ended up getting married. I was right about the nature of their involvement." He smiled whimsically. "I just jumped the gun by twelve years." Another deep sigh. "Then suddenly I had my friend back, Mother reconciled with Father and my whole family was put back together—just in Zohayd, where I could no longer be."

Swallowing what felt like a rock, she wondered if he'd elaborate on the intervening years, the "too much" he'd said with such aversion. He didn't.

He'd done what he'd set out to do, told her the story that explained his rift with Shaheen. Anything else would be for another day. If there would be one.

From the way her heart kept twisting, it wasn't advisable to have one. Exposure to him when she'd despised him, thought him a monster, had been bad enough. Now that she saw him as not only human but even empathetic, further exposure could have catastrophic consequences. For her.

His eyes seemed to see her again, seeming to intensify in vividness as he smiled like never before. A heartfelt smile. "Thank you."

Her heart fired so hard it had her sitting forward in her chair. "Wh-what for?"

The gentleness turning his beauty from breathtaking to heartbreaking deepened. "You listened. And made no judgments. I think you even…sympathized."

She struggled to stop the pins at the back of her eyes from dissolving in an admission of how moved she was. "I did. It was such a tragic and needless waste, all those years apart. For all of you."

His inhalation was sharp. The exhalation that followed was slow, measured. "Yes. But they're back together now."

They. Not we.

He didn't seem to consider he had his family and friend

back. Worse, it seemed he didn't consider himself part of the family anymore. And though his expression was now carefully neutral, she sensed he was…desolate over the belief. What he seemed to consider an unchangeable fact of his life now.

After that, as if by unspoken agreement, they spent the rest of their time in the Palm Court talking about a dozen things that weren't about lost years or ruined life plans.

After the rain stopped, he took her out walking, and they must have covered all of Central Park before it was dark.

She didn't even feel the distance, the exertion or the passage of time. She saw nothing, heard and smelled and felt nothing but him. His company was that engrossing, that gratifying. The one awful thing about spending time with him was that it would come to an end.

But it didn't. When she'd thought their impromptu outing was over, he insisted she wasn't going home until she was a full, exhausted mass unable to do anything but fall into bed. She hadn't even thought of resisting his unilateral plans for the rest of the evening. This time out of time would end soon enough, and she wasn't going to terminate it prematurely. She'd have plenty of time later to regret her decision not to.

Over dinner, their conversation took a turn for the funny, then the hilarious. On several occasions, his peals of goose-bump-raising laughter incited many openmouthed and swooning stares from besotted female patrons, while *she* was leveled with what's-*she*-doing-with-that-god glares, not to mention the times the whole restaurant seemed to be turning around to see if there was a hyena dining with them.

When he drove her back to her apartment building, he parked two blocks away—just an excuse to have another walk.

As they walked in companionable silence, she felt the impulsive urge to hook her arm in his, lean on him through the wind. It wasn't discretion that stopped her but the fact that he hadn't attempted even a courteous touch so far.

At her building's entrance, he turned to her with expectation blazing in those azure eyes. "So same time tomorrow?"

Her heart pirouetted in her chest at the prospect of another day with him.

But… "We went out at *one* today!"

He shrugged. "And?"

"And I have work."

He waved dismissively. "Take the day off."

"I can't. Johara…"

"Will shove you out of the office if she can to make you take some time off. She says you're a workaholic."

"Gee. She says the same about you."

"See? We both need a mental-health day."

"We already had one today."

"We worked our asses off for five hours in the morning. Tomorrow is a *real* day off. With all the trimmings. Sleeping in, then going crazy being lazy and doing nothing but eating and chatting and doing whatever pops into our minds till way past midnight."

And he'd just described her newfound vision of heaven.

Then she remembered something, and heaven seemed to blink out of sight. She groaned, "I really can't tomorrow."

Disappointment flooded his gaze, but only for a second. Then eagerness was back full steam ahead. "The day after tomorrow, then. And at noon. No…make it eleven. *Ten.*"

Her heart tap-danced. She did her best not to grin like a loon, to sound nonchalant as she said, "Oh, all right."

He stuck his hands at his hips. "Got something more enthusiastic than that?"

"Nope." She mock scowled. "That's the only brand available. Take it or…take it."

"I'll take it, and take it!" He took a step back as if to dodge a blow, whistled. "Jeez. How did something so tiny become so terrifying?"

She gave a sage nod. "It's an evolutionary compensatory mechanism to counteract the disadvantaged size."

"Vive la évolution." And he said it in perfect French, reminding her he spoke that fluently, too.

She burst out laughing.

Minutes later, she was still chuckling to herself as she entered her apartment. God, but that man was the most unprecedented, unpredictable, unparalleled fun she'd ever had.

She met her eyes in her foyer's mirror, wincing at what she'd never seen reflected back…until now. Unmistakable fever in her cheeks and soppy dreaminess in her eyes. Aram had put it all there without even meaning to.

Yeah. He was boatloads of fun. Too bad he was also a mine of danger.

And she'd just agreed to another daylong dose of deadly exposure.

Seven

"So how's my Tiny Terror doing this fine day?"

Kanza leaned against the wall to support legs that always went elastic on hearing Aram's voice. Not to mention the heart that forgot its rhythm.

You'd think after over a month of daily and intensive exposure, she'd have developed some immunity. But she only seemed to be getting progressively more susceptible.

She forced out a steady, "Why, thank you, I'm doing splendidly. And you, Hulking Horror?"

Right on cue, his expected laugh came, boisterous and unfettered. He kept telling her that she had the specific code that operated his humor, and almost everything she said tickled him mercilessly. She'd been liberally exercising that power over him, to both their delight.

In return, the gift of his laughter, and knowing that she could incite it, caused her various physical and emotional malfunctions.

She was dealing with the latest bout when he said, laughter still permeating his magnificent voice, "I'm doing spectacularly now that my Mighty Miniature has taken me well in hand. You ready? I'm downstairs." Yeah, he never even asked to come up. "And hurry! I have something to show you."

"Uh-uh. Don't play that game with me." She took a look in the mirror and groaned. Not a good idea to inspect herself right before she beheld him. The comparison was just too disheartening. She slammed out of her apartment in frustration and ran into the elevator that a neighbor had just exited. "Tell me what it is. I have severe allergies to surprises."

"Just so we won't end up in the E.R., I'll give you a hint." His voice had that vibrant edge of excitement she'd been hearing more of late as they planned trips they'd take and projects they'd do together. "It's things people live in."

Her heart sputtered in answering excitement. "You bought an apartment! Oh, congrats."

"Hey, you think me capable of making a decision without consulting my Mini Me?"

The elevator opened to reveal him. And it hit her all over again with even more force than last time. How…shattering his beauty was.

But with the evidence of his current glory, she knew he'd been right. When she'd met him again six weeks ago, he *had* been at his lowest ebb. Ever since then, he'd been steadily shedding any sign of haggardness. He was now at a level that should be prohibited by law, like any other health hazard.

And there she was, the self-destructive fool who willingly exposed herself to his emanations on a daily basis. And without any protection.

Not that there was any, or that she'd want it if there was. She'd decided to open herself up to the full exposure and to hell with the certain and devastating side effects.

As usual, without even taking her arm or touching her in any way whatsoever, he rushed ahead, gesturing eagerly for her to follow. She did. As she knew by now, she always would.

Once in his car and on their way, he turned to her. "I'm

taking you to see the candidates. I'm signing the contract of the one you'll determine I'll feel most comfortable in."

Her jaw dropped. "And I'm supposed to know that… how?"

His sideways glance was serenity itself. "Because you know everything."

"Hey." She turned in her seat. "Thanks for electing me your personal oracle or goddess or whatever, but no thanks. You can't saddle me with this kind of responsibility."

"It's your right and prerogative, O Diminutive Deity."

She rolled her eyes. "What ever happened to free will?"

"Who needs that when I have you?"

"If it was anyone else, I'd be laughing. But I know you're crazy enough to sign a contract if I as much as say a word in preference of one place." His nod reinforced her projection. "What if you end up hating my choice?"

"I won't." His smile was confidence incarnate. "And that's not crazy, but the logical conclusion to the evidence of experience. Everything you choose for me or advise me to do turns out to be the perfect solution for me. Case in point, look at me."

And she'd been trying her best not to. Not to stare, anyway. He gestured at his clothes. "You pointed this out in a shop yesterday, said I'd look good in it."

Yeah, because you'd look good in anything. You'd make a tattered sac look like haute couture.

"Even though I thought I'd look like a cyanotic parrot in this color…" A deep, intense purple that struck incredible hues off his hair and eyes. "I bought it on the way here based solely on your opinion. Now I think I've never worn anything more complimenting."

Her lips twisted in mockery, and with a twinge at how right he was. He looked the most vital and incandescent he'd ever been. "Pink frills would compliment you, Aram."

"Then I'll try those next."

A chuckle overpowered her as imaginings flooded her mind. "God, this I have to see."

His grin flashed, dazzling her. "Then you will." Suddenly his face settled into a seriousness that was even more hard-hitting. "All joking aside, I'm not being impulsive here. I'm a businessman, and I make my decisions built on what works best. And *you* work best."

"Uh, thanks. But in exactly what way do I do that?"

"Your perception is free from the distortions of inclinations. You cut to the essence of things, see people and situations for what they are, not what you'd prefer them to be, and don't let the background noise of others' opinions distract you." He slid her that proud, appreciative glance that he bestowed on her so frequently these days. "You proved that to me when you accepted my word and adjusted your opinion of me, guided only by your reading of me against overwhelming circumstantial evidence and long-standing misconceptions. It's because you're so welcoming of adjustments and so goal oriented that you achieve the best results in everything. I mean, look at me…"

Oh, God, not again. Didn't he have any idea what it did to her just being near him, let alone looking more closely at him than absolutely necessary?

No, he didn't.

He had no idea whatsoever how he made her feel.

She sighed. "I'm looking. And purple does become you. Anything else I should be looking at?"

"Yes, the miracle you worked. You took a fed-up man who was feeling a hundred years old and turned him into that eager kid who skips around doing all the things he'd long given up on. And you did it by just being your no-nonsense self, by just reading me right and telling me everything you thought and exactly what I have to hear."

She almost winced. She wasn't telling *everything* she thought. Not by a long shot. But her thoughts and feelings where he was concerned were her responsibility. She had no right to burden him with what didn't concern him.

But he was making it harder by the minute to contain those feelings within her being's meager boundaries.

He wasn't finished with his latest bout of unwitting torment. "You yanked me out of the downward spiral I was resigned to plunge into until I hit rock bottom. So, yes, I'm sure your choice of abodes will be the best one for me. Because you've been the best thing that has ever happened to me."

The heart that had been squeezing harder with every incredible word almost burst.

To have him so eloquently reinforcing her suspicion that he'd come to consider her the replacement best friend/sister he needed was both ecstasy and agony.

Feeling the now-familiar heat simmering behind her eyes, she attempted to take this back to lightness. "What's with the seriousness? And here I was secure in the fact that you're incapable of being that way around me."

His smile was so indulgent that she felt something coming undone right in her very essence. "I'm always serious around you. Just in a way that's the most fun I've ever had. But if you feel I'm burdening you with making this choice…"

And she had to laugh. "Oh, shut up, you gigantic weasel. After all the sucking up you did, and all the puppy-dog-eyed persuasion that you *have* perfected in front of that mirror, you have the audacity to pretend that I have a choice here?"

His guffaw belted out, almost made her collapse onto herself. "Ah, Kanza, *you* are the most fun I've ever had."

Yeah. What every girl wanted to hear from the most divine man on earth. That she made him laugh.

But she'd already settled for that. For anything with him. For as long as she could have it. Come what may.

He brought the car to a stop in front of a building that felt vaguely familiar. As he opened his door, she jumped out so he wouldn't come around to open hers, since opening doors and pulling back seats for her seemed to be the only acts that indicated that he considered her female.

When he fell into step beside her, she did a double take.

They were on Fifth Avenue. Specifically in front of one of the top Italian-renaissance palazzo-style apartment buildings in Manhattan.

Forgetting everything but the excitement of apartment hunting, she turned to him with a whoop. "I used to live a block from here." And she'd found the area only "vaguely familiar." He short-circuited her brain even more than she'd thought. "God, I loved that apartment. It was the only place that ever felt like home."

His eyebrows shot up. "Zohayd didn't feel like that?"

"Not really. You know what it was like."

He frowned and, if possible, became more edible than ever. "Actually, I have no idea how it was like for you there. Because you never told me." As soon as they entered the elevator, he turned to her with a probing glance. "How did we never get to talk about your life in Zohayd?"

She shrugged. "Guess we had more important things to discuss. Like how to pick the best avocado."

His lips pursed in displeasure. "That alone makes me realize how remiss I've been and that there is a big story here. One I won't rest until I hear."

She waved him off. "It's boring, really."

His pout was adamant. "I live to be bored by you."

The last thing she wanted to do was tell him about her disappointment-riddled life in Zohayd. But knowing him, he'd persist until she told him. The best she could hope for was to distract him for now.

She took the key from his hand as they got off the elevator. "Which apartment?"

He pointed out the one at the far end of the floor.

As they sauntered in that direction, he looked down at her. "So about this old place of yours—if it felt like home, and I'm assuming your new place doesn't, why did you move?"

"A friend from Zohayd begged me to room with her, as she couldn't live alone, and the new place was right by her work. Then she up and got married on me and went back to Zohayd, and I never got around to going back to my place. But now that you might be buying a place this close, it would save us a lot of commuting if I got it back. Hope it's still on the market."

"Choose this apartment, and I'll *make* it on the market."

"Oh. Watch out, world, for the big, bad tycoon. He snaps his fingers and the market yelps and rolls over."

He gave her a deep bow. "At your service."

They laughed and exchanged wit missiles as they entered the opulent duplex through a marble-framed doorway. Then she fell silent as she beheld what looked straight out of the pages of *Architectural Digest*. Sweeping, superbly organized layouts with long galleries, an elegant staircase, lush finishes, oversize windows, high ceilings and a spacious terrace that wrapped around two sides of the apartment. It was even furnished to the highest standards she'd ever seen and very, very much to her taste.

In only minutes of looking around, she turned to Aram. "Okay, no need to see anything more. Or any other place. I hereby proclaim that you will find utmost comfort here."

He again bowed deeply, azure flames of merriment leaping in his eyes. "My Minuscule Mistress, thy will be done."

And in the next hour, it was. He immediately called the Realtor, who zoomed over with the contracts. Aram passed them to her to read before he signed, and she made some amendments before giving him the green light. From then on, it took only minutes for the check to be handed over and the Realtor to leave the apartment almost bouncing in delight.

Aram came back from walking the lady to the front door, his smile flooding his magnificent new place in its radiance.

"Now to inaugurate the apartment with our first meal." He threw himself down beside her on the elegant couch. "So what are we eating?"

She cocked an eyebrow at him and tsked. "This inability to make decisions without my say-so is becoming worrisome."

He slid down farther on the couch, reclining his big, powerful body more comfortably. "I've been making business decisions for countless employees, clients and shareholders for the past eight years. I'm due for a perpetual vacation from making minor- to moderate-sized decisions for the rest of my personal life."

She gave him her best stern scowl, which she resignedly knew he thought was the most adorable thing ever. "And I'm the one who's supposed to pick up the slack and suddenly be responsible for your decisions as well as mine?"

He nodded in utmost complacency. "You do it so well, so naturally. And it's your fault. You're the one who got me used to this." His gaze became that cross between cajoling and imploring that he'd perfected. "You're not leaving me in the lurch now, are you?"

"Stop with the eyes!" she admonished. "Or I swear I'll blindfold you."

"What a brilliant idea. Then besides making decisions for me, you'll have to lead me around by the hand. Even more unaccountability for me to revel in."

She threw her hands up. "Sushi, okay. Here's your decision before I find myself taking over your business, too, while you go indulge in the teenage irresponsibility you evidently never had."

Chuckling, he got out his phone. Then he proceeded to ask her exactly what kind of sushi they were eating, piece by piece, until she had to slam him with a cushion.

After they'd wiped off the delicious feast, he was pouring her jasmine tea when she noticed him looking at her in an even more unsettling, contemplative way.

"What?" she croaked.

"I was wondering if you were always this interesting."

"And I'm wondering if you were always this condescending. Oh, wait, you were even worse. You used to look at me like I was a strange life-form."

"You *were* a strange life-form. I mean, green body makeup? And pink contacts? Pink? Did you have those custom-made?" He rejoined her on the couch with his own cup. "What statement were you making?"

She was loath to remember those times when she'd felt alone even while deluged by people. When she used to look at him and know that *nogoom el sama a'arablaha*—that the stars in the sky were closer than he was. Now, though he was a breath away, he remained as distant, as impossible to reach.

She sighed, shaking free from the wave of melancholy. "One of my stepmothers, Maysoon's mother, popularized Kanza the Monster's name until everyone was using it. So I decided to go the whole hog and look the part."

His eyes went grim, as if imagining having his hands on those who'd been so inconsiderate with her. Knowing him, she didn't put it past him that he would act on his outrage on behalf of her former self.

"What made you give it up?" His voice was dark with barely suppressed anger. "Then go all the way in the other direction, doing without any sort of enhancement?"

She shrugged. "I developed an allergy to makeup."

His lips twitched as his anger dissolved into wry humor. "Another allergy?"

"Not a real one. I just realized that regardless of whether makeup makes me look worse or better, I was focusing too much on what others thought of me. So I decided to focus on myself. Be myself."

That pride he showered on her flooded his gaze. "Good for you. You're perfect just the way you are."

Kanza stared at him. In any romantic movie, as the hero

professed those words, he would have suddenly seen his dorky best friend in a new light, would have realized she was beautiful in his eyes and that he wanted her for more than just a friend.

Before her heart imploded with futility, she slid down on the couch, pretending she thought it a good moment for one of those silent rituals they exercised together.

Inside her, there was only cacophony.

Aram considered her perfect.

Just not for him.

Eight

Aram sank further into tranquility and relaxation beside Kanza, savoring the companionable silence they excelled at together, just as they did at exhilarating repartee.

Just by being here, she'd turned this place, which he'd felt ambivalent toward until she'd entered it and decided she liked it, into a home. He'd decided to have one at last only because she'd said she would always stay in New York and make it hers.

He sighed, cherishing the knowledge that expanded inside him with each passing hour.

She was really her name. A treasure.

And to think that no one, even Shaheen and Johara, realized how much of one she really was.

He guessed she was too different, too unexpected, too unbelievable for others to be able to fathom, let alone to handle.

She was perfect to him.

It was hard to believe that only six weeks ago he hadn't had her in his life. It felt as if his existence had *become* a life only once she'd entered it.

And it seemed like a lifetime ago when Shaheen had

suggested her as a convenient bride, convinced she'd consider his assets and agree to the arrangement. If Shaheen only knew her, he would have known that she'd sign a contract of enslavement before she would a marriage of convenience. If he'd known how unique, how exceptional she was, he wouldn't have even thought of such an unworthy fate for her.

She'd achieved her success in pursuit of self-realization and accomplishment, not status and wealth—things she cared nothing about and would certainly never wish to attain through a man. She'd even made it clear she didn't consider marriage a viable option for herself. But among the many misconceptions about her had been his own worry that his initial fascination would fade, and she'd turn out to be just another opportunistic woman who'd use any means necessary to reel in a husband.

But the opposite had happened. His fascination, his admiration, his pleasure at being with her intensified by the minute. For the first time, he found himself attracted to the *whole* woman, his attraction not rooted in sexuality or sustained by it. He had to use Shaheen's word to describe what they were. Compatible. They were matched on every level—personally, professionally, mentally and emotionally. Her every quality and skill meshed with and complemented his own. She was his equal, and his superior in many areas.

She was *just* perfect.

Just yesterday, Shaheen had asked him for an update on whether he'd changed his mind about Kanza now that he'd gotten to know her.

He'd said only that he had, leaving it at that.

What he'd really meant was that he had changed his mind about *everything*.

The more he was with Kanza, the more everything he'd believed of himself—of his limits, inclinations, priorities and everything he'd felt before her—changed beyond all recognition.

She made him work hard for her respect and esteem, for the pleasure and privilege of his presence in her life, for her gracing his with hers. She gave him what no one had ever given him before, not even Shaheen or Johara. She *reveled* in being with him as much as he did with her. She *got* him on every level. She accepted him, challenged him, and when she felt there were things about him that needed fixing— and there were *many*—she just reached inside him with the magic wand of her candor and caring and put it right.

She'd turned his barren existence into a life of fulfillment, every day bringing with it deeper meanings, invigorating discoveries and uplifting experiences.

The only reason he'd fleetingly considered Shaheen's offer had been for the possibility of filling his emptiness with a new purpose in life and the proximity of his family. Now he found little reason to change his status quo. For what could possibly be better than this?

It was just perfection between them.

So when Shaheen had asked for an update, really asking about projected developments, he couldn't bear thinking of any. How could he when any might tamper with this blissful state? He was *terrified* anything would happen to change it.

They were both unconcerned about the world and its conventions, and things were flourishing between them. He only hoped they would continue to deepen in the exact same way. So even if he wanted to, he certainly wasn't introducing any new variable that might fracture the flawlessness.

For now, the only change he wanted to introduce was removing the last barrier inside him. He wanted to let her into his being, fully and totally.

So he did. "There's something I haven't told you yet. Something nobody knows."

She turned to him, her glorious mass of hair rustling as if it was alive, those unique obsidian eyes delving deep inside his recesses, letting him know she was there for him always.

Just gazing into them he felt invincible. And secure that he could share everything with her, even his shame.

"It happened a few months after I left Zohayd...." He paused, the long-repressed confession searing out of his depths. He braced himself against the pain, spit it out. "I got involved in something...that turned out to be illegal, with very dangerous people. I ended up in prison."

That had her sitting up. And what he saw on her face rocked through him. Instantaneous reassurance that, whatever had happened, whatever he told her, it wouldn't change her opinion of him. She was on his side. Unequivocally.

And as he'd needed to more frequently of late, he took a moment to suppress the desire to haul her to him and crush her in the depths of his embrace with all his strength.

The need to physically express his feelings for her had been intensifying every day. But she'd made no indication that she'd accept that. Worse. She didn't seem to want it.

It kept him from initiating anything, even as much as a touch. For what if even a caress on her cheek or hair changed the dynamic between them? What if it made her uneasy and put her on her guard around him? What if he then couldn't take it back and convince her that he'd settle for their previous hands-off status quo, forever if need be?

He brought the urge under control with even more difficulty than he had the last time it had assailed him, his voice sounding as harsh as broken glass as he went on, "I was sentenced to three years. I was paroled after only one."

Her solemn eyes were now meshed with his. He felt he was sinking into the depths of their unconditional support, felt understood, cosseted, protected. It was as if she was reaching to him through time, to offer him her strength to tide him through the incarceration, to soothe the wounds and erase his scars.

"For good behavior?" Her voice was the gentlest he'd ever heard it.

He barked a mirthless laugh. "Actually, they probably

wanted me out to get rid of me. I was too much trouble, gave them too many inmates to patch up. I almost killed a couple. I spent over nine months of that year in solitary. The moment they let me out, I put more inmates in the infirmary and I was shoved back there."

"You ended up being…solitary too many times throughout your life."

She'd mused that as if to herself. But he felt her soft, pondering words reaching down inside him to tear out the talons he'd long felt sunk into his heart. Making him realize that it hadn't been the solitude itself that had eaten at him but the notion that he'd never stop being alone.

But now she was here, and he'd never be alone again.

Her smile suddenly dawned, and it lit up his entire world. "But you still managed to make the best of a disastrous situation in your own inimitable way."

"It wasn't only my danger to criminal life-forms that got me out. I was a first-time offender, and I was lucky to find people who believed that I had made a mistake, not committed a crime. Those allies helped me get out, and afterward, they supported my efforts to…expunge my record."

The radiance of her smile intensified, scorching away any remnants of the ordeal's despondency and indignity. "So you're an old hand at expunging your record. And I wasn't the first one who believed in you."

He didn't know how he stopped himself from grabbing her hands, burying his lips and face in them, grabbing her and burying his whole being in her magnanimity and faith.

He expended the urge on a ragged breath. "You're the first and only one who did with only the evidence of my word."

She waved that away. "As you so astutely pointed out the first night, I do know Maysoon. That was a load of evidence in your favor, once I'd heard both sides of the story."

He wasn't about to accept her qualification. "No. You

employed this unerring truth-and-justice detector of yours without any backing evidence. You read *me*. You believed *me*."

Her eyes gleamed with that indulgence that melted him to his core. "Okay, okay, I did. Boy, you're pushy."

"And you believed me again now," he insisted, needing to hear her say it. "When I said I didn't knowingly commit a crime, even when I gave you no details, let alone evidence."

Teasing ebbed, as if she felt he needed the assurance of her seriousness. "Yes, I did, because I know you'd always tell me the truth, the bad before the good. If you'd been guilty, you would have told me. Because you know I can't accept anything but the truth and because you know that whatever it was, it wouldn't make a difference to me."

Hot thorns sprouted behind his eyes, inside his heart. Everything inside him surged, needing to mingle with her.

He had to end these sublime moments before he…expressed how moved he was by them, shattering them instead.

He first had to try to tell her what her belief meant to him. "Your trust in me is a privilege and a responsibility that I will always nurture with pride and pleasure."

Her gaze suddenly escaped his, flowed down his body.

By the time they rose back, he was hard all over. Thankfully, her eyes were intent on his, full of contemplation.

"Though you're so big, with no doubt proportionate strength, it never occurred to me you'd be that capable of physical violence."

The vice that had released his heart suddenly clamped around it again. "Does this…disturb you?"

Her laugh rang out. "Hello? Have you met me? It *thrills* me. I would have loved to see you decimate a few thugs and neuter some bullies."

His hands, his whole being itched, ached. He just wanted to squeeze the hell out of her. He wanted to contain her, assimilate her and never let her go again.

He again held back with all he had, then drawled, "And to think something so minuscule could be so bloodthirsty."

She grinned impishly. "You've got a lot to learn about just what this deceptive exterior hides, big man."

Though her words tickled him and her smile was unfettered, he was still unsettled. "Is it really no problem for you to change your perception of me from someone who's too civilized to use his brute strength to someone who relishes physical violence?"

She shook her head, her long, thick hair falling over her slight shoulders down to her waist. "I don't believe you 'relish' it, but you'll always do 'what works best.' At the time, violence was the one thing that would keep the sharks away. So you used it, and to maximum efficiency, as is your way with everything. I'm only lamenting that there's no video documentation of those events for *me* to cheer over."

The delight she always struck in his heart overflowed in an unbridled guffaw. "I can just see you, grabbing the popcorn and hollering at the screen for more gore. But I might be able to do something about your desire to see me on a rampage. I can pull some strings at the prison and get some surveillance-camera footage."

She jumped up to her knees on the couch, nimble and keen as a cat. "Yes, yes, please!"

"Uh…I'm already regretting making the offer. You might think you can withstand what you'd see, but it was no staged fight like those you see on TV. There was no showmanship involved, just brutality with only the intent to survive at whatever cost."

She tucked her legs as if she was starting a meditation session, her gaze ultraserious. "That only makes it even more imperative to see it, Aram. It was the ugliest, harshest, most humiliating test you've ever endured and your deepest scar. I need to experience it in more than imagination, even if in the cold distance of past images, so I'd be able to share it with you in the most profound way I need to."

Stirred through to his soul, he swallowed a jagged lump of gratitude. "You just have to want it and it's done."

"Oh, I so want it. Thank you." Before he pounced with a thank-*you,* she probed, "You've really been needing to confide this all this time. Why didn't you?"

She was killing him with her ability to see right into his depths. She was reviving him with it, reanimating him.

"I was…ashamed. Of my weakness and stupidity. I wanted to prove to Shaheen and his brothers that I didn't need their help after all, that I'd make it on my own. And I got myself involved in something that looked too good to be true because I was in such a hurry to do it. And I paid the price."

She tilted her head to the side, as if to look at him from another perspective. "I can't even imagine what it was like. When you were arrested, when you were sentenced, when you realized you might have destroyed your future, maybe even tainted that of your family. That year in prison…"

He wanted to tell her that she was imagining it just fine, that her compassion was dissipating the lingering darkness of that period, erasing the scars it had left behind. But his throat was closed, his voice gone.

The empathy in her gaze rose until it razed him. "But I can understand the ordeal was a link in the chain that led to your eventual decline. Not the experience itself as much as the reinforcement of your segregation. You couldn't share such a life-changing experience with your loved ones, mainly because you wanted to protect them from the agony they would have felt on your behalf. But that very inability to bare your soul to them made you pull further away emotionally, and actually exacerbated your solitude."

When he finally found his voice, it was a hoarse, ragged whisper. "See? You do know everything."

Her eyes gentled even more. "Not everything. I'm still unable to fill some spaces. You were going strong for years after your imprisonment. Was that only *halawet el roh?*"

Literally sweetness of the soul. What was said in Zohayd to describe a state of deceptive vigor, a clinging to life when warding off inevitable deterioration or death.

"Now that you mention it, that's the best explanation. I came out of prison with a rabid drive to wipe out what happened, to right my path, to make up for lost time. I guess I was trying to run hard and fast enough to escape the memories, to accumulate enough success and security to fix the chasm the experience had ripped inside me and that threatened to tear me open at any moment."

Her eyes now soothed him, had him almost begging her to let her hand join in their caress. "Johara told me you were at the peak of fitness, at least physically, three years ago when you attended their wedding in Zohayd. From her observations, you started deteriorating about two years ago. Was there a triggering event? Like when it sank in that they were a family now? Did their togetherness—especially with your parents' reconciliation—leave you feeling more alone than ever?"

He squeezed his eyes on a spasm of poignancy. "You get me so completely. You get me better than I get myself."

Wryness touched her lips. "It was Johara who gave me the code to decipher your hieroglyphics when she said she felt as if her and Shaheen's intimacy left you unable to connect with either of them on the same level as you used to."

"She's probably right. But it's not only my own hang-ups. Neither of them has enough left to devote to anyone else. A love like that fills up your being. And then there's the massive emotional investment in Gharam and their coming baby."

Something inscrutable came into her eyes, intensifying their already absolute darkness.

Seeming to shake herself out of it, whatever it was, she continued searching his recesses. "So *was* there a triggering physical event? That made your health start to deteriorate?"

"Nothing specific. I just started being unable to sleep

well, to eat as I should. Everything became harder, took longer and I did it worse. Then each time I got even a headache or caught a cold, it took me ages to bounce back. My focus, my stamina, my immunity were just shot. I guess my whole being was disintegrating."

"But you're back in tip-top shape now."

It was a question, not a statement, worry tingeing it.

He let his gaze cup her elfin face in lieu of his hands. "I've never been better. And it's thanks to you."

Her smile faltered as she again waved his assertion away. "There you go again, crediting me with miracles."

"You *are* a miracle. My Minute Miracle. Not that size has anything to do with your effect. *That's* supreme."

He jumped to his feet, feeling younger and more alive than he'd ever felt, needing to dive headfirst into the world, doing everything under the sun with her. He rushed to fetch their jackets, then dashed back to her. "Let's go run in the rain. Then let's hop on my jet and go have breakfast anywhere you want. Europe. South America. Australia. Anywhere."

She donned her jacket and ran after him out of the apartment with just as much zeal. "How about the moon?"

Delighted at her willingness to oblige him in whatever he got it in his mind to say or do, he said, "If it's what you want, then I'll make it happen."

She pulled one of those funny faces that he adored. "And I wouldn't put it past you, too. Nah…I'll settle for something on terra firma. And close by. I have to work in the morning, even if you're so big and important now you no longer have to."

He consulted his watch. "If we leave for Barbados in an hour, I'll have you at work by ten."

Her disbelief lasted only moments before mischief and excitement replaced it. "You're on."

Nine

"It's...good to hear your voice, Father."

Kanza hated that hesitation in her voice. Whatever her father's faults, she did love him. Did miss him.

Yeah. She did. But, and it was a huge but, after ten minutes of basking in the nostalgia of early and oblivious childhood when her father had been her hero, she always thudded back to reality and was ready not to see him again for months.

"It's great to hear yours, *ya bnayti*."

His calling her *my daughter,* instead of bestowing a personalized greeting with her name included, annoyed her. He called his other eight daughters that, with the same indiscrimination. She thought he used it most times because he forgot the name of the one he was talking to.

Curbing her irritation, and knowing her father never called unless he had something to ask of her, she said, "Anything I can do for you, Father?"

"*Ya Ullah,* yes. Only you can help me now, *ya bnayti.* I need you to come back to Zohayd at once."

Ten minutes later, she sat staring numbly into space.

She'd tried to wriggle out of saying yes. She'd failed.

She was really going back to Zohayd. Tonight.

Her father had begged her to board the first flight to Zohayd. Beyond confirming that no one was dead or severely injured, he'd said no more about why he needed her back so urgently.

She reserved a ticket online, then packed a few essentials. She wouldn't stay a minute longer than necessary.

Not that there was a reason to hurry back.

Not from the evidence of the past two weeks anyway.

It had been then, six weeks after that magical time in Aram's new apartment and the breakfast in Barbados, that Aram had suddenly become insanely busy. He'd neglected his work so much that the accumulation had become critical.

She understood. Of *course,* she did. She knew exactly how many people depended on him, what kind of money rode on his presence and expertise. She'd been neglecting her work, too, but Johara had picked up the slack, and she was not so indispensable that her absence would cause the same widespread ripples his had. She appreciated this fully. Mentally. But otherwise…

The fact was, he'd spoiled her. She'd gotten reliant on seeing him each and every day, on being able to pick up the phone, day or night, and he'd be eager and willing to grant her every wish, to be there with her at no notice. When that had suddenly come to an abrupt end, she'd gone into withdrawal.

God. She'd turned into one of those clingy, needy females. At least in her own mind and psyche. Outwardly, she was her devil-may-care self. At least, she hoped she was.

But she was something else, too. Moronic. The man had a life outside her, even if for three months straight it had seemed as if he didn't. She'd known real life would reassert itself at one point. So she should stop whining *now*.

And now that she thought of it without self-pity, going to Zohayd was a good thing. She'd been twiddling her thumbs until she and Johara started the next project. And by the time she was back, he would have sorted himself enough to be able to see her again—at least more than he had the past two weeks.

She speed-dialed his number. The voice she now lived to hear poured into her brain after the second ring.

"Kanza—a moment please…" His voice was muffled as he talked to someone.

Feeling guilty for interrupting him when he'd told her he wouldn't have a free moment before seven, she rushed on. "I just wanted to tell you I'm going home in a couple of hours."

More muffled words, then he came back to her. "That's fantastic. About time."

That she hadn't expected. "It—it is?"

"Sure, it is. Listen, Kanza, I'm sorry, but I *have* to finish this before the Saudi Stock Exchange opens. 'Bye now."

Then he hung up.

She stared at the phone.

Last night, he'd said he'd see her later tonight. But she'd just told him she wouldn't be able to see him because she was traveling and he'd sounded…glad?

Had she unwittingly let her disappointment show when he'd been unable to see her for the past two weeks, and he now thought it was a good idea if she did something other than wait for him until his preoccupation lightened and he could see her again?

But he hadn't even asked why she was going or how long she'd stay. Sure, he'd been in a hurry, but he could have said something other than *fantastic* or *about time.* He could have said he'd call later to get details.

So was it possible he was just glad to get her off his back? Could it be that what she'd thought were unfounded feelings of impending loss had just been premonition? Was the magical interlude with him really over?

She'd known from the start he'd just needed someone to help him through the worst slump in his life. Now that he was over it, was he over his need for her?

That made sense. Terrible sense. And it was only expected. She'd dreaded that day, but she'd known it would come. She'd just kept hoping it would not come so soon. She wasn't ready to give him up yet.

But when would she ever be? How could she ever be… when she loved him?

Suddenly a sob tore out of her. Then another, and another until she was bent over, tears raining on the ground, unable to contain the torrent of anguish anymore.

She loved him.

She would forever love him.

And she would have remained his friend forever, asking nothing more but to have the pleasure and privilege of his nearness, of his appreciation, of his completion. Of his need.

But it seemed he no longer needed her.

Now he'd recede, but never really end it as he would have with a lover. She would see him again and again whenever life threw them together. And each time, he'd expect her to be his buddy, would chat and tease and reminisce and not realize that she missed him like an amputee would a limb.

Maybe going to Zohayd now *was* a blessing in disguise.

Maybe she should stay until he totally forgot about her.

The moment Aram finished his last memo for the night, he pounced on his phone to call Kanza. Before he did, Shaheen walked into his office.

A groan escaped him that he had to postpone the call—and seeing her—for the length of Shaheen's visit.

His brother-in-law whistled. "*Ya Ullah,* you missed me *that* much?"

Aram winced. His impatience must be emblazoned across his whole body. And he'd been totally neglecting his friend as of late. But he'd been reserving every hour, every moment, every spare breath for Kanza.

"Actually I do miss you, but—" he groaned again, ran his fingers through his hair "—you know how it is."

Shaheen laughed. *"Menn la'ah ahbaboh nessi ashaboh."*
He who finds his loved ones forgets his friends.

He refused to comment on Shaheen's backhanded reference to Kanza as his loved one. "As much as I'd love to indulge your curiosity, Shaheen, I have to go to Kanza now. Let's get together some other time. Maybe I'll bring Kanza over to your home, hmm?"

Shaheen blinked in surprise. "You're going to Zohayd?"

Aram scowled. "Now, where did that come from? Why should I go to Zohayd?"

"Because you said that you're going to Kanza, who's on her way to Zohayd right now."

Aram glanced at his watch, then out of the jet's window, then back at his watch.

Had it always taken that long to get to Zohayd?

It felt as if it had been a day since he'd boarded his jet—barely an hour after Shaheen had said Kanza was heading there.

He was still reverberating with disbelief. With…panic.

His condition had been worsening since it had sunk in that the "home" Kanza had meant was Zohayd. According to Johara, Kanza was returning there at her father's urgent demand. Kanza herself didn't know why. Shaheen hadn't been able to understand why he'd be so agitated that she was visiting her family and would probably be back in a few days.

But he'd been unable to listen, to Shaheen or the voice of reason. Nothing had mattered but one thing.

The need to go after her.

A tornado was tearing through him. His gut told him something was wrong. Terribly wrong.

For how could she go like that without saying goodbye?

Even if she had to rush, even if he'd been swamped, the Kanza he knew would have let him see her before separation was imposed on them.

So why hadn't she? Why hadn't she made it clear where she was going? If he'd known, he would have rushed to her, would have paid the millions that would have been lost for a chance to see her even for a few minutes before she left. She had to know he would have. So why hadn't she given him the chance to? Hadn't it been as necessary for her to see him this last time as it was for him?

Was he not as necessary to her as she was to him?

He'd long been forced to believe his necessity to her differed from hers to him. He'd thought that as long as the intimacy remained the same, he'd just have to live with the fact that its…texture wasn't what he now yearned for.

But what if he was losing even that? What if not saying goodbye now meant that she *could* eventually say goodbye for real? What if that day was even closer than his worst nightmares?

What if that day was here?

He couldn't even face that possibility. He'd lost his solitariness from the first time he'd seen her. She'd proceeded to strip him of his self-containment, his autonomy. He'd known isolation. But he hadn't realized what loneliness was until he'd heard from Shaheen that she'd left.

She'd become more than vital to him. She'd become… home.

What if he could never be anything like that to her?

What if he caught up with her in Zohayd and she only thought he was out of his mind hurtling after her like that?

Maybe he was out of his mind. Maybe everything he'd just churned himself over had no basis in fact. Maybe…

His cell phone rang. He fumbled with it, his fingers going numb with brutal anticipation. *Kanza.* She'd tell him why she hadn't said goodbye. And he'd tell her he'd be with her in a couple of hours and she could say it to his face.

The next moment disappointment crashed through him. Johara.

He couldn't hold back his growl. "What is it, Johara?"

A silent beat. "Uh…don't kill the messenger, okay?"

"What the hell does that mean? Jo, I'm really not in any condition to have a nice, civil conversation right now. For both our sakes, just leave me alone."

"I'm sorry, Aram, but I really think you need to know, so you'd be prepared."

"Know what? Be prepared for what?" A thousand dreads swooped down on him, each one shrieking Kanza, Kanza, *Kanza*… "Just spit it out!"

"I just got off the phone with Kanza's father. He said he needed me to know as Kanza's best friend that Prince Kareem Aal Kahlawi has asked for her hand in marriage."

Kanza thought it was inevitable.

She would end up killing someone.

For now, storming through her father's house, slamming her old bedroom door behind her was all the venting she could do.

She leaned against it, letting out a furious shriek.

Of all the self-involved, self-serving, unfeeling… Argh!

To think that was why her father had dragged her back here!

Couldn't she kill him? And her sisters? Just a little bit…?

Her whole body lurched forward, every nerve firing at once.

She stopped. Moving. Breathing. Even her heart slowed down. Each boom so hard her ears rang.

That must be it. Why she thought she'd heard…

"Kanza."

Aram.

God. She was starting to hear things. Hear him. When he was seven thousand miles away. This was beyond pathetic.…

"Kanza. I know you're there."

Okay. She wasn't *that* pathetic.

"I saw you tearing out of the living room, saw you going

up. I know this is your room. I know you're in there now. Come to the window. *Now,* Kanza."

That last "now" catapulted her to the French doors. She barely stopped before she shot over the balcony's balustrade.

And standing down there, among the shrubs below, in all his mind-blowing glory, was Aram.

Azure bolts arced from his eyes and a wounded lion's growl came from his lips. "What are you *doing* here?"

Her head spun at the brunt of his beauty under Zohayd's declining sun and the absurdity of his question.

She blinked, as if it would reboot her brain. "What are *you* doing here? In Zohayd? And standing beneath my window?"

He stuck his fists at his hips. He looked…angry? And agitated. Why? "What does it look like? I'm here to see you."

She shook her head, confusion deepening. He must have left New York just a few hours after she had. Had he come all the way here to find out why she had? After he'd basically told her to scram? Why not just call? What did it all mean?

Okay. With the upheaval of this past day, her brain was on the fritz. She could no longer attempt to make any sense of it.

She pinched the bridge of her nose. "Well, you saw me. Now go away before all my family comes out and finds you here. With the way you've been shouting, they must be on their way."

He widened his stance, face adamant planes and ruthless slashes. "If you don't want them to see me, come down."

"I can't. If I go down and try to walk through the front door, I'll have twenty females on my case…and I don't want the ulcer I've acquired in the last hours to rupture."

"Then *climb* down."

That last whisper could have sandpapered the manor's facade. "Okay, Aram, I know you're crazy, but even in your insanity you can see that the last foothold is twenty feet above splat level."

He shrugged. "Fifteen max. I'll catch you."

Closing her mouth before it caught one of the birds zooming back to their nests at the approach of sunset, she echoed his pose, fists on hips. "If you want to reenact Shaheen's stunt with Johara, I have to remind you that she was six at the time."

That shrug again. "You're not that much bigger now."

She coughed a chagrined laugh. "Why, thanks. Just what every grown woman wants to hear."

He sighed. "I meant the ratio of your size to mine, compared to that of fourteen-year-old Shaheen to six-year-old Johara." He suddenly snarled again, his eyes blazing. "Stop arguing. I can catch you, easy. You know I've been exercising."

Yeah, she knew. She'd attended many a mind-scrambling session, seen what he looked like with minimal clothing, flexing, bulging, sweating, flooding a mile's radius with premium, lethal testosterone.

"But even in my worst days, I would have been able to catch you. I always knew I was that big for a reason, but I just never knew what it was. Now I know. It's so I could catch you."

Her mouth dropped open again.

What that man kept *saying*.

What would he say when he was actually in love…?

That thought made her feel like jumping off the balcony—and not so he could catch her.

She inhaled a steadying, sanity-laced breath. "Oh, all right. Just because I know you'll stand there until I do. Or worse, barge into the house to come up here and have a houseful of your old fans pick your bones. I hope you know I'm doing this to save your gorgeous hide."

His smile was terse. "Yes, of course. I'm, as always, eternally indebted to you. Now hurry."

Mumbling under her breath about him being a hulk-sized brat who expected to get his way in everything, she took one last bracing breath and climbed over the balustrade.

As she inched down over the steplike ledges, he kept a running encouragement. "You're doing fine. Don't look down. I'm right here."

Slipping, she clung to the building, wailed, "Shut *up,* Aram. God, I can't believe what you can talk me into."

He just kept going. "Keep your body firm, not tense, okay? Now let go." When she hesitated, his voice suddenly dropped into the darkest reaches of hypnosis. "Don't worry, I'll catch you, *ya kanzi.*"

My treasure.

All her nerves unraveled. She plummeted.

Her plunge came to a jarring, if firm and secure, end.

He'd caught her. Easy, as he'd said. As if he'd snatched her from a three-foot drop. And she was staring up into those vivid, luminescent eyes that now filled her existence.

Without one more word, he swept her along through the manicured grounds and out of her father's estate.

She reeled. Not from the drop, but from her first contact with him. His flesh pressed to hers, his warmth enveloping her, his strength cocooning her. Being in his arms, even if in this context, was like…like…going home.

Even if the feeling was imaginary, she'd savor it. He was here, for whatever reason, and their…closeness wasn't over.

Not yet.

She let go, let him take her wherever he would.

Aram brooded at Kanza as she walked one step ahead.

He could barely let her be this far away. He'd clutched her all the way out of her father's estate, almost unable to let her go to put her into the car. As if by agreement, they hadn't said anything during the drive. But it hadn't been the companionable silence they'd perfected. By the time they'd arrived, he'd expended his decimated willpower so he wouldn't roar, demanding she tell him what was wrong.

She turned every few steps, as if to check if he was maintaining the same distance. Her glances felt like the sustenance that would save him from starvation. But they didn't soothe him as they'd always done. There was something in them that sent his senses haywire. Something...wary.

He couldn't bear to interpret this. Any interpretation was just too mutilating. And could be dead wrong anyway. So he wouldn't even try.

She stopped at the railings of the upper-floor terrace, turning to him. "Don't tell me you bought this villa in your half hour in Zohayd before popping up beneath my window."

He barely caught back a groan of relief. Her voice. Her teasing. God, he *needed* them.

"Why? Do you think I'm not crazy enough to do it?"

Her smile resembled her usual ones. But not quite. "Excellent point. Since you're crazier, you might have also bought the sea and desert in a ten-mile radius."

A laugh caught in his throat, broke against the spastic barrier of tension. "It's Shaheen's. Now tell me what the hell you're doing here. And why you left without telling me."

Her eyes got even more enormous. "I did tell you."

He threw his arms wide in frustration. "How was I supposed to know you meant Zohayd when you said home?"

"Uh...is this a new crisis? What else could I have meant?"

"Your old New York apartment, of course. The one you said felt like home, the one I got you back the lease for. I thought you were finally ready to move there again."

"That's why you thought it fantastic when I said I was going home," she said, as if to herself. "You thought it was about time I was down the street from you."

He gaped at her. "Are you *nuts?* You thought I would *actually* think it fantastic for you to come out here and leave

me alone in New York? Contrary to popular belief, I'm not
that evolved. I might support your doing something that
doesn't involve me if it makes you happy, even accept that
it could take you away from me—for a little while—but be
okay, let alone ecstatic about it? No way."

Her eyes kept widening with his every word. At his last
bark, her smile flashed back to its unbridled vivacity.

"Thanks for letting me know the extent of your evolu-
tion. Now quit snarling at me. I have a big enough headache being saddled with making decisions for more than
you now, in not only one but *two* weddings."

It felt as if a missile had hit him.

No. She couldn't be talking about a wedding already. He
couldn't allow it. He wouldn't. He'd…

Two weddings?

His rumble was that of a beast bewildered with too many
blows. "What the hell are you talking about?"

"My last two unmarried sisters' weddings. With each
from a different mother and with how things are in Zohayd
where weddings are battlefields, they've reached a stand-
off with each other and with their bridegrooms' families. It
seems there's more hope of ending a war than reaching an
agreement on the details of the weddings. Enter me—what
Father thinks is his only hope of defusing the situation."

He frowned. "Why you?"

Her lips twisted whimsically. "Because I'm what Father calls the 'neutral zone.' With me as the one daughter
of the woman who gave birth to me then ran off with a big
chunk of my father's wealth, I am the one who has always
given him no trouble, having no mother to harass him on
my behalf. And being stuck as the middle sister between
eight half sisters, four each from a stepmother, it made me
the one in his brood of nine female offspring that no one is
jealous of, therefore not unreasonably contentious with."
She sighed dramatically. "I was always dragged to referee,
because both sides don't consider me a player in the fam-

ily power games at all. Now Father has recruited me to get all these hysterical females off his back and hopefully get those weddings under way and over with."

What about the groom who proposed to you? That... prince? Why aren't you telling me about him?

The questions backlashed in his chest. He couldn't give this preposterous subject credence by even mentioning it.

There was only one thing to ask now.

"Is it me?"

She stared up at him, standing against the winter sunset's backdrop, its fire reflecting gold on her skin and striking flames from the depths of her onyx eyes and the thick mahogany satin tresses that undulated around her in the breeze. She was the embodiment of his every taste and desire and aspiration. And the picture of incomprehension.

But he could no longer afford the luxury of caution. Not when he had the grenade of that...*prince's*...proposal lying there between them. Not when letting the status quo continue could give it a chance to explode and cost him everything.

He halved the step he'd been keeping between them. "You're the only one who's ever told me the whole truth, Kanza. I need you to give it to me now."

Her gaze flickered, but she only nodded. She would give him that truth. Always.

And that truth might end his world.

But he had to have it. "I believe in pure friendship between a man and a woman. But when they share... everything, I can't see how there'd be no physical attraction at all. So, again, is it me? Or are you generally not interested?"

No total truth came from her. Just total astonishment.

He groaned. "It's clear this has never even crossed your mind. And I've been content with what we share, delighted our friendship is rooted in intellectual and spiritual harmony—and I was willing to wait forever for anything else. But I feel I don't have forever anymore. And I can't live with the idea that maybe you just aren't aware of the possibilities, that if I can persuade you to give it a try, you might…not hate it."

Still nothing. Nothing but gaping.

And he put his worst fear into words. "Were you stating your personal preferences that first night? When you said I was disgustingly pretty? Do your tastes run toward something, I don't know, rougher or softer or just not…this?" He made a tense gesture at his face, his body. "Do you have an ideal of masculinity and I'm just not it?"

Her cheeks and lips were now hectic rose. Her voice wavered. "Uh… I'm really not sure…"

Neither was he. If it would be even adequate between them. If he could even please her.

But he felt everything for her, wanted everything with her, so he had to try.

He reached for her, cupped her precious head and gazed down into her shocked eyes. "There's one way to make sure."

Then he swooped down and took her lips.

At the first contact with her flesh, the first flay of her breath, a thousand volts crackled between them, unleashing everything inside him in a tidal wave.

Lashed by the ferocity of his response and immediacy of her surrender, he captured her dainty lower lip in a growling bite, stilling its tremors, attempting to moderate his greed. She only cried out, arched against him and opened her lips wider. And her taste inundated him.

God…her *taste*. He'd imagined but couldn't have possibly anticipated her unimaginable sweetness. Or the perfume of her breath or the sensory overload of her feel. Or what it would all do to him. Everything about her mixed in an aphrodisiac, a hallucinogen that eddied in his arteries and pounded through his system, snapping the tethers of his sanity.

He could have held back from acting on his insanity, could have moderated his onslaught if not for the way she melted against him, blasting away all doubts about her capacity for passion in the inferno of her response. Her moans and whimpers urged him on to take his possession from tasting to clinging to wrenching.

His hands shook with urgency as he gathered her thighs, opened her around his bulk, pinned her against the railings with the force of his hunger. Plundering her with his tongue, he drove inside her mouth, thrust against her heat, losing rhythm in the wildness, losing his mind.

But even without a mind or will, his love for this irreplaceable being was far more potent than even his will to live. She did mean more than life to him.

Tearing out of their merging, rumbling at the sting of separation, he looked down at the overpowering sight of the woman trembling in his arms. "Do you want this, Kanza? Do you want *me?*"

Her dark eyes scorched him with what he'd never dreamed of seeing in them: drugged sensuality and surrender. Then they squeezed in languorous acquiescence.

He needed more. A full disclosure, a knowing consent.

"I will take everything you have, devour everything you are, give you all of me. Do you understand? Is this what you want? What you need? *Everything* with me, now?"

His heart faltered, afraid to beat, waiting for her verdict. Then its valves almost burst as her parted, passion-swollen lips quivered on a ragged, drawn-out sigh.

A simple, devastating, "Yes."

Ten

Kanza heard herself moaning "yes" to Aram as if from the depths of a dream. What *had* to be a dream.

For how could this be reality? How could she be in Aram's arms? How could it be that he'd been devouring her and was now asking for more, for everything?

The only reason she believed it was real was that no dream could be this intense, this incredible. And because no dream of hers about him had been anything like this.

In her wildest fantasies, Aram, her indulgent friend, had been gentle in his approach, tender in his passion.

But the Aram she'd known was gone. In his place was a marauder: wild, almost rough and barely holding back to make certain she wanted his invasion and sanctioned his ferocity.

And she did. Oh, how she did. She'd said yes. Couldn't have said more. She could barely hold on to consciousness as she found herself swept up in the throes of his unexpected, shocking passion. The thrill of his dominance, the starkness of his lust tampered with everything that powered her, body and being. Her brain waves blipped, her heartbeat plunged into arrhythmia, her every cell swelled, throbbed, screamed for his possession and assuagement.

She'd thought she'd been aroused around him. Now she knew what arousal was. This mindlessness, this avalanche of sensations, this need to be conquered, dominated, ravished. By him, only him.

Almost swooning with the force of need, she delighted in openly devouring him, indulging her greed for his splendor. He loomed above her, the fiery palette of the horizon framing his bulk, accentuating his size, setting his beauty ablaze. The tempest in his eyes was precariously checked. He was giving her one last chance to recant her surrender. Before he devastated her.

She would die if he didn't.

The only confirmation she was capable of was to melt back into his embrace, arching against him in fuller surrender.

Growling something under his breath, he bent toward her. Thinking he'd scoop her up into his arms, carry her inside and take full possession of her, she felt shock reverberate when he started undoing her shirt. He planned to make love to her out here!

There was no one around in what looked like a hundred-mile radius, but she still squirmed. One arm firmed around her only enough to still her as his other hand drifted up her body and behind her to unclasp her bra. The relief of pressure on her swollen flesh buckled her legs.

He held her up, his eyes roving her body in fierce greed as he rid her of her jacket, shirt and bra. The moment her breasts spilled out, he bared his teeth, his lips emitting a soft snarl of hunger. Before she could beg for those lips and teeth on her, his hand undid her pants. She gaped as he dropped to his knees, spanning her hips in his hands' girdle of fire; his fingers hooked into both pants and panties and swept both off her, along with her shoes.

Suddenly his hands reversed their path, inflaming her flesh, rendering her breathless, and he stilled an inch from her core.

She shook—and not with cold. If it wasn't for the cooling air, she might have spontaneously combusted.

Then he lit her fuse, raising eyes like incendiary precious stones. *"Ma koll hada'l jamaal? Kaif konti tekhfeeh?"*

Hearing him raggedly speaking Arabic, asking how she had hidden all this beauty, made her writhe. "Aram… please…"

"Aih…I'll please you, *ya kanzi."* His face pressed to her thighs, her abdomen, his lips opening over her quivering flesh, sucking, nibbling everywhere like a starving man who didn't know where to start his feast. Her fingers convulsed in his silky hair, pressed his face to her flesh in an ecstasy of torment, unable to bear the stimulation, unable to get enough. He took her breasts in hands that trembled, pressed them, cradled them, kneaded and nuzzled them as if they were the most amazing things he'd ever felt. Tears broke through her fugue of arousal. "Please, Aram…"

He closed his eyes as if in pain and buried his face in her breasts, inhaling her, opening his mouth over her taut flesh, testing and tasting, lavishing her with his teeth and tongue. *"Sehr, jonoon, ehsasek, reehtek, taamek…"*

Magic, madness, your feel, your scent, your taste…

Her mind unraveled with every squeeze, each rub and nip and probe, each with the exact force, the exact roughness to extract maximum pleasure from her every nerve ending. He layered sensation with each press and bite until she felt devoured, set aflame. Something inside her was charring.

Her undulations against him became feverish, her clamoring flesh seeking any part of him in mindless pursuit of relief. Her begging became a litany until he dragged an electric hand between her thighs, tormenting his way to her core. The heel of his thumb delved between her outer lips at the same moment the damp furnace of his mouth finally clamped over one of the nipples that screamed for his possession. Sensations slashed her nerves.

Supporting her collapsing weight with an arm around

her hips, he slid two fingers between her molten inner lips, stilling at her entrance. "I didn't think that I'd ever see you like this, open for me, on fire, hunger shaking you apart, that I would be able to pleasure you like this…."

He spread her legs, placed one after the other over his shoulders, opening her core for his pleasure and possession. Her moans now merged into an incessant sound of suffering.

He inhaled her again, rumbling like a lion maddened at the scent of his female in heat, as she was. Then he blew a gust of acute sensation over the knot where her nerves converged. She bucked, her plea choking. It became a shriek when he pumped a finger inside her in a slow, slow glide. Sunset turned to darkest night as she convulsed, pleasure slamming through her in desperate surges.

Her sight burst back to an image from a fantasy. Aram, fully clothed, kneeling between her legs…her, naked, splayed open over his shoulders, amidst an empty planet all their own.

And he'd made her climax with one touch.

Among the mass of aftershocks, she felt his finger, still inside her, pumping…beckoning. Her gasp tore through her lungs as his tongue joined in, licked from where his finger was buried inside her upward, circling her bud. Each glide and graze and pull and thrust sent hotter lances skewering through her as if she hadn't just had the most intense orgasm of her life. It was only when she sobbed, bucked, pressed her burning flesh to his mouth, opening herself fully to his double assault, that his lips locked on her core and really gave it to her, had her quaking and screaming with an even more violent release.

She tumbled from the explosive peak, drained, sated. Stupefied. What had just happened?

Her drugged eyes sought his, as if for answers.

Even in the receding sunset they glowed azure, heavy with hunger and satisfaction. "You better have really en-

joyed this, because I'm now addicted to your taste and pleasure."

Something tightened inside her until it became almost
painful. She was flabbergasted to recognize it as an even
fiercer arousal. Her satisfaction had lasted only a minute,
and now she was even hungrier. No. Something else she'd
never felt before. Empty. As if there was a gnawing void inside her that demanded to be filled. By him. Only ever him.

She confessed it all to him. "The pleasure you gave me
is nothing like I ever imagined. But I hope you're not thinking of indulging your addiction again. I want pleasure *with*
you."

All lightness drained from his eyes as he reached for
her again. He cupped her, then squeezed her mound pos-
sessively, desensitizing her, the ferocious conqueror flaring
back to life. "And you will have it. I'll ride you to ecstasy
until you can't beg for more."

Her senses swam with the force of anticipation, with the
searing delight of his sensual threat. Her heart went haywire
as he swept her up in his arms and headed inside.

In minutes, he entered a huge, tastefully furnished suite
with marble floors, Persian carpets and soaring ceilings.
At the thought that it must be Johara and Shaheen's master
suite, a flush engulfed her body.

A gigantic circular bed draped in chocolate satin spread
beneath a domed skylight that glowed with the last tendrils
of sunset. Oil lamps blazed everywhere, swathing everything in a golden cast of mystery and intimacy.

Sinking deeper into sensory overload, she tried to drag
him down on top of her as he set her on the bed. He sowed
kisses over her face and clinging arms as he withdrew, then
stood back looking down at her.

His breath shuddered out. "Do you realize how incredible you are?" Elation, embarrassment, but mainly disbelief
gurgled in her throat. "Do you want to *see* how incredible
I find you?"

That got her voice working. "Yes, *please.*"

She struggled up to her elbows as he started to strip, exposing each sculpted inch, showing her how incredible *he* was. Her eyes and mouth watered, her hands stung with the intensity of need to explore him, revel in him. He did have the body of a higher being. It was a miracle he wore clothes at all, didn't go through life flaunting his perfection and driving poor inferior mortals crazy with lust and envy.

Then he stepped out of his boxers, released the…proof of how incredible he found her, and a spike of craving and intimidation had her collapsing onto her back.

She'd felt he was big when he'd pressed against her what felt like a lifetime ago back on the terrace. But this… What if she couldn't accommodate him, couldn't please him?

But she had to give him everything, had to take all he had. Her heart would stop beating if he didn't make her his now. *Now.*

His muscles bunched with barely suppressed desire as he came down onto the bed, his hunger crashing over her in drowning waves. "No more waiting, *ya kanzi.* Now I take you. And you take me."

"Yes." She held out shaking arms as he surged over her, impacted her. She cried out, reveling in how her softness cushioned his hardness. Perfect. No, sublime.

He dragged her legs apart even as she opened them for him. He guided them around his waist, his eyes seeking hers, solicitous and tempestuous, his erection seeking her entrance. Finding it both hot and molten, he bathed himself in her flowing readiness in one teasing stroke from her bud to her opening.

On the next stroke, he growled his surrender, sank inside her, fierce and full.

The world detonated in a crimson flash and then disappeared.

In the darkness, she heard keening as if from the end of

a tunnel, and everything was shuddering. Then she went nerveless, collapsed beneath him in profound sensual shock.

She didn't know how long existence was condensed into the exquisite agony. Then the world surged back on her with a flood of sensations, none she'd ever felt before.

She found him turned to stone on top of her, face and body, eyes wild with worry. "It's your first time."

As she quivered inside and out, a laugh burst out, startling them both. "As if this is a surprise. Have you met me?"

The consternation gripping his face vanished and was replaced by sensuality and tenderness. "Oh, yes, I have. And oh, yes, it is—*you* are a surprise a second."

He started withdrawing from her depths.

The emptiness he left behind made her feel as if she'd implode. "No, don't go...don't stop...."

Throwing his head back, he squeezed his eyes. "I'm going nowhere. In consideration of your mint condition, I'm just trying to adjust from the fast and furious first time I had in mind to something that's slower and more leisurely...." He opened his eyes and gazed down at her. "I would only stop if you wanted me to."

Feeling the emptiness inside her threatening to engulf her, she thrust her hips upward, uncaring about the burning, even needing it. "I'd die if you stop."

His groan was as pained, as if she'd hurt him, too. "Stopping would probably finish me, as well. For real."

She thrust up again, crying out at the razing sensations as he stretched her beyond her limits. "You'd still stop... if I asked?"

A hand stabbed through her hair, dragged her down by its tether to the mattress, pinning her there for his ferocious proclamation. "I'd die if you asked."

Her heart gave a thunderclap inside her chest, shaking her like an earthquake. Tears she'd long repressed rose and poured from her very depths.

She surged up, clung to him, crushed herself against his

steel-fleshed body. "*Ya Ullah, ya* Aram, I'd die for you, too. Take me, leave no part of me, finish me. Don't hold back, hurt me until you make it better...."

"*Aih, ya kanzi,* I'll make it better. I'll make it so much better...." He cupped her hips in both hands, tilted them into a fully surrendering cradle for his then ever so slowly thrust himself to the hilt inside her.

It was beyond overwhelming, being occupied by him, being full of him. The reality of it, the sheer meaning and carnality of it, rocked her to the core. She collapsed, buried under the sensations.

He withdrew again, and she cried out at the unbearable loss, urged him to sink back into her. He resisted her writhing pleas, his shaft resting at her entrance before he plunged inside her again. She cried out a hot gust of passion, opening wider for him.

He kept her gaze prisoner as he watched her, gauging her reactions, adjusting his movements to her every gasp and moan and grimace, waiting for pleasure to submerge the pain. He kept her at a fever pitch, caressing her all over, suckling her breasts, draining her lips, raining wonder over her.

Then her body poured new readiness and pleasure over him, and he bent to drive his tongue inside her to his plunging rhythm, quickening both, until she felt a storm gathering inside her, felt she'd shatter if it broke.

His groan reverberated inside her mouth. "Perfection, *ya kanzi,* inside and out. Everything about you, with you."

Everything inside her tightened unbearably, her depths rippling around him, reaching for that elusive something that she felt she'd perish if she didn't have it, now, now.

She cried out, "Please, Aram, please, give it to me now, everything, *everything....*"

And he obliged her. Tilting her toward him, angling his thrusts, he drove into her with the exact force and speed she needed until he did it, shattered the coil of tension.

She heaved up beneath him so hard she raised them both in the air before crashing back to the bed. Convulsion after convulsion tore through her, clamped her around him. Her insides splintered on pleasure too sharp to register at first, then to bear, then to bear having it end.

Then she felt it, the moment his body caught the current of her desperation, a moment she'd replay in her memory forever. The sight and feel of him as he surrendered inside her to the ecstasy the searing sweetness of their union had brought him.

She peaked again as he threw his head back to roar his pleasure, feeding her convulsions with his own, pouring his release on her conflagration, jetting it inside her in hot surges until she felt completely and utterly filled.

Nothingness consumed her. For a moment, or an hour. Then she was surging back into her body, shaking, weeping, aftershocks demolishing what was left of her.

He *had* finished her, as she'd begged him to.

Then he was moving, and panic surged. She clung to him, unable to be apart from him now. He pressed soothing kisses to her swollen eyes, murmuring reassurance in that voice that strummed everything in her as he swept her around, took her over him, careful not to jar her, ensuring he remained inside her.

Then she was lying on top of him, the biggest part of her soul, satiated in ways she couldn't have imagined, at once reverberating with the enormity of the experience, and in perfect peace for the first time in her life.

She lay there merged with him, fused to him, awe overtaking her at everything that had happened.

Then her heart stopped thundering enough to let her breathe properly, to raise her head, to access her voice.

She heard herself asking, "What—what was...that?"

He stared up at her, his eyes just as dazed, his lips twitching into a smile. "I...have absolutely no idea. So *that* was sex, huh?"

"Hey…that's my line."

"Then you'll have to share it with me."

He withdrew from her depths carefully, making her realize that his erection hadn't subsided. His groan echoed her moan at the burn of separation. He soothed her, suckling her nipples until she wrapped herself around him again.

Unclasping her thighs from around him, he gave a distressed laugh. "You might think you're ready for another round of devastation, but trust me, you're not." He propped himself on his elbow, gathered her along his length, looking down at her with such sensual indulgence, her core flowed again. "It's merciful I had no idea it would be like this between us or I would have pounced on you long ago."

Feeling free and incredibly wanton, she rubbed her hands down his chest and twined her legs through his. "You should have."

He pressed into her, daunting arousal undiminished, body buzzing with vitality and dominance and lust. "I should make you pay for all these times you looked at me as if I was the brother you never had."

She arched, opening for his erection, needing him back inside her. "You should."

He chuckled, a dozen devils dancing in his incredible eyes. "Behave. You're too sore now. Give it an hour or two, then I'll…make you pay."

"Make me pay now. I loved the way you made me sore so much I almost died of pleasure. Make me sore again, Aram."

"And all this time I was afraid you were this sexless tomboy. Then after one kiss, that disguise you wear comes off and there's the most perfectly formed and uninhibited sex goddess beneath it all. You almost did kill me with pleasure, too."

"How about we flirt with mortal danger some more?"

"Sahrah."

Calling her *enchantress,* he crushed her in his arms and

thrust against her, sliding his erection up and down between the lips of her core, nudging her nub over and over.

The pleasure was unimaginable, built so quickly, a sweet, sharp burn in her blood, a tightening in her depths that now knew exactly how to unfurl and undo her. She opened herself wide for him, let him pleasure her this way.

Feeling the advance tremors of a magnificent orgasm strengthening, she undulated faster against him. Her pleas became shrieks as pleasure tore through her.

He pinned her beneath him as she thrashed, bucked, gliding over his hardness to the exact pressure and rhythm to drain her of the last spark of pleasure her body needed to discharge.

Then, kneeling between her splayed legs, he pumped his erection a few last times and roared as he climaxed over her.

She'd never seen anything as incredible, as fulfilling as watching him take his pleasure, rain it over the body he'd just owned and pleasured. The sight of his face in the grip of orgasm…

Then he was coming down half over her, mingling the beats of their booming hearts.

"Now I might have a heart attack thinking of all the times I was hard as steel around you and didn't realize this—" he made an explicit gesture at all of her spread beneath him, no doubt the very sight of abandon "—was in store for me if I just grabbed you and plunged inside you."

"Sorry for wasting your time being so oblivious."

His eyes were suddenly anxious, fervent. "You wasted nothing. I was just joking. I can never describe how grateful I am that we became friends first. I wouldn't change a second we had together, *ya kanzi*. Say you believe that."

She brought him down to her. "I believe *you*. Always. And I feel exactly the same. I wouldn't change a thing."

She didn't know anything more but that she was surrounded by passion and protection and sinking into a realm of absolute safety and contentment….

* * *

She woke up to the best sight on the planet.

A naked Aram standing at the window, gazing outside through a crack in the shutters. From the spear of light, she judged it must be almost sunset again. He'd woken her up twice through the night and day, showed her again and again that there was no limit to the pleasure they could share.

As if feeling her eyes on him, he turned at once, his smile the best dawn she'd ever witnessed.

She struggled to sit up in bed as he brought her a tray. Then he sat beside her, feeding her, cossetting her. The blatant intimacy in his eyes suddenly made her blush as everything they'd done together washed over her. She buried her flaming face in his chest.

He laughed out loud. "You're just unbearably cute being shy now after you blew my mind and every cell in my body with how responsive and uninhibited you are."

"It's a side effect of being transfigured, being a first timer," she mumbled against the velvet overlying steel of his skin and flesh.

"I was a first timer, too." She frowned up at him. "I *was* as untried as you in what passion—towering, consuming, earth-shattering passion—was like. So the experience was just as transformative for me as it was for you."

Joy overwhelmed her, had her burrowing deeper in his chest. "I'll take your word for it."

He chuckled, raised her face. "Now I want to take *your* word. That you won't do what your sisters did."

"What do you mean?"

"That you won't ask for a million contradictory details. That you won't do a thing to postpone our wedding."

Eleven

"What do you mean *wedding?*"

Aram's smile widened as Kanza sprang up, sitting like the cat she reminded him of, switching from bone-deep relaxation to full-on alertness in a heartbeat. Everything inside him knotted and hardened again as his gaze roved down that body that had taught him the meaning of "almost died of pleasure."

He reached an aching hand to cup that breast that filled it as if it was made to its measurement. "I mean our wedding."

"Our…" Her face scrunched as if with pain. "Stop it right this second, okay? Just…don't. *Don't,* Aram."

His heart contracted so hard it hurt. "Don't what?"

"Don't start with 'doing the right thing.'"

He frowned. "What the hell do you mean by that?"

She rose to her knees to scowl down at him. "I mean you think you've seduced a 'virgin,' had unprotected sex with her a handful of times and probably put a kid inside her by now. Having long been infected with Zohaydan conservatism, you think it's unquestionable that you have to marry me."

He rose to his knees, too, towering over her, needing to

overwhelm her and her faulty assumptions before this got any further. "If there is a kid in there, I'd want with every fiber of my being to be its father...."

"And that's no reason to get married."

He pressed on. "And to be the best friend, lover and husband of its mother for as long as I live...and if there's really a beyond, I'd do anything to have dibs on that, too."

The chagrined look in her eyes faltered. "Well, that only applies if there was actually a...kid. I assure you there is no possibility of one. It's the wrong time completely. So don't worry about that."

He reached for her, pressing her slim but luscious form to his length. "Does this look like a worried man to you?"

She leaned back over his arm, her eyes wary. "This looks like a...high man to me."

"I am. High on you, on the explosively passionate chain reaction we shared." He ground his erection harder into her belly, sensed her ready surrender. "And it's really bad news there isn't a possibility of a kid in there right now. I really, really want to put one in there. Or two. Or more."

Her eyes grew hooded. "What's the rush all of a sudden, about all that life-changing stuff?"

"I don't know." He bent to suckle her earlobe, nip it, before traveling down her neck and lower. "Maybe it's my biological clock. Turning forty does things to a man, y'know?"

She squirmed out of his arms, put a few inches' distance between them. "Since you'll live to a gorgeous, vital hundred, you're not even at the midpoint yet, so chill."

He slammed her back against him. "I don't *want* to chill. I've been chilling in a deep freeze all my life. Now that I've found out what burning in searing passion is like, I'll never want anything else but the scorching of your being. I love you, *ya kanzi,* I more than love you. I adore and worship you. *Ana aashagek.*"

She lurched so hard, she almost broke his hold.

"You—you do?"

He stared into her eyes, a skewer twisting in his gut at what filled them. God, that vulnerability!

Unable to bear that she'd feel that way, he caught her back, holding her in the persuasion of his hands and eyes. "How can you even doubt that I do?"

That precious blush that he'd seen only since last night blazed all over her body. "It's not you I doubt, I guess."

He squeezed her tighter, getting mad at her. "How can you doubt yourself? Are you nuts? Don't you know—"

"How incredible I am? No, not really. Not when it comes to you, anyway. I couldn't even dream that you could have emotions for me. That's why I kept it so strictly chummy. I didn't see how you'd look at me as a woman, thought that I must appear a 'sexless tomboy' to you."

"I was afraid *you* thought you were that. This wasn't how *I* saw you." He filled his hand with her round, firm buttock, pushed the evidence of how he saw her against her hot flesh.

As she undulated against him, her voice thickened. "I was never sexless where you were concerned."

"Don't go overboard now. You were totally so at the beginning. Probably till last night."

Her undulations became languorous, as if he was already inside her, thrusting her to a leisurely rhythm. "If you only knew the thoughts I had where you were concerned."

"And what kind of thoughts were those?"

She rubbed her breasts against him, her nipples grazing against his hair-roughened chest. "Feverishly licentious ones. At least I thought they were. You proved me very uncreative."

He crushed her against him to stop her movements. He had to or he'd be inside her again, and they wouldn't get this out of the way. "If you'd had thoughts of even wanting to hold my hand, you hid them well. Too well, damn it."

Her hands cupped his face, her eyes filling with such tenderness, such remembered pain. "I couldn't risk putting you on edge or having you pull back if you realized

I was just another woman who couldn't resist you. I was afraid it would mar our friendship, that I wouldn't be able to give you the companionship you needed if you started being careful around me. I couldn't bear it if you lost your spontaneity with me."

The fact that she'd held back for him, as he'd done for her, was just more proof of how right they were for one another. "When did you start feeling this way about me?"

"When I was around seventeen."

That flabbergasted him. "But you hated the sight of me!"

"I hated that in spite of all your magnificent qualities you seemed to be just another predictable male who'd go for the prettiest female, no matter that she had nothing more to recommend her. Then I hated that you also seemed so callous—you could be cruel to someone who was so out of your league. But mostly, I hated how you of all men made me feel, when I knew I couldn't even dream of you."

"I beg you, dream of me now," he groaned, burrowing his face into her neck. "Dream of a lifetime with me. Let yourself love me, *ya kanzi.*"

"I far more than love you, Aram. *Ana aashagak kaman.*"

To hear her say she felt the same, *eshg,* stronger than adoration, more selfless than love, hotter than passion, was everything. What he had been born for. For her.

Lowering her onto the bed, he gazed deep into her eyes as she wound herself around him. "I've been waiting for you since I was eighteen. And you had to go get born so much later, make me wait that much longer."

Tears streamed among unbridled smiles. "You can take all the waiting out on me."

Taking her lips, her breath, he pledged, "Oh, I will. How I will."

Floating back to her father's house, Kanza felt like a totally different woman from the one who'd left it over twenty-four hours ago.

She was so high on bliss that she let her family subject her to their drama with a smile. She might have spent three years living autonomously in New York, but once on Zohaydan soil, she must act the unmarried "girl," who could do whatever she wanted during "respectable hours" provided she spent the nights under her father's roof.

To shut them up, she told them of Aram's proposal.

Her news boggled everyone's mind. It seemed beyond their comprehension that she, the one undesirable family member they'd thought would die a spinster, hadn't gotten only one, but two incredible proposals in the space of two days. One from a prince, which she'd dared turn down on the spot, and the other from Aram, someone far bigger and better than any prince. It seemed totally unacceptable to her sisters and stepmothers that she'd marry the incomparable Aram of all men, when *they* had all settled for *far* lesser men.

At least Maysoon was absent, as usual, pursuing her latest escapades outside Zohayd and unconcerned with the rest of her family or their events. Kanza would at least be spared what would have been personal venom, with her history with Aram.

Feeling decidedly Cinderella-like, she thought it was poetic when her prince strolled in. Reading the situation accurately, Aram proceeded to give her family strokes. Showing them he couldn't keep his eyes or hands or even lips off her, he declared he wouldn't wait more than three days for their wedding. A wedding he'd finance from A to Z—unlike her sisters' grooms who divided costs—and that the nuptials would be held at the royal palace of Zohayd.

As her family reeled that Kanza would get a wedding that topped that of a member of the ruling family and in the royal palace, too—where most of them had rarely set foot—Aram took her father aside to discuss her *mahr*. As the dowry or "bride's price" was paid to the father, Aram let everyone hear that her father could name *any* number.

As his *shabkah* to Kanza, the bride's gift, he was writing his main business in her name.

Kanza let him deluge her in extravagant gestures and tumbled deeper in love with him. He was defending her against her family's insensitivity and honoring her in front of them and all of Zohayd by showing them there were no lengths he wouldn't go to for the privilege of her hand.

She'd later tell him that her *mahr* was his heart and her *shabkah* was his body.

But then, he already knew that.

Now that she was as rock-stable certain of his love as he was of hers, she was ready to marry him right there on the spot. Three days felt like such an eternity. Couldn't they just elope?

Kanza really wished they *had* eloped.

Preparing for the wedding, even though Aram had taken care of most of the arrangements, was nerve-racking.

At least now it would be over in a few hours.

If only it would start *already*. The hour until it did felt like forever. Not that anyone else seemed to think so. Everyone kept lamenting that they didn't have more time.

"It's a curse."

Maram, the queen of Zohayd, and Johara's sister-in-law, threw her hands in the air as she turned from sending two of her ladies-in-waiting for last-minute adjustments in Kanza's bridal procession's bouquets. The florist had sent white and yellow roses instead of the cream and pale gold Aram had ordered, which would go with all the gowns.

"No matter what—" Johara explained Maram's exclamation "—we end up preparing royal weddings in less and less time."

Kanza grinned at all the ladies present, still shell-shocked that all the women of the royal houses of Zohayd, Azmahar and even Judar were here to help prepare her wedding. "Take heart, everyone. This is only a *quasi*-royal wedding."

"It is a bona fide royal one around here, Kanza." That was Talia Aal Shalaan, Johara's other sister-in-law. "It's par for the course when you're a friend or relative to any of the royal family members. And you and Aram are both to so many of us. But this is an all-time crunch, and there is no earthshaking cause for the haste as there was in the other royal weddings we've rushed through preparing here."

"Aram can't wait." Johara giggled, winking to her mother, then to Kanza. "That *is* earthshaking."

Talia chuckled. "Another imperious man, huh? He'll fit right in with our men's Brotherhood of Bigheadedness."

Maram pretended severity. "Since this haste is only at his whim, this Aram of yours deserves to be punished."

"Oh, I'll punish him." Kanza chuckled, then blushed as Jacqueline Nazaryan, her future mother-in-law, blinked.

Man, she liked her a lot, but it would be a while until the poised swan of a French lady got used to Kanza's brashness.

Maram rolled her eyes. "And if he's anything like my Amjad, he'll love it. I applaud you for taming that one. I never saw Amjad bristle around another man as he does around Aram. A sign he's in a class of his own in being intractable."

"Oh, Aram is nothing of the sort...." Kanza caught herself and laughed. "*Now.* He told me how he locked horns with Amjad when he lived here, and I think it's because they *are* too alike."

Maram laughed. "Really? Someone who's actually similar to my Amjad? *That* I'd like to see. We might need to put him in a museum."

As the ladies joined in laughter, Carmen Aal Masood came in. Carmen was the event planner extraordinaire whose services Aram had enlisted in return for contributing an unnamed fortune to a few of her favorite charities, and the wife of the eldest Aal Masood brother, Farooq, who gave up the throne of Judar to marry her. The Aal Masoods were also Kanza's relatives from their Aal Ajmaan mother's side.

Yeah, it was all tangled up around here.

"So you ready to hop into your dress, Kanza?" Carmen said, carrying said dress in its wrapping.

Kanza sprang to her feet. "Am I! I can't wait to get this show on the road."

Lujayn, yet another of Johara's sisters-in-law, the wife of Shaheen's half brother Jalal, sighed. "At least you're eager for your wedding to start. Almost every lady here had a rocky start, and our weddings felt like the end of the world."

Farah, the wife of the second-eldest Judarian prince, Shehab Aal Masood, raised her hand. "I had my end of the world *before* the wedding. So I was among the minority who were deliriously happy during it."

"Kanza doesn't seem deliriously happy." Aliyah, King Kamal Aal Masood of Judar's wife—the queen who wore black at her own wedding then rocked the whole region when she challenged her groom to a sword duel on global live feed—gave Kanza a contemplative look. "You're treating it all with the nonchalance of one of the guests. Worse, with the impatience of one of the caterers who just wants it over with so she can get the hell home."

Kanza belted a laugh as she ran behind the screen. "I just want to marry the man. Don't care one bit how I do it."

Feeling the groans of her half sisters flaying her, she undressed and jumped into her gown. They were almost *haybeedo*—going to lay eggs—to have anything like her wedding. And for her to not only have it but to not care about having it must be the ultimate insult to injury to them.

Sighing, she came out from behind the screen.

Her sisters and stepmothers all gaped at her. Yeah, she'd gaped, too, when she'd seen herself in that dress yesterday at the one and only fitting. If you could call it a dress. It was on par with a miracle. Another Aram had made come true.

Before she could get another look at herself in the mirror, the ladies flocked around her, adjusting her hair and veil and embellishing her with pieces of the Pride of Zohayd treasure that King Amjad and Maram were lending her.

Then they pulled back, and it was her turn to gasp.

Who was that woman looking back at her?

The dress's sumptuous gradations of cream and gold made everything about her coloring more vivid, and the incredible amalgam of chiffon, lace and tulle wrapped around her as if it was sculpted on her. The sleeveless, corsetlike, deep décolleté top made her breasts look full and nipped her waist to tiny proportions. Below that, the flare of her hips looked lush in a skirt that hugged them in crisscrossing pleats before falling to the floor in relaxed sweeps. And all over it was embroidered with about every ornament known to humankind, from pearls to sequins to cutwork to gemstones. Instead of looking busy, the amazing subtleness of colors and the denseness and ingeniousness of designs made it a unique work of art. Even more than that. A masterpiece.

Aram had promised he'd tell her how he'd had it made in only two days, if she was very, very, *very* good to him.

She intended to be superlative.

Looking at herself now—with subtle makeup and her thick hair swept up in a chignon that emphasized its shine and volume, with the veil held in place by a crown from the legendary royal treasure, along with the rest of the priceless, one-of-a-kind jewels adorning her throat, ears, arms and fingers—she had to admit she looked stunning.

She wanted to look like that more from now on.

For Aram.

The new bouquets had just arrived when the music that had accompanied bridal processions in the region since time immemorial rocked the palace.

Kanza ran out of the suite with her royalty-studded procession rushing after her, until Johara had to call out for her to slow down or they'd all break their ankles running in their high heels.

Kanza looked back, giggling, and was again dumbfounded by the magnitude of beauty those women packed. They themselves looked like a bouquet of the most perfect flowers in their luscious pale gold dresses. Those royal men of theirs sure knew how to pick women. They had been blessed by brides who were gorgeous inside and out.

As soon as they were out in the gallery leading to the central hall, Kanza was again awed by the sheer opulence of this wonderland of artistry they called the royal palace of Zohayd. A majestic blend of Persian, Ottoman and Mughal influences, it had taken thousands of artisans and craftsmen over three decades to finish it in the mid-seventeenth century. It felt as if the accumulation of history resonated in its halls, and the ancient bloodlines that had resided and ruled in it coursed through its walls.

Then they arrived at the hall's soaring double doors, heavily worked in embossed bronze, gold and silver Zohaydan motifs. Four footmen in beige-and-gold outfits pulled the massive doors open by their ringlike knobs. Even over the music blaring at the back, she heard the buzz of conversation pouring out, that of the thousand guests who'd come to pay Aram respects as one of the world's premier movers and shakers.

Inside was the octagonal hall that served as the palace's hub, ensconced below a hundred-foot high and wide marble dome. She'd never seen anything like it. Its walls were covered with breathtaking geometric designs and calligraphy, its eight soaring arches defining the space at ground level, each crowned by a second arch midway up, with the upper arches forming balconies.

At least, that had been what it was when she'd seen it yesterday. Now it had turned into a scene right out of *Arabian Nights*.

Among the swirling sweetness of *oud,* musk and amber

fumes, from every arch hung rows of incense burners and flaming torches, against every wall breathtaking arrangements of cream and gold roses. Each pillar was wrapped in gold satin worked heavily in silver patterns, while gold dust covered the glossy earth-tone marble floor.

Then came the dozens of tables that were lavishly decorated and set up in echoes of the hall's embellishment and surrounded by hundreds of guests who looked like ornaments themselves, polished and glittering. Everyone came from the exclusive realm of the world's most rich and famous. They sparkled under the ambient light like fairy-tale dwellers in Midas's vault.

Then the place was plunged into darkness. And silence.

Her heart boomed more loudly than the boisterous percussive music that had suddenly ended. After moments of stunned silence, a wildfire of curious murmuring spread.

Yeah. Them and her both. This wasn't part of the planned proceedings. Come to think of it, not much had been. Aram had been supposed to wait at the door to escort her in. She hadn't given it another thought when she hadn't found him there because she'd thought he'd just gotten restless as her procession took forever to get there, and that he'd simply gone to wait for her at the *kooshah,* where the bride and groom presided over the celebrations, keeping the *ma'zoon*—the cleric who'd perform the marriage ritual—company.

So what was going on? What was he up to?

Knowing Aram and his crazy stunts, she expected anything.

Her breathing followed her heartbeat in disarray as she waited, unmoving, certain that there was no one behind her anymore. Her procession had rustled away. This meant they were in on this. So this surprise was for her.

God, she hated surprises.

Okay, not Aram's. She downright adored those, and had,

in fact, gotten addicted to them, living in constant anticipation of the next delightful surprise that invariably came.

But really, now wasn't the time to spring something on her. She just wanted to get this over with. And get her hands back on him. Three days without him after that intensive… initiation had her in a constant state of arousal and frustration. By the end of this torture session, she'd probably attack and devour him the moment she had him alone….

"Elli shoftoh, gabl ma tshoofak ainayah.

Omr daye'e. Yehsebooh ezzai alaiah?"

Her heart stopped. Stumbled. Then stopped again.

Aram. His voice. Coming from…everywhere. And he'd just said…said…

All that I've seen, before my eyes saw you.

A lifetime wasted. How can it even be counted life?

Her heart began ricocheting inside her chest. Aram. Saying exactly what she felt. Every moment before she was with him, she no longer counted as life.

But those verses… They sounded familiar….

Suddenly a spotlight burst in the darkness. It took moments until her vision adjusted and she saw…saw…

Aram, rising as if from the ground at the far end of the gigantic ballroom, among swirling mist. In cream and gold all over, looking like a shining knight from a fantasy.

As he really was.

Music suddenly rose, played by an orchestra that rose on a huge platform behind him, wearing complementary colors.

She recognized the overture. *Enta Omri,* or *You Are My Lifetime.* One of the most passionate and profound love songs in the region. That was why the verses had struck a chord.

Not that their meaning had held any before. Before Aram, they'd just been another exercise in romantic hyperbole. Now that he was in her heart, every word took on a new meaning, each striking right to her foundations.

He now repeated the verses but not by speaking them. Aram was *singing*. Singing to *her*.

Everything inside her expanded to absorb every nuance of this exquisite moment as it unfolded, to assimilate it into her being.

She already knew he sang well, though it was his voice itself that was unparalleled, not his singing ability. They'd sung together while cooking, driving, playing. He always sang snippets of songs that suited a situation. But nothing local.

While his choice and intention overwhelmed her with gratitude and happiness, the fact that he knew enough about local music to pick this song for those momentous moments stunned her all over again with yet another proof that Aram knew more about her homeland than she did. Not to mention loved it way more.

He was descending the steps from the platform where the orchestra remained. Then he was walking toward her across the huge dance floor on an endless gold carpet flanked by banks of cream rose petals. All the time he sang, his magnificent, soul-scorching voice filling the air, overflowing inside her.

"Ad aih men omri ablak rah, w'adda ya habibi.
Wala da'a el galb ablak farhah wahda.
Wala da'a fel donia ghair ta'am el gerah."
How much of my lifetime before you passed and was lost.
With a heart tasting not a single joy but only wounds.
She shook, tears welling inside her.
Yes, yes. Yes. Exactly. *Oh, Aram...*

He kept coming nearer, his approach a hurricane that uprooted any lingering despondencies and disappointments, blowing them away, never to be seen again.

And he told her, only her, everything in his heart.
"Ebtadait delwa'ti bas, ahheb omri.
Ebtadait delwa'ti akhaf, lal omr yegri."
Only now I started to love my lifetime.

Only now I started to fear its hasty passage.

Every word, everything about him, overwhelmed her. It was impossible, but he was even more beautiful now, from the raven hair that now brushed his shoulders, to the face that had never looked more noble, more potent, every slash carved deeper, every emotion blazing brighter, to the body that she knew from extensive hands-on…investigation was awe incarnate. To make things worse and infinitely better, his outfit showcased his splendor to a level that would have left her speechless, breathless, even without the overkill of his choice of song and his spellbinding performance.

The costume echoed her dress in colors, from the cream-and-gold embroidered cape that accentuated his shoulders and made him look as if he'd fly up, up and away at any moment to the billowing-sleeved gold shirt that was gathered by a cream satin sash into formfitting coordinating pants, which gathered into light beige matte-leather boots.

She was looking at those when he stopped before her, unable to meet his eyes anymore. Her heart had been racing itself to a standstill, needed respite before she gazed up at him and into the full force of his love up close.

His hands reached for her, burned on her bare arms. Quivers became shudders. She raised her eyes, focused on the mike in front of lips that were still invoking the spell.

His hands caressed her face, cupped it in their warmth and tenderness, imbuing her with the purity of his emotions, the power of their union. And he asked her:

"Ya hayat galbi, ya aghla men hayati.
Laih ma abelneesh hawaak ya habibi badri?"
Life of my heart, more precious than my life.
Why didn't your love find me earlier, my love?

Shudders became quakes that dismantled her and dislodged tears from her depths. She waited, heart flailing uncontrollably, for the last verse to complete the perfection.

"Enti omri, elli ebtada b'noorek sabaho."
You are my lifetime, which only dawned with your light.

Music continued in the closing chords, but she no longer heard anything as she hurled herself into his arms.

She rained feverish kisses all over his face, shaking and quaking and sobbing. "Aram…Aram…too much… too much…everything you are, everything with you, from you…" She burrowed into his containment and wept until she felt she'd disintegrate.

He hugged her as if he'd assimilate her, bending to kiss her all over her face, her lips, raggedly reciting the verses, again and again.

She thought a storm raged in the background. It wasn't until she expended her tears and sobs that she realized what it was. The thunder of applause and whistles and hoots among the lightning of camera flashes *and the video floodlights*.

Drained, recharged, she looked up at her indescribable soul mate, her smile blazing through the upheaval. "This should get record hits on YouTube."

It was amazing, watching his face switch from poignancy to elation to devilry.

Only she could do this to him. As he was the one who could make her truly live.

"Maybe this won't." He winked. "But *this* surely will."

Before she could ask what "this" was, he turned and gestured, and for the second time tonight he managed to stun her out of her wits.

Openmouthed, she watched as hundreds of dancers in ethnic Zohaydan costumes, men in flowing black-and-white robes and women with waist-length hair and in vibrant, intricately embroidered floor-length dresses, poured onto the huge dance floor from all sides, *including* descending by invisible harnesses from the balconies. Drummers with all Zohaydan percussive instruments joined in as they formed facing queues and launched into infectiously energetic local dances.

He caught her around the waist, took her from gravity's

dominion into his. "Remember the dance we learned at that bar in Barbados?" She nodded hard enough to give herself a concussion. He swung her once in the air before tugging her behind him to the dance floor. "Then let's dance, *ya kanzi*."

Though the dance was designed to a totally different rhythm, somehow dancing to this melody worked and, spectacularly, turned out to be even more exhilarating.

Soon all the royal couples were dancing behind them as they led the way, and before long, the whole guest roster had left the tables and were circled around the dance floor clapping or joining the collective dances.

As she danced with him and hugged him and kissed him and laughed until she cried, she wondered how only he could do this—change the way she felt about anything to its opposite. This night she'd wished would be over soon, she suddenly wished would never end.

But even when it did, life with Aram would only begin.

Twelve

Aram clasped Kanza from behind, unable to let her go for even a moment as she handed back the Pride of Zohayd jewelry to the royal guards at the door.

He had to keep touching her to make himself believe this was all real. That she was his wife now. That they were in their home.

Their home.

The fact that it was in Zohayd made it even more unbelievable.

He'd thought he'd lost Zohayd forever. But she'd given it back to him, as she'd given him everything else. Though she'd never loved Zohayd as he loved it, she'd consented to make it her home again.

After seeing her among her family, he now realized why Zohayd had never held fond memories for her. But he was determined to set things right and would put those people in their place. They'd never impact her in any way again.

Now he hoped he could make her see Zohayd as he saw it.

But at any sign of discomfort, they'd leave. He just wanted

her happy, wanted her to have everything. Starting with him and his whole life.

She closed the door then turned and wrapped herself around him. "I just can never predict you."

He tasted her lips, her appreciation. "I hope this keeps me interesting."

Her lips clung to his as she kneaded his buttocks playfully, sensuously. He still couldn't believe, couldn't get enough of how uninhibited she was with him sexually. It was as if the moment he'd touched her she'd let him in all the way, no barriers.

"Don't you dare get more interesting or I'll expire."

"You let me know the level of 'interesting' I can keep that's optimum for your health."

"You're perfect now. You'll always be perfect." She squeezed him tighter. "Thank you, *ya habibi.* For the gift of your song. And every other incredible thing you did and are."

His lips explored her face, loving her so much it was an exquisite pain. "I had to give you a wedding to remember."

"As long as it had you, it would have been the best memory, as everything you are a part of is. *And* it would have been the best possible earthly event. But that…that was divine." Her eyes adored him, devoured him. "Have I told you lately just how out of my mind in love with you I am?"

His heart thundered, unable to wait anymore. He needed union with her. Now.

His hands shook as he undid her dress, slid it off her shoulders. "Last time was ten minutes ago. Too long. Tell me again. *Show* me. You haven't shown me in *three* damn days."

She tore back at his clothes. "Thought you'd never ask."

He shoved off the dress that he'd had ten dressmakers work on day and night, telling himself he couldn't savor her beauty now. He had to lose himself in her, claim her heart, body and soul.

The beast inside him was writhing. This. This flesh. This spirit. This tempest of a woman. Her. It demanded her. And it wouldn't have her slow or gentle. Their lifelong pact had to be sealed in flesh, forged in the fires of urgency and ferociousness. And she wanted that, too. Her eyes were engulfing him whole, her breathing as erratic as his, her hands as rabid as she rid him of his shackles.

He pressed her to the door, crashed his lips down on hers. Her cry tore through him when their mouths collided. He could only grind his lips, his all, against hers, no finesse, no restraint. The need to ram into her, ride her, spill himself inside her, drove him. Incessant groans of profound suffering filled his head, his and hers. He was in agony. Her flesh buzzed its equal torment beneath his burning hands.

He raised her thighs around his hips, growled as her moist heat singed his erection. His fingers dug into her buttocks as he freed himself, pushed her panties out of the way, and her breasts heaved, her hardened nipples branding his raw flesh where she'd torn his shirt off.

Her swollen lips quivered in her taut-with-need face. "Aram...fill me..."

The next moment, he did. He drove up into her, incoherent, roaring, invading her, overstretching her scorching honey. Her scream pierced his soul as she consumed him back, wrung him, razed him.

He rested his forehead against hers, completely immersed in her depths, loved and taken and accepted whole, overwhelmed, transported. He listened to her delirium, watching her through hooded eyes as she arched her graceful back, giving him her all, taking his. Blind, out of his mind and in her power—in her love—he lifted her, filled his starving mouth and hands with her flesh, with the music of her hunger. He withdrew all the way then thrust back, fierce and full, riding her wild cry. It took no more than that. One thrust finished her. And him. Her satin screams echoed his roars as he jetted his essence inside her. Her convulsions spiked with the first splash of his seed against her womb. Her heart hammered under his, both spiraling out of control as the devastating pleasure went on and on and on and the paroxysm of release destroyed the world around them.

Then it was another life. Their new life together, and they were merged as one, rocking together, riding the aftershocks, sharing the descent.

Then, as she always did, she both surprised and delighted him. "That was one hell of an inauguration at the very entrance of our new home. Who needs breaking a bottle across the threshold when you can shatter your bride with pleasure?"

Squeezing her tighter, he looked down at her, his heart soaring at the total satisfaction in her eyes. "I am one for better alternatives."

"That was the *best*. You redefine mind-blowing with every performance. I'm not even sure my head is still in place."

Chuckling, proud and grateful that he could satisfy her that fully, he gathered his sated bride into his arms and strode through the still-foreign terrain of their new home.

Reaching their bedroom suite, he laid her down on the twelve-foot four-poster bed draped in bedcovers the color of her flesh and sheets the color of her hair. She nestled into him and went still, soaking in the fusion of their souls and flesh.

Thankfulness seeped out in a long sigh. "One of the incredible things about your size is that I can bundle you all up and contain you."

She burrowed her face into his chest. "Not fair. I want to contain you, too."

Tightening his arms around her, he pledged, "You have. You do."

* * *

"It is such a relief to be back home in Zohayd."

Kanza looked up from her laptop as Johara waddled toward her, just about to pop.

Johara and her family had returned to Zohayd since her wedding to Aram two months ago. Their stay in New York *had* only been on Aram's account. The moment he'd come to Zohayd, they'd run home.

She smiled at her friend and now new sister-in-law. "I would have never agreed before, but with Aram, Zohayd has become the home it never was to me."

Johara, looking exhausted just crossing their new base of operations, plopped down beside her on the couch. "We knew you'd end up together."

Kanza's smile widened. "Then you knew something I didn't. I had no idea, or even hope, for the longest time."

"Yeah." Johara nodded absently, leafing through the latest status report. "When the situation revolves around you, it's hard to have a clear enough head to see the potential. But Shaheen and I knew you'd be perfect for each other and gave you a little shove."

Her smile faltered. "You did? When was that?"

Johara raised her head, unfocused. Then she blinked. "Oh, the night I sent you to look for that file."

A suspicion mushroomed then solidified into conviction within the same heartbeat. "There was no file, was there?"

Johara gave her a sheepish look. "Nope. I just had to get you both in one place."

Unease stirred as the incident that had changed her life was rewritten. "You sent him to look for the nonexistent file, too, so he'd stumble on me. You set us up."

Johara waved dismissively. "Oh, I just had you meet."

The unease tightened. "Did Aram realize what you did?"

"I'm sure he did when he found you there on his same mission."

So why had he given her different reasons when she'd asked him point-blank what he'd been doing there?

But… "He could have just thought you asked me to do the same thing. He had no reason to think you were setting us up."

"Of course he did. Shaheen had suggested you to him only a couple of weeks before."

"*Suggested* me…how?"

"How do you think? As the most suitable bride for him, of course." Johara's grin became triumphant. "Acting on my suggestion, I might add. And it turns out I was even more right than I knew. You and Aram are beyond perfect."

So their meeting hadn't been a coincidence.

But… "Why should Aram have considered your suggestion? It isn't as if he was looking for a bride."

Johara looked at her as if she asked the strangest things. "Because we showed him what a perfect all-around package you are for him—being you…*and* being Zohaydan. We told him if you married, you'd have each other, he'd have Zohayd back, I'd have my brother back, my parents their son and Shaheen his best friend."

Kanza didn't know how she'd functioned after Johara's blithe revelations.

She didn't remember how she'd walked out of the office or how she'd arrived home. Home. Hers and Aram's. Up until two hours ago, she'd been secure, certain it was. Now…now…

"*Kanzi.*"

He was here. Usually she'd either run to greet him or she'd already be at the door waiting for him.

This time she remained frozen where she'd fallen on the bed, dreading his approach. For what if when he did, when she asked the inevitable questions, nothing would be the same again?

She felt him enter their bedroom, heard the rustle of his

clothes as he took them off. He always came home starving for her, made love to her before anything else, both always gasping for assuagement that first time. Then they settled to a leisurely evening of being best friends and patient, inventive and very, very demanding lovers.

At least, that was what she'd believed.

If everything hadn't started as she'd thought, if his motivations hadn't been as pure as she'd believed them to be, how accurate was her perception of what they shared now?

The bed dipped under his weight, rolling her over to him. He completed the motion, coming half over her as soon as her eyes met his. He'd taken off his jacket and shirt, and he now loomed over her, sculpted by virility gods and unbending discipline and stamina, so hungry and impatient. And her heart almost splintered with doubt and insecurity.

Was it even possible this god among men could truly want her to that extent?

His lips devoured her sob of despair as he rid her of her clothes, sought her flesh and pleasure triggers, cupped the breasts and core that were swollen and aching with the need for him that not even impending heartbreak could diminish.

"Kanza...*habibati...wahashteeni...kam wahashteeni.*"

Her heart convulsed at hearing the ragged emotion in his voice as he called her his love, told her how much he'd missed her. When it had only been hours since he'd left her side.

He slid her pants off her legs, and they fell apart for him. He rose to free his erection, and as she felt it slap against her belly, hot and thick and heavy, everything inside her fell apart, needing his invasion, his affirmation.

Holding her head down to the mattress by a trembling grip in her hair, feeding her his tongue, rumbling his torment inside her, he bathed himself in her body's begging for his, then plunged into her.

That familiar expansion of her tissues at his potency's advance was as always at first unbearable. Then he with-

drew and thrust back, giving her more of him, and it got
better, then again and again until it was unbearable to have
him withdraw, to have him stop. He didn't stop, breaching
her to her womb, over and over, until he was slamming
inside her with the exact force and speed and depth that
would...would...

Then she was shrieking, bucking beneath him with a
sledgehammer of an orgasm, the force of it wrenching her
around him for every spark of pleasure her body was capable of, wringing him of every drop of his seed and satisfaction.

Before he collapsed on top of her in the enervation of
satiation, he as usual twisted around to his back, taking her
sprawling on top of him.

Instead of slowing down, her heart hurtled faster until
it was rattling her whole frame. It seemed it transmitted to
Aram as he slid out of their merging, turned her carefully
to her back and rose above her, his face gripped with worry.

"God, what is it, Kanza? Your heart is beating so hard."

And it would stop if she didn't ask. It might shrivel up
if she did and got the answers she dreaded.

She had no choice. She had to know.

"Why didn't you tell me that Johara and Shaheen nomi-
nated me as a bride for you?"

Thirteen

Kanza's question fell on Aram like an ax.

His first instinct was to deny that he knew what she was talking about. The next second, he almost groaned.

Why had he panicked like that? How could he even consider lying? It was clear Johara or Shaheen or both had told her, but why, he'd never know. But though it wasn't his favorite topic or memory, his reluctance to mention it had resulted in this awkward moment. But that was all it was. He'd pay for his omission with some tongue-lashings, and then she'd laugh off his failure to provide full disclosure about this subject as he did everything else, and that would be that.

He caressed her between the perfect orbs of her breasts, worry still squeezing his own heart at the hammering that wasn't subsiding beneath his palm. "I should have told you."

He waited with bated breath, anticipating the dawning of devilry, the launch of a session of stripping sarcasm.

Nothing came but a vacant, "Yes. You should have."

When that remained all she said and that heart beneath his palm slowed down to a sluggish rhythm, he rushed to qualify his moronically deficient answer. "There was nothing to tell, really. Shaheen made the suggestion a couple of weeks before I met you. I told him to forget it, and that was that."

Another intractable moment of blankness passed before she said, "But Johara set us up that first night. And you must have realized she had. Why didn't you say something then? Or later? When you started telling me everything?"

All through the past months, unease about this omission had niggled at him. He'd started to tell her many times, only for some vague…dread to hold him back.

"I just feared it might upset you."

"Why should it have, if it was nothing? It's not that I think I'm entitled to know everything that ever happened in your life, but this concerned me. I had a right to know."

He felt his skull starting to tighten around his brain. "With the exception of this one thing, I *did* tell you everything in my life. And it was because this concerned you that I chose not to mention it. Their nomination, as well-meaning as it was, was just…unworthy of you."

"But you did act on that nomination. It was why you considered me."

His skull tightened another notch. "No. *No.* I didn't even consider Shaheen's proposition. Okay, I did, for about two minutes. But that was before I saw you that night. If I thought about it again afterward, it was to marvel at how wrong Shaheen was when he thought you'd agree to marry me based on my potential benefits. There's no reason to be upset over this, *ya kanzi.* Johara and Shaheen's matchmaking had nothing to do with us or the soul-deep friendship and love that grew between us."

"Would you have considered me to start with if not for *my* potential benefits?"

"You had none!"

"Ah, but I do. Johara listed them. Stemming from being me and being Zohaydan, as she put it."

"Why the hell would she tell you something like that?

Those pregnancy hormones have been scrambling her brain of late."

"She was celebrating the fact that it all came together so well for all of us, especially you."

"I don't care what she or anyone else thinks. I care about nothing but you. You *know* that, Kanza."

She suddenly let go of his gaze, slipped out of his hold. He watched her with a burgeoning sense of helplessness as she got off the bed, then put on her clothes slowly and unsteadily.

He rose, too, as if from ten rounds with a heavyweight champion, stuffing himself back into his pants, feeling as if he'd been hurled from the sublime heights of their explosively passionate interlude to the bottom of an abyss.

Suddenly she spoke, in that voice that was hers but no longer hers. Expressionless, empty. Dead. "I was unable to rationalize the way you sought me out in the beginning. It was why I was so terrified of letting you close. I needed a logical explanation, and logic said I was nowhere in your league—nothing that could suit or appeal to you."

"You're *everything* that—"

Her subdued voice drowned the desperation of his interjection. "But I was dying to let you get close, so I pounced on Johara's claims that you needed a best friend, then did everything to explain to myself how I qualified as that to you. But her new revelations make much more sense why you were with me, why you married me."

"I was with you because you're everything I could want. I married you because I love you and can't live without you."

"You do appear to love me now."

"*Appear?* Damn it, Kanza, how can you even say this?"

"I can because no matter how much you showed me you loved me, I always wondered *how* you do. *What* I have that the thousands of women who pursued you don't." He again tried to protest the total insanity of her words when lashing pain gripped her face, silencing him more effectively than a skewer in his gut. "When I couldn't find a reason why, I thought you were responding to the intensity of my emotions for you. I thought it was my desire that ignited yours. I did know you needed a home and I thought you found it in me. But your home has always been Zohayd. You just needed someone to help you go home and to have the family and set down the roots you yearned for your entire life."

Unable to bear one more word, he swooped down on her, crushed her to him, stormed her face with kisses, scolding her all the while. "Every word you just said is total madness, do you hear me? You are everything I never dreamed to find, everything I *despaired* I'd never find. I've loved you from that first moment you turned and smacked me upside the head with your sarcasm, then proceeded to reignite my will to exist, then taught me the meaning of being alive."

He cradled her face in his hands, made her look at him. "*B'Ellahi, ya hayati,* if I ever needed your unconditional belief, it's now. My life depends on it, *ya habibati.* I beg you. Tell me you believe me."

Her reddened eyes wavered, then squeezed in consent.

Relief was so brutal his vision dimmed. He tightened his grip on her, reiterating his love.

Then she was pushing away, and alarm crashed back.

Her lips quivered on a smile as she squirmed out of his arms. "I'm just going to the bathroom."

He clung to her. "I'm coming with you."

"It's not that kind of bathroom visit."

"Then call me as soon as it is. There's these new incense and bath salts that I want to try, and a new massage oil."

Her eyes gentled, though they didn't heat as always, as she took another step away. "I'll just take a quick shower."

"Then I'll join you in that. I'll…"

Suddenly the bell rang. And rang.

Since they'd sent the servants away for the night as usual, so they'd have the house and grounds all to themselves, there was no one to answer the door. A door no one ever came to, anyway. So who could this be?

Cursing under his breath as Kanza slipped away, he ran to the door, prepared to blast whoever it was off the face of the earth.

He wrenched the door open, and frustration evaporated in a blast of anxiety when he found Shaheen on his doorstep half carrying an ashen-faced Johara.

He rushed them inside. "God, come in."

Shaheen lowered Johara onto the couch, remained bent over her as Aram came down beside her, each massaging a hand.

"What's wrong? Is she going into labor?"

"No, she's just worried sick," Shaheen said, looking almost sick himself.

Johara clung feebly to the shirt he hadn't buttoned up. "I talked with Kanza earlier, and I think I put my foot in it when I told her how we proposed her to you."

"You *think?*"

At his exclamation, Shaheen glared at him, an urgent head toss saying he wanted a word away from Johara.

Gritting his teeth, he kissed Johara's hot cheek. "Don't worry, sweetheart. It was nothing serious," he lied. "She just skewered me for never mentioning it, and that was it. Now rest, please. Do you need me to get you anything?"

She shook her head, clung to him as he started to rise. "Is it really okay? She's okay?"

He nodded, caressed her head then moved away when she closed her eyes on a sigh of relief.

He joined Shaheen out of her earshot. "God, Shaheen, you shouldn't be letting her around people nowadays. She unwittingly had Kanza on the verge of a breakdown."

Shaheen squeezed his eyes. "*Ya Ullah...* I'm sorry, Aram. Her pregnancy is taking a harder toll on her this time, and I'm scared witless. Her pressure is all over the place and she loses focus so easily. She said she was celebrating how well everything has turned out for you two and only re-membered when she came home that Kanza didn't know how things started." He winced. "Then she kept working herself up, recalling how subdued Kanza became during the conversation, the amount of questions she'd asked her, and she became convinced she'd made a terrible mistake."

"She did. God, Shaheen, Kanza kept putting two and two together and getting fives and tens and hundreds. But right before you came she'd calmed down at last."

Hope surged in his friend's eyes. "Then everything is going to be fine?"

He thought her spiraling doubts had been arrested, but he was still rattled.

He just nodded to end this conversation. He needed to get back to Kanza, close that door where he'd gotten a glimpse of hell once and for all.

Shaheen's face relaxed. "Phew. What a close call, eh? Now that that's settled, please tell me when are you going to take my job off my hands? In the past five months since I offered you the minister of economy job, juggling it with everything else—" he tossed a worried gesture in Johara's direction "—has become untenable. I really need you on it right away."

"So this is why you *have* to become Zohaydan."

Kanza's muffled voice startled Aram so much he staggered around. He found her a dozen feet away at the entrance to their private quarters. Her look of pained real-ization felt like a bullet through his heart.

Her gaze left his, darting around restlessly as if chasing chilling deductions. "Not just to make Zohayd your home, but you need to be Zohaydan to take on such a vital posi-tion. But as only members of the ruling house have ever held it, you have to become royalty, through a royal wife."

"Kanza…"

"Kanza…"

Both he and Shaheen started to talk at once.

Her subdued voice droned on, silencing them both more effectively than if she'd shouted. "Since there are no high-ranking princesses available, you had to choose from lower-ranking ones. And in those, I was your only viable possibility. The spinster who never got a proposal, who'd have no expectations, make no demands and pose no challenge or danger. I was your only safe, convenient choice."

He pounced on her, trembling with anxiety and dismay, squeezed her shoulders, trying to jog her out of her surrender to macabre projections. "No, Kanza, hell, *no.* You were the most challenging, *in*convenient person I've ever had the incredible fortune to find."

She raised that blank gaze to his. "But you didn't find me, Aram. You were pushed in my direction. And as a businessman, you gauged me as your best option. Now I know what you meant when you said I 'work best.' For I do. I'm the best possible piece that worked to make everything fall into place without resistance or potential for trouble."

He could swear he could see his sanity deserting him in thick, black fumes. "How can you think, let alone say, *any* of this? After all we've shared?"

Ignoring him, she looked over at Shaheen. "Didn't you rationalize proposing me to him with everything I just said?"

He swung around to order Shaheen to shut up. Every time he or Johara opened their mouths they made things worse.

But Shaheen was already answering her. "What I said was along those lines, but not at all—"

"Why didn't you all just tell me?" Kanza's butchered cry not only silenced Shaheen but stopped Aram's heart. And that was before her agonized gaze turned on him. "I would have given you the marriage of convenience you needed if just for Johara and Shaheen's sake, for Zohayd's. I would have recognized that you'd make the best minister of economy possible, would have done what I could to make it happen without asking for anything more. But now…now that you made me hope for more, made me believe I had more—all of you—I can't go back…and I can't go on."

"*Kanza*."

His roar did nothing to slow her dash back to the bedroom. It only woke Johara up with a cry of alarm.

Reading the situation at a glance, Johara struggled up off the couch, gasping, "I'll talk to her."

Unable to hold back anymore, dread racking him, he shouted, "*No*. You've talked enough for a lifetime, Johara. I was getting through to her, and you came here to *help* me some more and spoiled everything."

Shaheen's hand gripped his arm tight, admonishing him for talking to his sister this way for any reason, and in her condition. "Aram, get hold of yourself—"

He turned on him. "I *begged* you never to interfere between me and Kanza. Now she might never listen to me, never believe me again. So *please*, just leave. Leave me to try to salvage what I can of my wife's heart and her faith in me. Let me try to save what I can of our marriage, and our very lives."

Forgetting them as he turned away, he rushed into the bedroom. He came to a jarring halt when he found Kanza standing by the bed where they'd lost themselves in each other's arms so recently, looking smaller than he'd ever seen her, sobs racking her, tears pouring in sheets down her suffering face.

He flew to her side, tried to snatch her into his arms. Her feeble resistance, the tears that fell on his hands, corroded through to his soul.

Shaking as hard as she was, he tried to hold the hands that warded him off, moist agony filling his own eyes. "Oh, God, don't, Kanza…don't push me away, I beg you."

She shook like a leaf in his arms, sobs fracturing her words. "With everything in me…I do…I *do* want you to have everything you deserve. I was the happiest person on earth when I thought that I was a big part of what you need...to thrive, to be happy...."

"You are *everything* I need."

She shook her head, pushed against him again. "But I'll always wonder...always doubt. Every second from now on, I'll look at you and remember every moment we had together and...see it all differently with what I know now. It will...abort my spontaneity, my fantasies...twist my every thought...poison my every breath. *And I can't live like this.*"

Even in prison, during those endless, hopeless nights when he'd thought he'd be maimed or murdered, he'd never known terror.

But now...seeing and hearing Kanza's faith, in him—in herself—bleed out, he knew it.

Dark, drowning, devastating.

And he groveled. "No, I beg you, Kanza. I beg you, please...don't say it. Don't say it...."

She went still in his arms as if she'd been shot.

That ultimate display of defeat sundered his heart.

Her next words sentenced him to death.

"The moment you get your Zohaydan citizenship and become minister, let me go, Aram."

Fourteen

It was as harsh a test of character and stamina as Kanza had always heard it was.

But being in the presence of Amjad Aal Shalaan in Kanza's current condition was an even greater ordeal than she'd imagined.

She'd come to ask him as her distant cousin, but mainly as the king of Zohayd, to expedite proclaiming Aram a Zohaydan subject and appointing him to the position of minister.

After the storm of misery had racked her this past week, inescapable questions had forced their way from the depths of despair.

Could she leave Aram knowing that no matter what he stood to gain from their marriage, he did love her? Could she punish him and herself with a life apart because his love wasn't identical to hers, because of the difference in their circumstances?

Almost everyone thought she had far more to gain from their marriage than he did, especially with news spreading of the minister's position. Her family had explicitly expressed their belief that marrying him would raise her to undreamed-of status and wealth.

But she expected him to believe she cared nothing about those enormous material gains, to know for certain that they were only circumstantial. She would have married him had he been destitute. She would continue to love him, come what may. So how could she not believe him when he said the same about his own projected gains? Could she impose a separation on both of them because her ego had been injured and her confidence shaken?

No. She couldn't.

Even if she'd never be as certain as she'd been before the revelations, she would heal and relegate her doubts to the background, where they meant nothing compared to truly paramount matters.

Once she had reached that conclusion, she'd approached a devastated Aram and tried everything to persuade him that he must go ahead with his plans, to persuade him that she'd overreacted and was taking everything she'd said back.

He'd insisted he'd *never* had plans, didn't want anything but her and would never lift a finger to even save his life if it meant losing her faith and security in the purity of his love.

So here she was, taking matters into her own hands.

She was getting him what he needed, what he was now forgoing to prove himself to her.

Not that she seemed to be doing a good job of championing his cause.

That cunning, convoluted Amjad had been keeping her talking for the past half hour. It seemed he didn't buy the story that she wished Aram to be Zohaydan as soon as possible for the job's sake…that Shaheen needed Aram to take over before Johara gave birth.

He probed her with those legendary eyes of his, confirmed her suspicion. "So, Kanza, what's your *real* rush? Why do you want your husband to become Zohaydan so immediately? He can assume Shaheen's responsibilities without any official move. I'd prefer it, to see if my younger brother wants to hand his closest friend the kingdom's fate as a consolation prize for the 'lost years,' or if he is really the best man for the job."

"He is that, without any doubt."

Those eyes that were as vividly emerald as Aram's were azure flashed their mockery. "And of course, that's not the biased opinion of a woman whose head-over-heels display during her wedding caused my eyes to roll so far back in my skull it took weeks to get them back into their original position?"

"No, *ya maolai*." It was a struggle to call him "my lord," when all she wanted to do was chew him out and make him stop tormenting her. "It's the very objective opinion of a professional in Aram's field. While there's no denying that you, Shaheen and your father have been able to achieve great things running the ministry, I believe with the unique combination of his passion for the job and for Zohayd, and with the magnitude of his specific abilities and experience, Aram would surpass your combined efforts tenfold."

Amjad's eyebrows shot up into the hair that rained across his forehead. "Now, *that's* a testimony. I might be needing your ability to sell unsellable goods quite soon."

"As reputedly the most effective king Zohayd has ever known, I hear you've achieved that by employing only the best people where they'd do the most good. I trust you wouldn't let your feelings for Aram, whatever they are, interfere with the decision to make use of him where he is best suited."

He spread his palm over his chest in mock suffering. "Ah, my feelings for Aram. Did he tell you how he broke my heart?"

You, too? she almost scoffed.

Not that Aram had broken hers. It was she who'd churned herself out with her insecurities.

But that big, bored regal feline would keep swatting her until she coughed up an answer he liked.

She tried a new one. "I'm pregnant."

And she was.

She'd found out two days after Johara's revelations. She hadn't told Aram.

"I want Aram to be Zohaydan before our baby comes."

Amjad raised one eyebrow. "Okay. Good reason. But again, what's the rush? Looking at you, I'd say you have around seven months to go. And you seem to want this done last week."

"I need Aram settled into his new job and his schedule sorted out with big chunks of time for me and the baby."

"Okay. Another good reason. Want to add a better one?"

"I haven't told Aram he's going to be a father yet. I wish him to be Zohaydan before I do to make the announcement even more memorable."

His bedeviling inched to the next level. "You have this all figured out, haven't you?"

"Nothing to figure out when you're telling the truth."

Those eyes said "liar." Out loud he said, "You're tenacious and wily, and you're probably making Aram walk a tightrope to keep in your favor...."

"Like Queen Maram does with you, you mean?"

He threw his head back on a guffaw. "I like you. But even more than that, you must be keeping that pretty, pretty full-of-himself Aram in line. I like *that*."

"Are we still talking about Aram, *ya maolai?*"

His cruelly handsome face blazed with challenge and enjoyment. "And she can keep calling me *ya maolai* with a straight face, right after she as much as said, 'I'd put you over my knee, you entitled brat, if I possibly could.'"

Even though he didn't seem offended in the least by the subtext of her ill-advised retort, the worry that she might end up spoiling Aram's chances was brakes enough.

"I thought no such thing, *ya maolai.*"

He hooted. "Such a fantastic liar. And that gets you extra

points. Now let's see if you can get a gold star. Tell me the real reason you're here, Kanza."

Nothing less would suffice for this mercilessly shrewd man who had taken one of the most internally unstable kingdoms in the region, brought it to heel and was now leading it to unprecedented prosperity.

So she gave him the truth. "Because I love Aram. So much it's a constant pain if I can't give him everything he needs. And he *needs* a home. He needs *Zohayd*. It's part of his soul. It *is* his home. But until it is that for real, he'll continue to feel homeless, as he's felt for far too long. I don't want him to feel like that one second longer."

Amjad narrowed his eyes. He was still waiting. He knew there was just a bit more to the truth, damn him.

And she threw it in. "I didn't want to expose his vulnerability to you of all people, to disadvantage him in this rivalry you seem to have going."

His lips twisted. "You don't consider this rivalry would be moot and he'd be in a subordinate position once he becomes a minister in my cabinet, in a kingdom where I'm king?"

"No. On a public, professional level, Aram would always hold his own. No one's superior office, which has nothing to do with skill or worth, would disadvantage him. But I was reluctant to hand you such intimately personal power over him. I do now only because I trust you won't abuse it."

It seemed as if he gave her a soul and psyche scan, making sure he'd mined them for every last secret he'd been after.

Seemingly satisfied that he had, Amjad flashed her a grin. "Good girl. That took real guts. Putting the man you love at my mercy. And helluva insight, too. Because I am now bound by that honor pact you just forced on me to never abuse my power over your beloved, I'm definitely going to be making use of this acumen and power of persuasion of yours soon. And as your gold star, you get your wish."

Her heart boomed with relief.

He went on. "Just promise you will not be too good to Aram. You'd be doing him a favor exercising some...*severe* love. Otherwise his head will keep mushrooming, when it's already so big it's in danger of breaking off his neck."

She rose, gave him a tiny bow. "I will consult with Queen Maram about the best methods of limiting the cranial expansion of pretty, pretty full-of-themselves paragons, *ya maolai.*"

His laugh boomed.

She could hear him still laughing until she got out of hearing range. The moment she was, all fight went out of her.

This had been harder than she'd thought it would be.

But she'd done it. She'd gotten Aram the last things he needed. Now to convince him that it wouldn't mean losing her.

For though she was no longer secure in the absoluteness of his need for her, and only her, she'd already decided that anything with him would always remain everything she needed.

Amjad did far better than she'd expected.

The morning after her audience with him, he sent her a royal decree. It proclaimed that in only six hours, a ceremony would be held at the royal palace to pronounce her husband Zohaydan. And to appoint him as the new minister of economy.

She flew to Aram's home office and found him just sitting on the couch, vision turned inward.

The sharp, ragged intake of breath as she came down on his lap told her he'd been so lost in his dark reverie he hadn't noticed her entrance. Then as she straddled him, the flare of vulnerability, of entreaty in his eyes, made eversimmering tears almost burst free again.

Ya Ullah, how she loved him. And she'd starved for him.

She hadn't touched him since that night, unable to add passion to the volatile mix. He hadn't tried to persuade her again. Not because he didn't want to. She knew he did. He'd gone instantly hard between her legs now, his arousal buffeting her in waves. He'd been letting her guide him into what she'd allow, what she'd withstand.

She'd show him that for as long as he wanted her, she was his forever. That he was her everything.

She held his beloved head in her hands, moans of anguish spilling from her lips as they pressed hot, desperate kisses to his eyes, needing to take away the hurt in them and transfer it into herself. He groaned with every press, long and suffering, and remorse for the pain she'd caused him during her surrender to insecurity came pouring out.

"I'm sorry, Aram. Believe me, please. I *didn't* mean what I said. It was my insecurities talking."

He threw his head back on the couch, his glorious hair fanning to frame his haggard face. "*I'm* sorry. And you had every right to react as you did."

She pressed her lips to his, stopping him from taking responsibility. She wanted this behind them. "No, I didn't. And you have nothing to be sorry about."

His whole face twisted. "I just am. So cripplingly sorry that you felt pain on my account, no matter how it happened."

She kissed him again and again. "Don't be. It's okay."

"No, it's not. I can't bear your uncertainty, *ya habibati.* I can't breathe, I can't *be*...if I don't have your belief and serenity. I'd die if I lost you."

"I'm never going anywhere. I was being stupid, okay? Now quit worrying. You have more important things to worry about than my insecurities."

"I worry about nothing but what you think and feel, *ya kanzi.* Nothing else is important. Nothing else even matters."

"Then you have nothing to worry about. Since only

you…only us, like *this*…matters to me, too." Her hands feverishly roved over him, undoing his shirt, his pants. She rained bites and suckles over his formidable shoulders and torso, releasing his daunting erection. A week of desolation without him, knowing that his seed had taken root inside her, made the ache for him uncontrollable, the hunger unstoppable.

But it was clear he wouldn't take, wouldn't urge. He'd sit there and let her do what she wanted to him, show him what she needed…take all she wanted. And she couldn't wait.

She shrugged off her jacket, swept her blouse over her head, snapped off her bra and bunched up her skirt. She rose to her knees to offer him her breasts, to scale his length. He devoured her like a starving man, reiterating her name, his love.

Her core flowed as she pushed aside her panties then sank down on him in one stroke. Her back arched at the shock of his invasion. Sensations shredded her. *Aram.* Claiming her back, taking her home. Her only home.

She rose and fell over him, their mouths mating to the same rhythm of their bodies. He forged deeper and deeper with every plunge, each a more intense bolt of stimulation. She'd wanted it to last, but her body was already hurtling toward completion, every inch of him igniting the chain reaction that would consume her.

As always, he felt her distress and instinctively took over, taking her in his large palms, lifting her, thrusting her on that homestretch to oblivion until the coil of need broke, lashing through her in desperate surges of excruciating pleasure.

"Aram, *habibi,* come with me…."

He let go at her command, splashing her walls with his essence. And she cried out her love, her adoration, again and again. *"Ahebbak, ya hayati, aashagak."*

Aram looked up at Kanza as she cried out and writhed the last of her pleasure all over him, wrung every drop of his from depths he'd never known existed before collapsing over him, shuddering and keening her satisfaction.

She'd taken her sentence back, had again expunged his record, giving him the blessing of continuing as if nothing had happened. She'd called him her love and life again. She'd made soul-scorching love to him.

So why wasn't he feeling secure that this storm was over?

She was stirring, her smile dawning as she let him know she wanted to lie down.

Maneuvering so she was lying comfortably on her side on the couch, he got her the jacket she reached for. She fished an envelope from its pocket. At its sight, his heart fisted.

He recognized the seal. The king of Zohayd's. He was certain what this was.

With a radiant smile, she foisted it on him. And sure enough, it was what he'd expected. She'd gone and gotten him everything that just a week ago she'd thought he'd married her to get.

And she'd made love to him before presenting it to him to reassure him that accepting this wouldn't jeopardize their relationship. She was giving him everything she believed he needed. Zohayd as his home. The job that would be the culmination of his life's work, putting him on par with the ruling family.

He again tried to correct her assumptions about his needs. "I need only you, *ya kanzi....*"

"How many times will I tell you I'm okay now? I just showed you how okay I was."

"But we still need to talk."

She kissed him one last time before sitting up. "And we will. As much as you'd like. After the ceremony, okay? Just forget about everything else now."

Could *she* forget it, or would she just live with it? When she'd said before that she couldn't?

He feared *that* might be the truth. That she was just giving in to her love, her need for him, but even more, his love and need for her. But in her heart, she'd never regain her total faith in him, her absolute security in his love.

"Let's get you ready," she said as she pulled him to his feet. "This is the most important day of your life."

"It certainly isn't. That day is every day with you."

She grinned and he saw his old Kanza. "Second most important, then. Still pretty important if you ask me. C'mon, Shaheen said he'd send you the job's 'trimmings.'"

He'd always known she was one in a million, that he'd beaten impossible odds finding her. But what she was doing now, the extent to which she loved him, showed him how impossibly blessed he was.

And he was going to be worthy of her miracle.

Aram glanced around the ceremony hall.

It looked sedate and official, totally different than it had during his and Kanza's fairy-tale wedding. The hundreds present today were also dressed according to the gravity of the situation. This was the first time in the past six hundred years that a foreigner had been introduced into the royal house and had taken on one of the kingdom's highest offices.

As Amjad walked into the hall with his four brothers behind him, Aram stole a look back at Kanza. His heart swelled as she met his eyes, expectant, emotional, proud.

What had he done so right he'd deserved to find her? An angel wouldn't deserve her.

But he would. He'd do everything and anything to be worthy of her love.

Amjad now stood before his throne, with his brothers flanking him on both sides. Shaheen was to his right. He met Aram's eyes, his brimming with pride, pleasure, excitement and more than a little relief.

Aram came to stand before the royal brothers, in front

of Amjad, who wasn't making any effort to appear solemn, meeting his eyes with his signature irreverence.

Giving back as good as he got, he repeated the citizenship oath. But as he kneeled to have Amjad touch his head with the king's sword while reciting the subject proclamation, Amjad gave him what appeared to be an accidental whack on the head—intentionally, he was certain.

Aram rose, murmuring to Amjad that it was about time they did something about their long-standing annoyance with each other. Amjad whimsically told him he wished he could oblige him. But he'd promised Kanza he'd share his lunch with him in the playground from now on.

Pondering that Kanza had smoothed his path even with Amjad, he accepted the citizenship breastpin.

Yawning theatrically, Amjad went through the ritual of proclaiming him the minister of economy, pretending to nod off with the boredom of its length. Then it was the minister's breastpin's turn to join the other on Aram's chest. This time, Amjad made sure he pricked him.

Everyone in the hall rose to their feet, letting loose a storm of applause and cheers. He turned to salute them, caught Kanza's smile and tearful eyes across the distance. Then he turned back to the king.

In utmost tranquility, holding Amjad's goading gaze, he unfastened the breastpins one by one, then, holding them out in the two feet between them, he let them drop to the ground.

The applause that had faltered as he'd taken the breastpins off came to an abrupt halt. The moment the pins clanged on the ground, the silence fractured on a storm of collective gasps.

Aram watched as Amjad shrewdly transferred his gaze from Kanza's shocked face back to his.

Then that wolf of a man drawled, "So did my baby brother not explain the ritual to you? Or are you taking off your sharp objects to tackle me to the ground here and now?"

"I'll tackle you in the boardroom, Amjad. And I know exactly what casting the symbols of citizenship and status to the ground means. That I renounce both, irrevocably."

Amjad suddenly slapped him on the shoulder, grinning widely. "What do you know? You're not a stick-in-the-mud like your best friend. If you're as interesting as this act of madness suggests you are, I might swipe you from him."

"Since you did this for me to please Kanza, you're not unsalvageable yourself, after all, Amjad. Maybe I'll squeeze you in, when I'm not busy belonging to Kanza."

"Since I'm also busy belonging to Maram, we'll probably work a reasonable schedule. Say, an hour a year?"

Suddenly liking the guy, he grinned at him. "You're on."

As he turned around, Shaheen was all over him, and Harres, Haidar and Jalal immediately followed suit, scolding, disbelieving, furious.

He just smiled, squeezed Shaheen's shoulder then walked back among the stunned spectators and came to kneel at Kanza's feet. Looking as if she'd turned to stone, she gaped down at him, eyes turbid and uncomprehending.

He took her hands, pulled her to his embrace. "The only privileges I'd ever seek are your love and trust and certainty. Would you bestow them on me again, whole, pure and absolute? I can't and won't live without them, *ya kanzi.*"

And she exploded into action, grabbing him and dragging him behind her among the now-milling crowd.

"Undo this!"

Amjad turned at her imperative order, smiling sardonically. "No can do. Seems this Aram of yours *is* too much like me, poor girl. He's as crazy as I am."

She stamped her foot in frustration. "You *can* undo this. You're the king."

Amjad tsked. "And undo *his* grand gesture? Don't think so."

"So you can undo it!" she exclaimed.

Amjad shook his head. "Sorry, little cousin. Too many pesky witnesses and tribal laws. Your man knew exactly what he was doing and that it cannot be undone. But let me tell you, it makes him worthy of you. That took guts, and also shows he knows exactly what works for him, what's worthy. *You.* So just enjoy your pretty, pretty full-of-himself guy's efforts to worship you."

She looked between him and Amjad in complete and utter shock. "But…what will Shaheen do when Johara gives birth? What about Zohayd…"

"The only world that would collapse without your Aram is yours. And I guess that's why he's doing this. To make it—" Amjad winked at her "—impregnable."

As she continued to argue and plead, Aram swept her up in his arms and strode out of the palace, taking her back home.

Her protests kept coming even after he'd taken her home and made love to her twice.

He rose on his elbow, gathered her to him. "I'll work the job as if I'd taken the position, so I won't leave Shaheen in the lurch. All that'll be missing is the title, which I care nothing about. I want the work itself, the achievement. But contrary to what Shaheen said, I don't need to be always in Zohayd or need to belong here. I already belong. With you, to you."

She wound herself around him, inundating him with her love, which, to his eternal relief, was once again unmarred by uncertainty and fiercer than ever before. "You didn't have to do it. I would have gotten over the last traces of insecurity in a few weeks tops."

"I wouldn't leave you suffering uncertainty for a few minutes. You are more than my home, *ya kanzi.* You're my haven. You contain me whole, you ward off my own demons and anything else the world could throw at me. I haven't lost a thing, and I have gained everything. I *have* everything. Because I have you."

She threw herself at him again before pulling back to look at him with shyness spreading over that face that was his whole world.

"And you're going to have more of me. Literally. And in seven months I'll give you a replica of you."

He keeled over her. As she shrieked in alarm, he laughed, loud and unfettered, then kissed her breathless, mingling their tears.

A baby. There was no end to her blessings.

After yet another storm of rapture passed, he said, "I want a replica of *you*."

"Sorry, buddy, it'll be your replica. In Zohayd they say the baby looks like the parent who is loved more. Uh-uh-uh..." She silenced him as he protested. "I've loved you longer, so you can't do a thing about it. So there."

"I trust this applies only to the first baby. The second one doesn't follow those rules. Second one, your replica."

"But I want them all disgustingly pretty like you!"

He pounced on her, and soon the laughter turned to passion, then to delirium, frenzy and finally pervasive peace.

And through it all, he gave thanks for this unparalleled treasure, this hurricane who'd uprooted him from his seclusion and tossed him into the haven of her unconditional love.

* * * * *

"Why did you really want me here this summer?

"There are hundreds of terrific nannies in New York. You could have had your pick."

"I like your company. I thought you'd enjoy spending a couple months at the beach."

Her scrutiny intensified. "No ulterior motives?"

"Such as?" he prompted, voice silky smooth, wondering if she was brave enough to voice the challenge in her eyes.

"We haven't even been here two hours and already you've kissed me." The exaggerated rise and fall of her chest betrayed her agitation. She was practically vibrating with tension. "Do you expect me to sleep with you?"

"I'm considering the possibility," he admitted.

THE NANNY TRAP

BY
CAT SCHIELD

MILLS & BOON

Published in Great Britain 2013
by Mills & Boon, an imprint of Harlequin (UK) Limited,
Eton House, 18-24 Paradise Road, Richmond, Surrey TW9 1SR

© Catherine Schield 2013

ISBN: 978 0 263 90485 7
ebook ISBN: 978 1 472 00635 6

51-0913

Harlequin (UK) policy is to use papers that are natural, renewable and recyclable products and made from wood grown in sustainable forests. The logging and manufacturing processes conform to the legal environmental regulations of the country of origin.

Printed and bound in Spain
by Blackprint CPI, Barcelona

Cat Schield has been reading and writing romance since high school. Although she graduated from college with a BA in business, her idea of a perfect career was writing books for Mills & Boon. And now, after winning the Romance Writers of America 2010 Golden Heart Award for series contemporary romance, that dream has come true. Cat lives in Minnesota with her daughter, Emily, and their Burmese cat. When she's not writing sexy, romantic stories for Mills & Boon® Desire™, she can be found sailing with friends on the St Croix River or in more exotic locales like the Caribbean and Europe. She loves to hear from readers. Find her at www.catschield. com. Follow her on Twitter, @catschield.

To my wonderful editor, Charles Griemsman.

One

Sleek black limos were a common sight parked in front of St. Vincent's, one of Manhattan's premier private schools, and Bella McAndrews barely gave this one a thought as she knelt down on the sun-warmed sidewalk to say goodbye to her students. It was the last day of school; a procession of twelve kindergartners hugged her and then ran to waiting vehicles. She bumped her chin against their navy wool blazers, emblazoned with the St. Vincent's crest, her chest tightening as each pair of arms squeezed her. The children were precious and unique and she'd enjoyed having every one in her class. By the time her final student approached, she could barely speak past the lump in her throat.

"This is for you." The boy's blue eyes were solemn as he handed her a pencil drawing. "So you won't forget me."

"As if I could do that." Bella blinked away hot tears and glanced down at the self-portrait. What she held was no ordinary drawing by a six-year-old. Justin had shown talent early and his parents had given him private art lessons. Bella couldn't help but wonder what her brothers and sisters could have accomplished if they'd been given all the opportunities afforded Justin by his wealthy parents.

"This is very nicely done, Justin."

"Thank you." A grin transformed his solemn expression. Before Bella could be glad that he was acting like a normal six-year-old for a change, he became a serious man-child once more. "I hope you have a nice summer," he finished in formal tones.

"You, too."

Pasting on a bright smile, she got to her feet. Inside, her mood reflected the gray sky above. She watched, her chest heavy, until he got into the back of a black Town Car. Most of her fellow teachers were as excited as their students as the end of the school year approached, but Bella wasn't fond of partings. If she'd had her way, she'd keep her kindergartners forever. But that wasn't how life worked. Her job was to guide their growth and prepare them for new challenges. As difficult as it was for her, she had to set them free. How else could they soar?

"Bella."

The sound of her name cut through the excited chatter of children being released from their educational imprisonment. She stiffened, recognizing Blake Ford's deep voice, even though she hadn't heard it since late last summer. A rush of joy rooted her to the spot. Twenty feet away the heavy wood doors of St. Vincent's offered her a place to hide. Common sense urged her to flee. He would be perceptive enough to figure out how miserable she'd been these past nine months and curious enough to wonder why.

Acting as if she hadn't heard Blake, she pivoted toward the school. But before she could escape, she felt Blake's long fingers on her left arm. Apprehension shivered along her nerve endings. The light hold prevented her flight and agitated her pulse. He'd had this effect on her from the start.

Bracing herself against an unwelcome stab of delight, she turned in his direction.

His wide shoulders, encased in gray wool, blocked her view of the street and the long limo parked at the curb. She gathered a deep breath to steady herself and gulped in a heavy dose of Blake. He smelled of soap—the fresh, clean scent of a mountain stream. No fussy cologne for Blake Ford.

Enigmatic. Intense. Brooding. Blake had fascinated and frightened her at their first meeting at the fertility clinic. But the intuitiveness she'd inherited from Grandma Izzy, for whom she was named, had told her to hear him out on that occasion.

She'd come to New York City to be a surrogate for a couple who'd decided to give in vitro a try, but before she could meet with them, the wife's best friend offered to carry their child.

Around the same time, Blake and Victoria had come to accept that a surrogate was the only move left for them. Thinking Bella would be a good fit with the power couple, the doctor at the clinic had arranged for Bella to meet Blake and his wife.

Over a cup of coffee, as Blake and Victoria had shared their deep sadness at their inability to conceive, Bella had decided Blake was more than just the successful, driven CEO of a large investment management firm. He was a man with a deep yearning for family.

"Blake, how nice to see you." Her voice held a breathless edge. She dug her fingernails into her palm and told herself to get a grip. "What brings you to St. Vincent's?"

His hand fell away. He had no need to keep a physical hold on her. His resolute gaze held her transfixed. "You."

"Me?" Her stomach somersaulted. "I don't understand."

They'd not parted on the best of terms. He hadn't understood why she wanted no future contact with his family and she had no intention of enlightening him, no matter how insistently he'd pressed her for an explanation. Where did she start?

Her unexpected and unwished-for reluctance to give up the child she'd carried for nine months? The fact that his wife had told her in no uncertain terms that she was never to contact them again? The way his simplest touch sparked something elemental and forbidden? The certainty that she'd betray her moral code if he gave her the slightest inkling that he wanted her?

"You didn't go back to Iowa like you said you were going to."

She saw an unyielding wall of accusations in his steel-blue eyes. He was annoyed. Not glad to see her. So why had he come?

"St. Vincent's asked me back for a second year." Guilt poked at her, but Bella ignored it. She didn't owe him anything more than the explanation she gave most everyone. The real reason she'd stayed in New York was because she felt connected to the child she'd carried. But the truth was too troubling and deeply personal to share. "They pay better than the public schools back home." During their previous association, she'd let him believe she was preoccupied with money. It had kept him from questioning her motivations. "And I've really grown to love New York."

"So your mother said." He slid his hand into the pocket of his exquisitely tailored suit coat.

"You called my parents?"

"How else did you think I found you?" He regarded her impassively. "She and I had quite a chat. You didn't tell them the truth about what brought you to New York, did you?"

Bella regarded him with exasperation. Should she have shared with her conservative-leaning parents that she'd lent out her womb to strangers for nine months so she could stop the bank from repossessing the farm that had been in her father's family for four generations? Not likely. It was better that they believe she'd taken a high-paying job in New York City and been able to secure a personal loan because of that. Her mother had been very upset with her for going into debt for them, but Bella assured her it was something she felt strongly about doing for her family.

"I didn't want them to worry."

"In the last nine months, I've discovered that worrying is what parents do."

When his attention shifted to the car behind him, she relaxed slightly, happy to have his focus off her. "I imagine you have."

She had worries of her own. Was the child she'd given birth to happy? Did he get to see enough of his busy parents? Were they playing peekaboo with him? Reading him a bedtime story? She hated the ache in her heart. It exposed how badly she'd deceived herself.

"I assume my parents were curious about who you were and why you'd called looking for me. What did you tell them?"

"That I was someone you used to work for."

Which, in a twisted way, wasn't far from the truth. "Just that?" She couldn't believe that her mother had given up her whereabouts to a stranger on the phone. Hadn't she been the tiniest bit suspicious? Of course, Blake had a reassuring way about him. After all, after spending thirty minutes with him, Bella had agreed to act as the surrogate mother to his child. "Or did you have to tell them more?"

"I said you'd taken care of my son and I wanted to see how you were doing."

"I'm doing just fine."

His gaze slid over her as if to reassure himself she was indeed well. "You certainly look great."

"Thanks." While Blake's once-over carried no sexual intent, it still sparked unwelcome heat to run through her veins.

It would be humiliating if he ever discovered how her body reacted to his nearness. "How are you?"

"Busy."

"As usual," she quipped, wringing a disgruntled frown from him. Funny how they'd fallen back into familiar patterns. For a second it was as if three-quarters of a year hadn't separated them. "Always the workaholic."

He shook his head. "Not anymore. You'll be happy to know that I'm home every night by five o'clock. My son is too important for me to neglect."

He spoke firmly, determined to emphasize that his priorities were different from his father's, a man Blake grew up barely knowing because he spent so much time at the office or out of town on business. In the days before Bella had gotten pregnant with Blake and Victoria's baby, she'd been concerned about Blake's long hours, but a serious conversation about his childhood had reassured her that his son would be a top priority in his life.

"I'm glad."

"I know." His granite features softened for the space of a heartbeat, reminding her how he'd looked the day the ultrasound announced he was going to have a son.

Joy caused her pulse to spike. The months apart from him hadn't dimmed her reaction to his every mood. She remained enthralled by his powerful personality and susceptible to the dimples that dented his cheeks in those rare moments when he smiled.

"I knew you'd make a good father." It was why she'd agreed to be the surrogate for his child.

"It's a lot more work than I expected." His eyes lost focus. "And a lot more rewarding."

"How's Andrew?" She'd been equal parts thrilled and dismayed that Blake and Victoria had used part of her surname to christen their son.

"We call him Drew," Blake explained. "He's smart. Curious. Happy."

"He sounds delightful." Her longing to snuggle him—which had dimmed to an ache these past few months—flared up again. Bella crossed her arms against the sudden pain in her chest.

"What are your plans for the summer?"

The abruptness of his question caught her off guard. "My roommate and I are helping her cousin with her catering business." It was something she'd done regularly since moving in with Deidre, except for those months when pregnancy had made it too uncomfortable for Bella to spend hours on her feet. "Why?"

"I need a nanny for Drew this summer. The girl who's been taking care of him fell and broke her leg in three places a week ago and I need someone who can fill in for the next two months until she's recovered."

"Surely there are agencies that can help you out."

"I'm disinclined to look for someone that way. It took me thirty candidates before I found Talia. We are leaving for the Hamptons on Saturday. I'd like you to join us."

Besieged by conflicting emotions, Bella offered a neutral response. "It's nice that you thought of me."

Only it wasn't nice. It was unbearable. Walking away from the child who'd grown beneath her heart had shredded the tender organ. She'd cherished him when he'd been a flutter of movement in her belly. How was she supposed to take care of him for two months and not fall madly in love with his happy smile, his delighted giggle, his sweet scent?

She'd thought being a surrogate would be easy for her. In junior high she'd decided being a mom wasn't for her. She didn't want to be like her mother and have her life revolve around her kids. She'd grown up taking care of her brothers and sisters. She wanted to be free of that sort of responsibility. Being pregnant with Drew had challenged all she thought she believed.

Bella shied away from emotions as dangerous to her soul as splintered glass was to her bare feet. "But I really don't think I can."

He narrowed his eyes at her refusal. "I'll pay you more than you'd make as a waitress."

"That's generous."

Blake believed that she'd only acted as Drew's surrogate because of the money. That was only partially true. As much as she'd needed the money, she'd really wanted to help him and Victoria grow their family. All through her pregnancy, her intention had been to stay in touch. Blake encouraged her to maintain contact with his son, but Victoria had her own ideas.

She'd pleaded with Bella, asking her to stay out of Drew's life so she and Blake could focus on being a family. It was Victoria's right. And no matter how much it hurt her, Bella wouldn't dream of interfering between husband and wife.

"Have you discussed this with Victoria?" His wife didn't want Bella in the same city as Drew, much less the same house.

"She and I divorced two months ago."

"Oh, Blake." The news rocked her. What had happened to Victoria's determination to make her marriage work? It didn't make sense that she'd given up so easily.

"Turns out Vicky didn't take to being a mother." His unhappiness hit her like a January wind and Bella shivered. "She got a supporting role in an off-Broadway play and threw herself into acting."

Regret flared. Victoria had cut Bella out of Drew's life and then left him without a mother. "Did you have any idea she felt this way?"

"No. It came as a complete surprise." Blake's mouth tightened.

To Bella, as well.

Victoria had thrown herself into preparing the nursery and often quoted from parenting books. But it was Blake who'd accompanied Bella to every doctor's appointment while his wife immersed herself in auditions for off-Broadway shows. Bella had been worried about his long hours at the office, even though he genuinely seemed excited to be a father. She'd obviously focused her anxiety on the wrong parent-to-be.

"I'm so sorry."

Impulsively she touched his arm. The contact zinged from her fingers to her heart in a nanosecond, leaving her wobbly with reaction. She pulled back, but too late to save her composure from harm.

If he noticed her awkwardness, he gave no sign. "Now you understand why I need someone I trust to take care of Drew this summer," he said. "I could use your help."

Demands or bribes she could've easily refused. But turning down this request for help was like asking Superman to lift a truck-sized boulder of kryptonite. The superhero couldn't do it. She was no stronger.

And she was handicapped by her memories of her previous visit to the Hamptons. Early-morning walks on the beach. Sipping tea on the wraparound porch. Blake had invited her to spend two weeks at his vacation property toward the end of her pregnancy. The downside had been loneliness and too much time to think, but on the weekends when Blake and Vicky came with friends and family, the enormous house had been filled with laughter and conversation.

"Are you sure you wouldn't be better off keeping him in the city with you?"

"I'm planning on working most of the week from the beach house. I need someone to keep an eye on Drew during the day while I'm occupied. You can have your evenings free."

"How can you be away from the office that much?" Remembering the long hours he'd put in the year before, she couldn't imagine that Drew would get to spend much time with his father.

A ghost of a smile appeared at her shock. "I told you I've changed."

A warm glow filled her as she gazed at him, acknowledging the truth in his eyes. This was the Blake who fascinated her. A man with strong convictions and simmering passions. Intelligent. Wry. Sexy.

Tormented by temptation, she shook her head. A whole summer at the beach? With the son she had no claim to? With the man she had no right to desire?

She was already too susceptible to Blake. What if Drew took up residence in her heart, as well? Forming a lasting attachment to the child she'd carried wasn't part of her plan. After raising her seven brothers and sisters, she'd had enough of being a parent. Freedom was her watchword these days, but being unable to shake her anxiety about Drew's welfare worried her.

"Thank you for the offer. It sounds like a wonderful opportunity, but I have to pass."

A protest gathered on Blake's lips, but before he could voice it, the limo's door opened and an unhappy wail rode the fragrant spring wind blowing straight at them. Blake's tension switched off as his focus shifted to his son.

"Sounds like Drew wants a chance to convince you."

And before Bella could offer an objection, Blake crossed to his driver. The man had fetched the infant out of his car seat and now handed him to Blake. Drew's discontented cries turned to crows of delight as his father lifted him above his head. Bella's mouth went dry at the endearing picture of a powerful businessman in a tailored suit stealing a moment out of his busy schedule to hang out with his adorable nine-month-old baby. The tender connection between father and son made her throat ache.

At last Blake settled the baby against his chest and returned to where Bella stood. "Drew, this is Bella. She's the one I told you about."

As if the child could understand.

But when Drew's blue-gray eyes, so like his father's, settled on her in unblinking steadiness, Bella wondered if she'd misjudged the child's comprehension. She stretched out her hand, hoping that Blake wouldn't notice the slight tremor. Drew latched on with a surprisingly fierce grip. A lump of unhappiness swelled in Bella's chest, making it hard for her to breathe.

"Nice to meet you, Drew," she murmured. And when the infant gave her a broad grin, she tumbled head over heels in love.

While Bella stared at the baby she'd never held, Blake fought to keep his anger from showing. Drew was at his most adorable, plying her with happy smiles, which offered Blake a chance to scrutinize the twenty-eight-year-old woman who'd been his son's surrogate.

Lovely. Like a tranquil lake deep in the forest, her beauty was of the peaceful sort. With her dark brown hair and smooth, pale skin, Bella possessed a Midwestern-girl-next-door look. When he and Vicky had first hired her to act as their surrogate, Blake had worried that a big, impersonal city like New York would chew up an Iowa farm girl like Bella and spit her out. But, raised on love and clear values, she had a steel backbone and a practical view of the world.

Her expression was unreadable as she shook Drew's hand. Didn't she feel anything at all? She'd carried Drew for nine months. Surely that would forge an unbreakable bond. So what had happened? Why, after assuring him that she would be delighted to be a part of their extended family after Drew was born, had she done an abrupt about-face and walked away without a backward glance? Had it all been lies? Had he been so blinded by joy at his impending fatherhood that he'd let her deceive him into believing she was a loving, nurturing person? It wouldn't be the first time a woman had fooled him into seeing her as something she wasn't.

In the days following Drew's birth, he'd fought to keep his disappointment in Bella's startling decision from overshadowing his delight at being a father. The whole time she was pregnant she'd talked as if she would like to stay in touch with Drew. Obviously she'd been lying. Bella had seen acting as a surrogate as a means to fast cash. She'd performed a service. Blake didn't begrudge the money he'd paid her. He and Vicky had been desperate to start a family, and Bella had been instrumental in making that happen. He'd just been so damn stunned that the woman he'd thought he knew had made such a swift and unexpected about-face.

His anger with her for turning her back on Drew was irrational, but it was rooted in childhood hurt. Bella's abrupt departure reminded him how he felt when he was eight and his own mother had abandoned him and his father to return to her old life in Paris. But at least with his mother, and even with Vicky, there had been warning signs that they lacked a maternal instinct. With Bella, he'd been convinced that she was a caring, nurturing woman.

"He's very handsome." She might have been commenting on the weather as she released Drew's hand and stepped back. "He has your eyes."

"And Victoria's iron will." Blake kept his attention fixed on Drew as he reflected on his ex-wife's determination to pursue her career instead of being a mother. No amount of reasoning had convinced Vicky that her place was with her son.

Drew leaned away from Blake's chest, reaching for the ground and babbling insistently. More than anything Drew wanted to be put down so he could explore the unfamiliar place and shove into his mouth whatever he crawled across. He was at that age where it was dangerous to take your eyes off him for a second. Hoping to distract him, Blake pulled out the plastic key ring he'd shoved into his pocket earlier.

Ever since Vicky had walked out on him and Drew, Blake had wondered if Bella would be upset that the child she'd agreed to carry hadn't ended up in a perfect two-parent home. Then again, it wasn't as if they'd sold her a bill of goods. He certainly hadn't suspected that his wife would decide that motherhood didn't suit her less than a month after her son was born.

"You think so?" Bella watched as Drew threw the keys to the ground and renewed his appeals to be put down. "I think determination is a trait he got from his father."

"You make it sound like a bad thing," Blake said. His surly mood wasn't dissipating. Usually the second he hoisted Drew into his arms, all his cares fell away. But seeing Bella had churned up resentment and mistrust. "It's how I keep profits climbing in double digit percentages for Wilcox Investments."

"Of course."

Her dry smile needled Blake. *Damn.* He'd missed her sunny nature and optimism. Her bright mind and Midwestern take on things. While his wife found his business dealings deadly dull, Bella had been happy to listen and quick with questions when she didn't understand something.

He'd thought of her as a younger sister. A friend.

Her abrupt departure from his son's life had been unexpected and unsettling. They'd often discussed what would happen after Drew was born. She'd been excited to stay in touch with Drew, to return to New York City to visit him.

He'd appreciated that she intended to be part of his son's extended family because the closer Bella got to delivering Drew, the more worried Blake had become about Victoria's desire to be a mother. About the time Bella was starting her third trimester, Vicky had gotten a part in an off-Broadway show and started spending less and less time at home, re-awakening the anxiety Blake recalled from the months preceding his mother's move to Paris.

He and Vicky had begun to argue over her priorities. After Drew was born it got worse. She wasn't acting like Drew's mother; rather, she was a stranger who rarely ventured into his nursery. She complained that Blake put too much pressure on her. That his expectations were too much for her to bear. Brief, heated discussions soon led to long, heavy silences. Their marriage was unraveling.

Was it any surprise that she'd ended up having an affair with the show's producer, Gregory Marshall?

Blake's cell phone rang. "Here." He handed Drew to Bella and fished it out of his pocket. While he spoke with his assistant, he watched for some hint of emotion in Bella's face.

She tensed as Drew leaned forward and put his palms on her mouth. They stared deep into each other's eyes while Blake looked on. He wasn't sure if Bella was even breathing. Was she finally feeling something? Getting her to connect with Drew was why he'd approached her about being Drew's nanny. Now that Vicky had walked away from their family, he was damned if he was going to let his son grow up not knowing the woman who'd given him life, too.

"I need to get back to the office," he told Bella, gesturing with the phone toward the limo. "If you wouldn't mind putting him in his car seat."

"Sure."

She headed for the car, moving with a graceful stride that snagged his attention. The pregnancy weight was gone. She was back to the slim, delicate creature she'd been when he'd first met her at the fertility clinic.

She smiled at the driver when he opened the door for her. The car seat was on the opposite side of the vehicle and she had to maneuver to buckle Drew in. She chose to keep one foot on the sidewalk while the top half of her was swallowed up by the limo.

Blake raked his fingers through his hair. She had no idea what a charming picture she presented, her rear end wiggling as she fastened Drew into his safety seat. Abruptly, amusement became something much more compelling. He sucked in a hard breath, besieged by the desire to wrap his fingers around her hips and press up against her delicious curves.

Where the hell had that come from?

"Blake? What do you want me to tell Don?" His assistant's question made Blake realize he had no idea what she was talking about.

"I have to call you back." He hung up on her as the heat surging through his veins showed no signs of abating.

The feeling was as unwelcome as it was unexpected. Not once had he felt the slightest hint of lust toward the young woman while she'd acted as Drew's surrogate. He'd been married, committed to his wife, and it wasn't in his nature to cheat either physically or mentally. Bella had been for all intents and purposes an employee. They'd been friends. Nothing more.

But his marriage vows no longer stood between them and the attraction was an unexpected complication. He strode toward the car, his nerve endings tingling as he drew within touching distance of Bella.

"He's all secure." She backed away from the car, her hands clasped before her. Did she sense the riotous impulses that had surged to life in him, or was she just eager to get away from him and his request?

"Thank you." He gripped the car door, anchoring himself against the compulsion to brush a strand of hair off her cheek. "Having you take care of him this summer will be good for both of us."

"I really don't think it's a good idea, Blake."

Although she had refused his offer, Blake heard less conviction in her voice this time and sensed that Drew had already charmed her into agreeing to join them in the Hamptons.

"It's a wonderful idea. Take the night and think it over." He blasted her with his most engaging smile. "Do you still have my number?"

Lightning flashed in her eyes. The color of much-washed denim. They'd transfixed him from the start.

"Yes," she retorted, her voice gruff.

"Good. If you don't call me by nine tomorrow morning, I'll be forced to track you down again."

"Fine. I'll think about it." It wasn't enthusiastic agreement, but it wasn't a firm refusal either.

"Wonderful."

Despite his need to get going or risk running late for a meeting, Blake's gaze lingered on Bella until she entered St. Vincent's. For the first time since Vicky had abandoned their marriage, he was ready to move his personal life forward. Seeing Bella again reminded him how satisfying his situation had been a year ago. He'd been happily married and anticipating the birth of his son. And then Vicky had left and he was back to feeling incomplete. These past few months he'd known what would make his world whole again. All he needed was the right mother for Drew.

Today, he'd found her.

Two

Still shaken by her encounter with Blake and Drew, Bella let herself into the apartment she shared with Deidre and set a bag of groceries on the kitchen counter. The small two-bedroom was on the Upper West Side of Manhattan, not far from Central Park. Although the unit rented for a little over two thousand a month, because Bella's room was barely big enough for her double bed, her share was only eight hundred. It was a nice deal for her.

The location was a quick walk across Central Park to the school where she and Deidre worked and the low cost enabled her to send money home to her parents and still retain enough for herself. To have some fun. To build a small nest egg. Whatever she wanted.

Financial security was a luxury she'd never known growing up, and the cash cushion she now enjoyed filled her with a sense of power and confidence.

"There you are." Deidre appeared in the doorway to her room, her bright blond curls a wild tangle. She wore workout clothes and her skin had a light sheen of perspiration. "I wondered what happened to you. I'm almost done with my weights routine if you want to head to the park for some cardio."

"A run sounds good." Before stopping at the market to pick up the ingredients for dinner, Bella had taken the long way through the park, hoping the walk would clear her head. The exercise hadn't been strenuous enough. She was no more decisive now than when Blake's limo had pulled away from the curb.

Growing up with a houseful of siblings, the only way she got any peace was to disappear into the cornfields and make her way to the dirt path that led from their farm to the county road. In the winter the snow drifted in the fields, making it harder to escape her seven brothers and sisters, so she usually just sneaked into the barn and hid in the haymow.

"You're awfully quiet," Deidre said, reaching into the refrigerator and pulling out a bottle of water. "Did one of your students go into hysterics because it was the last day of school today and they couldn't bear to be parted from you for a whole summer?"

"What?" Bella shook her head at Deidre's question. "No. Nothing like that."

"I'm surprised. You are everyone's favorite teacher, you know."

"That's sweet, but we had no repeat of last year's drama." Warmed by her roommate's praise, Bella smiled. "I made sure I prepared them better this year."

"So what's up?"

"Blake came by the school today." Although she hadn't told her roommate everything that had transpired regarding the surrogacy, Bella had appreciated Deidre's sensible take on her mixed feelings about giving up Drew.

"Blake?" Deidre's concern reflected in her expression and her voice. "How did that go?"

"A lot better than you would expect, given how angry he was with me last fall."

"What did he want?"

"He wants me to be Drew's nanny for the summer."

Deidre looked appalled. "His nanny? He has a lot of nerve."

Some of Bella's anxiety eased in the face of her friend's fierceness. It was nice to have someone to support her for a change instead of always being the one people leaned on. "He doesn't have any idea how hard it was for me to give up Drew."

The cozy apartment fell away as Bella got lost in the memory of holding Drew. Beneath his soft skin, he was strong like his father. As she'd buckled him into his car seat, she'd inhaled his wonderful baby scent, so like her siblings' when they were little, and yet all his own. It had whipped her emotions into a muddled stew.

As much as she loved helping to raise her brothers and sisters, she'd lost her childhood to changing diapers, calming temper tantrums, making lunches and helping with homework. Her mother couldn't have kept up on her own. Plus there was always something around the farm that demanded Stella McAndrews's attention.

Bella knew she was a lot like her mother. A nurturer. Taking care of people was almost a compulsion. But it had left her little time or energy for herself and in the middle of her sophomore year in high school, she recognized the burning in her gut as resentment. She felt trapped by her siblings' neediness and began questioning her parents' decision to have eight children.

Soon, the farm, the small nearby town where they attended school, even her friends—their dreams no bigger than the rural community they lived in—began to feel like a prison she had to escape.

But to do so, she needed to make plans and promises.

She would focus on doing well in high school so she could get into college. Majoring in education was a logical choice. She'd grown up teaching her siblings and felt a sense of accomplishment when they did well in school.

She loved college and with each step toward graduation her future looked brighter. Between her course load and work, her time was still not her own, but now she was calling the shots and making all the decisions. It was a heady feeling. One she wasn't ready to surrender to a boyfriend. So she didn't date much. If something looked like it was getting serious, she broke it off. She liked her freedom and wasn't willing to give it up.

"He's beautiful." Bella summoned the energy for a weak smile. "Perfect."

"Blake?" Deidre looked puzzled.

Bella shook her head. "Drew."

"You saw him, too?"

"I did more than that." Her throat seized. "I held him."

Deidre made a disgusted noise. "So what was Blake's reaction when you told him no about the nanny job?"

"What do you think?" Bella winced at Deidre's disapproving scowl.

"He badgered you to say yes."

"*Badgered* is a little strong. He just didn't take no for an answer."

"Are you sure you really told him no?"

"I did."

"No hesitations?"

"Of course not."

Bella and Deidre might have started as roommates a year and a half ago, but as the months passed, they'd become good friends. Bella liked living in New York City, but once in a while the distance between her and that crowded farmhouse in Iowa felt farther than a thousand miles. She appreciated having someone to come home to. To cook for and to share the couch with. A friend she could confide in over a bottle of wine. For all her longing to be free, Bella couldn't deny she hated being alone.

"Not even when you picture that gorgeous mansion on the beach?" Deidre persisted.

Bella sighed in appreciation. "You know me too well. Okay, I'll admit the thought of a summer in the Hamptons is very tempting."

Deidre dug Bella's running shoes from under the bed while she changed. "So what are you going to do?"

"I really should turn him down."

"You really should. But are you sure that's what you want to do?"

"I promised Lisa I'd help with her events this summer."

"And you always keep your promises."

Bella thought about her bargain with Blake's ex-wife. Accepting the job as Drew's nanny wouldn't technically be breaking her promise to Victoria because their divorce meant the reason Bella had agreed to stay away no longer existed. Her presence in their life couldn't be considered a distraction to the tight family Victoria had hoped to have with Blake and Drew.

But staying out of Victoria's way hadn't been the only reason she'd cut off all contact. Bella had begun feeling things that ran contrary to what she'd determined for her life, and the conflict had disturbed her.

"I'll call Blake as soon as we're back from our run and tell him I can't be Drew's nanny."

"Why not now?"

"Because I need to plan what to say or he might just talk me into it."

As the limo eased toward the curb in front of his stepsister's building, Blake gathered up the baby and his bright blue diaper bag. Slinging it over his shoulder, lips quirking

as he contemplated how becoming a parent had domesticated him, Blake strode into Jeanne's building, nodding at
the doorman as he passed.

"You're late," his stepsister announced when he stepped
off the elevator. She raised her arms in welcome as she advanced to take her nephew. Murmuring in soothing tones,
she plucked Drew out of Blake's arms and cuddled him.
"I've been worried."

"I had to make a slight detour." Blake smiled when Drew
latched onto Jeanne's chunky gold necklace and blinked
sleepily up at her.

"Well, you're here now and just in time to hear my wonderful news." Jeanne's gaze cut to her stepbrother. "We're
going to be neighbors this summer. Isn't that great? Now
you don't need to worry about a nanny for Drew. I can take
care of him until Talia gets back on her feet."

"You found a rental this close to summer?"

"Connie and Gideon are getting divorced and they can't
agree on who gets the beach house, so they're letting Peter
and me lease it. We'll be living two doors away. It'll be such
great fun. Of course, Peter will only come up on the weekends, but I'm planning on spending as much time as I can
at the beach. Isn't it wonderful?"

"Wonderful," Blake echoed, his voice flat. He hadn't yet
shared his summer plans with Jeanne because he was certain she wouldn't approve. "But you don't need to watch
Drew this summer. I found someone to fill in as his nanny."

"Oh." Jeanne looked disappointed. Two months ago she'd
found out she was having a baby and her maternal instincts
had kicked into high gear. "I was hoping to spend the summer with my nephew. I hope the woman comes from a rep-
utable agency."

"I didn't use an agency." Blake decided to deliver his news
without preamble. "I asked Bella."

"Oh, Blake, no."

He ignored Jeanne's dismay. "You knew that she's been working at St. Vincent's this past year, didn't you?"

Jeanne had been the one who'd gotten Bella a job at the prestigious school a year ago last fall. It was her husband's alma mater and the endowment they gave to the school each year gave them a certain pull when it came to asking favors.

"Yes," his stepsister admitted with an exaggerated sigh.

"Why didn't you tell me?"

"Wasn't it you who said she didn't want to have anything to do with Drew?" Jeanne hadn't liked Bella, but she'd never explained why. "Why would you want to bother with her?"

Because he hadn't been completely satisfied with Bella's explanation for why she wanted to sever all contact. Because for reasons he couldn't rationalize, something unfinished lay between them.

"I need a nanny for Drew for a couple months until Talia's broken leg heals." This was what had prompted him to start looking for Bella. But it turned out that wasn't his only reason for tracking her down.

Jeanne's brow creased. "Let me help you hire someone."

Why couldn't she understand that he didn't want just anyone? "I'm leaving for the Hamptons in two days. I don't have time to interview a bunch of candidates. I know Bella. I trust her with Drew."

"Do you think that's wise?"

"Not only did she help raise her brothers and sisters, but she's a kindergarten teacher. Who could be better?"

"I don't think this is a good plan, Blake." Jeanne carried the sleeping Drew to the portable playpen set up in her stylish living room and settled the baby, fussing with his blanket until she was satisfied. "Bella declined contact with Drew. No pictures or updates. Why do you think she'd want to take care of him for two months?"

Jeanne's skepticism echoed Blake's own concerns. "She'll

do it." The money he intended to offer would be hard for her to refuse.

"Pick someone else. Anyone else."

"Why?"

"That girl is trouble."

Jeanne's proclamation was so ridiculous, Blake laughed. "Bella? She's the furthest thing from trouble."

"Are you going to tell me you never noticed the way she looked at you?"

Blake's amusement dried up. "What are you talking about? She and I were friends. Nothing more."

"Maybe nothing more from your perspective, but I think she was more than half in love with you." Jeanne crossed her arms and frowned. "Not that I blame her. You are wealthy, handsome and charming."

"In that order?" Blake muttered, unsettled by the interest that had flared inside him. Was Bella attracted to him? Maybe that's what accounted for his unexpected awareness of her—he was merely responding to her subliminal signals. Body language. The chemistry of pheromones. Building blocks of sexual desire. Easy to disregard now that he knew the root cause.

"But the two of you together alone in the Hamptons will give her ample opportunity to get her hooks into you."

"That isn't going to happen."

"No?"

"First of all, I believe I have some say in who I get involved with." Blake arched his eyebrows when Jeanne opened her mouth to protest. "Secondly, Bella isn't interested in getting her hooks in me. You said it yourself. She declined any contact with Drew. She told me she doesn't want to be a mother. She did enough parenting with her siblings. So you don't need to worry that I'm going to do something as foolish as fall for her."

"That's good to hear. But hasn't it occurred to you that

Drew needs more than a series of nannies? He needs a mother. Someone who will love him with all her heart."

"I've been thinking along those lines myself."

First Bella had turned her back on Drew. Then Vicky. He could do nothing about the latter. His ex-wife had let him believe she wanted a family when what she really wanted was for their relationship to remain unchanged, but Bella's values were different. She'd come from a large family. And if he'd learned anything at all about her in the months before Drew was born, he'd seen that she had a nurturing nature. Even if she was determined to deny it.

With Vicky there'd been no such mothering instinct. His ex-wife had insisted on hiring a nanny before Drew was born. She maintained she didn't have the temperament to be a full-time mother. He should have listened to her. But he'd been too set on having his son grow up in the perfect family Blake had not had growing up.

Jeanne lit up. "I'm so glad to hear you say that."

"Glad why?"

"Victoria ended her relationship with Gregory." His step-sister's animated expression warned Blake she was in full interference mode.

He'd heard something to that effect. "I suspect that had something to do with the fact that her play closed after two weeks?" Blake made no effort to hide his cynicism.

"That's not it at all," Jeanne insisted. "She never stopped loving you."

"She loves her career more."

It had been a bitter blow when he'd discovered how she'd fooled him into believing having a family was her first priority when her true passion was show business.

"That's not true," Jeanne insisted.

While Blake admired Jeanne's loyalty to her best friend, he was in no mood to forgive his ex-wife. "I know you want to defend her, but you're wasting your breath trying to convince me to take her back. She put her career before her family."

"I know it's something she'd never do again."

Despite her conviction, his stepsister's argument failed to shift Blake's opinion of Vicky's desires. "She left me. She left Drew." And it was the latter that prevented him from trusting her ever again.

"She knows she made a mistake."

"A mistake?" Past and present betrayals tangled in Blake's chest. "She chose her career over our family. That's more than just a mistake."

"You are not an easy man to please, Blake," Jeanne said, her tone firm. A second later, she put her hand on his arm. "She was overwhelmed at suddenly becoming a mother and retreated into something that was comfortable and familiar to her. She knows she didn't make the best choice."

"But she made it." He set aside his past disappointments and turned his gaze once more to the future. "And I made mine." Seeing that they weren't ever going to agree, Blake bent down and kissed his stepsister's cheek. "Drew needs a mother."

"And Vicky is ready to be that."

Blake shook his head. "She's not, and I need to put Drew's needs first."

"What does that mean?"

"I got married the first time because I fell in love, and it left my son without a mother. This time I'm going to do it differently."

Three

When Bella finished tying her shoes, she and Deidre left the apartment. They used the three-block walk along Eighty-Ninth Street to warm up their muscles. Reaching the park, they quickly stretched before starting off on an easy jog north along the bridle path. The two-and-a-half-mile run would be relatively easy, but long enough for Bella to reach that place where her mind opened up.

While their shoes thumped rhythmically on the pavement, Bella pulled crisp, fragrant air into her lungs and glanced around her. Late spring had always been her favorite time of year on the farm. Dreary skies, cold and snow gave way to green pastures and new life. It was time to stop planning and take action. Possibilities seemed as boundless as the fields that surrounded her family's farm.

It was no different in New York. As soon as the first buds formed on the trees, she'd felt a kick of excitement, as if anything she wanted could be hers. She and Deidre had begun to make plans for the summer and tossed ideas around for a winter vacation. And now that school was out, she reveled in her freedom from responsibility. Her life was turning out exactly the way she wanted.

"Do you ever regret it?" Deidre asked as their run wound down.

"Regret what?"

"The whole surrogacy thing." Obviously Bella hadn't been the only one mulling over her situation during the twenty minutes they'd been running. "I know you say you don't want to get married and have kids, but being pregnant and giving up the baby, that's different."

"I knew what I was getting into." She was a farm girl— when she was six she'd learned a difficult but important lesson about the difference between pets and livestock. As much time and energy that she put into raising a prizewinning calf, there was always a chance that it would be sold. "I wouldn't have done it if I thought I would have a problem. Besides, Drew isn't my baby. He belongs to Blake."

"And Victoria," Deidre prompted.

Bella shook her head. "She left him. Left them."

"What?"

"That's why he needs a nanny this summer. Victoria decided she didn't want to be a mother." Of course, she wasn't Drew's biological mother, but only Victoria and Bella knew the truth about that.

"So what are you going to do?"

"I don't know."

"A little sea air might be exactly what you need."

"Maybe." She wasn't thinking about sea air; she was mulling over the weeks of sleepless nights when she'd be battered by temptation, knowing Blake would be dreaming peacefully in the master bedroom down the hall. Keeping her attraction hidden had been easy when he was married to Victoria. That was a line she'd never cross. But now that he was single, would she send out vibes without even knowing it?

How humiliating to be fired from a nanny job because she had the hots for her employer.

Uncomfortable with the direction her thoughts had taken her, Bella made sure to shift the conversation away from Blake and Drew during the walk back to the apartment. Deidre had called dibs on the first shower, so Bella headed to her bedroom to pack away the supplies she'd brought home from her classroom. By the time she finished, she was ready to call Blake and turn down his offer. Picking up the phone, she noticed she'd missed a call during her run. The message was a giddy explosion of good news from her sister Kate: she'd been accepted into a global health program in Kenya.

It was impossible for Bella not to smile at her sister's enthusiasm. Kate had set her sights on this program since she'd started college three years ago and had worked diligently toward the goal. She would graduate next year with a major in social work and intended to get her master's in public health. Bella couldn't be more proud.

Kate was well on her way to making a life for herself beyond the fetters of the farm and her siblings' constant drain on her energy and resources. It was the dream Bella had for all her siblings, but thus far only Kate and Jess were poised to achieve it.

The phone rang before Bella had a chance to dial Kate's number to congratulate her.

"Hiya, Bella." It was Jess. At eighteen, she was the most practical of Bella's three sisters.

"What's up?"

"I heard Kate leaving you a message and just thought you should know that she's probably not going to be able to afford the semester abroad."

Bella's good mood crashed and burned. "Why not? Last I heard she'd gotten the scholarship and had enough saved." Kate had been working so hard for the past three years to make this trip happen.

"There were some extra costs she hadn't accounted for and Mom and Dad weren't able to give her the money she was counting on."

"How did that happen?" The long pause that followed Bella's question told her everything she needed to know. "What broke down?"

"The tractor. It was in the middle of planting. Mom and Dad didn't have a choice."

"Of course not," Bella mumbled bitterly and felt a stab of guilt over her tone.

It didn't do any good to complain that the money to fix the tractor was supposed to be given to Kate to make her dream come true. Their parents sacrificed so much to keep the farm running and raise a family. Clothes wore out before they were replaced. Food was home cooked and simple. Entertainment consisted of the games they played in their living room or around the dining table.

"I know she'd never ask," Jess continued. "But is there any way you can help her out? I'm giving her five hundred." Money earmarked for her college tuition next year. "Mom's going to give Kate the six hundred in egg money she'd put aside for Sean's truck."

Jess's voice trailed off. Guilt wrenched at Bella. What a horrible sister she was to selfishly cling to her nest egg when Kate needed help. This particular program was only offered once a year. She had to go now, because next year she would begin her graduate studies and the window would be closed.

But Bella had already sent money home to help with Paul's community-college expenses and Jess's activities. She'd helped with the medical bills when Scott broke his leg last fall and contributed to Laney's orthodontic treatments. As hard as her parents worked, sometimes they were caught short financially and Bella's sense of responsibility kicked into overdrive. How could she not help out her family when she had the resources to do so? But every once in a while, she wished there wasn't always someone needing something.

"How much is she short?"

"About three thousand."

Bella's heart sank, but she kept her dismay out of her voice. "Let me see what I can do."

"You're the best," Jess crowed, her unselfishness making Bella feel worse and worse about her resentment. "Elephant shoes."

"Elephant shoes right back," Bella echoed, her family's endearment failing to give her mood the lift it usually did. Shoulders slumping beneath the weight of responsibility, Bella dropped the phone onto her bed.

"Oh, dear." Deidre spoke from the doorway. "Which one of them called this time?"

"Kate and Jess. Kate got into the Kenya program, but she doesn't have enough money to go."

"And she wants you to help her out."

"She would never ask."

"But Jess would."

Bella nodded. Why deny it? Deidre knew how much Bella helped out her family. "It's only three thousand."

"That's the money you were going to use for our trip to the Virgin Islands during Christmas vacation."

"How could I possibly go and enjoy it if I didn't help Kate?"

"I get that, but why do you always have to be the one who gives up what you want to do?"

"Because I'm the oldest." Bella sighed. "And because I can."

"Don't beat yourself up for wanting to say no. You are always there when someone needs you. It's okay not to be once in a while."

"I know. It's just…" Bella trailed off, already knowing she wasn't going to disappoint her sister.

Deidre rolled her eyes. "You're just too responsible for your own good."

"If I was really responsible, I'd be living closer to home so I could be there when Laney needed help with math or Ben wanted to practice his goaltending skills." Instead, she'd stayed in New York, because here she could go hours without feeling weighed down by the never-ending demands of her large family.

"You need to stop feeling guilty for enjoying living so far away from Iowa." Deidre pulled the towel from her hair and wrapped it around her neck. Her brown eyes drilled into Bella. "Stop beating yourself up just because you like the freedom you have here. Your parents decided to have eight kids. They're the ones who should worry about taking care of your brothers and sisters."

"Worrying about each other is what families do." But Bella recognized the disparity between what she said and how she felt. She was burdened in equal parts by guilt and resentment.

"But at some point you're going to have your own family to focus on. What happens to them then?"

Bella shook her head. They'd had this conversation multiple times, but Deidre never listened. "I might someday get married, but you know how I feel about having kids. I don't want any."

"Your family really did a number on you," Deidre said, her expression glum. "You had to grow up way too fast."

"It's not their fault." But there was no denying that the yoke of responsibility Bella had shouldered at a young age had led to her decision never to have kids of her own. Just the thought of being trapped the way her mother had been filled her with dread.

It was why she'd thought she could carry a baby for Victoria and Blake without fear of becoming emotionally involved. Too bad she hadn't understood that her fundamental nature hadn't been altered by her frustration with her family's neediness. If she had, she'd have known she'd fall in love with the child she'd given birth to. A child she had no legal claim on.

"You know," Bella began, her pragmatic side taking over, "if I nanny for Blake this summer, I could afford to help out my sister and have enough for our Caribbean trip."

It was a job that would pay well. She needed the money. With it she could go on vacation this winter and feel no guilt, plus she could replenish her nest egg and still help out her family.

"I think it's a huge mistake."

"Seems more like a win-win situation. I get money. Blake gets a nanny."

With her head cocked to one side, Deidre studied her friend. "You forget that I know how hard it was for you to say no to Blake about staying in touch with Drew. And I know why you did it. Now that Blake is divorced, the reason you agreed to stay out of Drew's life no longer exists."

Bella felt a flutter of excitement in the pit of her stomach. Deidre was right. Blake wasn't married to Victoria any longer, so Bella's promise to disappear and give the three of them a chance to become a family was no longer binding.

But her agreement with Victoria wasn't her only reason for staying away. Giving up Drew had been the hardest thing she'd ever done. Being on the fringe of his life would never allow her ache for him to dull.

"Plus," Deidre continued, her eyes narrowing, "there's that little crush you have on Blake."

"Crush?" Bella's voice wobbled when she tried to sound indignant. "I don't have a crush on Blake."

"I think you do. Imagine all those lovely moonlit nights in the Hamptons. Perfect for romantic walks on the beach. A midnight swim, just the two of you. Clothing optional."

Deidre's eyebrows wagged suggestively. "You'd fall hard for the guy before the first week was over."

"Midnight swims? Romantic walks?" Bella gave a disgusted snort. "Not likely. I'll be sacked out. Exhausted from taking care of Drew all day, and Blake will be attending parties. Now that he's single again, he'll be swamped with invitations." Bella could see she wasn't getting through to her friend. "Besides, there's never been any hint of attraction between us."

"Of course not. He was married."

"He was in love with his wife. For all I know, he still is. They haven't even been divorced two months. I'm sure he isn't ready to move on."

"Keep telling yourself that, and when Blake suggests a nightcap one night after you put Drew to bed, call me the next morning so I can say *I told you so.*"

To Bella's dismay, a delicious, forbidden anticipation began to build. Crossing her arms over her chest, she felt the rapid pace of her heart and tried to ignore her body's troubling reaction to Deidre's warning. It was ridiculous to imagine Blake being interested in her. Her own feelings were more difficult to dismiss.

"That won't happen."

"It might if you spend much time around him."

"Any time we spend together will be with Drew for company. Nothing is going to happen between us."

"A baby in the house isn't going to stop a man like Blake Ford from taking what he wants." Deidre raised her eyebrows suggestively.

"That's not Blake's style." As tempting as it was to ponder whether Deidre was onto something, Bella knew better than to indulge in daydreams. "Blake and Drew are a package deal and he knows I'm not interested in having a family. He'll find someone who wants the same things he does."

"I think you're kidding yourself if you believe you'll ever

be happy without children of your own and a man at your side to share the responsibility with you."

Bella shook her head. "I'm sure my mother thought the same thing when she married my dad. But what happens when the responsibility gets to be too much for the two of you to handle?"

"So marry someone wealthy. Then you'd have staff to take care of your every desire, not to mention your kids." Having delivered her final bit of wisdom, Deidre retreated down the hall, leaving Bella to ponder her roommate's advice.

Would she be as reluctant to have children if money wasn't an issue? Bella had no clear answer. On the day she'd turned fifteen and had to spend her birthday in the emergency room because her two youngest siblings had stuck M&M'S up their noses on her watch, she'd decided she never wanted the responsibility of motherhood. Her opinion didn't change through college or the next few years of teaching when she'd moved away from the farm, although she continued to lend her family what support she could by sending money home. But it was never enough.

The emotions stirred up by her pregnancy had called into question a decade of wanting nothing but her freedom. She'd been plagued by doubts. Questioned her choices. But after Drew's birth, she'd decided that she'd been a victim of pregnancy hormones. Her heart continued to hurt at the absence of Drew from her life, but she knew he was part of a loving family that had his best interests at heart.

Only today she'd discovered that he might have a father who loved him dearly, but the woman who was supposed to be his mother had turned her back on him. Disgust rose at Victoria's actions. If Bella had suspected how things would turn out, she never would have agreed to carry Drew for Blake and his wife.

So what was Bella's responsibility to the child now? With Victoria out of the picture, Bella could be a part of Drew's life. Was that what she wanted? To be half in his life, always there, but never truly belonging? Blake had wanted her in his son's life before. But how long would it last? What happened when he remarried? Surely his next wife wouldn't want her around any more than his last one had.

There were no easy answers.

"So you're going to do it." Deidre shook her head as she came back into the room.

"I have to." Bella wished her friend would understand.

"You're going to miss a fabulous summer here. A friend of my brother works the door at that new club everyone has been talking about. He said he can get us in whenever we want."

Disappointment stirred. The reason she'd stayed in New York City was so she could enjoy being young and not have to be responsible for anyone but herself. Last summer she'd been pregnant, so this year she'd been looking forward to dancing the night away at the clubs. Sleeping late. Reading in the park. Being Drew's nanny meant she wouldn't get to do any of that.

But she'd have a week in the Caribbean to look forward to. And she had to help her sister.

"That club sounds like it's going to be so much fun. I wish I could be here to enjoy it with you."

"Then tell Blake to forget it. You don't have to make everyone around you happy all the time."

"I know that."

"But you never put yourself first. Does your family even appreciate all the things you do for them?"

Bella's spine stiffened. "They aren't taking advantage of me." This wasn't the first time Deidre had criticized her for helping her family. Being an only child, she didn't understand why Bella couldn't ignore that her family needed her help. She might feel anxious about working for Blake this summer, but she was willing to do it for Katie. "Look, if I can help my sister and go to the British Virgin Islands later this year, it will be worth spending a couple months as Drew's nanny."

Deidre stepped forward, her expression contrite. "I'm sorry if I made you feel bad. You know what you're doing. Let's go out tonight. You can borrow my new Michelle Mason dress. We'll celebrate the end of the school year and three months of freedom."

"Thanks," Bella said, grateful to have what she'd always wanted.

Freedom to do whatever she wanted with her time. Freedom to live where she was most content. Freedom to spend money on a fabulous vacation without guilt.

So, with all that freedom to revel in, why did she feel as if something was missing?

In the quiet Upper East Side apartment, Blake thanked his doorman and hung up the phone, his spirits lightening. Once he put Drew to bed, his mood always dipped. In the days before his son's arrival, he'd discovered just how much he hated being alone. Most nights Vicky had been at the theater preparing for her off-Broadway debut. The part had been small, but she'd been thrilled. Blake had indulged her, knowing his wife needed a diversion. Waiting to become parents had been hard on both of them.

Or so he'd thought.

It was his nature to be focused and driven. Setting goals and achieving them had made him wildly successful in his business. He'd applied the same principles to his personal life: first finding the perfect woman to marry, and then starting a family with her.

He'd taken Vicky at her word when she told him she wanted children someday. Two months after their divorce was final, he wasn't sure if she'd really wanted to be a mother before being an actress came along and got in the way, or if she'd told him what he wanted to hear so that he'd marry her.

Either way, the results were the same. He and Drew were alone—the same way Blake and his father had been in the ten years following his mother's return to Paris—and Blake had no intention of letting his son grow up without a mother who loved him.

The doorbell chimed, startling Blake out of his reverie. He glanced at his watch as he headed for the front door. Ten-thirty was late for his sister to be out. But when he opened the door, he saw it wasn't Jeanne.

Rocking her weight from one black stiletto sandal to another, Bella looked like a kid caught midprank. But she wasn't a kid. Nor was she the guileless Iowa farm girl she'd been last summer. In the nine months since he'd last seen her, New York City had transformed her into a sophisticated woman who looked at ease in a one-shoulder black mini-dress that showed off miles of toned leg and bared slender arms adorned with eight inches' worth of jangling bracelets.

Her inability to meet his gaze gave him hope that the woman he'd befriended wasn't gone, only hiding beneath her expensive wardrobe. She'd done something with brown eye shadow to make her large, pale blue eyes dominate her face. Not even the bright red she'd applied to her lips could eclipse their haunting beauty. But the stark color did emphasize her mouth's downward cant. The urge to smear her perfect lipstick with hot, demanding kisses demonstrated that his reaction to her this afternoon hadn't been a fluke.

Damn this sudden attraction.

He didn't want to be distracted from his important mission by a fleeting, if forceful, craving to take her to bed. He had to keep the focus on Bella and Drew's relationship. She needed to become so attached to Drew that she couldn't imagine not being a part of his life. That would be jeopardized if Blake got physically involved with her.

He stepped back. The move wasn't an invitation for her to enter, but a retreat from the way she affected him.

"Come in," he offered, covering his lapse of control.

"I can't stay long. I'm meeting friends." She glanced around as she took three steps into the foyer and stopped.

Blake shut the door, trapping them together in the foyer's dimness. Intimacy crowded them as the silence lengthened.

A year ago they'd been friends. He'd thought her one of the kindest, warmest people he'd ever met. She was everything he imagined the perfect mother to be. Gentle, but resolute. A natural caretaker with a loving heart. Dedicated to her family.

His heartbeat quickened as images of her in the apartment rushed through his mind. The evening she came over for dinner to celebrate her agreeing to act as their surrogate. The afternoon she'd perched on the edge of a chair in the living room while they awaited the results of her pregnancy test. Her, cranky and uncomfortable the morning before she gave birth, four days past her due date and annoyed with him for being so positive despite the extended wait.

Thinking about that day made his heart clench. Twenty-four hours later, she'd exited his son's life without a backward glance. "What brings you by?"

"I came to tell you my decision."

"You could have called." He softened his tone to take the edge off the words. A hint of anxiety tightened his muscles. Having her company in the Hamptons this summer was instrumental to his plans. Unfortunately, at the moment he wasn't thinking as a father concerned about his motherless child, but as a man who knew how to appreciate a beautiful woman.

"I should have." She gnawed on her lower lip. "But something has come up and I was wondering if I could borrow three thousand against my salary before we leave New York."

Any elation he might have felt at her decision was tempered by her request. He'd hoped that meeting Drew would have made his offer irresistible, but here she was thinking only of the money. "I think that can be done."

He tightened his jaw against the urge to ask why she needed the money. He'd paid her thirty thousand dollars to act as Drew's surrogate. Had she gone through all that money already? If that was why she'd agreed to be his nanny for a couple months, getting her maternal instinct to kick in might be more of a challenge that it was worth.

"Thank you." She sounded very relieved.

He paused, considering her. "Don't you want to know how much I'm going to pay you?"

"I know you'll be fair."

"Ten thousand."

Her eyes widened. "Very fair."

"Never fear, you'll earn it."

As if to punctuate his statement, a wail came from his study, where Blake had left the baby monitor.

Her gaze reached beyond him, delving into the apartment. "Is Drew still up?"

"No. I put him down an hour ago."

That caught her attention. "You put him down?"

"I am his father."

"Of course you are."

"You didn't expect me to take care of my own son?"

"It's not that."

"Then what?"

A line appeared between her delicately arched eyebrows. "I guess I never pictured you doing anything so domestic."

"You don't think I'm domesticated?"

That made her lips soften and the edges curve up. "Not really."

He wasn't sure what to make of her smile or the way such a minute shifting of facial muscles made his gut twist. "I assure you, I'm quite tame."

"Then things have changed a lot since Drew was born."

"And it's those changes that brought us to where we are right now."

"You mean being a single dad."

"Partially." He noted her quicksilver frown and guessed he'd sparked her curiosity. Before she could question him further, he said, "I'm planning to head to the beach house on Saturday. Can you be ready?"

"Sure. All I need to pack are some shorts and tops."

"And a bathing suit. Drew loves the water."

"Since your current nanny is out of commission, do you want me to stop by tomorrow and help Mrs. Gordon pack for Drew?"

Blake wasn't surprised by her offer. He'd noticed that Bella often went that extra mile when it came to helping people out. "I'm sure she'd appreciate that."

"Tell her I'll be by around ten."

She was turning to go when Blake spoke. "Want to help me check on him?"

The impulsive request caught both of them by surprise.

Bella gestured over her shoulder. "If I'm late my friends will worry."

"I understand." But he didn't move from the foyer, despite his son's continued distress. "Text them. Tell them where you are."

His reluctance to let her go wasn't logical or sensible. Until he'd gone to her school today, he hadn't realized just how much he'd missed her company. The way her eyes danced with mischief. How easily she made him smile.

He'd spent the past nine months being angry with her; it had blocked out all the good memories. Now, thinking back on how well they'd gotten along and confronted with his startling sexual attraction, Blake was forced to face that his plan was not going to be as straightforward as he'd originally thought.

"They're waiting for me." She sidled toward the door, but her attention remained on the source of the unhappy sounds deeper in the apartment. "You'd better go see what's wrong."

And she was out the door before his emotional chaos sorted itself out. He headed to his son's room, contemplating the changes in Bella.

The city had hardened her. Her warmth was no longer as accessible as it once had been. Of course, their final conversation right after Drew's birth hadn't been in any way congenial. He'd been harsh, caught off guard by her insistence that she wanted no contact with Drew.

He still didn't fully believe her explanation. The decision had been such an about-face from everything he believed he knew about her. Well, he would have two uninterrupted months to get to the bottom of her abrupt turnaround.

And before those months were up, he expected to excavate all her secrets.

Four

Little about Blake's East Hampton home had changed since she'd been here last summer. Painted a soothing pearl gray, trimmed in white, it was expansive and elegant on the outside, with dormer windows that overlooked the sprawling front lawn and gardens. Now Bella stood in the middle of the elegant entry drinking in the vast open floor plan before her attention was drawn to the expensive white furniture.

Everything about the house inspired awe. Including the owner.

Blake stood before the two-story windows at the back of the house, staring toward the beach. Bella couldn't see past his broad shoulders, clad in a pale blue oxford button-down, to see the pool and glittering ocean beyond. Behind him, a large portrait of his ex-wife stared at him from above the fireplace.

Casting about, Bella noticed several other photos of the stunningly beautiful Victoria Ford, alone and smiling bliss-fully from the circle of Blake's arms. Given how dismissive he'd been of his ex-wife and her disregard for her son, she was surprised so many mementos had been permitted to remain.

"I'll have Mrs. Farnes remove those," Blake said, noticing what had captured her interest. "Damn," he muttered. "There's probably more in the master bedroom." Blake crossed the room with his long, hungry stride and plucked Drew from her arms, tossing the infant into the air. The boy's delighted cries drowned out the thump of Bella's heart as she watched father and son. "And while we're at it, we'll have Mrs. Farnes ship the pictures to Victoria in New York."

Tearing her gaze from Blake's relaxed face, Bella strode into the living room and took stock of all the potential trouble the nine-month-old boy could get into if she took her eyes off him for a second. "The house could use some baby proofing."

An unhappy wail followed her words. Bella glanced over her shoulder at the truculent child. Drew wanted to be put down. The forty-five-minute helicopter ride from the East Thirty-Fourth Street heliport hadn't been particularly restful for Bella, but Drew had taken full advantage of the rocking motion and napped. This meant he was full of energy and ready to go.

"Tell Mrs. Farnes what you need done," Blake said, giving in to Drew's demands to be put down.

The baby crawled to the couch and stood up. He required very little help to stay standing. She'd already observed how confidently he walked as long as he had something to hold on to. In no time at all, he'd be walking on his own. Then running. Bella sighed.

"Hello?" a female voice called from the entry. "Anybody home?"

While Blake headed to the front door to greet his stepsister, Drew began working his way along the couch. Bella wished Blake had mentioned that Jeanne would be staying with them this weekend. She would have appreciated the opportunity to prepare herself for the other woman's chilly dislike.

Bella raced forward and caught Drew's hand before it snagged a heavy crystal bowl on the end table.

"Where's my darling nephew?" Jeanne called, sweeping into the living room with great style. She wore a melon-hued linen dress that drew attention to her perfect complexion and played up the reddish highlights in her dark brown hair. A diamond tennis bracelet glittered at her wrist as she descended on her nephew, hands outstretched.

Bella backed away from Drew as his aunt reached him. Jeanne had a knack for making Bella feel like an employee—necessary when the socialite needed something, forgotten otherwise.

"You are going to love it in the Hamptons," she crooned to Drew, snuggling him close despite his incoherent protests. "We are going to have so much fun this summer."

Dismayed to hear that Jeanne would be around so much, Bella glanced in Blake's direction and discovered he was directing the man who'd picked them up at the East Hampton airport on where to put their luggage. The caretaker—Blake had introduced him as Woody—had already brought in several bags belonging to Drew and Blake and had fetched her single suitcase. Alarm stirred as he headed upstairs with it.

"Wait," Bella called after him. "That's mine. It belongs in the pool house."

Blake stopped her. "You'll be staying in the house. I thought it best if you slept across the hall from Drew."

She'd expected Blake would assign her the same accommodations as last summer and was distressed by the idea that she would be sleeping a short distance from him. "Why?" she blurted out.

"He's been waking up in the middle of the night lately. I've been having a hard time getting him back to sleep. I thought you'd have better luck."

"Oh, sure," she said, failing to keep the dismay out of her voice.

"Problem?"

She couldn't help but feel as if the walls were closing in on her. This was how it began with her family, too. She'd agree to a simple request to adjust a hemline and the next thing she knew she was sewing a brand-new dress.

"You did mention that I could have my evenings off."

"Is it your plan to be out all night?" Blake glowered at her.

She steeled herself against a sudden thrill, reminding herself that his concern about her going out—and staying out—was because he expected her to be at Drew's beck and call. Not because he wanted her company himself.

"Of course not." She'd much rather spend her nights with Blake and Drew, but he couldn't know that. He'd start wondering why. "It's just that I was hoping to have a little fun this summer and I really enjoyed the pool house." She'd appreciated the privacy. If not the solitude.

"And I'd like you to be close by."

"Blake, let the girl stay in the pool house if that's what she wants," Jeanne broke in, her exasperation plain. "I really don't see why she's here at all. I'm perfectly capable of watching Drew this summer."

Jeanne's negative attitude toward her had never been this overt and Bella wondered what she'd done to turn the woman against her.

Blake's stepsister gave up the battle with the squirmy Drew and set him down on the foyer's cool marble. Immediately he began crawling toward the open door. Bella chased after him, deciding it would be easier to wear out the adventurous infant than to try to contain him. Glad to escape the stare-down between siblings, Bella scooped up Drew and marched him outside.

"You will be far too busy lunching with friends and shopping to be a full-time babysitter," Blake countered, his voice calm but steely. "Bella will give him her full attention."

To keep him out of trouble, she'd have to. Bella steered Drew away from roses that flanked the sidewalk and aimed for the large expanse of smooth, green lawn. As soon as she'd gauged Drew was a safe distance from the flowerbeds that enclosed the mansion in graceful, bright waves, she plopped onto the grass with a heavy sigh and began tickling Drew's round belly.

His hearty giggles made her smile. She lost herself in his darling grin and ran her fingers through his soft hair. Sighing, she snuggled him close and imprinted his scent in her memories. He endured it all with good humor and took his own turn investigating her nose and mouth with his chubby fingers.

The late-afternoon sunlight cast long shadows across the lawn and Bella knew she couldn't hide out here with Drew much longer. The wind coming off the ocean was growing cooler by the minute. She was psyching herself up to return to the house when she heard the slam of a car door and an engine starting.

Glancing over her shoulder, she spied Jeanne's silver Lexus heading away from the house and Blake striding across the lawn toward them. Her pulse jerked erratically at his somber expression and she wondered if he was going to send her back to the city.

"Where's Jeanne going?" she asked, startled when he sat beside her.

Hoisting Drew onto his lap, Blake stared after his sister. "She's heading home."

"Back to New York?" It distressed Bella to think she'd come between the siblings.

"She and Peter have a rental just down the beach."

"Then she's not staying here?" She couldn't stop relief from overwhelming her voice.

"No." Blake's eyebrow lifted. "I take it you're glad."

Bella plucked at the lawn. "Your sister doesn't like me."

"It's not that she doesn't like you," he explained, weariness twisting his mouth into an unhappy line.

"You could have fooled me."

"She doesn't want us spending the summer together." Blake was watching Drew crawl toward a butterfly that had flitted across his path and spoke almost absently.

"Why not?"

"She thinks you have feelings for me."

Bella couldn't have been more shocked. "What?" she sputtered, sounding anything but amused or incredulous. She sounded guilty. "That's crazy."

Blake's gaze sharpened as it swung in her direction. "I don't know. She was pretty convinced. It was something about the way you looked at me last year."

Sucking in a breath, intending further protest, Bella was silenced by the heat in his eyes. The chilly afternoon suddenly seemed like a midsummer scorcher.

"She's making that up." Bella quivered. "I've never thought of you as anything more than a friend. You were married."

"I'm not married anymore." His fingers grazed her cheek and slipped beneath her hair.

Her nape tingled as he stroked her skin.

"Sure. But that doesn't mean anything has changed."

"Hasn't it?"

Transfixed by the intent glowing in the blue-gray depths of his eyes, she forgot to breathe. The desire that had haunted her for months exploded in her midsection. Reason melted like spring snow on a sunny day.

She wanted him. Badly.

"Tell me you've never imagined me kissing you," Blake demanded, cupping the back of her head and urging her forward. He frowned as the distance between them narrowed.

This could not be happening. If he came any closer, she was going to make a huge fool out of herself.

"I've never."

His lips stopped a mere whisper from hers. "Say it again and make me believe it."

"I've—"

He didn't let her finish.

Blake meant the kiss to put an end to his craving for her. A quick taste and she'd be out of his system.

That's the way it was supposed to work. He didn't expect her soft moan to scatter all rational thought. Or the way her lips parted beneath his to rob him of control. He'd intended to keep the upper hand, but when her fingers tunneled into his hair and tightened almost painfully, he lost the willpower to set her free.

He rubbed his mouth back and forth against hers, felt her body soften. Almost from the first, she surrendered herself completely to the moment. To him. Despite her earlier protests, she offered herself without reservation.

Deepening the pressure on her mouth, he let his tongue slip past her even, white teeth. He thrust into the warm wetness of her mouth, licking at all the sweetness awaiting him. Her ardent reception evoked another moan. This one his.

In a flash he knew this was no experiment. It wasn't going to end easily with him lifting his lips from hers. Stopping the kiss was going to take effort. Way more than it should.

Heat poured through him. He was consumed by desire. Intense. Inappropriate toward the woman who was his son's nanny.

Right and wrong. Simple and complicated.

This had been a mistake. But one he wasn't going to quit making until it was certain to haunt him for the rest of the summer. Maybe beyond.

Drew's sharp cry sliced through the air, severing their

kiss. Bella jerked away and scrambled to her feet faster than Drew could draw breath for a second shriek. Cursing the way his heart was pounding, Blake followed her across the lawn to where his son sat on the grass, his features crumpled in torment.

Recognizing that it wasn't a regular old temper tantrum, Bella had fallen to her knees beside Drew. Her hands skimmed over his face and arms, searching for the damage. Blake joined them just as she found the red spot on the back of his hand.

"I think he was stung by something." She scooped the child into her arms and held him close. "You poor baby."

"Are you sure he was stung?"

Bella shot him a stern look. "I grew up on a farm. I know what a sting looks like." She cupped Drew's cheek and surveyed him. "Is there any history of allergic reactions to bees or wasps in your family?"

"No." He helped her stand, hating the feeling of helplessness that always came over him when Drew cried. "Do you know what to look for if he has a reaction?"

"Difficulty breathing. Severe swelling."

"Someone in your family is allergic?" he quizzed, concern growing as he imagined Drew being afflicted by those symptoms.

She shook her head. "No, but I had a student who carried an EpiPen in case she got stung, which of course she did. About a week into my first year as a teacher. Luckily our classroom was close to the playground so we could get the epinephrine into her before her throat swelled shut."

As they reached the house, they met up with Mrs. Farnes at the front door. She looked from Drew to Bella.

"What's happened?"

"He's been stung," Bella answered, her pace slowing as she entered the house.

"Wasp or bee?" Mrs. Farnes quizzed, catching Drew's

flailing hand so she could peer at the red spot. "Looks like it's swelling some."

"I didn't see a stinger, so I'm assuming it was a wasp." Bella shifted Drew higher on her hip. "Do you think you could pour some vinegar in a bowl?"

"Of course." Mrs. Farnes raced back to the kitchen.

Bella followed, wiping tears from Drew's cheeks as she went.

"Vinegar?" Blake demanded, suspicious.

"It's what we always used on the farm. The acid neutralizes the venom."

"What about a doctor?"

She kissed Drew on the temple and snuggled him close. "He's not showing any signs of a reaction. I think he'll be just fine once his hand stops hurting."

As difficult as it was to entrust his son's welfare to another person, Blake knew that if he interfered, he would disrupt the attachment sparking between Bella and Drew. And this was exactly the sort of situation where Bella shone. Taking care of someone who needed her was as natural as breathing for her. She just needed to stop denying who she was.

Drew's sobs had devolved into ragged inhalations that shook his whole body, followed by a keening cry that had Bella blinking back tears of her own. Blake watched them. Was this the moment Bella transformed into a concerned parent, or was she merely distraught because Drew was so upset?

"All set," Mrs. Farnes said, gesturing to the kitchen table where she'd set a bowl and some dishcloths. "I gave you some ice as well to numb the area. Is that all you need? I could make a baking soda paste."

"My mother never had much luck with baking soda." Bella sat down with Drew in her lap. She dipped a towel in the water and applied it to the back of his hand.

While Drew screamed with renewed enthusiasm, Blake marveled at the range of home remedies these two women knew. He hunkered down beside his son and touched Drew's cheek.

"He seems hot," Blake said.

"I'm not surprised," Mrs. Farnes murmured, handing Drew a cookie. "He's worked himself into quite a lather. This should help."

Hiccupping, Drew stuffed the cookie into his mouth. He smacked noisily, distracted from the pain in his hand. Bella and Mrs. Farnes exchanged a knowing glance. As the level of estrogen in the room peaked, Blake was assailed by a renewed sense of urgency. Drew needed a mother who would tear up when he was hurt and fiercely protect him from the world's dangers. She would teach him respect for women and how to be both strong and gentle at the same time.

He would not grow up with a hole in his heart and a head full of questions about why his mother had abandoned him.

"I think it's working," Bella said, her gaze shifting to Blake. "Will you hold him for me while I fix a bottle?" She dipped the cloth in the vinegar once more and handed it to Blake before she shifted Drew to him. Her fingers slipped over Blake's hand as he sat down, the tender contact a warm reminder of their earlier kiss. "He's going to be all right," she told him softly, her voice encouraging.

Blake tracked her progress across the kitchen, his skin tingling in the aftermath of her light touch. She'd managed his worries over Drew's wasp sting with the same calm reassurance she'd used with his son. As much as she denied that she was cut out for motherhood, she was a natural. More than a natural. She was innately driven to make those around her happy.

The large kitchen became more homey as the smell of cooking onions filled the air, the sound of them sizzling in the pan blending harmoniously with the hum of female voices as Mrs. Farnes began dinner preparations.

Lifting the damp cloth off Drew's wasp sting, Blake noticed the red mark on his son's hand had been reduced to a dot the diameter of a pencil. The progress pleased him.

"It looks a lot better," Bella commented, peering over Blake's shoulder.

Her dark brown hair fell forward, brushing his cheek. He had a quick second to fill his lungs with the scent of vanilla before she swept the wayward strands behind her ear. While she peered at Drew, Blake studied her profile. Her nose had a slight bump from being broken when she was ten while rescuing her three-year-old brother from a charging billy goat owned by her grandmother.

It was the only imperfection in an otherwise lovely face. Softly rounded cheekbones, a well-shaped mouth and pale blue eyes that tilted up at the corners gave her a fresh, girl-next-door look so unlike his ex-wife's sleek sophistication. Combine that with a smile that went from uncertain to delighted in the blink of an eye, and Blake had a hard time keeping his mind focused on his plans and off the delectable kiss they'd just shared.

Already he'd done something he'd intended to avoid. But what Jeanne had said to him about Bella finding him attractive had been gnawing at him. He'd gone over every memory he had of Bella and found no sign that she'd been anything but friendly toward him. Today he'd thrown Jeanne's words in Bella's face, expecting her to hotly deny it. Instead, her protest had lacked conviction. He'd expected her to slap his hand away. To get angry.

His groin stirred at the memory of her impassioned moan. She'd sounded both confounded and thrilled. Beneath his kiss she'd come alive. Her ardent surrender had carried both of them into a place where they alone existed. Blake frowned. How far would things have gone if Drew hadn't brought them back?

"Here's his bottle."

While he'd been lost in thought, Bella had finished preparing Drew's bottle. She held it out to Blake, but he shook his head.

"Why don't you feed him," he said. "I have to call Jeanne and tell her I'm not going to make dinner."

"You shouldn't cancel on your sister," Bella said, carrying baby and bottle out of the kitchen. "Drew is fine. After he finishes this, we're going to read a little and if he isn't sleepy, I'll give him some dinner, a bath and then straight to bed."

Her words had set the scene for the sort of evening he'd been hoping to enjoy, just the three of them.

"You were pretty determined that your nights would be free, remember?" Blake had followed her into the living room. "Besides, I don't feel right about leaving Drew after what happened."

She settled onto the pale blue couch and started feeding Drew before she answered. "Really, Blake, it's only a wasp sting. He's perfectly fine and there's no need for you to stay."

"Are you trying to get rid of me?" He sat beside her, immediately realizing he was too close when his thigh bumped against hers. The contact delighted him. So did the way she bit down on her lower lip.

"Of course not."

"I don't believe you."

She shifted on the soft cushion, but there was nowhere for her to go. He'd boxed her in.

"It has nothing to do with you. I don't want your sister thinking you don't trust me to take care of Drew."

"She'll understand that I'm staying home because otherwise I'll be wondering how he is the whole time and be terrible company."

"She's going to blame me for not keeping a close enough eye on him."

"I will tell her it was my fault." Blake's lips thinned. "I'll explain I had you thoroughly distracted."

"You really shouldn't do that." Concern thrummed in her voice. "She will think we're…"

A rosy flush spilled over her cheeks. The sight of it confounded him. Why was she acting embarrassed? The kiss they'd shared had given him a clear picture of the attraction between them. She'd responded boldly to every sweep of his tongue. He hadn't anticipated that she'd throw herself into the kiss with sweet abandon, or that he'd be equally swept away by the softness of her skin and the heat of her mouth.

"That we're…?" He prompted.

She kept her attention fixed on Drew. "Why did you kiss me?"

Her voice was so low he almost didn't catch the question.

"Because I wanted to."

"It complicates things between us."

More than she knew.

"Things are already complicated between us."

She eyed Blake as she handed him the empty bottle. "Why did you really want me here this summer? There are hundreds of terrific nannies in New York. You could have had your pick."

"I like your company. I thought you'd enjoy spending a couple months at the beach."

Her scrutiny intensified. "No ulterior motives?"

"Such as?" he prompted, voice silky smooth, wondering if she was brave enough to voice the challenge in her eyes.

"We haven't even been here two hours and already you've kissed me." The exaggerated rise and fall of her chest betrayed her agitation. She was practically vibrating with tension. "Do you expect me to sleep with you?"

"I'm considering the possibility," he admitted. At some

point during that explosive kiss, he'd lost control. Her effect on him was both intriguing and disturbing.

"You don't mean that."

Blake forced his tone neutral. "I do."

"But you've never given any indication that you're interested in me." Her soft blue eyes grew incredibly large in her pale face.

"As you pointed out earlier, I was married. These days I'm free to be attracted to any woman I want."

"Sure, but there are hundreds for you to pick from who are much more suitable."

"Maybe I'm not looking for suitable." He took her chin and forced her to meet his gaze. "Maybe all I'm interested in is a woman who moans when I kiss her."

Her lips parted on a sharp inhale. "You caught me by surprise."

"And if I gave you fair warning? Would that make a difference?"

"You can't be serious."

He stared at her soft mouth, remembering how it felt beneath his. The passionate tangle of her tongue with his. If Drew wasn't snuggled in her arms, his eyes focused on Bella's face, Blake would lean over and show her just how powerful the chemistry between them could be.

"Would you like me to demonstrate just how serious I am?"

"No." She shook her head vehemently. "Don't toy with me, Blake."

"I assure you, that's the last thing I intend to do." Deciding he'd pushed her to the very edge of her comfort zone, Blake got to his feet. "We'll talk more about this later. Right now I need to change if I'm going to make it to Jeanne's on time."

Brain reeling from her exchange with Blake, Bella stared after him. What had she gotten herself into? Had coming to the Hamptons with Blake and Drew been a huge mistake? The last thing she'd ever expected was that Deidre would have been right about Blake. What had his kiss meant? Was she a naive fool to read anything into it at all?

Blake was single. She was a warm body. Was it as simple as that? But why would he choose her when the Hamptons were filled with far more suitable women? Maybe she shouldn't ask questions. Maybe she should just pack and get the hell out.

Unfortunately, now that she'd given her sister the three-thousand-dollar advance on her salary, she would have to stay and be Drew's nanny for at least two weeks.

Besides, she couldn't just leave father and son in the lurch. No matter how often she tried to put her needs first, it was inevitable that she would put acting responsibly before self-preservation. She was trapped here. Incarcerated by her belief system.

When Blake came home from his stepsister's dinner party, she would simply tell him that nothing like that kiss could ever happen between them ever again. Blake would understand and agree. Surely he didn't want to complicate their working relationship. It had been a one-time misstep, incongruous and regrettable, and never to be repeated.

The baby in her arms was stirring back to full wakefulness. She carried him upstairs and found a large bedroom with pale blue walls, decorated with sailboats and furnished with a dark cherry crib, dresser and changing table. The last time she'd been here, the room had just been finished. The stuffed animals that now filled the window seat that overlooked the ocean hadn't been here. There'd been no baskets on the floor filled with stacking cups and electronic games. No well-worn books had filled the shelves.

Now the space looked lived-in. Loved.

Bella set Drew on the floor near the basket of toys and began unpacking his clothes. A fire truck with a siren held his attention for as long as it took Bella to fill one drawer. After that he crawled to the low bookcase and began pulling out one story after another. Seeing the mess he was making, Bella left the rest of the unpacking for later and joined him on the floor.

"What should we read first?" She scanned the books.

"He's particularly fond of *Belly Button Book*," Blake said from the doorway.

Bella located the story and turned to thank him for the suggestion, but the words faltered on her lips at the sight of him in khakis, a white polo shirt and navy blazer. The casual clothes reminded her of those days last summer when they'd sat on the back porch and he'd told her about his favorite places in the Virgin Islands and about how he'd first tried *cinghiale*—wild boar—in a small village in Tuscany. She'd been surprised to learn that they hunted wild boar in Italy and that it was a favorite dish in the region.

He'd opened her eyes to adventures she'd never imagined when she'd been growing up on a small farm in Iowa and her dreams had expanded to include traveling beyond the borders of the U.S.

"I should be back in time to put him to bed," Blake told her.

"Don't feel the need to rush back. We'll be just fine." She lifted the baby onto her lap and opened the book. "Enjoy your dinner."

"Thank you," Blake said.

It wasn't until he was gone that Bella realized she'd been holding her breath. She released the air in a gusty sigh and kissed Drew on top of his head. "That daddy of yours sure ties me in knots," she confided to the baby. "Did you see the way he kissed me this afternoon?"

Drew smacked the book with his hands and made impatient noises.

"Typical guy," Bella teased. "When it comes to talking

about feelings, you aren't interested in hearing what a woman has to say."

And without further delay, she began to read.

Five

Blake cursed as he turned into the driveway of the house Jeanne and Peter had rented and spied three cars parked in front. His stepsister had lied to him. This wasn't a quiet family dinner. It was a setup.

One of her numerous socialite friends from New York? An oil baron's daughter from Texas? Hopefully she hadn't fixed him up with the actress from Los Angeles she'd met the previous week. The possibilities were endless, considering Jeanne's vast social connections and vivacious personality.

"Blake." Jeanne flung open the door before he had a chance to ring the bell. "I'm so glad you could join us." She grabbed his arm and pulled him toward the living room.

Her over-the-top gaiety deepened Blake's suspicions. She was trying too hard.

Peter met him in the living room doorway and handed him a cut-crystal tumbler with a three-finger shot of whiskey. "I told her this was a bad idea."

Blake's chest vibrated with a suppressed growl. "Jeanne, what's going on?"

He loved his stepsister, but sometimes she didn't know when to stop her well-meaning machinations. She liked the world organized to her specific standards. And most of the time she got her way.

"Look who was able to get away from New York to join us for the weekend." Jeanne maneuvered him around Peter and into the contemporary monstrosity of a living room where Blake's ex-wife stood, her expression a mask of delight, her eyes flaring defiance.

"Damn it, Jeanne," he began, biting off the rest of the sentence when his stepsister gripped his hand hard.

"Don't be mad. You two are my favorite people in the world." Her husband made a disgusted sound behind her that she ignored. "I can't have you refusing to be in the same room. There's going to be harmony in this house when the baby comes." Her lovely features wore the determined expression they all knew too well. "I mean it."

Blake took a healthy swallow of his drink and relished the burn in his throat and chest. He concentrated on getting a handle on his annoyance before he spoke. "So, this isn't a setup?" He thought he sounded cool and relaxed, but Peter winced, Jeanne's eyes went wide and Vicky grew pale.

"Must you suspect everyone's motives?"

"Not everyone's," he retorted smoothly, saluting his stepsister with the glass. "Just yours."

Jeanne rolled her shoulders in an elegant shrug and nudged him toward Vicky. "Go be nice while I have Peter refresh your drink."

Tension marred his ex-wife's lovely features as he approached her. Stunning in a figure-hugging black dress that showed off a significant amount of cleavage, she'd obviously spent a great deal of time on her hair and makeup. If she was hoping he'd be moved that she'd gone to so much trouble for him, she was destined for disappointment.

"I don't need to ask how you've been," she murmured. "You look wonderful."

"Fatherhood agrees with me."

"I knew it would."

The flow of conversation was interrupted when Peter handed him a tumbler of scotch. When they began again, Vicky changed the topic to recent gossip about their friends. She didn't ask after Drew. Eight months ago this would have annoyed Blake. In the months since she'd left, he'd grudgingly accepted that he'd been too blinded by his desire to be a parent to realize his wife didn't share his enthusiasm. In the week after they'd brought their son home from the hospital, Vicky hadn't held the baby more than a half dozen times, each for less than ten minutes. Pity he hadn't recognized her lack of maternal instinct earlier. It would have saved them both a great deal of heartache.

"I heard that your play closed," he said. "I'm sorry to hear it didn't work out."

She shrugged. "There will be others."

Blake spied telltale signs of anxiety in the lines bracketing her mouth. "I thought you were very good."

"You saw it?"

"Of course. Don't sound so surprised. You know I've always been your biggest fan."

News of her affair had left him angry and raw for twenty-four hours. It had taken him that long to process the abrupt end of his five-year marriage and to remember that his energy was better spent caring for his son.

"But I thought..." She looked baffled.

"That I hated you?" He shook his head. "We wanted different things. You, a career. Me, a family. I didn't appreciate the way you ended things, but I've been told that I can be a bit difficult to say no to." He snagged her gaze and let his lips drift into a conciliatory curve.

"That's so reasonable of you." Her tone reflected doubt.

"I told you fatherhood agrees with me."

"I guess it does."

"Drew's terrific. Stop by the house anytime if you'd like to see him." He made the offer knowing she'd never do that.

"I will." She nodded. "I'm heading to Los Angeles next week. Maybe we could have lunch at the Saw Grass Grill before I leave?"

The restaurant where they'd agreed to start a family. Had she been honest in her agreement, or had it merely been a way to preserve their marriage? He'd never be sure whether what she'd told him was the truth or merely what she'd believed he wanted to hear. One thing he did know, he'd missed all the warning signs that Vicky wasn't interested in being a mother.

He was saved from having to answer by the arrival of the housekeeper announcing dinner was ready. Blake lingered in the living room while the other three made their way into the dining room. Blake wasn't surprised to see that Jeanne had placed him next to Victoria to suit her matchmaking scheme.

His sister wasn't behaving as if she'd listened when he told her he intended to put his son's needs first. Of course, he wasn't exactly walking the walk either. Kissing Bella this afternoon had been a mistake. There was no denying he wanted her, but she was far too determined to remain childless. Getting involved with her was contrary to everything he wanted for Drew. Better to heed her warning. Pursuing her would complicate things between them and he needed their relationship to be trouble free, for Drew's sake.

That decided, he returned his attention to the dinner conversation, ignoring the burn of disappointment in his gut.

* * *

Bella stared down at a sleeping Drew, unable to obey the logical side of her brain that told her to grab the baby monitor and go. She needed to remember that Drew was nothing more than a job. She was his nanny. This tightness in her chest would go away the instant she accepted that Drew belonged to Blake and only Blake. She had no claim on him. No reason to ache for all the firsts she'd already missed and all the ones still to come that she wouldn't get to experience.

Damn Blake. It was all his fault. First he'd tracked her down. Then he'd offered her the financial means to help her sister and not feel guilty for spending money on a fabulous trip to the Caribbean. If not for him, she might be broke and resentful, but she'd be blissfully free of the emotional chaos churning in her gut. Free of the anxiety that came with being responsible for another human being.

Reaching down, she grazed her knuckles across Drew's soft cheek. This afternoon when he'd been stung, she'd longed to take on his pain as her own. She hadn't been able to separate herself from his hurt the way she did when something harmed her brothers and sisters. It was as if despite being apart for nine months, she and Drew shared a bond. He would always be hers no matter how many miles separated them.

It was a disquieting thought that she wished she could unthink.

Her phone buzzed in her back pocket, alerting her that a text had come in. She suspected that it was Blake checking in again, so relief surged through her when she saw Deidre's name on the display. Bella exited the nursery, pulling the door closed behind her, and went to sit on the steps that descended toward the darkened first floor. She keyed up her friend's message and grimaced at the video of Deidre dancing with three guys.

There's too many gorgeous guys for me to keep happy all by myself.

That could be her. Young, single and ready to break hearts all over town. No responsibilities. No worries. Just fun.

Bella texted her friend back.

I've seen you in action and have faith that you can do it.

A minute later her phone rang.

"We miss you." Deidre's fervent voice sounded loud in the still house as she made it sound like Bella had been gone for weeks instead of hours.

"I miss you, too."

"How are things there?" From the background noise, it sounded like Deidre was in the ladies' room.

Bella waffled over how much to tell her friend and finally decided to ease into it. "A little weird."

"Weird how?"

"You were right about Blake."

"Aha!" Deidre crowed. A second later her voice quieted. Tension gathered in her tone. "What do you mean I was right?"

"He kissed me." A stunned silence followed Bella's declaration. With her nerves frayed by too much self-doubt, Bella wished her friend would say something. She could really use Deidre's sensible council. "Did you hear me?"

"I did. I'm just trying to figure out how to respond." Another pause. "Yippee?"

"No, not yippee," Bella shot back. "Yikes."

Deidre laughed. "Yikes, indeed. Boy, does he work fast. What sort of a kiss was it?"

"What do you mean, what sort of a kiss?"

"Friendly? Some people kiss on the lips to say hello or goodbye. Was it that sort of a kiss?"

Despite the hysteria bubbling up, Bella appreciated her roommate's matter-of-fact way of assessing the situation.

"No. It was not a friendly kiss."

"Juicy, then." Deidre's voice barely missed sounding like a triumphant whoop. "Did he rock your world?"

The question aroused an untimely urge to giggle. "He does that just by walking in the room."

"You've got it worse than I thought."

"So much worse." Bella set her forehead on her knees and cradled the phone against her ear. "I keep telling myself it was just a one-time thing and it won't happen again."

"Is that what you believe?"

"No." Hot flashes surged through Bella's body. "What should I do?"

"You're asking the wrong girl. I'd sleep with him in a New York minute. He's gorgeous and sexy. Nothing wrong with two single people enjoying each other's company. But that's me. What do you want to do?"

Bella had never been able to cultivate Deidre's casual attitude toward sex. As much as she'd love to be a sophisticated woman taking large bites out of the Big Apple, in truth, she was still a girl who'd grown up on a farm in Iowa. Granted, she didn't want to get married and start a family, but that didn't mean that she could see herself jumping into bed with someone where there was no possibility of a future.

"What I want to do goes against my nature."

"Bella, you've been stuck on this guy way too long. Offer him a couple months of uncomplicated sex and get him out of your system." Voices called Deidre's name from somewhere close by. "I have to go. Call me tomorrow and we'll talk more about this."

"I will. Have fun tonight."

Without Deidre's vibrant voice filling her ear, Bella's anxiety returned in spades. It was crazy to contemplate what could happen with Blake. She'd already decided against repeating this afternoon's kiss. It would be easier on her heart that way.

Beside her Drew's baby monitor picked up a soft cry. Blake had warned her that he'd been having trouble staying asleep lately and she wondered at the source of his restlessness. Was he cutting new teeth? The discomfort of that had kept her youngest sister up nights for two solid months.

Drew quieted before Bella could stand. Ears keyed to the tiniest noise, she heard the sound of approaching footsteps from below. Blake was back earlier than she expected. And he was humming. What had put him in such a good mood?

"How was your evening?" she asked as he rounded the landing.

His eyes lit up as he spied her sitting on the steps. "Waiting up for me?"

"No." The last thing she needed was for him to think she'd spent the evening missing him. "I just got off the phone with my friend. She couldn't wait to tell me how much fun she was having at this new club."

Blake stretched out on the stair beside her. His knee bumped her thigh. The casual contact zinged through her body. Shifting away would betray her agitation. Holding still took all her concentration.

"Wish you were there?" A lazy smile appeared on his well-formed lips, but the eyes that surveyed her were keen and curious.

"A little."

She tried to keep her eyes off him, but the dim stairwell offered little of interest to distract her. And there was a whole lot of wonderful occupying far too much of her personal space. In complete contrast to her tense muscles, he looked entirely at ease beside her. His elbow rested on the top step, fingers interlocked loosely. Beneath his navy blazer, a white shirt stretched across his broad chest, the top button undone to reveal the strong column of his throat.

He was strong, masculine, utterly confident in every situation, and Bella could feature him in a hundred fantasies without taxing her imagination. Deidre was right. She'd been hung up on Blake for too long. But was a brief, casual affair the best way to get him out of her system?

"Tomorrow night I'll stay home with Drew," he offered. "You can go out and have some fun of your own."

"By myself?" She didn't mean for the question to come out sounding as grim as it did, and Blake's eyes brimmed with amusement. "What I mean is I don't know anyone here. I'm not sure I want to go to a bar alone."

"I'll get Jeanne to watch Drew and I'll take you."

His offer made her pulse race. She imagined herself in a bar with Blake. A glass of wine to relax her. The throb of electronic music making her blood run hot. How long before she dragged him onto the crowded dance floor and gave in to the hunger he aroused?

"That's nice of you to suggest, but I don't think you and I going out is a good idea."

Her repressive manner put him on instant alert. He regarded her through narrowed eyes for a long moment before asking, "Any reason why not?"

"I've been doing some thinking since earlier."

"About what?"

"About what happened between us today."

His lips arced in a predatory smile. "I've been thinking about it, as well."

"Then you'll agree that it was a mistake."

"I can't say that."

His declaration gave Bella pause. This was not going as planned. "I'm your son's nanny."

"If you're worried that things will become uncomfortable between us, I have no intention of letting that happen."

She relaxed. "Good. I think it's for the best if nothing further happens."

"I truly wish I could make that promise." Blake's exhalation sounded weary. "Earlier tonight, I thought I could. But now I realize I can't."

"Why not?" Her voice pitched higher than normal as she asked the question.

"Because it's not that easy to keep my hands off you."

Six

Sitting on the steps was not an ideal place to begin a seduction, but Blake wasn't about to risk Bella bolting for the safety of her bedroom if he let her get to her feet. Her resistance amused him. It was as if all her arguing against an affair between them was aimed at convincing herself. He was confident she wanted him. He just needed her to admit it.

He cupped her neck to hold her still while he slid his lips into the hollow above her collarbone. The contact made her shiver. Her skin was warm silk. Softer than he'd expected. He pulled in a long, slow breath, taking in the scent of her. Vanilla and jasmine. Simple fragrances for an uncomplicated woman.

"Blake—" She whispered his name, objecting even as she leaned into his searching lips.

"Yes, Bella?" He sampled more of her skin, grazing his mouth up her neck. Her soft sigh made him smile in satisfaction.

"We really shouldn't."

"Are you telling me to stop?" Instead of waiting for her to answer, he let his fingertips slip from her neck to her shoulder, drawing her into his space. He wanted to overwhelm her with intent. Compel her understanding. He wanted her. Very much. "Just say stop. I'll quit."

His teeth grazed her throat. She moaned something, but the word that left her lips wasn't *stop*. Her fingers bit into his shoulders. He felt their fierce hold through his blazer. For a woman who wanted him to believe she was opposed to letting the chemistry between them run its course, she was not resisting.

"Let's go." Suddenly impatient, he got to his feet and swept her into his arms.

She looked dazed for a moment, but as he strode toward his bedroom, her eyes cleared. "Go where?"

"I'm going to make love to you, Bella."

Her big blue eyes regarded him in consternation. "I don't want that."

He set her on her feet in the doorway to his bedroom, but didn't dare set her free. "Then we'll only do as much as you do want."

"You'll stop?"

"Whenever you say." His finger found her chin and elevated it until her face was at a perfect angle. He placed his lips on hers in a gentle kiss meant to reassure her. The tension humming in her muscles eased slightly, so he set his palm against her spine and drew her ever so slowly against him.

Her breath quickened as their hips came together. Restraint came at a price as her hands slid beneath his jacket. Fingers fanning over his rib cage, she took the kiss up a notch, parting her lips and flicking her tongue across his teeth. He let her in, captured her breath in his lungs and held it while she grew bolder.

Sliding one foot between hers, he backed her against the

doorframe. Her surprised inhalation barely registered as he pressed his thigh against the heat of her core. They rocked together in a languid rhythm, matched by the dueling feint and retreat of their tongues. Keenly focused on her every sigh and the trembling of her body, he was rapidly losing faith that if she asked him to stop he could.

"Do you want to stop?" he questioned, sliding his fingers beneath her simple T-shirt. Her skin was impossibly hot, as if she was on fire for him.

The modest neckline had gaped when he'd lifted her into his arms, offering him a peek at her flesh-colored bra. So practical. Nothing seductive about it. Yet he couldn't wait to see her in it.

She pushed him to arm's length. "I think we should."

Gusting out a sigh, Blake stepped back. As his hands fell to his side, she studied him.

"As you wish."

"That's just it, don't you see?" Her expression reflected frustration. "I don't want to stop. I want to keep going. Until we're naked and rolling around in that big bed over there." She gestured to where his king-size bed sat between two patches of moonlight. "But I think that would be a huge mistake."

Her breath rasped, the cadence agitated. Blake wanted to snatch her into his arms and kiss away all her angst. With her eyes glowing, her mouth soft from his kisses, she was spectacular. And worth waiting for.

He took her hands and turned her palms upward. Bending, he placed a kiss in each one. "It's late. Why don't we call it a night?"

"You've changed your mind?" She sounded heartbroken. "Just like that?"

"You said stop."

She yanked her hands free. "I didn't say stop. I simply said it would be a mistake."

Her logic escaped him. "How is that different than stop?"

"You are so exasperating."

Before he had a clue to her intentions, she'd stripped her shirt over her head and eliminated the distance between them. He had about a second to appreciate the curves of her breasts before they slammed into his chest.

His arms came about her, binding her to him. She was silk and fire in his grasp. With a low groan, Blake dropped his mouth onto hers and found her lips parted in invitation. Any hesitation she might have demonstrated these past ten minutes was lost in the heat of her ardent response to his kiss.

Taking things slowly—savoring her surrender—was proving difficult. While their mouths melded in passionate harmony, in the back of his mind he braced for her doubts to resurface. They didn't. Once committed, she was a siren calling him to lose all touch with reality and follow her anywhere.

Chest heaving, Blake eased back. As much as he hated to risk giving her time to come to her senses, standing in his doorway was an awkward place to romance her properly. Her eyes were heavy lidded and slightly unfocused as he led her toward the bed.

In a flash he'd stripped off his blazer and pulled his shirt over his head. She gazed at his chest in fascination. He flinched as her fingertips settled on his skin.

"You acted as if that hurt," she said, absorbed in her study of his bare chest.

"Your touch has a strong effect on me."

"It does?" She traced his pectoral muscles, fascinated by every curve she encountered. "Is that good or bad?"

"It's very good." Although he was dying to let his own fingers do some exploring, he kept his hands on her hips. He would have all night to discover her body. "I like being touched by you."

Her smile came and went. "You are as beautiful as I imagined." Did she realize what she'd let slip?

"My turn." He guided her onto the mattress and followed her down, his lips drifting along her throat and across her chest to the edge of her bra. "You are perfect."

She squirmed beneath him as he grazed her nipple through the fabric of her bra. "That feels amazing." Reaching behind her, she unfastened the catch. With a quick jerk, she freed herself from the bra and tossed it aside. "This will be even better."

Blake groaned as he closed his mouth around one tight bud. He laved her with his tongue and then sucked until she arched off the mattress. Whimpering, she clutched at his hair. Never had he been with a woman as sensitive as Bella. Suddenly he was hungry for more. He blazed a trail down her stomach. Unzipping her pants took only a second. With fingers that trembled, he hooked her waistband and slid the fabric down her thighs. She lifted her hips to aid him and in no time she lay in the middle of his bed clad in nothing but her panties.

It was a moment worth appreciating, and Blake was a man who knew the value of doing so. First with his gaze, then with his hands, he learned the arch of her feet, the slenderness of her ankles, the muscular thrust of her calves, the lean length of her thighs, the flare of her hips and flatness of her abdomen. He lingered over each ripple in her rib cage, drawing out the suspense until his fingers circled her breasts.

When she grabbed his hands and cupped them over her breasts, Blake knew she'd suffered all she could take. Leaning down, he captured her mouth, branding her with a sizzling kiss.

Bella had never felt anything like Blake's hands on her body. He paid attention to every inch of her skin, as if he wanted to know all of her, not just the "good parts." It made her feel adored, something she'd never known before.

The crushing weight of his body lifted off her as he abandoned her mouth to blaze a trail of delicious sensation down her body. Expecting he would turn his attention back to her breasts, she was disappointed when he paused only long enough to draw a wet circle around one nipple before following her ribs downward. He lingered on her abdomen, dipping his tongue into her navel and awakening a series of shudders. By the time his lips drifted over her hip bone, Bella was half-mad with wanting.

Her thighs had parted ages ago. Between them she throbbed with increasing hunger. She craved his hard length buried inside her. The need grew with each circle of his tongue and press of his lips against her feverish skin. But it wasn't until his broad shoulders nudged her legs wide did she awaken to what he intended.

She gasped. "Blake."

He looked up at her call. His chin bumped against her hot core, sending a spear of pleasure lancing through her. Her breath suspended as their gazes locked.

"Are you asking me to stop?" he challenged, letting his lips drift over her mound.

Stop? Was he mad?

The slight tug of fabric against her sensitized flesh rendered her incoherent. If it was like this before his lips found her bare skin, what would it be like when he'd stripped away the last of her clothes?

"It's…"

She broke off as he trailed his tongue along the edge of her panties. Sliding his hands down her legs, he gripped her behind the thighs and bent her knees until her feet were flat on the mattress. Every movement caused an escalation in the commotion inside her. Her fingers gripped the sheet beneath her. She'd never had anyone kiss her there.

"I'll go slowly," he told her, capturing her gaze. "You tell me when to stop."

Stop?

It was glorious to watch his pleasure in her body's every reaction. How could she possibly stop him from indulging his power over her? Helplessly, she waited, her breath shallow and ragged as his warm breath washed over her. And then he pressed a kiss there and a strangled groan broke from her throat. She was lost as the bold stroke of his tongue licked over her. Her hips bucked. A wild laugh erupted from her tight chest.

"Stop?" He ceased all movement.

She wanted to weep with longing. "Don't..."

"More?"

Amusement edged his tone. Part of her recognized she should be angry with him for taunting her, but she was on the edge of something glorious and devastating.

"Yes."

"It would be easier if I took these off." He hooked his fingers in her panties and tugged.

She lifted her hips. "Do it."

The fabric skimmed off her body far too slowly. Bella's head thrashed from side to side as she felt the air hit her overheated flesh. With her eyes closed, it felt safer. She could pretend it was anyone between her thighs, but the second Blake spoke, she became grounded in the moment once more.

"I'm going to kiss you now." But he didn't immediately follow through with his promise. Bella's heart thumped hard against her ribs as she waited. "Care to watch?"

Enticed by the question, her lashes drifted upward. He was waiting for her. He wanted her to see what he intended to do. Bella shuddered at the intensity in his eyes, but couldn't look away as his tongue stroked against her.

She cried out, an incoherent sound barely loud enough to escape the confines of the bed. Blake's gaze electrified her. His kiss set her ablaze. He was thorough. Each wet circle of his tongue sent her spiraling higher. The ache in her belly coiled into a tight knot. Her world shrank to the feel of Blake's mouth on her and the rapid approach of cresting pleasure.

Her hips rose off the mattress, frantically searching for the fulfillment that eluded her. She was whimpering, her breath coming in erratic and short bursts.

"Let go," he urged. "Come for me."

And then she felt the slide of his finger inside her. The penetration touched off her orgasm and her spine bowed as she exploded like a firework, splintering into a million hot shards before returning to earth in a gentle waterfall.

Bella's cries were the sweetest music Blake had ever heard. Beneath him she continued to tremble in the aftermath of her powerful orgasm. At long last her lashes fluttered and her gaze focused on him. There was such wonder in the much-washed blue of her eyes. Blake's heart clenched.

"That was amazing," she murmured.

He kissed his way up her body until he reached her mouth. "There's more to come," he murmured against her lips.

Bella coasted her fingertips over his lower lip before settling her palm against his cheek. Her gentle touch was as much about claiming him as surrendering to his will.

"I'm glad."

Moving quickly, he stripped off his pants and rolled on a condom. Her arms came around him as he rejoined her on the bed. Where a second earlier her body had been limp and sated, as he positioned himself between her thighs and sucked her nipple between his lips, she became a living flame once more. Her fingers wandered across his shoulders and down his spine. The scratch of her nails along his sides startled him.

Before he could ask her if she wanted to stop, she spoke.

"Enough with the preliminaries. I need to feel you inside me."

She bumped her hips upward, nudging his erection and making him quake with yearning. Never one to keep a woman waiting, he positioned himself at her entrance and claimed her mouth in a long, deep kiss. Then he thrust gently. She was so wet and aroused that he was nearly seated all the way in before he stopped himself. After a brief pause to gather much-needed air, he began moving with a smooth rocking motion that she matched as fluidly as if they'd made love a thousand times.

The ease of their connection caught Blake by surprise. It occurred to him that he knew Bella well and at the same time didn't know her at all. From the first she'd intrigued him. Later, her contrary behavior had frustrated him. There was so much yet to discover about her. So many unanswered questions. And he would have most of the summer to ferret them out.

"Blake." Her clutching fingers told him she was close to another climax.

He'd been distracting his mind to prolong their encounter, but as her nails dug into his back and her cries grew more frantic, Blake loosened the hold on his willpower and thrust powerfully into her. Capturing her pleasure in a hot, demanding kiss, he slipped his hand between their bodies and touched the knot of nerves that would send her spinning into another orgasm.

As her body contracted, he let his own climax catch him. With a final thrust, he buried his face in her neck and gave her everything. Shuddering, his arm muscles unable to support him any longer, he collapsed on her.

"Now, that was amazing," he said, chest heaving as he struggled to recover.

Eyes glowing with contentment, Bella parted her lips to respond, but before she could, a cry erupted from beyond the room. Recognizing the quality of the cry, Blake nevertheless willed his son back to sleep. It was a fruitless proposition.

Another unhappy wail filtered in from the nursery, this one of longer duration than the last. Drew didn't sound as if he was going to settle down on his own.

Blake put his forehead against Bella's shoulder and heaved a sigh. "I'd better get him."

"Let me."

With an abrupt shake of his head, Blake pushed away from her warm, silken skin, grinding his teeth as he was pummeled by the room's cool air. "I've been through this with him. I'll have an easier time getting him back to sleep." He covered her with the sheet and bent down to buss her cheek. "Sleep."

"Sure." She gave him an uncertain smile.

Blake's movements felt jerky and uncoordinated as he slid back into his clothes. His muscles hadn't fully recovered from the mind-blowing sex with Bella. He cast a final look her way before he headed for the doorway. What he saw gave him pause.

If not for his son's escalating distress, Blake would have lingered to reassure Bella that he too had been affected by the power of what had happened between them. The last thing he wanted with any woman was to take her to a vulnerable place and abandon her there. He sensed Bella wasn't the sort of woman who took sex lightly.

Which meant leaving her so soon after being intimate would undo some of the rapport they'd established. She'd had her doubts earlier, but he'd been able to reassure her. Abandoning her in his bed would give her ample time to re-establish her defenses.

But there was nothing to do about that. His son needed him. It was something Bella understood. She'd often put her family's needs above her own; it was a big part of what appealed to him about her. On the other hand, when she'd decided to cut off all ties with Drew, she'd demonstrated that like his ex-wife, she had a selfish side.

And what of his decision a mere three hours ago not to complicate their relationship by acting on his desire for her? He certainly hadn't been thinking about what was best for his son while he made love to her. What he needed was a mother for Drew. Bella wasn't interested in the role.

So why had he felt compelled to have her spend part of the summer with them? Had he hoped if she spent time with Drew her maternal instincts would awaken?

When he got to the nursery, Blake lifted his son into his arms and rocked him the way he knew Drew loved. Almost immediately the infant's cries waned. He met Drew's eyes and felt peace wash through him. He wanted the world for his son, but right now he would settle for a mother who would love him with her whole heart.

Which was why making love to Bella tonight had been a mistake. They could no longer pretend to be simply boss and employee. But he couldn't promise to keep his hands off her in the future. He'd told Jeanne he intended to put Drew first the next time he married. Getting involved with a woman who didn't want to be a mother ran contrary to that determination. But being with her felt so right. What the hell was he supposed to do?

Seven

Abandoned in Blake's enormous bed, Bella pressed a pillow against her stomach and curved her naked body around it, coiling herself into a tight ball. The instant he'd left the room, her sense of belonging had vanished with him.

Earlier, while Blake was dining with his stepsister, she'd glanced into the master bedroom. Residual traces of Victoria—like the photographs in the living room—lingered in the large, beautifully decorated space. Blake's ex-wife remained a presence in the house, and Bella felt like an imposter. An interloper. Had she really just made love to Blake?

The riotous sensations still buffeting her body as well as the residual tingle left behind by the imprint of Blake's lips told her she had stepped across a line. And now that she'd left footprints in forbidden territory, there was no taking it back. But was that what she wanted? To unmake the memories of the past hour?

Bella rubbed her hot cheeks against the cool sheets. Nothing could have prepared her for the explosive quality of Blake's mouth on her body. The things he'd done. No one had ever kissed her like that before. Done things to her body that made her go wild. To say they were unmatched in experience was woefully inadequate. She'd had so much to learn. Tonight it had been all she could do just to hang on for dear life as he took her on an epic ride. In the aftermath, she recognized that a man as sophisticated as Blake would expect his lover to match him in skill and knowledge.

Through the door Blake had closed behind him, Bella could hear Drew's continuing cries. The instinct to go to him thundered through her. He was her baby. Comforting him was her job. Her responsibility.

Except that it wasn't. Drew belonged to Blake. And in a way, to Victoria. She might have abandoned him, but as far as the world knew, Blake's ex-wife was his mother. Bella was just someone who'd acted as a surrogate. A living incubator. Well paid and insignificant the second Drew was born.

But his cries tore at her. No matter how hard she tried to be sensible, the need to cuddle him until his tears dried up was so much more compelling than her desire to be free of responsibility. The war between her brain and her emotions was leaving her confidence in tatters. Her doubts about the choices she'd made about Drew were growing stronger day by day.

As Bella threw back the covers, the house went silent. She held her breath, waiting for the cries to start again, but no sound stirred. Far from anything resembling sleepiness, Bella dressed and eased out of the room. Drew's door was shut, but a faint light glimmered beneath. Tiptoeing forward, she drew close and heard Blake's deep voice. He was telling Drew a story, his tone pitched to engage an infant.

Reluctant to enter the nursery and disturb what Blake had accomplished, Bella retreated toward her room, but instead of heading inside, she took the stairs to the first floor.

In bare feet she was able to move soundlessly across the

polished wood floor of the living room. Drawn by the light of the moon, she crossed to the windows that overlooked the ocean. Snagging a throw from a nearby chair, she wrapped it around her shoulders before letting herself out the door.

A wide porch stretched across the back half of the house, offering a place to rest and enjoy the view. White wood lounge chairs covered with thick, cobalt-blue cushions were scattered here and there. Straight ahead a wide set of steps led to an expansive lawn. At the far end, a boardwalk split the vegetation capping the low dunes lining the beach. A light wind carried the sound of the surf to Bella's ears. She headed down the steps and across the lawn.

From her first glimpse at the ocean last summer, it had been love at first sight. Everything about the beach had fascinated her, from the birds to the myriad of trinkets left behind by the tide to the pulse of the ocean itself. With her toes gripping the sand, she'd stared at the horizon and pulled the briny air into her lungs, letting the sights, sounds and smells fill her with peace.

She'd been close to her due date and riddled with doubts that she was doing the right thing by herself and her son. She'd hoped that spending a couple weeks with Blake and Victoria and seeing their eagerness to be parents would enable her to set aside her misgivings. The beach had settled her anxiety and allowed her to gain perspective.

By the end of the first week, she'd accepted that the baby she carried would be brought up by loving parents who could provide everything he could ever want or need. At peace with her decision to help Blake and Victoria, she'd given birth to Drew and walked out of the hospital, never imagining that she'd see him again.

Yet here she was nine months later, taking care of Drew once more, pretending that a conflict wasn't raging inside her. Once again grappling to make sense of what her heart wanted versus what she believed would make her happy. In the long run she knew being a mom would only make her resentful, yet every fiber of her being longed for Drew. And after what had happened between her and Blake tonight, she yearned for him, as well.

It would be so easy to surrender her heart to them. Equal parts charming and aggravating, they'd slipped beneath her skin in a disturbingly short period of time. She had no trouble imagining herself becoming a part of their lives. Taking care of them. Falling into a routine that would leave little time or energy for the things she wanted.

Bella retraced her steps to the house. Earlier tonight she'd discovered the power Blake held over her. She'd been disappointed they'd had no chance to cement the connection they'd forged during their lovemaking, but relieved for the opportunity to gain perspective before facing Blake again.

Not one thing she'd experienced tonight had left her unaffected. Should she get out before it was too late? She could tell Blake she'd changed her mind. It wasn't too late to back away from the edge.

And never make love to him? Her body ached at the thought.

Bella stopped halfway across the lawn and faced the ocean. Lifting her face to the wind, she quieted her mind and listened for the truth.

In the past two years she'd learned a great deal about herself. She'd reimagined her dreams. She'd learned more about her strengths and desires. And she'd enjoy her time with Blake as long as it lasted. A day, a week or a month. Whatever she could have. If she was smart and kept her head on straight, she could do exactly as Deidre suggested and enjoy his company for as long as it lasted.

When it was done, they would part friends.

With Victoria and Blake's marriage over, it was no longer necessary for Bella to keep away from Drew. But what sort of relationship did she want with him? Back when she'd given birth, Blake had expected her to stay in touch. Come to Drew's birthday parties. Join them for dinner. Take him to the park. She would have been a family friend, an honorary aunt. That had been her intention until Victoria had asked her to stay away.

But Victoria was no longer in the picture. She'd chosen her career over her son. Rejected the baby that was supposed to keep her marriage together. Now the only women in Drew's life were his nanny and Blake's stepsister. And with Jeanne expecting a child of her own, how much time would she have to spend with Drew?

Bella could fill in here and there, but Drew deserved a full-time mother. Soon Blake would get past any lingering feelings of distrust left over from Victoria's duplicity and remarry. That would leave Bella on the outside looking in again.

Which shouldn't bother her. She didn't want the responsibility of a child. But she didn't like being an outsider looking in on her son's life, either. As hard as it had been to cut all ties, each day she'd missed Drew a little less. Who knew—in a year or ten, she might have forgotten all about Blake and Drew if he had never found her at St. Vincent's.

Bella laughed bitterly at her foolishness and lifted her face to the wind. The brine from the ocean mingled with the salt of her tears.

Instead, in less than three days, she'd made memories that would haunt her to her dying day.

Like the master bedroom, the nursery faced the back of the house. Blake stood before the large picture window, one hand on his son's crib, and watched Bella return from the beach. Their lovemaking had been spectacular. Bella's innocence refreshing. Her enthusiasm addictive. The play of emotion on her face fascinating. When he'd set his mouth on her, she'd been surprised. Shocked, even. Discovering each thing that pleasured her made him feverish to learn more. How many things could he introduce her to? The possibilities appeared to be endless.

The moon was three-quarters full and high overhead, providing enough light for him to follow the lone figure as she made her way across the lawn. Despite the distance between them, Blake could see the determined set of her shoulders. She strode toward the house as if marching into battle. What a fascinating woman she was. A perplexing blend of determination and insecurity, as if she knew what she wanted, but was afraid to grab it with both hands.

And tonight she'd wanted him. Her boldness had been a delightful surprise. After the way she'd pushed him away this afternoon, he'd assumed he'd spend the next week convincing her to fall into his arms. He'd never expected she'd arrive at the decision all on her own.

Not that he believed for one second that what had happened between them earlier meant that their relationship would proceed smoothly. Jeanne's presence down the road and her goal of reuniting him with Victoria was a complication that wouldn't just go away. If his stepsister had any inkling of what he intended for Bella, she would move heaven and earth to stop him.

The muffled sound of a closing door roused him out of his thoughts. Bella had returned to her room, not to his. As tempting as it was to follow her and resume what Drew had interrupted, Blake stayed put.

Earlier that evening he'd reaffirmed that he intended to put Drew's needs before his own, and what his son required was a mother. So what was he doing with Bella? He couldn't see their relationship going anywhere, because Bella wasn't interested in being a part of the sort of family he wanted. One night of sex, no matter how amazing, wasn't going to change her mind on that score.

But as he'd slipped between her thighs and claimed her

as his, he hadn't been thinking about convincing her how wonderful it would be for her to take on the role of Drew's mother. He hadn't been thinking at all. He'd been feeling. Desire. Possessiveness. Pleasure.

He'd stormed past her defenses. Made her surrender. Claimed her in the most elemental way possible. He'd been careful, used a condom, but he was spellbound by the compelling fantasy of her big and round with another child, this one theirs alone, created in the throes of passion.

Last time he hadn't been able to share the experience with her the way he now wanted to. To feel his child move inside her. To indulge her every craving. To observe every miraculous change in her body.

He wanted what was best for his son, but couldn't deny his longing for many more sensational nights with Bella. The dilemma haunted him long into the night.

Tired and grouchy from lack of sleep, Blake woke the next morning at eight and went to check on Drew, only to discover both he and Bella were nowhere to be found.

Mrs. Farnes had breakfast waiting for him when he entered the kitchen. Beyond the sliding glass door that led out to the side yard, sunshine spilled across the large patio where he'd had an outdoor kitchen installed. Victoria had enjoyed entertaining. They threw two large parties every summer to raise money for some charity or another and her birthday party in July was always an elaborate affair.

His ex-wife liked being the center of attention, and Blake had indulged her need to be adored.

Life with Bella would be quieter. He wouldn't be expected to entertain people he scarcely knew and barely liked after spending a long week at the office. The relief of it hit him square in the forehead. Until this moment, he hadn't realized how much he'd craved a weekend alone with his wife when they were still together.

"Have you seen Bella and Drew this morning?"

"She took him for a run."

He had no idea she jogged. The last time she'd stayed at the beach house, she'd been eight months pregnant and moving no faster than a swift waddle.

How many other things were there about her that he didn't know?

"Any idea when they'll be back?"

"She said she intended to go five miles and they've been gone forty-five minutes. Do you want breakfast now or did you want to wait and eat with them?"

"I'll take the paper and a cup of coffee for now and eat later."

His study was at the back of the house, overlooking the formal gardens. On cool mornings like this, he enjoyed opening the windows to take in the tantalizing scent of roses. As he crossed the foyer, the front door opened and a flushed, animated Bella pushed a jogging stroller inside. She wore thin black shorts and a snug hot pink tank top that showed off her lean form.

Blake's gaze slid over her in appreciation. She was sporting a sassy high ponytail that drew attention to her heart-shaped face and expressive blue eyes. As soon as she spotted him, her expression brightened even more.

"What a gorgeous morning for a run."

"You should have let me know you were going out. I would have joined you."

Running was something Victoria had never been keen on. She found it monotonous. Her exercise program involved a very expensive trainer and the comfort of a home gym. She claimed that when it came to working out, she needed someone to push her.

"I wasn't sure how late you were up with Drew and didn't want to disturb you."

"Mrs. Farnes said you intended to run five miles. Is that what you normally do?"

"I fluctuate between two and seven depending on how much time I have."

"How long have you been running?"

She began unbuckling Drew from the stroller. The little boy reached for her, indicating he wanted to be picked up. "All my life. The only way I got any time by myself was if I put on my running shoes and hit the road."

"So if I offer to keep you company tomorrow, you'll turn me down?"

She shook her head. "I'd love to have you come along." She lifted Drew high in the air and spun him around. As his laughter filled the spacious foyer, she snuggled him against her chest and dropped a kiss on his head. "Have you had breakfast?"

Blake was so captivated by the mother/son moment that her question didn't initially register. After a pause, he said, "No. I was waiting until you got back."

"Then let's go eat. I'm starving."

She carried Drew into the kitchen and put him in the high chair Mrs. Farnes had set up at the table in the breakfast nook. While Blake fastened on Drew's bib, Bella helped the housekeeper carry over plates of eggs, bacon, pancakes, toast and fruit. Blake cut up a variety of things he knew Drew liked and placed them before his son.

"What are your plans for the day?" he asked, keeping one eye on Drew in case he decided the food wasn't to his liking and began to throw it.

"I thought I'd take Drew to the beach this morning. Maybe take him for a swim later this afternoon if it's warm enough."

"There's a car in the garage for you to use if you want to get out," Blake said. "There's the children's museum and a petting zoo at the Wilkinson Farm. With all the things to do in the area, I'm sure it will be easy to keep Drew entertained."

Bella gave him a wry smile. "At his age you can sit him in the kitchen with a pot and a wooden spoon to bang on it and he would be perfectly content."

Blake pictured the myriad of toys that crowded his son's room and realized what Bella said was completely true. Everything engaged Drew's imagination, from a brightly colored train that played songs when he pressed its buttons to a stainless-steel pot that made a racket when he banged on it.

"The beach sounds nice. Mind if I join you?"

Her smile was shy as she answered, "That would be nice."

"We can go out for lunch later."

"I'm sure Drew would like that." The phone strapped to her upper arm began to buzz. She unfastened the band and eyed the screen. "It's my brother. Excuse me for a second."

She got up from the table and strode out of the kitchen. Blake's gaze followed her departing form until Drew banged on his tray to get his father's attention.

"More banana?" Blake sliced the fruit for his son, then turned his attention to Bella's low voice.

"Another nine hundred?" she quizzed, her tone concerned. "But I already gave you five to buy the truck. What is the nine hundred for?" A long pause followed her question. "Is that the cheapest quote you got?" More silence. "I realize that the truck does you no good if it doesn't run. Okay. I'll see what I can do about the money." Her voice grew louder as she approached. "Elephant shoes," she said as she sat back down. With a sigh, she disconnected the call.

"That's a strange way to say goodbye."

She offered him a wan grin. "It's a family joke."

"Feel like telling me about it?" Blake buttered more toast and set it on her plate, then pushed the bowl of preserves her way.

"It started with my parents." Her mood perked up as she

began her tale. "They met through 4-H when they were teenagers, but lived in towns an hour apart so they didn't go to the same high school. But their schools competed against each other in football and basketball. My dad played both." Bella slathered preserves on her toast and cast a wry look Blake's way. "Naturally, my mom was a cheerleader so she was always rooting against my dad."

Blake had little trouble picturing the atmosphere in the small-town gymnasium where rivalries were fierce between the various communities. "Nothing like a little competition to keep things interesting."

"And apparently things were very interesting. My parents' senior year, Dad and some of his teammates crashed my mom's homecoming dance. I guess things got a little out of hand and my dad ended up getting his nose broken by his best friend when Dad stepped in to protect my mom from being hassled."

"And the rest is history?"

Bella shook her head. "Not even close. It became a Romeo and Juliet story. The two high schools were always pretty contentious, but after the fight at the homecoming dance, things got even worse."

"So your parents were star-crossed lovers?"

"Something like that. Anyway, they had to keep their romance a secret, and when they met in public, instead of saying 'I love you,' they'd say 'elephant shoes.'"

Her wistful grin told him the story had great meaning for her, but the punch line eluded him. "Why elephant shoes?"

"Read my lips." She paused a beat. "Elephant shoes. See?"

Lost in the pleasure of watching her mouth form the words, he neglected to notice what she was trying to tell him. "Sorry, I missed it. Do it again."

She rolled her eyes, but complied. "Elephant shoes."

This time he paid attention and the message came through

loud and clear. "It looks like you're saying 'I love you,'" he said with a short laugh. "Very clever."

"My mother came up with it."

Drew banged his palms on the high-chair tray and made happy noises, adding to the cheery vibe surrounding the small table.

"I think he likes the story, as well," Blake said with a chuckle. He caught a glimpse of the clock. They'd lingered over breakfast for more than an hour. Once again Bella's stories made time vanish. How could she be so against having a family of her own when hers was such an integral part of her life?

Blake was pouring a third cup of coffee as Mrs. Farnes approached the table and began to clear the dishes.

Bella got to her feet. "Let me help."

"No, dear. You've got enough to keep you busy." She nodded to Drew, who was busy smashing scrambled eggs and banana into his hair.

"Oh, Drew." Bella ran for a washcloth. By the time she returned, Mrs. Farnes had swept the last bits of food from the tray. "Thanks for your help," she told the housekeeper. "It really does take a village." Bella caught one of Drew's chubby hands and began applying the wet cloth. "I can't imagine how my mother did it. Before I was old enough to help, she had to handle three children under the age of six all on her own."

"Sounds like you grew up fast," Blake said, amused at the faces his son made while Bella cleaned food from his hair.

While Mrs. Farnes kept an eye on him, Bella and Blake ran upstairs for some warmer clothes. Although the day was heating up, the breeze on the beach would be cool, and she didn't want Drew catching cold on her watch. Blake followed Bella and Drew outside, a blanket and some plastic beach toys in his arms.

Because his house sat on five acres of land, the stretch

of beach in front of his property didn't see a lot of traffic. Bella spread out the blanket on the soft white sand and sat Drew in the middle of it. Blake lay on his side, his position perfect to watch both Bella and Drew. The infant showed little interest in the beauty surrounding them, preferring to focus his attention on the sand. This meant they had to watch him like a hawk, because he was determined to fill his mouth with handfuls of sand.

"Last night," Blake began.

Bella thrust her hand up, forestalling him. "I did some thinking."

"As did I."

"Me first," she insisted, determined to lay her cards on the table. "I imagine the idea of trusting another woman with your heart is unnerving."

His eyebrows twitched upward at her opening salvo. "It's positively terrifying," he retorted dryly.

She plowed on, ignoring his sarcasm. "You have to know that every woman in your social circle is going to set her sights on you."

"I am quite a catch." He was playing with her, letting her lead the conversation instead of demanding she get to the point.

"Yes, you are." Bella paused, her gaze on the horizon, her thoughts elsewhere.

"Bella?" he prompted. "Were you done making your point?"

His question jolted her back on track. "Not quite." She pulled the shovel out of Drew's mouth and demonstrated how it could be used to dig in the sand. "You are also the most guarded person I've ever met. You have to be doubly so after your divorce."

Blake could tell she was winding up to deliver a knock-out punch and awaited the results with keen interest. What notions had she bandied about in that adorable brain of hers these last few hours? He couldn't decide if this was a pre-amble to goodbye or a lecture on the evils of sexually ha-rassing someone in his employ.

"Let me see if I'm clear on what you're saying. Women want me, but I've been burned."

"Exactly." Her rain-washed blue eyes regarded him sol-emnly. "That's why you picked me."

Now they were getting somewhere. At her heart, Bella was a practical woman. She would need to reconcile how, after they'd been nothing but friends for the months she was carrying Drew, he could suddenly desire her. Blake cursed himself for moving too fast. She would be skeptical of any explanation he offered. And how could he get her to accept why his desire for her had struck him so powerfully when he didn't fully understand it himself?

"I'm not following," he said, playing for time. "Why do you think I picked you?"

"Because I'm safe."

Blake couldn't believe what he was hearing. Safe? She had to be kidding. "Is that how you see yourself?"

"I'm a kindergarten teacher from a tiny town in Iowa. You are a sophisticated, wealthy businessman from New York City. When it comes to experience, I'm no match for you."

And that was a huge part of her charm. He liked her au-thenticity. She was a woman of substance and depth. She intrigued his mind in addition to captivating his body.

Blake stared at her profile and fell into the memory of their lovemaking. Desire hummed pleasantly along his nerves, the sensation muted, but poised to sharpen with the least provocation. She might be right to be concerned.

"I can see where you might get that idea," he said. But where was she headed with her analysis? Was she treating him to a tongue-in-cheek jab at his forceful personality, or was she worried he'd be too physically demanding?

"Also, you know I have no interest in marrying you. So there's no pressure."

She had everything all figured out, didn't she?

"You have no interest in marrying me?" Blake's amusement dimmed. If anyone other than Bella had made that statement, he would write it off as a woman willing to say anything to keep a man from bolting. But this was Bella, determined to stay childless.

"You probably find that hard to believe." She gave him a smug look. "But it's true. Plus, you don't have to worry whether or not I'll fall for you because you already know I won't."

"Am I so undesirable?" She was certainly making him feel that way.

"You know you're not," she retorted, treating him to a scowl. "In fact, you're very charming and terribly handsome."

"Which explains why you're completely immune."

She sighed. "Even if I believed Cinderella stories can come true—which I don't—the fact of the matter is you and Drew are a package deal. At some point you're going to want to get remarried to someone who can be a mother to him. That's not me."

She'd certainly thought the whole thing through. Too bad for her, he'd done some comprehensive strategizing of his own.

"Where does that leave us?"

"I was thinking a casual summer romance. Something to bridge the gap between your divorce from Victoria and the next Mrs. Blake Ford."

Blake couldn't believe what he was hearing. "How casual, exactly?"

"Great sex. No strings."

She looked so pleased with herself that Blake wanted to shake her until the ridiculous idea tumbled out of her mind.

Great sex. No strings. What man wouldn't jump at the opportunity?

It was impossible. And insulting. Did she really think he could spend the next two months getting to know her, making love to her and then just let her go?

Blake pitched his voice to disguise his annoyance and asked, "If we were to begin a no-strings arrangement, have you considered how we might go about it?"

"Not really. But if we were to do consider one, it would have to remain a secret."

This was just getting better and better. "Are you embarrassed to be with me?"

"I'm only thinking of your reputation."

"Why don't you let me worry about my reputation."

He brushed her hair off her shoulder and grazed his thumb along the line of her neck, feeling her tremble beneath his touch. Her eyes widened as he tugged her off balance. She wasn't quick enough to save herself and ended up tumbling onto the blanket beside him.

"Blake," she muttered in obvious warning.

He cupped her head and drew her closer. His lips grazed hers and he smiled when he felt her kissing him back. "Are you asking me to stop?"

"Yes." Rattled and flushed though she was, her tone was firm.

After several quick heartbeats, he complied.

"I think it's time I took Drew back up to the house. He'll need a bath before lunch." She got quickly to her feet and picked up Drew. "Do you mind bringing the blanket and his toys?"

"Not at all," he said. "I'll be up shortly."

Eight

With her nerves all stirred up, Bella was breathless by the time she reached the house. The mirror in the hall between the kitchen and foyer reflected a wild-eyed woman with windblown hair and bright red cheeks.

Why was it every time he touched her she came apart? Only the fact that they were on a public beach kept her from surrendering to the sensual light shimmering in his eyes.

"Hello?" a voice called from the entry.

Bella's heart plummeted when she spied Blake's ex-wife. For her impromptu visit, Victoria had chosen to wear a pair of wide-legged white linen pants and a sheer white blouse over a lacy camisole. Her long blond hair was fastened into a messy knot atop her head with loose tendrils framing her face. She wore gold sandals with four-inch heels. The look was perfect for a party at the yacht club or demonstrating to your ex-husband how much he was missing.

"Hello, Victoria." Bella shifted Drew's weight higher on her hip. "I didn't realize you were in the Hamptons."

"I'm staying with Blake's sister." Victoria's perfect lips curved into a smug smile.

It took a second to register that Blake's ex-wife wasn't the least bit surprised to see her. "I heard Jeanne rented a house nearby."

"Just three houses down. We're neighbors. Isn't that nice?"

While Bella wondered why Blake had neglected to mention this, Victoria rattled on. "I tried calling him earlier, but got his voice mail, so I thought I'd pop over and invite him out for lunch."

"He's down at the beach."

"Looks like you all were." For an instant Victoria's perfectly arched eyebrows came together. "It didn't take you long after my divorce to break your promise."

"Blake needed my help." Bella glanced behind her, wondering where he was. She would appreciate him running interference with his ex. "And the reason I made the promise was no longer valid."

"I'm still Drew's mother. We're still a family." Except for her initial greeting, Victoria hadn't paid Drew a bit of attention. Her focus was all on Bella.

Bella bit down on the inside of her lip to keep from firing back at Victoria. No need for the model-turned-actress to know how much Blake had shared about the reasons for his divorce.

"Of course you are." Bella decided the safest thing to do was change the subject. "How have you been?"

"Just terrible," Victoria said, her tone turning tragic. "I miss Blake. I made such a mistake leaving him."

Bella was at a loss for what to say. Last night Blake had held her in his arms, made her come alive. Not once had he mentioned that he'd had dinner with Victoria or that she was staying with his stepsister.

"I'm sure you did what you felt was best at the time,"

Bella murmured, grateful that Drew was beginning to fuss so she didn't have to meet Victoria's gaze.

"I was afraid. Blake put so much pressure on me to be the perfect mother. He has all these expectations because of what happened with his own mother."

Curiosity aroused by Victoria's declaration, Bella pinched her lips together to contain the questions that flooded her mind. Blake's past was none of her business. But her silence acted to prod Victoria to more revelations.

"He never really recovered from her abandonment. He was only eight at the time. It's why he expected me to stay at home and spend every waking second with Drew. But that's not who I am. My career makes me happy."

"Victoria—" Bella began, only to have the woman interrupt her.

"You can talk to him. You can make him understand that a woman can do both. Have a career and be a mother."

"I really don't want to get involved in what's going on between you and Blake."

"Aren't you already involved?" Victoria's gaze grew laser sharp. "Look at you. Blake and I have been divorced scarcely a few months and you're already moved into his house and taking care of his son. You're just one happy little family, aren't you?"

"I'm Drew's nanny. That's it." Unbidden memories of previous night rose into her mind and Bella felt heat rush into her cheeks.

Victoria's lips thinned. "You've wanted him all along, haven't you?"

"That's not true."

"Sure it is. I knew from the moment Blake introduced us that you would fall for him. A naive little farm girl from Iowa. What a laugh. I should have argued harder for a different surrogate."

Bella's breath caught in her throat. Victoria was a better

actress than any of them gave her credit for. Bella had had no idea Blake's ex-wife disliked her so much.

"I don't think we should be talking about this in front of Drew," she told Victoria.

The stunning former fashion model regarded her in disgust. "He's nine months old."

"He might not understand the words, but he's sensitive to tone and body language."

"Fine." Victoria leaned toward Bella and lowered her voice. "Since you're so worried about Drew, you'll want to make sure I only have to say this once. Keep your little crush on Blake to yourself. He and I are meant to be together. That's the way it is."

That she made no mention of Drew irritated Bella. "They're a package deal," she reminded the other woman. "Blake is devoted to his son. He's going to expect the woman he marries to be equally committed to Drew."

"And I suppose you think that's you?"

Bella was stunned by Victoria's vehemence. How was it possible that such a beautiful, successful woman could be intimidated by her? "I have no interest in marrying Blake."

"Why not? It would set you up for life. All your family's financial problems would be a thing of the past."

The slap of Victoria's words loosened Bella's tongue. "Like you, I don't want to be a mother."

"Yet here you are playing one to Drew."

"I'm his nanny," Bella repeated, enunciating each word so her message was clear. "Blake needed someone to fill in for a couple months. I needed money for my sister. It's nothing more than that."

"Then make sure it stays that way, because if anything you do keeps me from getting him back, I'll make sure he knows the truth about Drew."

Instinctively Bella clutched Drew tighter. Her heart jerked in alarm. "That will only hurt your relationship with Blake."

"Remember the mother who abandoned him? If he finds out you've done the same thing to your son, he will hate you forever."

Bella flinched away from the malice in Victoria's eyes. "My relationship with Blake is strictly professional. I'm his son's nanny," she reiterated. "If he doesn't want to reunite with you, it will not be because of anything I've said or done." Shaken by her encounter with Victoria, Bella headed for the stairs. "If you're looking for Blake, try the beach."

Without another word Victoria marched off, leaving Bella to ascend the stairs on shaky legs. Thanks to their little chat, Bella was no longer certain a summer fling with Blake was a good idea. As tempting as it was to spend the next couple of months *getting him out her system,* as Deidre had termed it, with Victoria back in the picture and angling for a reunion, Bella was better off returning her relationship with Blake to a professional footing.

While she ran Drew's bathwater, Bella stripped him out of his sandy attire. Either he was still energized by his time on the beach or Victoria's hostility had riled him up; whichever was the case, Bella had a heck of a time keeping the sand from scattering all over the bathroom. Once he was seated in the water, splashing happily, she sat down against the wall and wiped her forehead with the back of her hand, following Drew's antics with only half her attention.

It was peaceful sitting here. How many times had she watched her brothers or sisters in the tub? Too many to count.

Bella plucked Drew from the water and wrapped him in a thick towel. Cuddling him against her, she turned toward the door and spied Blake. How long had he been standing there? He'd showered but hadn't taken time to dry his hair. It had a tendency to curl when it was wet. The sight struck her as adorable, a ridiculous term to use for someone as vigorous and masculine as Blake.

"I'm sorry Drew's bath took so long." She stumbled over

her apology, thrown off balance by his clean scent and penetrating regard. "Give me a second to get him dressed for your lunch with Victoria. Is she still here or are you picking her up?"

"Neither."

He continued to loom in the doorway, barring her way. Butterflies swirled in her midsection at the way he overpowered the generous space with his strong personality and commanding form.

"But I thought…?"

Blake hooked his free hand around her neck and drew her close. Bella was too startled to avoid the lips that came down to claim hers. Hard and demanding, the kiss stole her breath. She had no choice but to yield to the hunger that surged through her. He devoured her in slow, deliberate strokes of his tongue and lips.

She murmured in protest as he eased back, but the sound of Drew's babbling reached through the fog of passion that held her enthralled. She twisted away from his kiss.

"Blake." Her fingers clutched Drew's towel. "You have to stop doing that."

"I like doing that." His voice was flat and emotionless. "I think you do, too."

She refused to respond to the challenge in his eyes. "We can't." She took a hurried step back when she realized her close proximity might be misconstrued as further invitation.

"You were singing a different tune half an hour ago." He kept his hands to himself, but his hot gaze was just as devastating to her willpower.

"I haven't been thinking straight for the past twenty-four hours." Seeing that he wasn't buying her explanation, Bella hurried on. "You have no idea how charming you can be."

"I know exactly how charming I can be, but you can't seriously expect me to believe that's why you slept with me."

"I'm attracted to you." Bella gave him a one-shoulder

shrug, but wouldn't meet his eyes. "I won't deny I wanted you. But after some more soul-searching, I realized the two of us engaging in a casual romp is just ridiculous."

"And naturally this has nothing to do with Victoria showing up here today? What did she say to you?"

"She wants you back." The breath Bella gathered was less steady than she would have wanted. "You, her and Drew are a family. I think you owe it to yourself to give it another try with her."

"The three of us are not a family. She left us." The way his own mother had left him.

Bella winced. Convincing Blake he was better off with his ex-wife wasn't going to be easy. "And she regrets that."

"Is that what she told you?"

"Yes."

"What else did she say?"

Here's where she had not wanted to go. "I told Victoria—and I'm going to tell you—I don't want to be involved in whatever's going on between you two."

"There's nothing going on."

"I don't think your ex-wife sees it that way."

"I don't care which way she sees it. The reality is she's not willing to give up her career to be a mother to Drew."

"Does she have to? Can't she do both?"

Victoria had been right about Blake's expectations. He wanted his wife to surrender everything she was in order to be Drew's mother. It was one thing if a woman wanted to put her family first, the way that Bella's mother had. It was something else for a man to insist that she do it.

"Her career isn't something that Vicky can do halfway. With her last play, I was lucky if she was home before ten at night. And that was before the play opened. She spent at most an hour or two with Drew a week."

"I would have made a rotten marriage counselor," Bella grumbled, beginning to see Blake's point. Both he and Victoria had valid issues. Irreconcilable differences had caused their marriage to end. "Maybe you two can find a way to compromise. Figure out some middle ground."

"She came by today to tell me she has an audition for a television series in Los Angeles. How are we supposed to be a family if we're on two different coasts?"

"She invited you to lunch. Why not go and hear her out?"

"Because I already have a date with you."

At the word *date* a sensation lanced along Bella's nerve endings. Excitement? Anxiety? Her emotions were too scrambled for her to distinguish one from the other. The last thing she needed right now was to be seen in public lunching with Blake. How was she supposed to keep Victoria from getting the wrong idea once the gossip began to spread?

"I know I agreed earlier to have lunch with you and Drew, but maybe it's not such a good idea for us to be seen together like that? People might get the wrong impression."

"People in general?" he echoed. "Or someone in particular?"

She had no intention of answering him. "Won't it look odd for you to be seen lunching with the help?"

His mouth twisted with displeasure. "Is it really my reputation you're worried about, or is it yours?"

"Mine." The instant the admission left her lips, she wished it back. "You probably think it's dumb that I value my privacy, but after growing up in a small town where everyone knew your business and having to share a house with seven nosy siblings, I've discovered that being anonymous is one of my favorite things about living in New York City."

Blake regarded her for a long, silent moment before nodding. "Fine. We'll drive up the coast to a little out-of-the-way place I know. The food is terrific and you won't have to worry about anyone spotting you with me. Happy?" He sounded anything but.

"Delirious." She gave the word the same sarcastic spin

he'd used, but her insides were dancing with joy. "Give me ten minutes to shower and get dressed."

"Take twenty. I'll dress Drew and meet you downstairs."

The second half of June vanished before Blake could tear himself away from East Hampton and return to New York City. He, Drew and Bella had settled into a nice routine.

They ran five miles before breakfast, ate eggs or pancakes, then Bella and Drew went to the beach while Blake worked in his office. They reconnected for lunch and while Drew napped, Blake discovered all sorts of new and interesting ways to make Bella moan. She had a delightful range of impassioned sounds and he was happy cataloging each one.

Once Drew woke, he and Bella would go for a swim and then play until dinner while Blake made calls to New York. They almost never went out. The beach house had become a cozy world for just the three of them. Leaving it would mean confronting reality. And Blake was certain neither he nor Bella wanted to do that.

He suspected his friends were wondering if he'd ever stop turning down invitations. He had little trouble imagining the gossip being exchanged over drinks at the club or shopping in town. His divorce from Vicky had been fast and quiet. He'd kept the reasons for it private, but something as juicy as Victoria Ford having an affair with Gregory Marshall wasn't something that could remain undiscovered.

His relationship with Bella was too new, too tenuous to survive the curiosity of his social circle. Nor was he ready to share her with anyone. He was enjoying having her to himself far too much.

After a long day at the office, he was glad to head home. The penthouse was a hollow shell without Drew, and he realized how easy it had been to forget his ordinary life in Manhattan and live a fantasy in East Hampton with his son and a woman who was a nurturing caretaker and an outstanding mistress.

Blake stood in the living room, a scotch in his hand, and contemplated Central Park. In another year Drew would be running over the grass with Blake in hot pursuit. He could almost hear his son's joyful giggles. And the woman who stood by and watched? Bella.

His breath caught. She'd been appearing more and more in his thoughts about the future. He'd pictured quiet dinners with her in the penthouse. Them pushing a stroller around the zoo. Attending Drew's soccer matches together. It was a very different life than he'd had with Vicky.

"Mr. Ford." Blake's housekeeper stood in the arch between the living room and front hallway.

He glanced at his watch. "Is it time for dinner already?"

"No." She advanced. "I was cleaning out the closet in the third bedroom. Mrs. Ford came by earlier this week and wanted to pick up some things she'd left behind." Mrs. Gordon paused and looked uncomfortable. "I told her I couldn't let her in without your say-so, but that I would pack everything up and get it delivered to her."

"That's fine." Blake was about to turn back to contemplating the view when he noticed an envelope in Mrs. Gordon's hand. "Is there something else?"

"This." She advanced toward him. "It fell out of a box filled with her old tax records."

Vicky had always handled her own money. Early in her career, a friend of hers had lost everything when her business manager embezzled from her. Blake had always enjoyed watching his wife sit at her desk and work her financial data. As frustrated as he often became with her frivolous nature, this was one aspect of her personality that he wholeheartedly appreciated.

"What is it?" Blake quizzed, taking the envelope from

his housekeeper. It had already been slit open, allowing him to remove the contents.

"It's a bill from the fertility clinic." Mrs. Marshall sounded worried.

Blake scanned the statement. It was indeed a bill. One that had only his wife's name on it. The bottom line was a great deal less than what they'd been told to expect for in vitro fertilization.

Probably because the services rendered had been for artificial insemination instead.

As the import of what he was reading sunk in, Blake felt his stomach drop. Thoughts spinning, he double-checked. Yes, Bella was listed as the patient. But she hadn't been implanted with fertilized eggs. She'd been impregnated with his sperm.

Drew wasn't Vicky's son.

He was Bella's.

With Blake in the city for a few days, Bella decided to take Drew on a tour of some local museums. East Hampton had a rich history that fascinated her. Established in 1648, it was one of America's earliest settlements. Fishing and farming was the way most made their living until the early part of the twentieth century, when the town began attracting the wealthy as well as artists and writers.

She started at Mulford Farm. Built around 1680, the house was remarkable in that it remained unchanged since 1750. In addition to being architecturally interesting, the fact that the Mulford family had owned the house for most of its existence offered insight into how they used the land and the buildings.

While Bella explored the rooms furnished with period pieces, Drew fell asleep in his stroller. He was exhausted after a difficult night of teething. Bella sympathized. She too was worn out, but her scholarly interest was stimulated by the house and the barn. She took a lot of pictures, knowing her father would find the layout of the barn intriguing.

Her phone rang as she was buckling Drew into his car seat. Thinking it was Blake, she answered.

"Hiya, sis." It was her sister Laney. At thirteen, she was the most social of all Bella's siblings.

Laney had two close friends who lived in town and when the three girls weren't together, they were texting or chatting through social media. To save her parents the cost of an additional line, Bella had put Laney on her cell plan. Plus, it offered her an opportunity to see how much time her sister spent "connecting."

"What's up?"

"I don't know if I told you that our choir got invited to Chicago to perform in August."

"That's fantastic."

"Mom and Dad aren't going to be able to chaperone and I was wondering if you could."

Bella sighed at her sister's request. It was something she'd done in the past. Laney had been in the choir since she turned nine. They'd often traveled to sing, but never to a city as big or as far away as Chicago.

"When is it?"

"August first through the sixth. We've raised almost all the money we need, but we're short two chaperones."

The timing of the trip wasn't great. Bella didn't know when Talia would be back and she didn't want to leave Blake in the lurch for that long. "I'm not sure I'm going to be able to do that."

"Come on, Bella, you've done it for me before." Which was why Laney expected her sister to drop everything and do it again. "We might not be able to go if we don't have enough chaperones."

The despair in Laney's voice was real and Bella winced.

She hated disappointing her sister, but she had an obligation to Blake, as well.

"I'm not saying no because I don't want to," she explained, ignoring the way Laney's request had caused a dip in her mood. "It's just that I have a job this summer and I'm not sure I can get away."

"Can't you ask them? Tell them how important it is. I'm sure they'll understand."

"This is important, too." Bella cursed her rising temper.

She didn't want to be cross with her sister. Laney was thirteen and excited about going to Chicago. Bella didn't blame her. If she'd had an opportunity to spend a few days there when she was her sister's age, she would have been over the moon.

"Please. Please. Please."

With each pleading syllable, Bella felt herself weakening. "I'll have to check and see if I can have the time off. I'll let you know later in the week."

"I need to know tomorrow. That's when they're deciding if they need to cancel the trip or not."

Behind Laney, Bella heard her mother's voice. A second later, Laney was replaced by her mother.

"Bella, we have everything in hand here. You don't need to ask your boss for time off."

As much as it would relieve Bella to believe that, she'd grown up hearing her mother utter the exact same phrase when things weren't the slightest bit under control.

"That's not the way it sounded."

"Your sister cannot expect you to fly to home so you can chaperone."

The weariness beneath her mother's exasperation tugged at Bella. She should be home helping out instead of living the good life in New York. It had been selfish of her to move so far away.

"I'm sure it will be okay with Blake," she assured her mother.

"Blake Ford? That nice man who called us a few weeks ago?"

Bella rolled her eyes at her mother's description of Blake. Many words could be used to describe the attractive CEO. *Nice* was probably not top on the list. Forceful. Determined. Persuasive. Sexy as hell. *Nice* was too tame.

"I'm working as his son's nanny for a couple months while his regular nanny recovers from a broken leg."

"It's wonderful that you can help him out. Don't you worry about Laney. Someone will step forward and be their chaperone."

Even though Bella had been relieved of responsibility, her sense of obligation lingered. "If no one does, give me a call back. I'm sure I can figure something out."

"Of course."

But Bella knew her mother wouldn't call. She never asked for help. She just tried to get it all done on her own. Only she never did. There was always something left undone. Pieces to be picked up by Bella. And now her other siblings. But were they helping out?

"How are things going there, Mom?"

"Terrific."

Bella wasn't sure why she asked. Her mother never showed any signs of stress. But it was always there, just below the unruffled surface. When Bella had lived on the farm, it had been easy to pitch in. These days, Bella worried all the time about what was going on, but she was too far away to help.

Except with money.

It was how she assuaged her guilt over living so far away. Sending money let her feel as if she was still able to make things easier on her parents.

"I'm glad to hear things are good."

"Oh dear, Laney has another call coming in. We'll talk soon. Elephant shoes."

And as Bella was echoing her mother's *I love you,* the phone went dead.

She slid behind the wheel, her enthusiasm for the outing fading fast. The familiar burden of responsibility had descended on her shoulders. Her mind told her to shake it off, but a lifetime of habit kept the weight right where it was.

Nine

The empty stretch of road before them taxed Blake's driving skills very little and gave him lots of time to brood. Beside him, Bella watched the landscape race past, as lost in her thoughts as he was. The only sound in the car was the musical toy attached to Drew's car seat. The tinny nursery rhymes kept the atmosphere from becoming completely awkward.

Three days had passed since he'd learned that Drew was Bella's biological child. Three days for him to run a gamut of emotions from shock to anger to deep sadness. When he'd thought she was only Drew's surrogate, he'd been dismayed that she'd decided that she didn't want any contact after Drew was born. The realization that she'd given up her own flesh and blood troubled him to the point where he had difficulty speaking to her.

How could Bella give up her child?

The question pounded him over and over.

So why hadn't he asked her?

Because he was afraid her explanation would answer an

even older question. How could Blake's mother have abandoned him? Deep down he'd never truly accepted that his mother was too miserable with his father to stay married to him. If she had to move back to France, couldn't Blake have spent some time with her? Summers? Holidays?

As a child it had been too painful to accept that she'd never really loved him. He'd made excuses that continued to be plausible today. His father was a controlling bastard who'd probably paid her well to disappear out of his son's life. But could a woman who loved her child be bought off?

Blake's grip tightened on the steering wheel as he thought about the thirty thousand dollars he'd paid Bella to be Drew's surrogate. She'd had no problems taking the money in exchange for her son.

"Tell me more about the vineyard we're going to," Bella prompted, breaking the heavy silence. Blake had arrived back at the beach house just that morning and announced they would be visiting some friends. "How do you know the owner?"

"He and I went to college together. We were both business majors, but even back then he had a passion for wine. His father expected him to take over the family business. They haven't spoken in five years."

"Because he bought the winery?" Bella shook her head in dismay. "What sort of parent cuts ties with their child because they don't do exactly what the parent expects?"

Incredulous, Blake glanced her way. "There are all kinds of reasons why parents turn their backs on their children." He hadn't meant to start this particular conversation with Bella when they were on their way to visit his friends, but he couldn't let the topic go without commenting.

"Is that a shot at Victoria or at me?"

Thanks to this week's revelations, Blake now understood that Vicky didn't care if she was in Drew's life. He was far more interested in why Bella had turned her back on him.

"Why did you walk away last fall?"

"Because he didn't need me. He had you and Victoria."

Her practical answer didn't make him feel any better. "And now that Victoria and I are divorced?" Blake knew it was too early to push his agenda, but he was too irritated to be patient. "Have you changed your mind about being a part of his life?"

"Don't you think that will confuse him when he's old enough to understand how he was conceived?"

More excuses. Blake unclenched his teeth and relaxed his jaw. "I think he'll be more confused when he finds out there's a woman who carried him for nine months who isn't in his life."

"And what happens when you remarry?" Her tone took on an aggressive note. "Do you really think your new wife will appreciate me hanging around when she's trying to develop a relationship with him?"

"That's a poor excuse."

"It's not. It's what happened." Bella must have heard the slip because she rushed on. "What will happen. If it was me, I wouldn't want another woman hanging around. Interfering."

The explanation Bella gave didn't sound like her rationale.

"Vicky asked you to stay away." Suddenly it all made sense. "That's why you took yourself out of the picture after Drew was born."

"She was terribly insecure about becoming a mother. If she'd been able to carry Drew, she wouldn't have felt so disengaged from the process."

"There's nothing wrong with Vicky that would keep her from getting pregnant," Blake said, curious how much his ex-wife had told Bella. "She was afraid of the damage a pregnancy would do to her body."

"But—" Bella sputtered to a stop. When Blake looked

over, she was staring at him in horror. "How do you know that?"

"A year ago, I found out she lied to me about her infertility."

Blake remembered finding his wife's birth control pills. He'd been too focused on starting a family to see that his wife wasn't ready—wasn't interested—in having children. And instead of being honest with him, she'd lied and gone along with his desire for a family. In the end, she'd chosen her career over him.

But now that she'd discovered that becoming an actress was tougher than she'd thought, she wanted him back. Did she really think him such a fool? Nothing about her had changed. When the next opportunity presented itself, she would leave them once more.

Bella stared at him in shock. "Is that why you are so resistant to reconciling?"

"It's part of the reason. A marriage based on lies doesn't have much hope of lasting, wouldn't you agree?"

"Absolutely." She knitted her fingers together in her lap. "I don't understand why she would do something like that."

"Maybe at first she hoped I'd eventually give up my desire to become a father and then we could continue our active social schedule. She'd gotten her first taste of acting and wanted to do more. That would be impossible if she was pregnant."

Blake had thought he'd gotten past his bitterness, but it rose in his gut like acid. "Perhaps you can understand now why I'm going to put Drew's needs first the next time I marry."

"I do. But Victoria is pretty determined to win you back."

"I agree. And it's even more complicated because my stepsister is encouraging her." Blake took his gaze off the road long enough to gauge Bella's readiness for his next words. She had no idea what was coming. "But I know when they see you and me together, both Jeanne and Vicky will realize I've determined to go forward with my life."

"Me?" Her voice cracked with skepticism. "I'm sure there are dozens of women that would be a better choice."

"Not better for Drew." Blake decided it was time for the gloves to come off. "I've thought about you a lot these last nine months."

"You thought about me?"

"I had a hard time with your refusal to be in Drew's life."

Bella's lips parted. She appeared to be grappling with what to say. Blake waited her out, wondering if she was ready to give him a different explanation than she had nine months ago.

At last she said, "I did it because Victoria asked me to."

That was a relief. It meant she wasn't the coldhearted woman she'd led him to believe.

"I understand and appreciate what you tried to do, however misguided." Blake took one of her hands in his and played with her fingers. "And that means there's nothing standing in the way of you being in Drew's life." *Or in mine.*

Bella pulled her hand free and stared out the side window. "In his life as what, exactly?" Her low voice was almost impossible to hear over the music coming from the backseat.

It was too early for Blake to reveal his true intentions. "As his mother."

Her huge sigh told him she'd been expecting his words. "But I'm not his mother."

"You gave him life."

"As part of a business arrangement."

Her answer kicked him hard in the gut. He ignored the ache and kept all pain from his voice. "Don't tell me that's all it was."

"What do you want me to say?" Heartache thrummed in her tone.

"All I want from you is the truth."

"Then here it is. If I'd had any hint how hard it would be to give him up, I would never have agreed to be your surrogate." She gathered a shaky breath. "Never in a million years would I have guessed how attached I would get to the child I was carrying."

Accepting her explanation gave him some peace. "You gave no indication that you felt that way while you were pregnant."

Her lips drooped at the corners. "I was supposed to be carrying a child that could never be mine. How would you have felt if I'd told you I never wanted to let Drew go?"

"Devastated."

She gave a tight nod. "Every day that went by I fell more deeply in love," Bella continued. "By the time I was in my final trimester, I was seriously considering breaking our contract and going back to Iowa with Drew."

Blake's pulse hitched at how close he'd come to losing his son. "What stopped you?"

"I thought I was ready to do anything to keep him until I came here and spent those two weeks with you…and Victoria. I couldn't put my happiness above yours."

He sensed she hadn't included Vicky in her deliberations. "Thank you. The gift you've given me is something I can never repay."

"You're welcome." A ghost of a smile flitted across her lips. "But you're wrong. The money you paid me saved my parents' farm."

"You never told me what you did with the money."

Her eyes glittered. "And from your tone, I gather you thought I blew it on stupid things like clothes and partying?"

"New York can be an expensive place to live and you did give me the impression you'd been sucked in by the glamour."

"I've always valued my privacy. When you live with nine other people, it's a rare commodity."

"So your parents kept their farm and I have a wonderful son." His anger at her deception about being Drew's biological mother was tempered by yet another example of her generous nature. "How exactly did *you* benefit from our arrangement?"

Her eyes widened at his question, as if she'd never thought to include herself in the equation. "I guess what I got out of it was a wonderful new life in New York City. I never would have stayed here if we hadn't met. The couple I originally came out here to meet chose a different surrogate and I was on the verge of returning to Iowa when I got a call from the clinic about you and Victoria needing a surrogate."

She appeared perfectly happy with how things had turned out, but Blake couldn't help but believe she deserved more.

"I think you are the most unselfish person I've ever met."

"I'm not as altruistic as you believe."

"Really?" He recalled the bits he'd overheard from her phone conversations over the last several weeks. "What did you do with the salary advance I gave you?"

"I gave it to my sister Kate for her semester studying abroad in Kenya."

"And the money you gave to Sean?"

"Repairs to the truck he just bought."

"A truck you helped him buy?"

"He got a job in town this summer. If he doesn't have a car, he won't be able to get to work. He's planning on going to college after high school. He'll need to save as much as possible. If I can help in this small way, it will make things a little easier on him."

"Does everyone in your family turn to you for financial help?"

"My parents do the best they can. Mom promised Sean six hundred dollars toward a truck, but then the tractor needed repairs." Bella looked resigned. "There's always something that needs fixing on the farm."

"I was wrong earlier," Blake said, amazed how she down-played the number of sacrifices she made on behalf of her siblings. "You're a saint."

She laughed. "Hardly."

It seemed as if her family didn't hesitate to ask for all sorts of help. He considered how easy it would be for people to take advantage of her generous nature. Obviously Vicky had. He was beginning to understand why she'd be so reluctant to take on more responsibility with a family of her own.

"So who takes care of you?"

Her brows came together at his question. "I guess I do."

Blake picked up her hand and carried it to his lips. Kissing her reverently, he declared, "You deserve someone who is willing to put you first."

"I wouldn't know what that's like," she admitted, tugging to free herself. "I'm compulsively drawn to people who need my help. It's a pattern I've had no luck breaking. All my life I've taken care of my brothers and sisters. I don't know how to do anything else."

"That changes now." Blake saw the sign for the Rosewood Winery and braked. "From this moment forward, I'm going to satisfy your every whim. It's time you see what you've been missing."

While the car rolled along a long driveway lined with neat rows of grapes that stretched endlessly in either direction, Blake's promise reverberated in Bella's mind. He was going to satisfy her every whim? Did he have any idea how incredibly tempted she was to let him do just that?

What would it be like to have Blake spoil her rotten? Just being with him brought her a joy she'd never known before. At the deepest level, his strength lulled her anxieties. Bella knew that if she stopped pushing him away, he would make her deliriously happy. But for how long? What he wanted for himself and for Drew was someone who would be completely dedicated to being a wife and a mother.

Long ago Bella had promised herself if she ever married it would be to someone who didn't want to be tied down with kids. She wanted the freedom to travel, to be spontaneous, to not constantly worry about money. To put herself first.

The way Blake's ex-wife had.

There were many things to criticize about Victoria's behavior, but sometimes Bella envied the ex-model's capacity for guilt-free self-indulgence. It would be nice to keep the money Blake was paying her instead of doling it out to her siblings. At the rate things were going back home, would her nest egg still be intact when it came time for the winter trip to the Caribbean?

"I need to warn you," Blake said as he stopped the car in front of a house straight out of the Tuscan countryside. "If Sam starts talking about making wine, he will not stop unless you tell him to. I think I mentioned that he's been obsessed with wine as long as I've known him. The same thing goes for growing grapes."

"But we're here to visit his winery." Bella stepped out of the car and stretched. The drive had taken a little less than an hour, but their conversation hadn't been an easy one and all her tension had sunk deep in her muscles. "Won't he expect us to be interested in it?"

Before Blake could answer, the front door opened and a woman appeared. While Bella unfastened Drew's car seat, the leggy redhead threw her arms around Blake.

"How wonderful to see you," she cried. "And you brought Drew."

"Julie, this is Bella."

"What a pleasure to meet you," Julie said.

Bella couldn't help but like the woman's energy. "Likewise."

"Where's Sam?" Blake asked as Julie coaxed a smile from a suddenly shy Drew.

"Do you really need to ask?" Julie hitched her head toward a group of buildings. "Why don't you go say hello and tell him lunch will be served in fifteen minutes. Bella, Drew and I will go get acquainted."

Julie led Bella around the house to a shady patio where several wicker chairs had been placed to take advantage of the views of the surrounding gardens and the acres of neatly planted grapes.

"I can't get over how beautiful it is," Bella exclaimed. "It looks just like the pictures I've seen of Italy. How big is your property?"

"About a hundred acres. Fifty-five of it is planted with grapes. The rest is pasture and my training facilities."

"Blake mentioned you train horses. How long have you been doing that?"

"Professionally for about five years, but I grew up competing in dressage and eventing. It was Sam's idea. I don't know if Blake mentioned to you how obsessed my husband is about his wine."

"He said Sam would talk my ear off if I let him."

Julie laughed. "That he will. Before he and I got married, I was worried how I was going to keep myself occupied. I don't share my husband's passion for grapes and fermenting. Sam suggested I open a training facility and then found us a vineyard with a large stable, riding ring and extensive paddocks. Our activities couldn't be more different, and yet somehow it feels as if we're working together."

"It sounds like a perfect arrangement."

Julie's blissful expression gave Bella a momentary pang. This was the sort of harmony her parents shared. Dad was in charge of the fields and the livestock. Mom looked after the heart and soul of the farm: her husband and her children. Together they kept the farm running and the family solid.

Resentment over her parents' decision to have so many children had kept Bella from recognizing how well they worked together. Sure, her brothers and sisters had complained about wearing hand-me-downs and having to share toys and electronic devices, but there was no question they'd all grown up in a loving household.

"I hope you don't mind my asking," Julie began. "But how is it you are spending the summer with Blake and Drew? I thought you told Blake you didn't want any contact with Drew."

The question caused Bella's stomach to wrench. Obviously Julie knew a great deal about Blake's business. Bella debated how to answer, then decided he wouldn't mind if she explained. "You probably think there's something wrong with me." She wouldn't blame Julie if she did. "I must be a horrible person to not want this amazing child in my life."

"*Horrible* is a little strong." Julie's hesitation made Bella like her all the more. "At first I assumed you were just in it for the money. But the way Blake had described you, that didn't make sense."

Curiosity got the better of her. "How did Blake describe me?"

"I believe he called you the perfect mother."

Bella felt the jolt clear to her toes. Her muscles quivered in the aftermath of the shock. "When did he say that?"

"Last summer. I've known Blake for a lot of years and I don't remember ever seeing him as happy as he was last year. When he and Victoria came to our five-year anniversary party last August, you and the baby were all he talked about."

"Oh, dear," Bella murmured beneath her breath.

Had Victoria overheard Blake's description? Was that what had prompted her to demand Bella stay away from Drew? If Blake was right and Victoria was feeling insecure about being a mother, that could explain why she acted as she had. "I think he was really stunned when you left. He thought you were planning to be a part of Drew's life."

"I did what I thought was best for all of them," Bella explained. "And to be honest, it was no easier for me." Feeling tears burn her eyes, Bella inhaled deeply, striving for calm. Those days following Drew's birth had been some of the darkest she'd ever known.

"I think I understand. It would have killed me to give up my daughter." Julie's quiet sympathy pulled Bella back from the edge. "And it looks like you're making up for it now. He obviously adores you."

Bella glanced down and realized Drew was staring up at her in that unnerving way he had. Their eyes met and he grinned. His expression was so adorable Bella couldn't help but smile back. She knew it was crazy to feel as if Drew recognized her as his mother. After all, she'd only been back in his life for a few weeks. But every time she thought about having to leave him again, a ball of agony settled in her chest.

"Here come the boys," Julie announced. "And my daughter, Lindsay. I can't believe Blake got Sam away from his tanks in time for lunch."

Blake and a tall blond man, carrying a four-year-old with copper ringlets, closed the distance to the patio with matching long strides. Setting down the little girl, Sam introduced himself to Bella with a bone-crushing handshake and tossed Drew in the air, making the boy scream with delight.

Since the weather was perfect, Julie insisted they eat outside. Halfway through the meal, Drew began to fuss and Bella went into the kitchen to heat up a bottle. By the time she returned, Blake had calmed the boy down and insisted on feeding him so Bella could finish her lunch.

Remembering what he'd said about satisfying her every whim, she couldn't help but appreciate his actions. Granted, Drew was his son, but she was the one getting paid to take care of him. Blake could have expected her to let her meal go uneaten while he continued his uninterrupted. But that wasn't his parenting style.

Each night they traded off who got up when Drew began to cry. Heat crowded Bella's cheeks at the memory of what they were usually doing in the moments before the boy awakened. The easy intimacy between her and Blake continued to amaze her. Was it possible only weeks had passed since he'd shown up at her school? Her level of familiarity with father and son made it feel as if she'd been with them for months.

Bella's phone buzzed, signaling she had a text. Thinking it was Deidre or maybe her brother, she peeked at the screen. The message leached the afternoon of all its pleasure.

Mrs. Farnes said you are having lunch with Blake. I warned you.

"Bella?" Julie's voice brought back the sunshine. "Are you all right? You look as if you've gotten some bad news."

"No. I'm fine," she lied, smoothing her expression into a half smile. "With a family as large as mine, there's always drama."

"You have to tell me all about it," Julie insisted. "I'm an only child and I've always wondered what it would be like to have a big family."

Glad for the distraction, Bella began regaling Julie with stories of her family in Iowa, while in the back of her mind she replayed Victoria's message over and over. Would Blake's ex-wife follow through on her threat?

Now that Bella realized having Drew in her life was as necessary as breathing, would Blake find out the truth and hate her for abandoning her son? He'd been so angry at her decision when she'd only been Drew's surrogate. How betrayed would he feel if he knew that Bella was Drew's biological mother?

Of course, that bombshell would have devastating repercussions for Victoria, as well. Blake's ex-wife had to know that he would be unlikely to forgive her deception. But would she realize that in time to stop all their lives from being ruined?

Ten

Blake stood in the hallway outside his son's nursery and listened to Bella rambling in a soothing tone to Drew. Her words weren't exceptional, just a list of all the things they would do the following day if he would just settle down and go to sleep, but something about the quality of her voice captured his attention.

She sounded sad.

Who was to blame? Blake ran the day through his mind. Their conversation on the ride to the winery had been serious, but he'd stayed away from anything that would upset her. Bella had enjoyed meeting Julie and Sam. They'd all laughed a great deal at lunch as Bella regaled them with tales of her family.

She was a natural storyteller, blending drama and comedy to keep them completely engaged. Was this what she did for her students? No wonder they'd all given her such fierce hugs goodbye.

The day he'd stopped by her school, he'd sat in the car for

a long time watching her. For nine long months, she'd been on his mind. He'd gone through an entire emotional range after she'd walked out of Drew's life. When he'd found out the truth about Bella being Drew's biological mother, the elusive piece of the puzzle had fallen into place: he'd understood why Vicky had lacked any maternal instinct toward Drew. But until today, Bella's behavior had been less clear. The question that had plagued him all his life had one answer.

Why did a mother abandon her child?

In Bella's case it was because she'd sacrificed her own happiness to give Drew two parents who adored him. Or so she'd been led to believe.

"Elephant shoes."

Despite their being spoken softly, the words reached Blake's ear. His heart thumped hard. If he'd had any lingering doubts about Bella's true feelings for her son, they were completely eradicated. She loved Drew.

Blake entered the room and spoke softly. "How's he doing?"

"He's finally asleep." She smiled as Blake joined her at the crib. "It was touch and go for the last fifteen minutes, but I think exhaustion finally won out."

"That's fast work. Usually when he's fighting sleep it takes me an hour to get him down."

Her left shoulder rose and fell. "I've had a lot more practice with stubborn children than you have. My brother Scott was the worst. He used to stand in his crib and cry for hours. Ever try getting your homework done while a kid is screaming at the top of his lungs?"

"As an only child, I never had that problem."

Bella sighed. "It would have been wonderful to grow up an only child."

"It would have been nice to grow up with a houseful of siblings."

"I guess everyone wants what they don't have," Bella said.

"That's not always true." Blake slid his arms around her waist and pulled her snug against his body. "Some of us appreciate the things we do have."

When he bent to kiss her, her lips were parted and waiting. All his anger and doubts about this being the right thing for any of them vanished as he pulled her breath into his lungs and claimed her mouth. Her soft moan unleashed the fierce hunger he'd been holding back all day. She belonged in his arms. In his bed. He turned his back on logic and sent his palms gliding along her curves.

She rose onto her toes and tunneled her fingers into his hair. The hot, urgent dance of her tongue with his said that she'd missed him.

"Make love to me, Blake."

He needed no further urging. Sweeping her into his arms, he carried her from the nursery. His room was a few steps down the hall, but his impatience to have her naked beneath him made his bed seem a lot farther away. The mattress yielded beneath their combined weight. Bella sighed as he stripped off her shirt and set his mouth against her throat. Her fingers worked at his buttons, their progress unsteady. Then it was his turn to groan as she spread the edges of his shirt wide and coasted her palms along his skin. She skimmed the shirt off his shoulders and down his arms. He tossed the garment aside and bent to glide his tongue along the lacy border of her bra.

"You're beautiful," he murmured, grazing his teeth against her tight nipple.

She gasped. "Do that again."

He complied with a smile. Her hips moved restlessly as he teased her through the bra's thin fabric. Once again he was captivated by how responsive she was to his touch. He kissed his way down her flat stomach, the muscles quivering beneath his lips, to the waistband of her pants. Moving with deliberate intent, he unfastened the button and slid down the zipper. She raised her hips as he applied downward pressure to the material. In seconds she lay before him clad only in her underwear.

Blake paused to admire her delectable curves and long legs before stripping out of his pants and returning naked to slip between Bella's legs. With his erection sandwiched between them, Blake enjoyed the torment of her hands as she coasted her palms over his back and butt. He caught her hips and rolled them until he lay on his back with her on top of him.

Setting her palms on his shoulder, she pushed into a sitting position. For a long moment she stared down at him, her expression a study in wonder as she acclimatized herself to this new position. Then she trailed her fingers over his chest, taking a long moment to tease his nipples until they tightened in delight. Beneath her his erection jumped. She grinned.

"You like that," she said.

"I like everything you do to me."

"I haven't done much." She looked him over. "You pretty much take me by storm every time we make love."

"Tonight it can be lady's choice." He'd gladly surrender himself to her hands.

She hummed, considering. "Well, if that's the case…"

With a sly smile, she lowered her torso, placed her elbows on either side of his head and kissed him with rising passion. Her position offered Blake the perfect access to the most sensitive places on her body. Imitating what she'd done to him earlier, he eased his palms down her back, paying homage to each inch of silky skin and every bump of spine. Anticipation had rubbed him raw by the time he curved his fingers over the soft mounds of her backside. He stroked his fingertips along the seam between her buttocks and felt her shudder as he grazed down the heat between her thighs.

She'd soaked through the fabric, as aroused as he by their

foreplay. Her hips shifted in rhythm to his light touch while her breath rushed in and out of her lungs. She pushed back until she could glare down at him.

"This is supposed to be my turn," she reminded him, her voice unsteady.

"You can't seriously expect me to just lie here and take it." He watched her bite her lip as he slipped his finger beneath her underwear.

Reaching back, she seized his hands and pinned them to the mattress. "That's exactly what I expect."

"For how long?"

She considered the clock on his nightstand. "Half an hour?"

"Three minutes," he suggested, convinced that was all he could bear.

"Fifteen."

The urge to drive up inside her and feel her tight walls close around him would overtake him long before that. "Four."

His counteroffer wasn't to her liking. Her expression grew stern. "When negotiating you're supposed to meet the other party halfway."

"That's not how I made my millions."

"Ten."

"Five."

She nodded. "Five." And then she reached up and unfastened her bra. It flew across the room and before it landed, she'd settled her mouth over one of his nipples. The hot, wet tug shot a bolt of lust straight to his groin. Blake gathered two handfuls of sheet as a groan erupted from his throat.

In the end he lasted four and a half minutes, each second counted out as her exploration taxed his willpower. But she was having such a fine time trailing her lips over his chest, her fingertips over his legs that he endured the sweet torment until she seized his erection and nearly put an end to their interlude with one swift stroke.

"Time's up," he announced, catching her by the wrist. Before she could protest, he flipped her onto her back and pinned her beneath him. "It's my turn."

"That wasn't five minutes."

"Are you sure? Damn it, Bella."

She'd wrapped her thighs around his hips, bringing him into contact with her core. Only her panties kept them apart.

"Take these off." Fingers bit into his hand as she guided him to her underwear. "Or rip them off. I don't care. I need to feel you inside me."

"Your wish is my command."

But first he sheathed himself in protection. He knew how fast his willpower diminished once she was completely naked. By the time he turned back to Bella, she'd stripped herself bare and knelt behind him.

Her lips on his shoulder made him smile. Her eager fingers trailing up his thighs, however, shortened his breath. In a flash he'd snatched her into his arms and rolled them across the mattress. Once again, he stopped with her above him.

Without words, she understood what he wanted and positioned herself so that just the head of his erection penetrated her. Her lips curved in a blissful smile as she slowly lowered herself onto his shaft. By the time she'd fully encased him, Blake was certain he'd never seen a more beautiful sight.

The first hint of orgasm hit Bella before she'd taken in all of Blake's considerable length. Being on top offered her a whole new sensation. The bite of his fingers on her hips heightened the wildness rampaging through her. So did his expression of utter satisfaction.

As the first wave of pleasure hit her, she rotated her hips, experimenting with driving herself against his pelvic bone, and then had nothing more to do but hang on for dear life as he gently pumped into her. She bit her lip to hold back her cries, not wanting to disturb Drew. Maybe if they were very lucky, he would sleep through the night and Bella could linger in Blake's bed until dawn.

Suddenly she couldn't breathe. Her focus intensified on the bliss crashing through her body. It spun her in circles and catapulted her outward in a thousand different directions. Dimly she heard a raspy voice fill the room, but didn't realize it belonged to her until she returned to her body and spied Blake grinning at her.

"That was spectacular," he told her, reverence below the delight in his tone. "You are a firecracker."

With the heat of her orgasm blazing beneath her skin, Bella would never have believed she could feel hotter, but Blake's compliment turned her into an inferno.

She clapped her hands to her hot cheeks. "I've never been this way before. You bring it out of me."

Blake drew her palms to his lips and kissed each one, setting her body to tingling all over again. In turn, she grasped his hands and brought them to her breasts. He fondled her, tweaking her sensitized nipples and reawakening the desire momentarily sated by her climax. She rocked her hips. Inside her, Blake remained thick and hard. He hissed through his teeth as she began to move up and down on him.

"That's it," he told her, abandoning her breasts to show her exactly the way he wanted her to move.

She only had enough breath for one word. "Wow!"

As fast as she'd peaked before, this time the climb was slower. She had time to imprint Blake's scent. The salty taste of his skin. His low murmurs of encouragement. By the time he quickened his pace and began thrusting his way to his own completion, Bella knew she'd never escape the memory of this night.

Blake's movements grew more frantic. He was close. Bella felt the leading edge of another abyss, but she wasn't going to get there before Blake finished, until his fingers slid between their bodies.

"Come with me," he growled, touching her with the perfect pressure to make her explode. A second later he began to shudder with the power of his orgasm.

And then she was following him. Their cries were little more than low eruptions of satisfaction, but they crescendoed in harmony.

In the aftermath, Bella settled against his side, her cheek on his strong chest. With Blake's fingers drifting up and down her spine, she floated on a cloud of contentment. Telling him about her family this afternoon had torn down the last of the walls she'd erected to keep him at bay. She'd opened herself to him and the intimacy left her wanting to understand him better.

"Today you let me go on and on about growing up on the farm. I'd love to hear a little bit about your childhood."

Beneath her cheek, Blake's chest froze as if his breath had stopped. It was a long moment before he spoke. "Mostly it was lonely."

"Because your dad worked so much?"

"And because my mother spent more than half the year in Paris. Then she moved there permanently shortly after I turned eight."

He was so terse that Bella wondered if she should have left well enough alone. "Is that why you never talk about her?"

"There isn't much to talk about. She was beautiful and sang in French when she was happy. Often when I came home from school, she would be sitting by the window staring out at the park."

Bella's chest ached at the images of his childhood that his words conjured. No wonder he'd been so furious with her for deciding against staying in Drew's life. He didn't want his son to lack for a mother's love. Even a surrogate mom. "Do you ever speak with her?"

"Every birthday she sends me a card. It's the only contact we have."

"Is that a mutual decision?"

"When I was a kid, she never responded to any of my letters or answered when I called her. In time I gave up. After my dad died, she tried to get ahold of me, but I was old enough not to need her anymore."

Blake's blunt words and neutral tone wrenched at Bella, but there was more she had to know.

"Do you know why she left?"

"My father told me she missed her family in Paris. I imagine she thought he would make all her dreams come true when she married him, but he worked all the time and she was lonely."

"I'm sure that was very hard on you."

Another man with Blake's experience might never open himself up to love and marriage. It said a great deal about his strong, passionate heart that he'd let Victoria in. Bella could only hope the next woman he chose would be worthy of him.

"It took me a long time to accept that it wasn't my fault she left."

Bella ached for every day that Blake had carried the burden of his mother's abandonment. Often when Mommy or Daddy left, the remaining parent didn't explain to their children that adults could be selfish. She suspected Blake's father had been one of those.

"Now perhaps you understand why it was so important that you be in Drew's life."

"I've been doing a lot of thinking about that," she began, pushing up on her elbow so she could gaze into Blake's eyes. "I want to be in Drew's life. Our connection might be a bit unconventional, but I should be there for him whether or not he needs me."

Blake cupped her cheek and pulled her toward him for

a long, slow kiss. There was more gratitude than passion in the contact, but Bella was smiling when he released her.

His intense blue-gray eyes were soft with appreciation as he gazed at her. "Thank you."

"I should be the one to thank you. Drew is special. I'm so glad to be a part of his life."

"I intend for you to be part of my life, as well," Blake declared as he rolled her onto her back and blurred her thoughts with another heart-stopping kiss.

As he began making love to her all over again, Bella mulled his words and wondered what the future would hold once they returned to New York City and settled back into their separate lives. The freedom she'd craved grew less and less appealing with each day that passed, and it was becoming more and more clear that the obligations she hoped to avoid by not having a family were not easy to shake even if she wanted to.

And now she was caught in a dilemma of her own making. She was falling in love with the man who'd fathered the child she'd given up. The responsibilities she'd hoped to avoid were now what she longed to have. Marriage. Children. She wanted it all. And with the man who, if he ever discovered how she'd conspired with his wife to deceive him, would never be able to forgive her.

While the hallways and offices of his New York City investment company hummed industriously beyond his closed door, Blake sat in the stillness of his large corner office and eyed the selection of engagement rings the jeweler had brought for his inspection. There were probably a hundred carats of diamonds twinkling at him, each more beautiful than the last. The decision was easy. His eye had fallen on the ring immediately. It was simply a matter of indicating his choice.

The jeweler sat across the desk from him as if he had all

the time in the world. Blake appreciated the silence, because he wasn't just picking out a ring—he was making a decision that would affect the rest of his life.

Was marrying Bella the best idea? He'd been unable to answer the question in the ten days since they'd visited Sam and Julie, despite the increased intimacy he and Bella now shared. Talking about how she helped out her family and discussing his mother's abandonment had given him a deeper sense of connection with her.

But she'd kept from him that she—not Vicky—was Drew's biological mother. Could he trust that Bella wouldn't feel burdened by responsibility at any point in the future and change her mind about parenting her son? It was obvious that she loved Drew and he adored her, but was she ready to commit to being a family?

Should he let her remain as a part-time mom who saw Drew a few times a week? He'd rather she be fully in their lives, the full-time mother who got Drew up in the morning, took care of him all day and put him to bed at night. A mother who then became a wife. His wife. A wife he could worship with his body and cherish with his heart. But could that happen while he held on to his doubts?

Blake picked up the ring he'd chosen and gazed at it while the jeweler took care of the paperwork.

An enormous lie still lay between them.

After much deliberation, he'd decided not to confront her with his son's true biology. She must never believe he was marrying her because Drew was her biological child.

His first priority was his son's happiness. Drew deserved a mother who was willing to give him everything. He wanted Drew to have the sort of childhood Blake had been denied. To feel secure and loved. He should never need to question if there was something he'd done to cause his mother to leave.

Whatever it took to make his son happy, Blake would do. Any benefit he derived was a fortuitous byproduct. That he and Bella were good together was secondary to his son having a mother who loved him.

And while Bella was keeping Drew happy, Blake would make certain he took care of her. In every way possible.

A breeze off the Atlantic and the shade of a large umbrella kept Bella and Drew from feeling the worst of the afternoon sun. She'd still applied a liberal amount of sunscreen to his skin. Despite her sunglasses, she squinted against the glare coming off the pool's reflective surface. Humming along with the children's songs playing from speakers attached to the outside of the pool house, Bella carried Drew into the cool water.

The pool had been designed with a shallow shelf large enough to hold two lounge chairs. It was ideal for Drew because he could stand in the water. In the past two weeks, he'd become increasingly impatient with being held and when set down liked to pull himself up on the closest piece of furniture to him.

Bella had taken to walking with him on the lawn to strengthen his legs and improve his balance. Before long he would be walking on his own and she was determined to be around to witness his first steps.

Her phone began to ring as she was drying off Drew. It was Sean. She sighed, hoping he wasn't calling to borrow more money for repairs. She never should have lent him the money to buy the truck if she'd known he hadn't had their dad check it out first.

"You are the best sister ever," he exclaimed, barely giving her a chance to say hello.

"Thanks?" She wasn't sure what had brought on such enthusiastic accolades.

"It's absolutely the best."

"It's the best what?"

"Truck."

"I'm glad," she said, relieved that her savings account wasn't going to suffer any further withdrawals. "So nothing else has gone wrong with it?"

"How could anything go wrong with it?" He crowed. "It's brand-new."

Bella felt as if she and Sean were having two completely different conversations. "What's brand-new?"

"The truck."

"You mean it's *like* brand-new." Bella was developing a sinking feeling in her gut.

"No. I mean it *is* brand-new. The guy from the dealership delivered it an hour ago. He said I should thank my sister."

"Sean, I didn't buy you a new truck." But she had an idea who might have. "Let me call you back."

She hung up on her brother and scooped up Drew. As she marched up to the house, uneasy thoughts tumbled through her mind. There was only one way a brand-new truck could have been delivered to her brother.

Bella rushed into Blake's office. "Did you buy my brother a truck and say it came from me?"

"Yes."

Drew squirmed in her arms and she set him on the ground at her feet.

"Why would you do that?"

"Because you were giving him all your hard-earned money to repair the truck he had."

His matter-of-fact tone increased her exasperation. Bella glared at Blake, barely registering the chill of Drew's damp fingers against her bare legs as he pushed himself to his feet.

"It's too much. How am I supposed to repay you?"

"I don't expect you to."

Why was he helping her like this? She was an employee. He was paying her to watch his son.

But they were also sleeping together. And even though her heart wanted more, she'd never expected their relationship to be anything other than a casual summer fling. Now he was helping her in a huge way. What was she supposed to think?

Blake got up and came around his desk. His expression warned her that he intended to kiss away her concerns. She backed up two steps and lifted her hand to ward him off. His attention shifted to the space she'd just vacated.

"Look," Blake exclaimed, breaking into a broad grin.

Bella followed his gaze in time to see Drew toddle three steps to reach his father. Her annoyance vanished as Drew clutched his father's pant leg and gave a triumphant cry. His first steps and she'd been there to share the moment with Blake. At the same instant the momentous occasion registered, Blake's gaze shifted to her and she realized that he recognized the significance, as well.

"Marry me."

The proposal wasn't at all what she'd expected Blake to say. Her mouth dropped open, but she had no words. Blake scooped Drew into his arms, seeming not to notice that his son wore a wet bathing suit, and caught Bella about the waist.

"Marry me," he repeated, his eyes burning fiercely. "I want us to be a family."

This same longing had been growing in her ever since coming to the Hamptons, but Bella shook her head. "That's what I want, too—"

But before she could go on to explain the improbability of that happening, Blake gave her a kiss that was impulsive yet tender. Her body came to life as it always did when he touched her, but it was her heart that escaped the protective walls she'd built and soared free.

Blake loved her. The knowledge gave her the confidence she needed to trust her own heart. To accept that the right path for her was not to be free of responsibilities and obligations, but to embrace them the way Blake was embracing her. No wonder her mother had wanted a whole bunch of kids. They were a tangible reflection of her great love for Bella's father and for the life they had together.

As soon as Blake let her come up for air, she answered his proposal with all the joy in her. "Yes. Oh, yes." She set her head on Blake's shoulder and stared down at her son. "I want us to be a family."

Drew babbled at her, adding his own opinion to the mix.

Blake laughed. "I think we have a unanimous vote."

"It sounds that way." Bella rose on tiptoe and gave Blake a quick kiss. "And now I think we should get out of these wet clothes."

"While I love the way your mind works—" his hand slid downward from the small of her back, fingers trailing along the edge of her bikini bottoms "—I still have a couple calls to make before I'm free for the afternoon."

"That's not what I meant," she said, plucking Drew from his grasp. "We came straight from the pool…" Bella suddenly remembered why she'd charged up here in the first place. "You bought my brother a truck. Why?"

"I want to take care of you. Helping out your family is one way I can do that."

Relief made her knees wobble. She'd been the strong one for so long. "No one has ever taken care of me before."

"That's about to change. I don't ever want you to feel anxious or worried again."

The relief that washed through her was like a tsunami. It mowed down all her feelings of obligation, resentment and guilt and left behind a clean slate that she could use to build her new life upon.

"Thank you." The words were inadequate. She'd been transformed by his commitment to her. A tear escaped her eye. Not wanting to spoil the moment by losing control and sobbing in front of him, Bella dashed away the moisture with the back of her hand and set her cheek against the top of Drew's head. "I'd better get him changed."

Blake accompanied them upstairs and headed into his room for dry clothes. Bella carried Drew into her bathroom and stripped them both out of their swimming suits. She'd found that the easiest way to keep an eye on Drew and at the same time get them both cleaned up after visiting the beach or the pool was to bring him into the shower with her. There was plenty of space for Drew to sit at one end, out of the range of the spray, and play in the water while she rinsed off sand or chlorine.

Today, however, he'd discovered walking and used the wall for balance as he navigated from one end of the shower stall to the other. By the time she turned off the water and wrapped towels around them both, Drew was babbling happily at his newly acquired skills. It was then that Bella realized keeping track of him was going to be a full-time job.

The thought made her knees weak. She dropped to the bed and replayed the conversation she'd had with Victoria. Blake would expect Bella to give up her job at St. Vincent's and become a full-time mother. Drew squirmed on her lap, impatient at being held. She set him on the floor and quickly dressed. She braided her damp hair and chased after him into the hall. He was nowhere to be found and she raced to the open stairs, worried that he'd fallen down them.

Behind her came a wail and Bella spun around in relief. The sound had come from the nursery. And that's when it hit her that whether she was ready to accept it or not, in her heart, she was Drew's full-time mom and she would be miserable if she wasn't spending every waking minute taking care of him.

Eleven

Pushing Drew's stroller along Main Street in East Hampton was slow going. Bella had to stop frequently to avoid running over the people who were window-shopping along the thoroughfare. She was taking Drew for ice cream at a place she'd discovered the summer before. This was only her second trip into town. Drew was an active child. He preferred the beach and the pool to sitting in his stroller.

After purchasing a scoop of chocolate, Bella found a shady bench and sat down to share the treat with Drew. Where he'd been cranky the moment before, bored with his enforced immobility, the second the ice cream hit his taste buds, he was all delighted smiles and happy baby sounds.

She'd scraped the last of the chocolate from the cup and was steering the spoon toward Drew's open mouth when a woman's voice hailed them.

"Hello."

Bella looked up and saw Blake's stepsister sailing up the sidewalk toward them. Her attention was fixed on Drew, but she shot a friendly smile at Bella before joining her on the bench.

"You should have told me you were bringing Drew into town. We could have come shopping together." Jeanne set down her purchases. Half a dozen bags of various sizes pooled around her feet.

"We just came in for ice cream," Bella explained, noticing one of the bags had the logo of a maternity store. She recalled Blake mentioning that Jeanne was pregnant. "The stores here are out of my price range."

"Isn't my brother paying you enough?" Jeanne's question sounded like lighthearted teasing, but something beneath her tone raised Bella's defenses.

"He's paying me very well." She could see Jeanne's curiosity, but refused to explain further.

"Then you should be able to buy yourself a little something. I saw a darling dress at Martini's."

"I really can't."

"Well, if not an outfit for you—" Jeanne tugged Bella to her feet "—how about a toy for Drew?"

"He has more than he could ever play with," Bella protested, although she was less resistant to this suggestion.

"Have you been in the Pea Pod?" Jeanne gathered up her packages and sifted through the bags until she located the one she wanted. "I got this there." She showed off a colorful toy, rich with textures and interesting shapes. "You probably think it's crazy of me to buy toys when I've only just reached my second trimester, but shopping makes the time pass faster."

"Congratulations. Peter must be thrilled."

Jeanne made a face. "My husband is not like Blake. He's ambivalent at best about having a family. Not that he would ever say no to our having children," she hurried to explain. "It's just that he's not close with either of his brothers or his sister so he doesn't see how family benefits him."

Bella followed Jeanne across the street, pondering how important family was to Blake despite growing up with parents who hadn't been there for him and how she, who'd enjoyed a close relationship with her parents and siblings, had been determined never to have any children at all.

"That's the dress I was talking about," Jeanne said, pointing to a shop window. "I think it would be perfect on you."

Bella admired the party dress. It had a dark purple bodice with a gathered skirt that shaded to soft pink flowers at the hem.

"My sister would love it."

Bella smiled, imagining Jess's joy at receiving something so frivolously East Coast. Since Bella had moved to New York, her sister had become consumed with all things Manhattan. She'd watched every episode of *Sex and the City,* much to their mother's dismay, and imagined Bella living an exciting life of roaming around the city and hanging out with her fabulous friends in the gorgeous clothes that graced the glossy fashion magazines.

Of course, Jess knew that wasn't the reality, but she'd always been one to set her sights high. Her dream was to be a writer living in New York. She'd already had a couple stories published in small magazines. She planned to major in creative writing in college. Bella had little trouble imagining Jess succeeding in her goals.

"You should get it for her."

"She wouldn't have any place to wear it."

"She would if she came to visit you in New York."

"That won't happen until next summer. She's saving money for a plane ticket."

"Is it lonely being so far from home?"

"I miss my family, but I love living in New York."

"So you aren't going back to…where are you from?"

It was then that Bella realized Blake hadn't told his stepsister about his engagement. It might have upset her that he hadn't shared the news if she'd called Deidre or her family to tell them she was engaged. Normally she shared big news like hers right away. Instead, resistance rose inside her every time she went to dial home. It made her question if she was doing the right thing.

But how could marrying Blake be wrong? She loved him. She loved their son.

"I'm from Iowa. But I'm in New York to stay."

Bella continued down the street toward the store Jeanne had suggested they visit. The Pea Pod specialized in unique baby clothes as well as creative toys. She pushed the door open with her left hand and guided the stroller inside. As she held the door open for Blake's sister, she noticed Jeanne's attention snag on the four-carat diamond Blake had put on her finger yesterday.

"You're engaged?" Jeanne's tone held accusation as she glared at the ring. "To my brother?"

"Yes." At that second, Bella wished herself a hundred miles away. "He asked me yesterday."

Shock and disappointment reflected in Jeanne's expression. She was Victoria's best friend. Bella was certain Jeanne had been keen to have Victoria and Blake reconcile.

"Are you in love with him?"

"Of course." Bella couldn't believe the question. She yanked her hand free. "Why would you even ask that?"

"For someone like you, my brother must seem like a gold mine."

"I suppose that makes me a gold digger?" Shaking with suppressed fury, Bella still managed to keep her tone civil. "Do you think your brother is that gullible?"

Was this what Blake had been avoiding by not telling Jeanne about their engagement? No, Blake didn't dodge problems. He met them head-on. Bella was certain it was simply a timing issue between him and his stepsister.

"I think that because you were Drew's surrogate, Blake has a blind spot where you're concerned."

"Are you implying I would use Drew in some way to get to Blake?" Any joy she'd felt in the day was long gone. "That's not who I am."

Bella's throat closed over further words. She glanced around the store, reassured to see their discussion hadn't garnered any attention. Moving awkwardly in the tight space between displays, Bella navigated Drew's stroller until it was pointing toward the exit. Outside, Bella looked around, unsure where she'd left her car.

"I never said it was." Jeanne had followed her outside. "But aren't you moving too fast? You've only been back in Drew's life for a month."

"I love Drew."

"You abandoned him nine month ago."

Bella needed to get away from Blake's sister. She needed time to process what Jeanne was telling her. But as she headed back the way they'd come, Blake's stepsister was at her side. Feeling like a cornered animal, Bella rounded on her. "Victoria asked me to go. She said she and Blake needed time and space with Drew to become a family. So I left and I stayed away." At the end of the block she stopped to let several cars go before it was safe to cross.

"Does Blake know that?"

"I told him."

"No wonder he doesn't want to get back together with Victoria."

"There's more to their situation than that."

"Tell me."

Bella clamped her lips together and shook her head. "I've said enough. You need to get anything more from either Victoria or Blake."

"Then that's what I'll do." Jeanne stared at Bella a moment longer before turning on her heel and marching away.

Bella's gaze followed her. Was that what everyone in Blake's circle would assume? That she was marrying him for his money? The anonymity she'd enjoyed as a simple kindergarten teacher in New York City would be shattered as soon as news of their engagement reached the gossip columnists. It didn't take much imagination to picture the announcement on Page Six.

Wealthy CEO saves Iowa farm girl from a life of poverty by marrying her.

It would then be a short step to *Blake Ford weds son's surrogate.*

Hopefully by then they would become old news and the press wouldn't dig any deeper. Fertility clinics were supposed to be private, but there was no telling what an individual employee might be paid to reveal. Drew's true parentage might come to light.

Suddenly overwhelmed by the afternoon heat, Bella headed into the closest shop in search of some cooler air. Ironically, it was the boutique where Jeanne had seen the dress she thought would suit Bella.

The bell tinkled above the door, announcing Bella's entrance to the shop clerks. They gave her a once-over, but didn't approach. Her shorts and top weren't expensive enough to signal she was a serious shopper. Bella recognized the signs from when Deidre dragged her into the stores in Manhattan.

The air conditioning felt good against her overheated skin. She decided to take a closer look at the merchandise, specifically the dress displayed in the front window. Her target was on a rack near the front. Bella surreptitiously checked the price and sucked in a short, sharp breath. Four hundred dollars was a lot to spend. She stared at the garment and realized that soon she would be able to buy it without a second thought. Once she married Blake, there would no longer be a need to zealously guard every penny. The thought gave her pause.

The diamond on her finger felt heavier than ever. She glanced down at the sparkling token of Blake's promise and reminded herself she was marrying him in spite of his vast wealth. If it all vanished tomorrow she'd still want to be his wife. But that was unlikely to happen and questions crowded her. She didn't want to believe her motives were mercenary. She loved Blake. But money, or the lack of it, had been a burden for so long, she couldn't deny a small part of her wanted to buy things without checking a price tag or giving a single thought to where the money was going to come from.

In the end she left the store without making a purchase and returned to her car. Jeanne's words had bitten deeper than Bella had realized. She started the engine and headed back to the beach house.

Wasn't it enough for her to know she loved Blake and not his money? Did she really need the world to accept that as truth?

Blake was enjoying a vodka and tonic on the deck when he heard the front door close. He probably should have popped the cork on a bottle of champagne, such was the successful day he'd had, but that could wait until Drew was in bed. Then he and Bella could celebrate properly.

Listening to the brisk click of heels crossing the wood floor, he swung his feet off the lounge chair and stood. The woman passing through the living room was not the one he expected.

"Blake, where are you?"

He pushed open the sliding glass door and called to his stepsister. "Hello, Jeanne, what brings you here this afternoon?"

His stepsister whirled at the sound of his voice and

stormed toward him, outrage swirling around her like a cape. "You asked that girl to marry you?"

Her accusation made him realize he'd delayed too long informing her of his engagement. "If by *that girl* you mean Bella, then yes."

"You don't even know her." Instead of stopping when she reached where he stood, Jeanne began to pace along the windows.

"I've known her for almost two years. She is kind, nurturing and beautiful. Most importantly, she loves Drew."

"Don't you think you're moving way too fast?"

"When have you known me to do anything without thinking it through first?"

Jeanne's eyes flashed. "When you divorced Victoria."

"That decision was not made lightly." Blake kept his voice even as annoyance flared. "She gave me no choice."

"Why, because she didn't want to be a full-time mother?"

"There's more to it than that."

"What does that mean?"

Victoria might have felt okay about involving Jeanne in her campaign to reconcile and then pitting his sister against him when her plan failed, but Blake was not about to cause friction between the best friends by telling Jeanne all the reasons why their marriage had fallen apart.

"That means that Victoria hasn't told you the full story."

Uncertainty dampened Jeanne's irritation. "What is the full story?"

"She's your friend. Ask her."

"You're my brother. I'm asking you."

Blake crossed his arms and regarded his stepsister in determined silence until she growled his name. "I'm not going to involve you in a battle of he said, she said. Ask Victoria. If he chooses to tell you then you and I can discuss it further."

"And in the meantime you're planning on marrying Bella."

"I am." Blake led Jeanne to the couch and went to fetch a bottle of her favorite water. When he returned, she looked more troubled than angry. Handing her the bottle, he sat beside her on the sofa, his arm slung across the back, and waited for what was to come next.

Jeanne took a long sip of water and replaced the cap. "You don't think she's marrying you for your money?"

"Not in the least."

"But you paid her to be Drew's surrogate. You're paying her to be his nanny. Aren't you the least bit curious where all that money has gone?"

Blake's irritation faded to weariness. "This isn't any of your business, Jeanne."

"I'm your sister and I love you. Of course it's my business. What happened to all that money, Blake?"

"She sent it home," he told her, realizing Jeanne wasn't going to let up until she got answers. "To her parents, her brothers and sisters. Everything she can spare goes to help them out."

"So she says."

He shook his head. "It's the truth. I made my own inquiries."

"See," Jeanne exclaimed as if Blake had made her point for her. "You didn't trust her, either."

"Not after she refused to have any contact with Drew." Blake stared out the large windows at the far-off ocean. He liked the way the expansive view let his mind open to all sorts of possibilities. "But I've recently learned why that happened."

"She told me Victoria told her to stay away."

"Did she?" Blake shifted his attention back to Jeanne. "What else did she say?"

"That she loves you."

"Damn." He hadn't expected her to feel that way about

him. It was a precious burden he would carry the rest of his life.

"Do you love her?"

Bella froze at Jeanne's question. When she'd pulled into the driveway, she'd seen the familiar car parked by the front door and realized Jeanne must have raced over here as soon as she'd left Bella in town to tell Blake what a mistake he was making.

"What I feel doesn't matter," he said, his tone impatient.

Bella's heart constricted as it occurred to her that Blake had never spoken those three words. Deep down she'd feared being more emotionally invested in their relationship than Blake. It hurt to realize she'd been right.

"I loved Victoria," he continued, "and look how that turned out for Drew. She abandoned him to pursue her career. Much like my mother left me to return to Paris." A great deal of pain filled the silence that followed. No matter how perfect his life became, Blake would never fully get over his mother's abandonment. It afflicted every aspect of his personal life. "What is important is that Drew will have a mother who will care for him and love him completely."

Was that all Blake wanted from her? All the times they'd made love, the way he'd touched her with adoration as well as passion, was he only looking to cement her loyalty to him so she wouldn't ever leave?

"But why Bella? She's far from the most beautiful woman you've ever dated. Socially, she'll be utterly out of her element." Jeanne's comments echoed Bella's own worries. What would she talk to these people about? Her only contact with most of them was as a teacher. "There are a hundred women in Manhattan who would be a better choice for you and Drew."

"She's Drew's mother," Blake said firmly.

"Victoria is Drew's mother."

"She could have been, but she didn't want the role." And his tone said he didn't want to discuss the matter further. "And there's something else about the situation you don't understand."

Was Blake going to tell Jeanne about Victoria's infidelity? He sounded frustrated enough with his stepsister to set her straight on all counts.

"Like what?" Jeanne demanded.

"Bella is Drew's biological mother."

The shock of hearing this from Blake made Bella sway.

"That's impossible," Jeanne exclaimed. "She was just acting as Victoria's surrogate."

"It's true. I have billing statements from the fertility clinic as proof. Drew is not Victoria's biological son. He's Bella's."

Blake knew? How long? Why hadn't he said something to her about it?

Fearing she might drop Drew, she set him on the ground. He immediately began to crawl forward.

Blake spotted Drew about the same moment the little boy pulled himself to his feet with a happy cry and began toddling toward the kitchen. As if in slow motion, Bella watched his head swing from Drew toward her. She met his gaze, saw the determination in his eyes and for a second couldn't breathe.

Was that why he'd asked her to become his nanny? Why he'd sought her out? Why he'd asked her to marry him?

"Jeanne," he said, his voice low and even, his eyes never leaving Bella. "I think Bella and I need to talk in private."

"Sure." She sounded uncertain, as if the pressure in the room was set to explode at any moment. Moving with far less confident grace than usual, she left the sofa and circled around the room, giving Bella a wide berth.

The front door opened and closed.

Leaving Bella and Blake alone.

Twelve

"You knew?" Bella was shocked by how calm she sounded. "Why didn't you say something?" When Blake didn't answer her question immediately, she hit him with another. "Were you ever planning on telling me you knew? What would have happened when we had a second child and he looked exactly like Drew? Were you planning on ignoring that?"

"That's a question both of us should answer, don't you think?" Blake closed the distance until mere inches separated them. His voice lowered to a rumble. "Were you ever planning on telling me?"

Blood pounded in Bella's ears. Her earlier dizziness returned. What was she going to say to make this right?

"I don't know. Everything between us happened so fast. And then you proposed and…" Bella swayed forward and his arms came around her, a strong circle she never wanted to leave. "I was afraid I would lose you if I told you Drew was mine."

Heavy silence followed her declaration. As she waited for

Blake to decide whether to forgive her or send her packing, each second that ticked by was like another hole in the life raft that kept her from drowning.

"How long have you known?" she asked, muffling the question against his shoulder.

"A couple weeks."

Before he proposed to her.

Although it made her whole body ache to do so, Bella pushed out of Blake's arms. "That's why you want to marry me. Not because you love me. You told Jeanne you just wanted a mother for Drew. His real mother. Marrying someone you love wasn't in your plans."

"I'm sorry you overheard that."

But he wasn't sorry he felt that way.

"How long were you planning on keeping up the charade?" Bella demanded. "Did you think I wouldn't figure out eventually that ours wasn't a real marriage?"

"I care for you. I'm not pretending. You shouldn't be upset because I put Drew's needs above my own—when you left after he was born, you did the exact same thing. No matter how much it hurt to walk away."

"Does the thought of marrying me hurt?" Her voice sounded impossibly small, but it was hard speaking past the tightness in her throat and chest.

"Don't be ridiculous. I'm thrilled that we're going to be a family."

"But you don't love me."

"Stop harping on that."

"But it's important to me. The reason I resisted having children for so long is that I was afraid to be trapped in a situation like my mother was. There were so many of us to take care of. There was never enough money. She seemed exhausted and worried all the time. I didn't want that for myself. I refused ever to settle for less than what made me happy."

"What are you saying?"

"That I now find myself trapped in an untenable situation. I can't marry you knowing that you don't love me, but I want more than anything to be Drew's mother."

"But you could marry me knowing that I will be forever faithful as well as grateful for the gift of Drew and any other children we might have."

Grateful?

Bella crossed her arms to ward off a sudden chill. Could she be happy with half a marriage? It was unrealistic to believe that anyone enjoyed a life of complete bliss, but for two short days she'd thought Blake loved her and she'd never been happier. Sure, she'd had a few concerns, but not when Blake held her in his arms. Not when she snuggled Drew.

"I need some time to think."

She eased sideways in the direction of the stairs, tugging off the expensive ring as she went. As it came free of her finger, a burden seemed to lift off her shoulders. Marrying Blake had been a pipe dream. She'd been a fool to think he could love her. Now she'd never have to struggle to make herself acceptable to his friends or worry that they would believe she'd married him for his money.

Blake caught her wrist before she could set the ring down on a nearby table. His grip was firm, but not painful. "Keep the ring. It's a symbol of how much I want us to be a family."

"If you're worried that I'm going to abandon Drew," she said, "don't be. I don't need a ring or a marriage proposal to keep me around. I love Drew. He's the most important person in my life. I'd never turn my back on him."

"What about me? Do you think I proposed marriage on a whim? I want you in my life, as well. This last month I realized just how important you are to me."

With a strong tug, Bella freed her wrist and pressed the ring into Blake's palm, closing his fingers around it. "I couldn't be happy knowing I was standing in the way of you finding someone you love and making a life with her."

Then, with her sight blurred by tears, Bella raced upstairs, leaving behind the two men she loved most in the world.

Blake stared after Bella until a crash sounded behind him. Drew's wail erupted a second later. He'd jostled an end table and caused a picture frame to fall. Blake scooped him off the floor and saw that he wasn't hurt, just startled.

With his son riding his shoulders, Blake strode upstairs. His conversation with Bella had been a disaster, but Blake wasn't ready to just let all his plans fall apart. Her bedroom door was closed, signaling she wasn't in the mood to talk. He considered knocking for a brief moment before Drew began to yawn. His son needed a diaper change and a nap. There would be time to approach Bella after Drew was asleep.

But by the time Drew was settled, Bella was in the midst of packing.

"Where do you think you're going?" Blake demanded, unsettled by this new development.

"I need some time to think. So I thought I'd go home for a few days."

"I'll make arrangements for you to fly back to New York. Will four days be enough time? We're supposed to attend the Weavers' anniversary party."

"I'm not going to New York. I'm heading back to Iowa.'

She'd told him she was returning home after Drew's birth and then she ended up staying in New York. This time he believed she was going to Iowa. He was less confident she would be coming back.

"What's a few days?"

"Five. Maybe a week."

Was he on the brink of losing her all over again? "Drew will miss you if you're gone too long."

"I know. But he has you. And Jeanne and Mrs. Farnes.'

"That's not the same as having his mother."

"I'm not leaving forever, Blake. It's just a week."

"Why don't you stay here and think. If it's space you need, I can return to New York. I'll take Drew with me if you'd like."

She shook her head. "I can't let you leave your home. Don't worry about me. I'll be fine."

He'd met this same wall of stubborn determination after Drew was born, when she'd refused contact with him. The familiarity of the situation put him on edge.

"You'll call me?"

"Of course." She zipped up her suitcase and slipped her purse over her shoulder. "Now I really need to get going. There's a bus heading back to New York in an hour."

"I'll drive you into town."

"No need. I've ordered a taxi."

Suddenly Blake couldn't bear to let her go. "Stay."

"I can't. Not right now."

He stepped into her path and cupped her face in his hands, holding her steady while his lips dipped to hers. He kissed her as if she was the only woman for him and she responded in kind, but in the end, she was still holding on to the handle of her suitcase, and the way she averted her gaze said she was still determined to make her bus.

"Come back to us," Blake told her.

"I will." But her expression was sad rather than reassuring. "Goodbye, Blake. Give Drew a kiss for me. Tell him…" A gentle smile flitted across her lips. "Elephant shoes."

A heartbeat later she was gone.

And Blake was left feeling that this time it was no one's fault but his that the most important woman in his life was walking away.

When Bella entered the apartment she shared with Deidre, her roommate was waiting. Bella had called from the bus, saying she was coming home, but didn't get into detail about what happened.

"Are you okay?" Deidre opened her arms and swallowed Bella in a tight embrace.

It was hard to maintain an unflappable demeanor with so much sympathy and understanding pouring down on her. The emotional outburst she'd kept locked inside the entire afternoon burst free. Sobs wrenched at her. All the disappointment and hurt at finding out that Blake didn't love her tore her apart until Bella was certain she'd never feel whole again.

When at last she'd gotten past the worst of it, Deidre spoke.

"What happened?"

"Blake knew I was Drew's biological mom."

"Was he angry?"

"No." She'd been so convinced that if he found out about how she and Victoria had deceived him he would never want to speak to her again. "I think he's known for a while."

"Did Victoria tell him?"

Bella shook her head. "He said something about having a medical bill from the fertility clinic?"

"Why is this a big deal?" Deidre knew only that Bella and Blake had been intimate. Now her friend needed to hear the rest of the story.

"He asked me to marry him." She rubbed her bare ring finger. "We were engaged for two whole days."

"What?" Deidre erupted in shocked tones. "And you didn't immediately call and tell me?"

"I didn't tell anyone."

"Not even your family?"

Bella rubbed a new batch of tears from her cheeks. "No. And I can't explain why. I think maybe I was afraid something like this would happen."

"Who broke off the engagement?"

"I did."

"Why?"

"Because he's only marrying me because I'm Drew's mother. He doesn't love me."

"Did he tell you that before or after you agreed to marry him?"

Bella hit her roommate with a hard expression. "I found out today. And as soon as I did, I broke off the engagement. How am I supposed to marry him knowing he only wanted me around for my maternal instincts?"

"Oh, I can see where being married to a handsome, charming billionaire would be one of the worst things that could happen to a girl," Deidre taunted. "But do you really expect me to believe that a man who could have any woman in Manhattan would settle for a loveless marriage for the sake of his son?" She shook her head. "I don't see it."

"But that's exactly what he wanted."

"You said you two were sensational together in bed. It can't be that great without some emotional connection."

Deidre's arguments weren't helping Bella's peace of mind.

"Well, sure, we like each other."

"You were marrying a man you only liked?"

Bella's breath gusted out. "Okay, I'm in love with him."

"Madly? Passionately?"

"Deeply. Irrevocably."

"So, the man you adore—the father of the baby you've been missing like crazy for almost a year—likes you and wants to marry you." Deidre paused and waited for Bella's reluctant nod. "And you turned him down because it's not enough?"

"Put that way, I sound like a complete idiot."

"Not an idiot. But you do sound afraid. Haven't you spent your whole life running from anything that you didn't think was perfect? Your mother's choices are not ones you would have made, but from what you've told me, she's completely happy with her life."

"I've been thinking a lot about that. I think I've been so determined not to have children because I'm just like her and I know once I got started, I'd want to keep going until eventually I'd be financially strapped and tied down with no hope of getting free."

"That doesn't have to be what happens to you. Marry Blake and you'll have more money than you can spend and an army of nannies to take care of your brood."

Deidre's pragmatism echoed what Jeanne had said. She glared at her friend. "And have everyone assume I'm only marrying him for his money?"

"Why do you care what anyone thinks? As long as your motives are pure, they can all go jump off a bridge." Deidre went to the kitchen and came back with two glasses filled with red wine. "We are going to drink this wonderful Cab I got from my friend Tony and then you are going to tell me what club you'd like to hit tonight. Before you decide Blake isn't the one for you, I suggest you remember what life is like as a single girl. Then you can tell me if that's really what you want."

"What if it is?"

"Then I'll support you one hundred percent. But if it's not I expect you to call Blake and tell him you want a long engagement followed by a sensational New York City wedding with all the trimmings." Deidre held out her hand. "Deal?"

Wondering what sort of trimmings Deidre was talking about, Bella shook her roommate's hand. "Deal."

The beach house echoed with loneliness. Blake sat in the darkness, an untouched tumbler of scotch at his elbow, and stared out into the night. Bella had been gone for three days.

Blake woke every morning to an empty bed and a sick feeling in his gut. Nor was he the only one to feel the impact of Bella's absence. Drew was fussier than ever. Exhausting himself by crying for hours at night and then refusing to settle down for naptime. If Blake thought his son was too young to notice that Bella wasn't around, he'd misjudged the bond that had formed between mother and son.

She hadn't answered any of his numerous phone calls, but had texted him that she was fine and simply needed some time and space to think. He was beginning to worry she wouldn't come back to them. No, he amended. She would return and take up her role as Drew's mother. She loved her son and would fight to stay in his life.

Even if that meant suffering a relationship with Blake to do it.

His cell rang. Heart leaping in joy, he checked the display, but it was only Jeanne.

"We are having a few people over for dinner, tonight," she told him, her tone authoritative. "You should join us."

"I'm not sure that's a good idea."

"Bring Bella. I'm sure Mrs. Farnes wouldn't mind watching Drew tonight."

"Bella's not here." He wanted to blame Jeanne for his predicament, but in all fairness, couldn't pass on the blame for Bella's leaving. "She went home to Iowa for a week or so."

"Is everything all right?" Jeanne's concern came through the phone.

"I don't know. She won't answer my calls."

"Is this because she overheard our conversation?"

"What do you think?"

"I think you're annoyed with me," Jeanne retorted. "It's not my fault that Bella left. You are the one who proposed to her under false pretenses."

"They weren't false. I intended for us to be a family. I wouldn't ever do anything to hurt her or make her regret marrying me."

"And there's nothing you can do about that tonight. Come have dinner with us."

"Another night."

Blake hung up on his stepsister. He was unfit company for anyone.

Less than ten minutes later, his doorbell rang. Cursing, he went to answer, expecting Jeanne, but it was Victoria who stood on his doorstep.

"If you've come to persuade me to have dinner at Jeanne's, you are wasting your breath."

"That's not why I'm here." Victoria strode past him into the home they'd shared for five years. "Jeanne said you hadn't taken down any of the pictures of me until the beginning of summer."

"Don't read anything into it."

"Have you asked yourself why?"

"Because I hadn't gotten around to it."

"I think there's a lot more to it than that." Vicky gave him a crafty smile as she took the glass he offered. "Jeanne said you and Bella are getting married."

"Did she also tell you that she and I are having problems?"

"She said you don't love her."

"I loved you and look how our marriage turned out."

"Do you think a marriage without love will have better luck?" Victoria quizzed. "Or are you afraid to fail at love a second time?"

Her question cut him. "I'm putting Drew's needs before my own."

"That's not going to work for you."

For the better part of the past five days, he'd pondered his marriage to Vicky and the way things had gone down hill toward the end. He could blame her for choosing her career over Drew, and her disinterest in being a mother had definitely led to trouble between them, but he'd married her knowing how much she identified with being a model.

He'd been proud of her ambition. Enjoyed how she'd looked on his arm. Disregarded her insecurity as the mod eling jobs dried up. She was beautiful and self-centered, exciting and infuriating. Demanding his complete attention and sulking when she didn't receive it. Keeping her happy had required a great deal of his energy and there were days when he didn't even try. They hadn't had a partnership. They'd had a nonstop power struggle.

Being with Vicky had been exciting, but many days had felt joyless. There had been weeks when being married reminded him of the loneliness he'd felt as a child when his mother stayed in Paris for long periods of time.

"Did you know I told Bella never to contact us after Drew was born?"

"She told me." He wondered where his ex-wife was going with her confession. "She said it was because having her around would create confusion and complications for Drew."

"Partly. Mostly I hated the way you two got along. She was happy to listen to you talk about your business. The same things that bored me to death fascinated her. She made you laugh. You ate up the stories of her family. When you two were together, I felt like an outsider."

"We were friends," Blake protested. "Nothing more."

"It was a lot. You two connected in a way that we never did. I didn't like it."

"I wasn't interested in her beyond simple friendship."

"Because you and I were married and you are an honorable man. But she was in love with you. It was obvious to me. So I asked her to leave us in peace."

Blake couldn't believe what he was hearing. "She was not in love with me."

"From the start, I think. And who could blame her? I fell for you the first night we went out."

"Why are you telling me this?"

"Because you're not in love with her and that's going to break her heart one day. Do you really want to do that to her?"

The news that Bella had once been in love with him dominated his attention. Blake heard Vicky continuing the conversation, but her words were indistinct. Was that the way Bella still felt? And he'd just let her go? Would she ever forgive him?

"Even though you and I want different things, when my play failed, all I wanted to do was run back and have you take care of me the way you used to."

But he didn't want to take care of Vicky any longer. She'd chosen her career over being a family with him. Her lies and infidelity might have put an end to their marriage, but it had been in trouble for a long time before that.

"You and I are done," he told her, getting to his feet.

Not once in the month that he'd been with Bella had he longed for something different or better. Her even temper, quick mind and dry sense of humor made her wonderful company. She took care of everyone around her and didn't expect anything in return. He'd been a skeptical fool to think she'd refuse contact with Drew because she didn't care about him. In truth, she'd cared too much.

Loving her was easy. Comfortable. Being with her brought him utter contentment. He hadn't recognized the sensation as love because that wasn't how love had been for him growing up. The love he'd known made him feel empty. Alone. He'd never known completeness.

He'd never known real love.

Blake plucked the glass from Vicky's hand and tugged her to her feet. He loved Bella. Her sweetness. Her passion. Her sunny disposition and her stubbornness. She might be afraid to acknowledge it, but she wanted what he did: a family. Someone to love and sacrifice for. Someone who would be there when you needed them.

Ignoring his ex-wife's sputtering protests, he guided her firmly toward the front door. "Vicky, you are not the woman I want to be with anymore."

Her eyes narrowed in icy calculation. "You're serious about marrying that farm girl? Think about your friends. They'll never accept her. Your lifestyle in New York City. She'll do nothing but make a fool of herself at the events you attend."

"Bella is everything I could want in a woman. If my friends don't like her, I need new friends. And I only went to the parties because you insisted we had to be seen. I intend to be there for my son in a way my father wasn't." To ensure that Vicky understood this wasn't a game and that he actually wanted her gone, Blake walked her out to her car. "I wish you all the best."

But his ex-wife wasn't done. "You're making a huge mistake."

"The only mistake I've made is not realizing sooner that I'm in love with Bella." He opened Vicky's car door and gestured her in. "But I've finally come to my senses and I have you to thank."

He didn't linger to watch his ex-wife drive off. He had plans to make. Disturbed that he'd let Bella leave thinking he didn't love her, Blake knew he had to do something to win her back. But what? Impressing her with a grand financial gesture would not be the best way to apologize. Anything he did would have to come from the heart. For a man who was able to buy everything he needed, this was a daunting realization.

The first thing he needed to do was head to Iowa and meet her family. He never should have proposed to her without seeing where she was from and getting acquainted with the people who knew her best.

Despite the late hour, Blake contacted his personal assistant and got her started making arrangements. Then he headed upstairs to pack and figure out what he could do for the woman who never seemed to want anything for herself.

* * *

The next morning Blake and Drew headed for Iowa. He would do whatever it took to win Bella back. He loved her. Could he convince her that he'd been a fool or would she simply believe that he was saying what she wanted to hear?

In Dubuque, he rented a car and drove the hour and a half to the town where Bella had been born. With each mile that passed, the declarations he went over in his head grew less eloquent. By the time he turned onto the long driveway that would take him to the house, Blake had only pleading left in his arsenal.

With a family as large as Bella's, a strange car approaching the house was cause for curiosity. As the vehicle rolled to a stop, he was surrounded by two dogs, a goat and four children ranging in age from about five to the midteens.

Blake exited the car, stretching as his feet hit the gravel driveway, and smiled in as friendly a manner as possible. "Hello," he said. "I'm Blake Ford. I'm here to see Bella."

"She's in New York," one of the boys said.

"Why do you want to see Bella?"

A dog drew close and growled.

"She told me she was coming home for a visit."

"We haven't seen her since Christmas," the oldest girl said. "Is that your baby?"

"Yes." Before Blake could stop her, she'd opened the car door and unfastened him from the seat. "His name is Drew."

"He looks exactly like Ben when he was a baby."

"I'm sure all babies look alike."

"Maybe." The girl carried Drew toward the house. "Come inside and I'll show you Ben's baby pictures. You'll see for yourself."

Blake trailed after the girl. As they neared the farmhouse, a woman stepped through the screen door. She dried her hands on a dishcloth and looked from Blake to Drew.

"Hello," he said, coming forward to offer her his hand. "I'm Blake Ford. We spoke on the phone a month ago."

"I remember," the woman said, taking Drew from her daughter. "You said Bella took care of your son. Is this him?"

"Yes."

"Mama, don't you think he looks like Ben when he was a baby?"

"He does." Bella's mother fastened a hard look on Blake. "Why is that, Mr. Ford?"

"I think that's something we should go inside and discuss."

Thirteen

It only took one night of clubbing with Deidre for Bella to realize this wasn't what she should be doing. They were out until dawn, going from club to party to breakfast with some of Deidre's friends. By the time Bella fell into bed at five in the morning, she'd wished a hundred times that she'd spent the evening with Blake and Drew.

During the trip back to the city, she'd decided against going to Iowa. Her family's farm wasn't where she belonged anymore. Home was wherever Drew lived.

While she struggled against what her heart told her to do, Bella moped around her apartment. Restless, edgy, eating little, sleeping badly, by the fifth night, Bella's nerves were stretched thin.

She lay awake, staring at her ceiling, watching the day brighten and feeling as if she'd made nothing but a series of bad decisions. Yesterday, Deidre had sat her down for a reality check. Her roommate made a great deal of sense. There was no perfect relationship. If she spent her life chasing after one, she'd probably end up miserable and alone.

But could she marry Blake and be a family with him and Drew knowing that he didn't love her?

Yes.

Being with him and Drew had made her happy this summer. Deep down she'd known he didn't love her, but she'd been more content than ever before. She belonged with Drew. And with Blake.

The bus trip back to the Hamptons seemed endless, offering her way too much time to rehearse what she was going to say to Blake. She imagined a dozen scenarios. Each one ended with Blake throwing her out of the house and telling her never to return.

Telling the taxi driver to wait, Bella headed up the front walk to the beach house. She rang the bell rather than use her key. Blake might be more receptive to her return if she didn't barge in with a presumptuous air.

Mrs. Farnes answered the door and looked surprised to see Bella. "You're here?"

Bella's heart sank. "I came to see Blake."

"He's not here."

"Did he return to New York?" She should have called before making the trip, but what she had to say needed to be said in person. She couldn't risk Blake hanging up on her before she'd spoken her heart.

Mrs. Farnes stepped back and gestured Bella inside. "He's in Iowa." The housekeeper looked amused. "Visiting you."

"But I didn't go to Iowa." She thought of all those phone calls from Blake that she'd not answered and her spirits rose. "How long has he been gone?"

"He left yesterday morning."

That meant he'd been with her family for almost twenty-four hours. "I'd better call him."

Bella returned to the taxi and paid the driver. For the moment she wasn't going anywhere. On her way back inside the beach house, she dialed Blake. He answered on the third ring.

"Where are you?" he demanded.

His concerned tone set her heart to pounding madly. "I'm at the beach house. Where are you?"

"At your family's farm. I'm helping your father repair the tractor. Apparently the starter has been giving him trouble."

"Why are you there?"

"Because this is where you said you were coming." Blake spoke to someone in the background before returning to their conversation. "What are you doing at the beach house?"

"I thought you'd be here and I came back to tell you that I'm sorry I left the way I did. I want you, Drew and me to be a family if you still want me."

"I chased after you all the way to Iowa." Blake's deep voice took on a somber note. "Of course I want you. If we were in the same state, I'd show you just how much."

Helpless laughter seized Bella. "We have terrible timing, don't we?"

"I think both of us have been afraid to acknowledge what we really want for fear of being hurt."

Bella was impressed by his insight. "I'm not afraid anymore. That's what I came here to tell you. For so long I've been running from what I wanted most—a family. I thought it would be a burden, not a joy."

"The way I proposed to you was so wrong. I should never have let you believe I was only thinking of Drew. The truth is I could have found any number of women who would have made Drew a good mother. Not one of them would have been the wife for me. Only you. It was awfully convenient that you were Drew's biological mom because it gave me a way to make us a family without having to admit that I was the one who couldn't live without you."

Tears wound their way down Bella's cheeks. "Damn you Blake. Why do you have to be so far away?"

"Whatever impulse you're feeling, hang on to it. I'll be there in six hours to pick you up and bring you back."

"You don't need to do that. I can fly commercial."

"Don't be ridiculous. I'll call you en route to tell you what time we're going to land."

"Please hurry," Bella murmured, too overcome by emotion to be able to speak louder than a whisper. "I've really missed you."

"Elephant shoes," Blake said in return. "See you in a few hours."

Bella stared at the now silent phone. "He loves me." She looked up and realized Mrs. Farnes was returning from the kitchen, a cup of hot tea in her hand. "He loves me," she repeated, still stunned by the realization.

"Of course he does," said the housekeeper with a broad smile. "That's been obvious for a long time."

As soon as the Gulfstream touched down and rolled to a halt at East Hampton Airport, Blake was on his feet and waiting at the door for his crew to lower the stairs. With the way cleared, he rushed down, eyes scanning the hangar for Bella. She stood off to one side, her suitcase at her feet, blue eyes seeming larger than ever in her pale face.

Her uncertainty touched him. She wanted so badly to make others happy that most times she forgot about her own needs. He would spend the rest of his life making sure she lacked for nothing.

Half a dozen long strides brought him within reach. He snatched her off her feet and swung her in a wide circle. Her laugh bounced off the walls of the hangar as she clutched at his shoulders. As soon as he set her down, his mouth captured hers in a long, hungry kiss that disclosed his feelings for her.

"I missed you," he said at long last, framing her face with his hands while he refreshed his memories of her features.

"I missed you, too." She gave him a shy smile. "And I can't wait to see Drew."

"It's going to be a couple hours until that happens. I left him with your family."

"You left him?" She looked horrified. "Do you realize my dad will probably take him for a ride on the tractor? Or one of my brothers might think it's a great idea to introduce him to the calves. Or the girls will make him play tea party. There's no telling what could happen."

Blake gave her an odd look. "I'm sure he'll be fine. I thought you and I could use a few hours to ourselves." He picked up her suitcase and wrapped his arm around her waist. "By the way, your mother figured out Drew is your son."

Bella stumbled, but Blake's arm kept her stable and she quickly recovered. "How?"

"Apparently he looks just like Ben did when he was a baby."

"That's impossible. Drew takes after you."

"Not according to your family. And I've seen the pictures. They're right. He has the McAndrews chin and nose."

"Did you explain to your mother what happened?"

"Since I'm unsure on all the details, I thought it would be better if you told her." It was a gentle nudge to share the story with him.

As soon as they sat down on the plane, Bella snuggled beside Blake in one of the comfortable leather chairs, her head on his shoulder.

"How did you find out that Victoria isn't Drew's mother?"

"I came across some of the paperwork from the clinic. The treatment was a lot less expensive than it should have been. When I looked at the itemized statement, I noticed that the charges weren't for in vitro, but for artificial insemination."

"Victoria told me her eggs weren't viable," Bella explained, remembering her shock when the former model had asked to use Bella's eggs as well as have her carry the baby.

"As far as I know that's not true," Blake said.

"I guess I'm just a gullible farm girl from Iowa." Bella burned with humiliation at being so easily duped. "I believed her."

"My ex-wife excelled at telling a person what they wanted to hear." There was a hint of frustration beneath Blake's even tone. "For years she let me believe she wanted to have a family."

"Maybe she didn't know what she wanted until it was too late," she suggested. "I know that she was determined to hold on to you."

"Is that how she talked you into letting us use one of your eggs?"

"She was frantic, telling me that your marriage would be over because she couldn't give you a baby. It was entirely plausible. Infertility can tear apart a marriage."

"But how did she think she could get away with lying to me about our son's parentage?"

"Desperate people do foolish things sometimes." Bella stared up at his strong profile, saw the muscle move in his cheek. "I should know. I gave away my son in exchange for the money to help my parents keep their farm."

Blake cupped her cheek in his hand and kissed her with slow, thorough adoration. "And every day that goes by I thank heavens your parents had financial difficulties, because otherwise we never would have met and I wouldn't have my son."

"I'm not sure they'd appreciate hearing you say that," Bella teased, sliding her hand along his muscular arm, enjoying the strength of him beneath her fingertips.

"They're going to be my family now. I hope you realize I'm going to take good care of all your siblings."

Bella groaned. "Please don't tell them that. They already see me as the cash cow. If they have any idea how generous you are, they'll never leave you alone."

"Don't worry. I can handle them." His lips covered hers, silencing any further protest she might make.

Relaxing into the familiar press and retreat of his kiss, Bella hummed in appreciation of the masterful way he could make her forget everything but what was happening at that moment. For too long she'd worried about the future. Blake kept her completely grounded in the present.

"I love the sounds you make," he murmured, gliding his lips along her neck.

She shivered in delight as he lightly sucked on her sensitive skin. "What sounds?"

"Your moans have terrific range. They tell me how much you like something. And then there's the way you purr. I know you're really happy when that happens."

"I do all that?" Despite the level of physical intimacy she'd experienced with him, hearing his praise sent heat spiraling into her cheeks.

"All that and more." He kissed her forehead. "You make me happier than I've ever been."

Was that possible? His marriage to Victoria had seemed perfect. They'd been an it couple. Attractive, talented, wealthy. Bella couldn't remember a time when they were in the same room and didn't touch in some way. She'd envied their obvious passion for each other.

"I'm glad."

Blake's intent blue eyes grew sharp. "You don't sound convinced."

"You forget, I saw you with Victoria."

"She didn't make me feel like you do. Living with her was often exhausting. She loved drama. When it didn't present itself organically, she created it."

"But you seemed so happy."

"Our marriage worked as long as Victoria got what she wanted. And I was happy to give her whatever. All I wanted was for us to be parents. Things began to change as soon as she agreed to try for a baby."

Bella kept silent. The best thing she could do was trust that Blake knew what he was getting into by marrying her. He was telling her that he was tired of beautiful and exciting. He wanted…what? Plain and dull? She sighed.

"With you, I feel as if we're a partnership," he continued. "So you can stop sighing. It's great with you. I know we're on the same page."

"Are you sure you're not going to be…"

"Bored?"

His knack for reading her mind never ceased to surprise her. "You might miss all the drama."

A slow smile spread across his lips. "I'll take your brand of passion over Vicky's love of chaos any day."

And the hot, sexy kiss he planted on her demonstrated just how true that was.

Bella expected a mob scene when she arrived at her parents' farm and her family didn't disappoint her. The last time she'd been home was for a week at Christmas. The crowded, noisy farmhouse had seemed claustrophobic after her quiet apartment in New York. Plus, she'd been unable to answer their questions about what she'd been doing during the year since she'd last visited.

More than anything she'd wanted to be able to share the truth with her mother. Giving up Drew had been an open wound and she longed for nothing more than to sob out her pain in her mother's arms. But taking comfort was something she'd never learned how to do. It was always her supporting others. So she'd put on a brave face and bottled up her sadness.

"You're home." Jess was the first to reach her. As soon as Blake stopped the car, Bella's sister yanked open the door and wrapped her arms around Bella, practically falling into her lap as she did so. "I missed you," she said softly.

"Me, too," Bella whispered back.

Blake stuck close to her side as they entered the house, his fingers entwined with hers. He was a solid buffer against her boisterous family as they pummeled her with dozens of questions she didn't know how to answer.

"I'd like to see Drew," she told him, angling toward the stairs.

"Your mother put him in your old room. When Drew and I arrived, she insisted we spend the night here rather than in town."

Bella nodded. "There's only two motels and neither one is up to your standards." She entered her old room and saw immediately that Jess had taken over the space. As the oldest girl still living at home, it made sense that she would get it. "Oh, look. He's awake."

Drew was standing in the crib, his chubby fists gripping the railing. He bounced excitedly when he spotted her.

"He looks none the worse for wear," Blake said. "Your family didn't play too rough."

It wasn't until Bella had him in her arms that the tension of the past week melted away. How had she been stupid enough to walk away from Drew twice? "I'll never leave you again," she murmured into the baby's soft neck.

"Blake, would it be all right if I had a moment alone with my daughter?"

"Certainly."

Turning around, Bella saw her mother in the doorway. Remembering what Blake had told her as they boarded the plane, her stomach twisted into knots of dread. As soon as they were alone, Bella sat down on the bed, Drew cradled against her chest like a shield.

"I know what you're going to say," she began.

"Do you?" Her mother sat down on the bed beside her. "What exactly am I going to say?"

"You are going to tell me what I did was thoughtless and wrong."

"Since I'm not exactly sure what you did, that's not what I was going to say at all." Her mother cupped Drew's head with gentle fingers. "How did all this come to be?"

"When I went to New York, I went there to answer an ad placed by a firm that matched infertile couples with surrogates." When her mother didn't react, Bella continued. "That's where I met Blake. He and his wife were having trouble conceiving and so they decided to use a surrogate."

"But usually a surrogate doesn't supply the egg, correct?"

"Victoria told me her eggs were no good."

"She told you?" Bella's mother echoed. "Was that the case?"

Bella shook her head. "At the time all I knew was that she was desperate to save her marriage by having a baby. I felt sorry for her so I…helped."

"Bella." Her mother sounded aghast. "That was your child you were giving up."

"You didn't see the expression on Blake's face the day he took me for the ultrasound. He was thrilled I was carrying his son. I knew at that moment that I would do anything to make him happy, even sacrifice my own happiness by never seeing Drew ever again so that Blake and Victoria could be the happy family he wanted." Bella kissed Drew's head. "Besides, I'd never planned on having any children. It never occurred to me I would get so attached."

"When did you realize something changed?"

"The first time I felt him kick. By then it was too late. And Blake was so excited about becoming a father."

"Are you in love with him?"

"More than anything."

"He asked your father permission to marry you."

"Really?" Bella was utterly charmed that Blake would do something so old-fashioned. It wasn't what she would have expected.

"Are you going to marry him?"

"I don't know." She grinned at her mother. "Did Dad say yes or no?"

"That's between them." Her mother was silent for a long time. "You probably don't think I've realized just how much you've done for this family."

Bella scrunched up her face. "I would do whatever I could to help you."

"You've given more than your fair share of time and money to help us out. That stops now. Living in New York City isn't the dream I had for you, but I can see Blake and Drew make you happy. I'm glad you found a man who loves you the way your father loves me."

And love was what made her mother's burden lighter, Bella realized. Love for her husband. His for her. The love she had for the farm and her children. The financial struggles, the vast amount of work that needed to be done on a daily basis, the petty spats between her kids, all of that rolled off Stella's back because she was happy with the life she'd chosen.

What a blessing that was.

"It's time for you to get a little selfish," her mother continued. "Promise me you'll put yourself first at least once a week."

Blake appeared in the doorway and grinned at both women. "I intend to take excellent care of her."

Bella's mother smiled. "It's nice to see someone worrying about you for a change." She stood and plucked Drew from his mother's arms. "I'm going to take Drew downstairs and find him a snack."

Once they were alone, Blake came to kneel beside Bella. He pulled out the diamond ring she'd returned to him earlier that week. "The last time I did this all wrong. I'd like to try again."

Nodding, unable to speak past the lump in her throat, Bella stared at the ring Blake slipped on her finger.

"Bella McAndrews, I love you with all my heart. Will you do me the honor of becoming my wife?"

She slid her hands around his neck and leaned forward until their lips were inches apart. "Blake Ford, you are my heart and my life. I will marry you and spend the rest of my days making you happy."

A reverent kiss sealed their commitment to each other. When Blake released her, Bella's whole body was tingling with passion and joy.

"Shall we go tell your family the news?"

"I'm sure three of them are outside the door listening to us," she retorted, kissing him hard and fast. "In this house there is no privacy."

Blake stood. "Then perhaps we should go downstairs and accept their congratulations."

"We should." She let him pull her to her feet.

As they left her childhood bedroom, Bella thought back over all the nights she'd lain here and plotted how her life would go. Not once had she contemplated living in New York City, being married to a billionaire and raising a family.

With her fingers laced with Blake's, she marveled at how despite her best efforts to avoid it, she'd gotten what her heart truly wanted all along.

* * * * *

A sneaky peek at next month...

Desire™

PASSIONATE AND DRAMATIC LOVE STORIES

My wish list for next month's titles...

In stores from 20th September 2013:

☐ The Lone Star Cinderella – Maureen Child

& A Cowboy's Temptation – Barbara Dunlop

☐ Sunset Seduction – Charlene Sands

& A Beauty Uncovered – Andrea Laurence

☐ Stern – Brenda Jackson

& A Wolff at Heart – Janice Maynard

2 stories in each book - only £5.49!

Just can't wait?

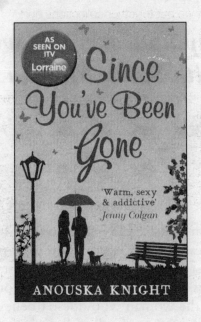

Special Offers

Every month we put together collections and longer reads written by your favourite authors.

Here are some of next month's highlights— and don't miss our fabulous discount online!

On sale 20th September

On sale 4th October

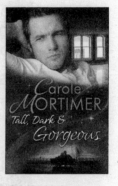

On sale 4th October

Save 20%
on all Special Releases

Join the Mills & Boon Book Club

Subscribe to **Desire**™ today for 3, 6 or 12 months and you could **save over £30!**

We'll also treat you to these fabulous extras:

- **FREE L'Occitane gift set** worth £10

- **FREE home delivery**

- **Rewards scheme, exclusive** offers…and much more!

Subscribe now and save over £30
www.millsandboon.co.uk/subscribeme

Mills & Boon® Online

Discover more romance at
www.millsandboon.co.uk

- **FREE** online reads
- **Books** up to one
  month before shops
- **Browse our books**
  before you buy

...and much more!

The World of Mills & Boon®

There's a Mills & Boon® series that's perfect for you. We publish ten series and, with new titles every month, you never have to wait long for your favourite to come along.

Blaze
Scorching hot, sexy reads
4 new stories every month

By Request
Relive the romance with the best of the best
9 new stories every month

Cherish™
Romance to melt the heart every time
12 new stories every month

Desire™
Passionate and dramatic love stories
8 new stories every month

CONVENIENTLY
HIS PRINCESS

BY
OLIVIA GATES

Published in Great Britain 2013
by Mills & Boon, an imprint of Harlequin (UK) Limited,
Eton House, 18-24 Paradise Road, Richmond, Surrey TW9 1SR

© Olivia Gates 2013

ISBN: 978 0 263 90485 7
ebook ISBN: 978 1 472 00634 9

51-0913

Harlequin (UK) policy is to use papers that are natural, renewable and recyclable products and made from wood grown in sustainable forests. The logging and manufacturing processes conform to the legal environmental regulations of the country of origin.

Printed and bound in Spain
by Blackprint CPI, Barcelona

Olivia Gates has always pursued creative passions such as singing and handicrafts. She still does, but only one of her passions grew gratifying enough, consuming enough, to become an ongoing career—writing.

She is most fulfilled when she is creating worlds and conflicts for her characters, then exploring and untangling them bit by bit, sharing her protagonists' every heart-wrenching heartache and hope, their every heart-pounding doubt and trial, until she leads them to an indisputably earned and gloriously satisfying happy ending.

When she's not writing, she is a doctor, a wife to her own alpha male and a mother to one brilliant girl and one demanding Angora cat. Visit Olivia at www.oliviagates.com.

To my family and friends, who give me all I need…
love, understanding, encouragement and space, to
keep on writing…and enjoying it. Love you all.